LONG CREEK

JIM NICOLSON

iUNIVERSE, INC.
NEW YORK   BLOOMINGTON

Long Creek

This is a work of fiction. All of the characters, names, incidents, organizations, and dialogue in this novel are either the products of the author's imagination or are used fictitiously.

iUniverse books may be ordered through booksellers or by contacting:

iUniverse
1663 Liberty Drive
Bloomington, IN 47403
www.iuniverse.com
1-800-Authors (1-800-288-4677)

Because of the dynamic nature of the Internet, any Web addresses or links contained in this book may have changed since publication and may no longer be valid. The views expressed in this work are solely those of the author and do not necessarily reflect the views of the publisher, and the publisher hereby disclaims any responsibility for them.

ISBN: 978-1-4502-4223-3 (sc)
ISBN: 978-1-4502-4225-7 (dj)
ISBN: 978-1-4502-4224-0 (ebk)

Library of Congress Control Number: 2010909961

Printed in the United States of America

iUniverse rev. date: 7/19/2010

For Alexander, Kylie, Rachel, Sharon and Isabelle

Contents

PREFACE

This novel is historical fiction. The principal settings are two cattle runs (ranches) in Australia's Northern Territory over sixty years ago, when Australia's far north was much more of a frontier than it is today. In 1947, Darwin's population was 2,538, and Katherine's 331. Today these are close to 125,000 and 10,000 respectively.

The Aboriginal beliefs and legends have been drawn from a number of groups. This is consistent with the fact that individuals from different groups mingled and worked on cattle runs and mission stations. And it was this mingling—together with the influence of British and European settlers as well as Chinese, Japanese, Afghan and other migrants—that led to the development, in the 1930s, of a new and very widely used Aboriginal language. This language used to be called Creole. Today it's known as Kriol.

To ensure authenticity, a number of dialectal words and phrases appear that would've been routinely used back then on far-north cattle runs. A glossary of Kriol, Aboriginal, and Australian historical terms can be found on page 365 and 366.

J. N.

PART ONE

ALL MINE TO CHERISH AND SURVEY

Mother why don't you enfold me as you used to in the long long ago
Your morning breath was sweetness to my soul
The daily scent of wood smoke was a benediction in the air
The coolness when you wore your cloak of green after the rain was
mine
All mine to cherish and survey.

—Jack Davis

CHAPTER 1

RETRIBUTION

THE NORTHERN TERRITORY'S BIG RIVER, 1952

Hank had a quick glance skyward. The clouds now looked as if they'd been pulled apart, and the sun was beginning to peer through. This tranquil riverbank glade with its dappled shade was cool and still. There was only the twittering of birds and the gurgling wash of the river's slow-moving water. For the umpteenth time, Hank blamed himself for what had happened. He considered their captive: a depraved man who enjoyed inflicting his horrific barbarity on women. *Yes*, he thought, *you're goddamn evil personified.*

The conviction that life was incongruous rose to the top of his consciousness, rather like a green frog that suddenly bobs up and then floats wide legged on a *billabong's* brown surface. For it seemed to him that it was only yesterday when, consumed by fear, he and his company had been pinned down on Omaha Beach by murderous enemy fire. Again, images of floating GI corpses being washed over by wavelets, dyed red with blood, flashed into his mind. He shook his head to clear it. Right now his only companions were a *Murri* and a *yeller feller*, and he wouldn't have had it any other way.

He saw that Jalyerri had finished daubing his water-and-white-clay design onto Brian's upper body. Then their captive's whining voice intruded.

"Fair go, fellers! I've got to have water. Them damn niggers wouldn't give me any. An' *me*, a white man too."

Hank saw that the man had struggled to his feet and was leaning against the River Red Gum's variegated trunk, while imploringly holding out his bound wrists. The guilt that'd been nagging at him retreated abruptly. Thin lipped, he walked over and savagely kicked the man's ankles from under him. The man screamed in agony and fell heavily to the ground. The urge to kill gripped Hank hard. Taken by surprise, he had to struggle momentarily to control himself. He regarded the bound man with cold, narrowed eyes.

"You're a fucking obscenity," he spat. He continued to study the man. Then he smiled chillingly. "Now, is the woodcock near the gin," he mocked.

The man stared at him, wide-eyed. "That's bullshit," he whined. "I haven't been near any *gins*. I never go into them Abo camps." The man began to whimper. "I've got to have water," he begged. "I'm *dying* of thirst, I tell you."

"Good," Hank replied coldly. "I need you to suffer."

"I've done nothing wrong. Christ, why won't you take me to Fitzpatrick? Take me, *please*."

"No way." Hank's lips tightened. "And 'twas writ that even shit gets to strut and fret its hour upon a stage."

"You're bloody raving mad!" The man sobbed, "An' what's that yeller feller there having done to him, for Crissake?"

"I believe that the Lord High Executioner is having his stage make-up applied."

"You're raving mad!" Their captive screamed hysterically. "Anyone who won't give a man water in this country is mad. Mad, I tell you. You're *mad*."

"Aren't we all? Just a bit?"

"Give me water, *please*."

"Suffer."

Jalyerri had finally finished. He and Brian moved next to Hank and stood silently.

Eventually, Brian spoke. "We're waiting for you, Hank. Are you joining us?"

Hank glanced at them, half-smiled and nodded his assent. He and Jalyerri went to the man, grabbed an arm each and hauled him roughly to his feet. Brian silently passed a length of thick vine under their captive's arms and firmly bound him to the River Red Gum's trunk.

Hank regarded Brian. "I don't mind doing it, really," he said. "I blame myself for what happened. And I'd like to do it."

Brian shook his head firmly. "No, mate," he said. "You know this has to be me."

He reached for one of the spears that'd been left standing against the River Red and met the man's eyes. They were blank with the coldness of terror. Brian didn't hesitate and, grimacing with the effort, drove the spear powerfully through the man's right shoulder below the collarbone. It shattered the shoulder blade on its way through and stayed deeply embedded in the River Red's trunk. The sudden startled look on the man's face was instantly replaced by one of shock and pain. He shrieked in agony, his shrill shouts echoing like demented screams through the surrounding bush.

"Oh Christ! Christ, *no*. Help me. Help me, *someone*."

The man continued to shriek; his face contorted with agony. Brian reached for the other spear and abruptly drove it right through the man's left thigh, deep into the River Red's trunk, while taking care to avoid the femoral artery. He glanced briefly at his handiwork and then walked back a few paces before squatting. Hank and Jalyerri squatted on either side of him. All three silently watched the agony of their impaled captive.

Now that he had done it, Brian felt sick. He was used to killing animals, but—he shuddered—a human being was something else again. Christ, even the blood smelled different.

Soon, the sound of more and more flies, buzzing on the man's blood, dominated. The three of them sat silently and watched the man alternate between screams, sobs and desperate begging. They were watching the last tenuous grip on life, of someone who should've been jailed years ago. Who, now that he was dying, begged for the mercy that he'd never shown to women. He offered his watchers every penny in his bank account. He prayed to God through pain-contorted lips.

And he continually begged and screamed for water. Of the watchers, only Hank spoke. His rage wouldn't leave him, and he spoke, just once, in his slow Texas drawl.

"Think about what you did, you stinkin' bastard. And I'll sure be gratified if you take a long time to die. Yes, I surely will."

Then carnivorous, Red Beef Ant scouts discovered where his blood had dripped onto the ground. They quickly crawled up his legs and commenced their vicious biting. Their bites stung and stung and caused numerous welts to appear, almost immediately.

Soon, numberless Red Beef Ants found their way to the speared man. They swarmed en masse over his body and started to eat at his orifices, particularly where his bloody flesh girdled both spears. The man's shrieking immediately soared to a shriller crescendo. Then it ebbed and flowed.

Countless more voracious Red Beef Ants appeared. Then large, metallic-green, egg-laying Blowflies, settled on his blood. And, as was their preference, their hatched maggots would soon be feeding on flesh next to the shrieking man's wounds.

Hank dispassionately watched the man's suffering. He felt no pity, and every now and again, his rage flared up like hot, just-fanned flames.

The speared man didn't last as long as Hank had hoped. And when he died, Hank felt cheated because he hadn't suffered longer. Moments later, the appalling screech of a Barking Owl pierced the surrounding stillness.

"Murder bird," Jalyerri observed, wide-eyed.

The three rose to their feet and cut down the dead man. Brian and Hank each grabbed an ankle and dragged the body through trees and scrub, to the river's bank. Once there, they tossed it into the water. It floated downstream for twenty yards before becoming entangled in the waterlogged, dark branches of a half-submerged, dead tree. Awestruck, they saw the head and cold eyes of a giant Estuarine Crocodile suddenly break the surface. It opened its enormous, yellowish-pink maw and clamped its irregularly toothed jaws across the body. It briefly gazed at them with expressionless, unblinking eyes before closing its thin, transparent eyelids and silently sinking below the surface. The coffee-coloured water briefly swirled to acknowledge the giant reptile's departure, before continuing its onward meander.

"For Crissake," Brian gasped. "Did you see the size of that damn lizard?"

"Terrifying!" Hank drew in his breath sharply. He noticed that Brian's face now looked pale. "You feeling okay, partner?"

"It's starting to hit me now that it's over, know what I mean?"

"That's understandable." Hank's voice grew bleak. "But don't forget what that animal did. And remember," he emphasized quietly, "it'd be best if nobody knew we caught up to him."

"Yeah," Brian murmured. "I'm definitely with you on that one."

"Coming?" Hank asked.

"Yeah."

The three of them turned and headed toward their horses. Only Jalyerri broke the silence, and he spoke just once. "No goot shit bugger, dat one," he said with feeling.

The slight, dark figure of the *Kaditje* man continued to watch them. When they were out of sight, he emerged from behind his tree, walked to the riverbank and stood, and looked at the spot where the giant reptile had disappeared. And being a polite person, he thanked the ancestral Crocodile Man in the same way that he thanked him whenever he lit a fire. For it was the Crocodile Man who first gave his people fire. Now, he thanked him for sending somebody to take that evil body to where those keepers of white feller, right-side *bijnitch* would never find it. He stared one last time at the river. Then, breathing in deeply, he turned and walked to the River Red to collect his two spears that Jalyerri had left against its trunk.

CHAPTER 2

CALUM

LONG CREEK CATTLE RUN, MARCH 1947

The youth sat nervously in the passenger's seat of the sturdy, Bedford truck as it headed up the rutted dirt track toward the two men that were leaning against the top rail of a holding yard. He desperately needed a job and was worried that he was fast running out of cattle runs. So far, none of the runs at which they'd called, on Perce's mail round, had been interested in employing an inexperienced young ringer.

"That's Mr. Jackson there, leanin' against the rail o' that yard, young feller," Perce informed him. "He'll decide quick whether yer gets a job here."

Beyond the two men ahead lay a sparsely-treed, seemingly endless plain covered with knee-high Mitchell and Flinders grasses that surged in the breeze. These green surges looked, for all money, like rolling, green waves.

Already it was a warm eighty degrees plus, and swarms of sticky Black Flies seethed over the men's khaki-shirted backs. Les Jackson, the heavy, big-boned Station Manager, turned his head and glanced at his Head Stockman.

"When'll you be right to start mustering fats, Hank?" he impatiently asked.

"I'll leave by the end of the week, Boss."

"Even if you're a *ringer* short?"

"Fats don't stay fat forever." The tall Head Stockman looked out over the green plain before them. "Now ain't that new grass really somethin', Boss?" he stated admiringly.

"Yeah, there's enough of it," the other agreed, shortly.

They turned and watched the Bedford truck brake and stop. Its overweight, sweating driver alighted and, panting in the heat, carried a bundle of mail over to them.

"G'day, Mr. Jackson. Goin' awright, Hank?"

"G'day, Perce."

Les Jackson eyed the slightly built youth who had alighted from the truck's cabin. He flashed Perce a hard look of annoyance. "Who's *that* boy, Perce?" he demanded.

"Young ringer lookin' for work. Name's Calum McNicol. I come across him in Catriona." Perce regarded Les Jackson obediently. "But if yer don't want him, I'll take him on with me, no worries."

Les Jackson briefly appraised the boy, standing self-consciously in his Cuban-heeled riding boots. He noted the brand-new, khaki shirt, *moleskins* and plaited, kangaroo-hide belt. *Young McNicol looks nervous*, he thought and decided that his nervousness didn't sit well with his expensive clothing.

"Where you from, boy?" he curtly asked.

"I've been helping on a Queensland cattle run, in Brigalow country."

"How big was this run?"

"Seven-thousand acres."

"And how many runs've turned you down so far?"

"A few," Calum admitted defensively; then he raised his chin and added defiantly, "They didn't have any vacancies."

Les Jackson puffed out his chest, and Hank couldn't help grinning to himself. *The goddamn, silly bastard*, he thought. *Now he's starting to look like some damn, great Pouter pigeon. And Christ alone knows why he sweats so much, when the only exercise he gets is fornicating with Murri women. Yes, he surely is a goddamn, two-faced bastard! Because, damn me, if he doesn't keep reminding the men that the Government's made it illegal for them to screw black women.*

Les Jackson started to speak again. "This here is *the* Long Creek, boy," he announced pompously. "We're owned by First Northern Pastoral, and we've got eighty-five-hundred-plus *square miles* of the finest Tablelands and Gulf Country cattle country. And our herd is fifty-thousand, give or take a few thousand!" He fixed Calum with an intimidating stare. "What're you running from, boy?"

Calum lifted his chin, straightened his skinny shoulders, and met the heavy-set Station Manager's eyes. "I'm not running from the police. And I earn my wages."

Les Jackson turned to his Head Stockman, and they looked briefly at each other. Hank had never before seen anyone with this boy's unusual colouring; the fair complexion, coal-black hair and blue eyes that were almost startling; so intense was their blue. He couldn't help wondering about his background.

"You can ride, I suppose?" Hank asked, smiling.

"Yes, if it's a quiet horse."

Now that's a sensible answer, Hank thought. *The kid knows I could set him up by putting him on a rough one. Well, I still need to find out just how badly you want a job, young feller. Hell, I can sure do without some kid, in camp, who suddenly wants out because the going's too tough.*

"Perce, take this boy to the stock camp kitchen," Les Jackson ordered dismissively. "Charlie'll be hanging about, and he'll give you both a feed."

"No worries, Mr. Jackson, an' thanks. See yer later, eh."

"Yeah."

Perce led the way, and Calum followed. When they were out of earshot, he turned and grinned at Calum. "Didn't I tell you we'd get a feed here?"

"Yes, and I'm starving!"

Perce briefly kissed the grouped fingers of his right hand and gave his protruding belly a rub. "Don't yer worry, mate," he said, "there'll be *real* bread too. None of that unleavened damper what's so dry it binds a bloke up. Yeah, the cook here is Corn Beef Charlie hisself. Bit of a gossip, mind you, same as all bloody cooks. An' always waitin' fer someone ter put a foot wrong! But," he added admiringly, and then loftily explained, "Corn Beef Charlie is the *gen-u-ine* article. Yer see, young feller, cooks is graded up here. On top yer gets cooks. After 'em comes tucker fuckers. Then bait layers. An' last of all yer gets yer willful bloody murderers."

"Shit!"

Alarmed, Calum quickly resolved to watch out for any willful bloody murderers. Clearly, their food had to be totally indigestible, if not halfway poisonous.

"And," Perce continued conversationally, "I wish Charlie'd get a set of those store teeth what fit. The ones he's got are so bloody loose they click like fuckin' Abo, music sticks when he speaks."

****

Les Jackson continued to regard Hank dubiously. "Hell, Hank," he complained. "That kid's so skinny you'll lose him if he stands sideways! Now, how in God's name could anyone get a solid day's work out of him?"

"After he's eaten, I'll put him up on Quiet As. If he looks like he can ride, he'll earn his half wage all right."

"You'll kill the skinny bastard. Hell, he hasn't even lived yet." Les Jackson shook his head impatiently. "Anyway, he's got to be sillier than a two bob watch if he gets up on that rough, bloody animal."

"Maybe he won't get on the horse. If that's the case, he leaves with Perce. End of story."

"Don't waste your bloody time, Hank. Just piss him off!"

Hank thought that Les Jackson was being judgmental and unfair, and he promptly decided that he'd find a way to get young McNicol hired. "I liked it when he said he earned his wages," he told Les Jackson brightly. "Anyway, I'm going to tell him to be here at one. You want to watch?" He smiled disarmingly. "What've you got to lose, Boss? He won't cost you much, and I'm the one who has to make him earn it."

"Yeah, I hadn't thought of that. And you know, there's nothing to stop you promotin' those two, Abo horse tailers. Abo ringers mostly only cost me food and clothes, remember."

"Right. See you, Boss."

"Yeah."

Hank turned on his heel and walked toward the stock camp kitchen. His thoughts as they so often did, when alone, returned to the family ranch in Texas and the wife he'd married in '43, before the Twenty-ninth Infantry Division had embarked for Europe. His indescribable shock and hurt and sense of betrayal were fading at long last, thank God. And, yes, he hadn't telegrammed Donna to tell her that he'd been discharged because he'd wanted to surprise her. Well, he'd sure surprised his yellow rose of Texas. He'd also surprised his younger brother. The two had been in the shower together. The worst kind of betrayal! Yeah, well he *had* exploded. He'd hit his brother clean through the bathroom door. He'd never felt such rage. Then the frightening realization that he'd been capable of killing them both had shocked him. In fact, he had wanted to kill them. That still shocked him.

Donna had come to him while he'd been packing civilian clothes into a small suitcase. He'd always remember the words that she'd wailed. They hadn't made any sense then. And they didn't make any sense now.

"Ah surely don't know how it happened, Hank dahlin'. Exceptin' I was awful lonely, an' Billy Jack kinda made me feel close to you."

Jesus, what a rotten mess. He'd needed to get as far away from both of them as was possible—and as quickly as possible. Australia had looked like a good bet. It was even farther away than Europe. Besides, he'd had about as much of Europe as he could take. Yes, the ever-present smell of cordite plus the rotting fetidity of all the battleground corpses had ensured that Europe would forever be associated, in his mind, with the stomach-turning stench of the decaying dead.

On reaching the stock camp kitchen, Hank poked his head around the latticed, open doorway. "Be at that holding yard at one, kid," he ordered. "I want to see you ride before you get a job." He nodded at the mail truck driver. "And don't you leave, Perce, till I tell you."

"I hear you, Hank," Perce called out at the Head Stockman's departing back.

Calum hungrily ate the meal of steak, topped with two fried eggs; freshly baked white bread; and sugared black tea that Charlie had placed in front of him. When he'd finished, he moved his chair back and stood up.

"Thanks, Mr. Charlie," he said. "That's the best meal I've had in ages."

The elderly cook pushed back the brim of his grey, Fedora hat, and his mail-order teeth clicked disconcertingly when he spoke. "Yer all right, son, because yer've got yer manners. An' jus' call me Charlie." He sniffed and looked disparagingly at Perce. "That's more'n I can say about some blow-ins who don't appear ter appreciate grouse tucker."

Perce knew that top cooks, on cattle runs, were as scarce as hens' teeth. He also knew that humouring them was an important unwritten rule. He inwardly winced at the thought of future breadless visits.

"Of course, I like yer food, Charlie," he protested vigorously. "I never come across a better cook anywhere!"

"Well, that's awright then."

Charlie hadn't always been a cook. But he'd decided, forty years ago, that cooks had it easier than ringers. Also, their wages were much better. Besides, a good cook commanded a fair bit of power and esteem. And all the ringers in Hank's crew recognized his skill. It was just that they didn't praise him enough. Mostly, it was only Hank who complimented him. The rest seemed to think that what Hank had said sufficed. But it didn't. Charlie craved a ton of appreciation from everyone.

Outside, in the harsh sunlight, Calum looked about him. The home station consisted of five, bush timber and tin-roofed buildings with their mandatory, corrugated iron, water tanks. The buildings seemed to possess an ageless, sturdy feel. Overshadowing the few acacias were special plantings. These were two, tall, Mango trees plus a *Mangan*. Calum noted that the homestead possessed bamboo-latticed, timber-floored verandahs on all four sides. Its front garden was fenced with chicken wire. There were no flowers, just a scraggy lawn bisected by a dirt path, which led to the front door.

During the long drive to Long Creek, Calum had been told by Perce that a Mr. Jackson was the Station Manager.

"He carries the whip on Long Creek, an' he lives alone, in the house." Perce had grinned lasciviously. "Likes the gins he does. He's a fair dinkum, gin jockey." Perce had winked. "I heard he favours them as got a bit of meat on 'em! An' they don' need ter be real young neither."

Calum had looked puzzled.

"Yer know," Perce had airily explained, "those whose bums, when they walk, look like a coupla pups bouncin' around in a sack."

Calum had reddened and had looked away.

Perce had picked up his discomfort and had quickly changed the subject. "Long Creek's got four, permanent stock camps yer know," he'd said. "An' out of the four Head Stockmen, they reckon that the Yank, what Brisbane hired, is the best ter work for." He'd glanced at Calum, to check whether Calum'd been listening, before continuing. "And that Hank feller is dinkum educated. Went to one of them colleges in the States, I heard. An' there's a ringer named Murranji Bill who's also educated, but he got his learnin' from all the books he gets sent ter him, from Adelaide. Been getting books mailed ter 'im fer years."

Perce had been doing the same, mail run for fourteen years. It was a lonely life, and he'd never married. His father had been a battler, and he used to whine to Perce that it was all the fault of his wastrel wife. Maybe that's why Perce'd never made the long trip to Adelaide, in South Australia, to find a wife.

Perce had a profitable sideline, rum. He carried enough boxes with him to help out any isolated run, which had temporarily run out. He constantly worried about the price he charged and spent a lot of time wondering, when driving, if he could get away with a price hike. But the thought of being abused as a rip-off merchant always made him go to water.

The light sou'easterly blustered fitfully and swirled dirt into Calum's eyes. Discordant, *metallic-sounding* screeches coming from one of the Mango trees announced the presence of a flock of large, sooty-black Red-tailed Black-Cockatoos—so named for their distinctive long, red-panelled, black tails—while above the towering, steadily creaking windmill that supplied a fifty-yard long water trough, Calum noticed a flock of Galahs. These large cockatoos wheeled sharply in close formation and, in doing so, alternately revealed their powder-grey backs and wings and rosy-pink breasts. And high in the hot, blue sky, a pair of pale-coloured, carrion-eating Whistling Kites soared and banked on motionless wings while, higher still, a massive, dark-brown Wedge-tailed Eagle, steered by its wedge-shaped tail, effortlessly rode a thermal.

Calum had already concluded that this was a hard country. He had noticed from the truck that carrion was never far away, for these plains often revealed small, brown-coloured humps, at which perching crows and kites tore greedily. These were the carcasses of calves born to mothers whose milk had run dry. And the remains of adult cattle also weren't uncommon. He'd wondered whether these had succumbed to bloat, caused by the rich new grass.

****

As he walked toward Long Creek's Aboriginal camp, Murranji Bill, one of Hank's ringers, noticed the youth ahead of him. Word had spread, and he knew exactly what Hank had in mind. And for the past twenty years or so, Murranji Bill hadn't been able to resist siding with the underdog. His biggest regret was that this hadn't always been the case. It was a nagging guilt that never left him.

"Hang on, young feller," he cheerfully called out. "I want to show you where you'd best climb up on the horse you'll be riding for Hank."

Murranji Bill was slim and middle-aged. His deeply tanned features were creased white at the corners of his eyes and mouth; he was a man who smiled a lot. And once he'd caught up to Calum, he held out his hand, his brown eyes crinkling and his smile open and friendly.

"The name's Bill Taylor," he said. "Some folks call me Murranji Bill."

"Calum McNicol."

"Come with me, son. I'll show you a dry, creek bed filled with sand." He grinned engagingly. "If a man's going to come off a horse, I reckon sand's got to be a helluva lot softer than trampled-down dirt in a stock yard, don't you?"

"Yes."

"An' another thing. Hank's only testing to see how bad you want a job," Murranji Bill advised. "If I were you, I'd hang on for a couple of minutes an' then slide off into this soft sand. An' don't get back on. I know the horse Hank's got in mind. It's a rough bugger with all the tricks an' then some."

"Yes."

"Now, I know Hank admires a man who stands up to him, so you hold your ground, son, know what I mean?"

Calum frowned and looked away. "But if I don't get back on," he said, "it'll mean Mr. Nelson's won, won't it?"

Murranji Bill gave Calum a curious look. "An' that's important is it, young feller?"

"Yes."

"Course, you know you'll be providin' laughs for all the entertainment-starved bastards around here, don't you?"

Calum carefully considered this. Finally, he just nodded and then changed the subject. "I've only seen Shorthorns here, you know," he said in a curious voice.

"They're best for this country, young feller. An' the Long Creek Shorthorns are quality. All the herd bulls are Munro-breed, an' we cull out any white beasts because the bloodsucking aphids really go for 'em, leaving only skin an' bone."

"And I've never seen so much grass," Calum exclaimed, wide-eyed.

"That's because these are black soil plains. An' *this*," Murranji Bill said, indicating with a boot toe, "is what makes it special. That's Mitchell grass. It's here all year. An' this other here is Flinders grass. It only comes up after the Wet an', by the end of the Dry, all that's left is bare patches between the Mitchell grass tussocks."

"I didn't mean to sound nosey," Calum said apologetically.

"Hell, I admire a young feller who wants to learn an' has the sense to ask. In my book, asking beats the hell outta having to learn the hard way."

"And is the whole run on these plains?"

"No, only some of the south end. And these plains are crossed by red ridges, harsh as desert country, an' covered with Snapping Gums an' Bloodwoods; also there's red grass that grows between the red, ant beds." Murranji Bill paused. "An' you also get patches of red soil. There, you'll find low trees like Mimosa scrub an' Mulga."

"Charlie said that if I get a job, I'll be mustering the northwest section."

"Right. Well, that's sort of Bay of Biscay country, young feller. The flats have good Mitchell grass, but it gets hilly an' stony with thick Bulwaddy an' Lancewood scrubs." Murranji Bill collected his thoughts before continuing. "An' it's jumbled country, mate. Hills, gorges, boulders and billabongs. And Pandanus trees and Paperbarks."

A low movement in a nearby patch of scrub caught Calum's eye. For a long moment he found himself looking into oval, dark-brown eyes that weren't afraid. The strong, canine neck held a broad head with forward-pointing, erect ears. A deep chest, strong shoulders and a low, bannerlike, sweeping tail completed the image. Then the reddish-yellow vision just seemed to melt away, and Calum found himself staring into vacant scrub. He glanced, in surprise, at Murranji Bill.

"Is that the first dingo you've seen, mate?" the other asked.

"It looked so strong and quick," Calum exclaimed.

"Best you don't sound too keen on the dogs, especially when you're around cattlemen."

"Oh, do they kill lots of cattle?"

Murranji Bill smiled. "That's one argument that's been goin' on, between sensible folk, since I was a boy."

"Oh?"

"They kill calves, for sure," Murranji Bill explained. "But it's mostly during drought when tucker's scarce. An', yeah, they'll hamstring an' kill a yearling. But I reckon they do good too, by cleaning out the sick an' weedy beasts."

"I heard they can't be tamed?"

Murranji Bill smiled gently. "I don't know about that," he offered. "I knew a feller who had one. He reckoned, in play, he was often stalked an' nipped on the bum. But that's how they stop 'roos, by hamstringing 'em. And they've got all the guts in the world. I've seen it myself. Yeah, a dingo'll stand its ground against any dog its own size, or bigger."

"Oh."

"An' it climbs an' jumps almost like a cat. Good watchdog too. You'll soon know if something's about, because your dingo'll have its hair raised from between its ears to the start of its tail. An' it won't settle till it's checked out everywhere."

They reached a sandy, dry, creek bed fringed with Coolibah trees. Murranji Bill watched Calum scrape at the sand with his boot, in order to gauge its depth, before looking up with a pleased smile.

"Thanks," he said. "I owe you."

"No worries, young feller. An' remember you don't have to prove you're the best rough-horse rider in the Territory."

"I know. But I'm going to try and stay with it."

"Suit yourself. Anyway here's where I leave you." Murranji Bill grinned. "I need to see someone in the Murri camp for half a minute."

"And Murranji?"

17

Smiling, Murranji Bill glanced back over his shoulder.

Calum smiled back, self-consciously. "I'm trying for a ringer's job. And I haven't heard that word before."

"It comes from being able to ring a mob of bullocks that're rushin' back into themselves."

"Oh."

For a moment Calum watched Murranji Bill continue up the creek bed. Then he turned and went back the way that he'd come.

The mail truck hadn't been moved. He grabbed his saddle, swung it over his right shoulder and headed for the holding yard. There, he balanced it on a rail, sat on the ground with his back against a fence post and shaded his eyes with his broad-brimmed, stock hat. He tried to visualize eighty-five-hundred square miles. And he tried to imagine living in cattle camps for eight months of the year. First, mustering bullocks and then branding the run's *cleanskin* calves. This was what he wanted, he told himself. He'd never seen so much space before, or so few people in it. There was no way his father would be able to find him now providing, of course; he managed to get a job here.

He thought some more about the father who'd never given him much. That is, if you discounted all the violent, drunken abuse. He frowned to himself. But at least his father had taught him about horses. He supposed that had to count for something. And when he was older, he'd had to learn to stick up for himself; otherwise, his father would've walked all over him. He wondered dispassionately whether his father was the only racehorse trainer who'd personally managed the preparation of his own, Pakenham Cup winner while in the middle of a two-month bender. But don't knock it, mate, he told himself, because the winnings and prize money that you stole, when the bastard was drunk and snoring, were your escape from his run-down stables; as well as your ticket up north. He inwardly recoiled when he recalled his father's drunken abuse. *Well you shit*, he thought, *I'm the one who took your dough. And I'm the one who's laughing 'cause it's bought me clothes, a stock saddle, stock whip, and the latest 30/30 lever action Winchester. And there's plenty left. Yes, you bastard, you didn't win with me. And it serves you right because you should've treated me better. And you should've treated Mum better too.*

Calum made himself stop thinking about his father, stood up, ducked through the fence and walked to the stock trough. He moved easily through the cows lying around the bore, many of which lumbered to their feet and moved protectively toward their calves. Without apparent effort, he avoided walking between any cow and its calf. At the trough, he rinsed his hands and sloshed water over his face and hair. Farther up, he noticed that a cow, moving in to drink, gave the one beside it a solid horn in the ribs, before taking over the quickly vacated space. Calum grimaced. Apparently, bullies, like his father, also existed in the animal world.

Calum's progress to and from the trough had been observed approvingly by Hank, Les Jackson and a newly returned Murranji Bill. On seeing the tall Head Stockman, Murranji gave him a mocking grin. Hank smiled back and wondered what Murranji'd been up to. Again, he became aware that the undercurrent between them had surfaced and wondered, once more, if it was due to envy because he, Hank, had enjoyed a formal education.

Hank turned his attention to Calum and watched him to see if there was any reaction when an Aboriginal horse tailer led a good-looking, bay gelding into the stockyard. There was none.

Calum walked over to the gelding. He tried to ignore the good-humoured spectators who had draped themselves along the yard's rails. Laughing and joking among themselves, they were clearly looking forward to the impending entertainment. Calum felt a quick stab of annoyance. Shit! Hank Nelson had him trapped because if he didn't ride this horse, word would quickly get around. And then no cattle run would give him a job. He tightened his lips. He'd show that Yank bastard. He nodded to the Aboriginal horse tailer.

"This horse tame?" he asked.

"Him no cranky bugger. Him no kick, Boss."

"I'm not a boss. And my name's Calum."

"*Yu-ai.*" The Aborigine grinned, showing very white teeth. "You savvy this country?"

"No."

"Eh, look out!"

Hank watched on impassively.

"What's this horse's name?" Calum called out to him.

"Quiet As."

"Like in 'as a mouse'?"

"Yeah, something like that."

"Shit."

Calum took the reins from the Aborigine and then removed the heavy, station saddle.

"What're you doing, kid?"

"I'm going to put my own saddle on him, Mr. Nelson. And also check you haven't put anything prickly under the saddle blanket."

"We don't do that on this run."

"I bet," Calum responded angrily.

"Kid, you won't last long up here, unless you learn to trust people."

Calum led the bay over to the Head Stockman. He had the station saddle balanced over his right shoulder. He put it on the rail in front of Hank Nelson and met his eyes. "Trust?" He grimaced sarcastically. "I told you I could ride a quiet horse, and you bring out this outlaw."

Ah, so the boy's got a bit of a temper, Hank thought. He smiled pleasantly. "Relax, kid," he said. "That's no outlaw. Has he tried to chop at you, with his front hooves?"

"Where I come from, a horse that chops with its front feet gets shot."

"Yep, I guess that's the same here." Hank grinned. "Look, all he'll do, kid, is buck a bit."

"A big bit or a little bit?"

"Climb up and find out. Unless you haven't you got the guts to be a ringer?"

Calum turned up his top lip scornfully and walked away.

"Stroppy young bugger isn't he, Hank?" Les Jackson remarked.

"Yeah, but I like a bit of spirit, Boss."

Calum controlled the gelding's head with the reins in his left hand and checked the saddle blanket for thorns before swinging his own saddle onto its back with his right hand. He tightened the girth and waited for the gelding to exhale before tightening the girth another couple of notches. Again, he studied the bay. It had an intelligent eye, small ears and a head with a definite dish. *Bit of Arab back there*, he thought. Yes, you only had to look at the short back, slim legs, small hooves and the flow to its mane and tail. He saw that its ears were now flat, that its nostrils were dilated, and that its eyes were wide and rolling and were showing their whites. He offered it the unthreatening back of his hand to smell. Said that it was a fine horse but he was going to ride it. And he wouldn't hurt it. Look, he wasn't even wearing spurs or carrying a quirt. But he *was* going to ride it. And it would learn to trust him, and they would become friends. He saw that the bay was listening to him because its ears were moving, and its eyes weren't rolling so much. He continued talking while he stroked its neck. He told it he suspected that somebody had once treated it badly and that he was aware that it knew the difference between right and wrong. And so did he. Finally, he looked at Hank Nelson and nodded to him.

"I'm going to the dry, creek bed," he said. "I'll climb on there."

"Makes sense."

Les Jackson turned to his Head Stockman. "Hank, do you reckon I've been wrong about this boy?"

"I guess we'll both know the answer to that in around ten minutes, Boss."

"I didn't reckon he'd get on that animal," Les Jackson said.

"I thought he might. He strikes me as kind of stubborn."

At the creek bed, Calum continued to ignore the onlookers who now leaned against the dark-trunked, blue-green leafed, Coolibah trees. He shortened his left rein till the bay's head was turned toward him, took both reins in his left hand and then grasped the bridle's cheek strap with the same hand. He placed the ball of his left foot in the stirrup iron and smoothly swung himself into the saddle. But the instant that he released his grip on its cheek strap, the bay exploded. What followed was brutal. First, the bay produced a rapid succession of near-vertical jumps with stiff-legged landings. And each time that it landed, Calum felt a shuddering shock travel right up his backbone. Then the gelding spun like a top, lightning fast, on virtually the same spot. Calum sat it easily as he anticipated its movement. Then he lost his left, stirrup iron. Now, without any loss of momentum, the gelding launched itself into a series of very fast, very violent bucks. It soon became obvious to the spectators that Calum was in trouble. He'd lost the rhythm and was like a dancer, out of step and struggling to regain his balance. He knew that it'd be only a matter of time before he came off, and the power beneath him astonished him. *Bloody hell,* he thought, *this must be about the strongest horse I've ever been on.*

"Not long now," murmured Hank.

After yet another vicious buck, Calum became airborne. He half-turned slowly, in midair, before landing with a dull thud. The gelding stood motionless. Its ears were pricked, its head was down and its reins were dangling. Its eyes stayed fixed on its dislodged rider. Calum and the bay considered each other.

"You haven't won yet, mate," he told it. "That was only the first round."

It didn't concern Murranji Bill that the gelding had dislodged its rider. No, he liked what he'd seen of the boy, so far. The way, when saddling up, he'd used the reins and bridle, cheek strap to control the bay's head, and hence its rear end. The safe way that he'd mounted a horse, about which he'd known nothing. Yes, the boy had done everything right. No way was he going to find himself only halfway mounted when the bay started its bucking. But most of all, Murranji'd liked the way the boy had sat close behind the pommel, right over the bay's centre of gravity. He'd known that the farther back he sat, the more he'd be lifted by the gelding's bucking. Finally, Murranji Bill had liked the sensible way that the youth, when thrown, had lain prone on his stomach and had protected his head with his arms. Yes, he'd known all right that a thrown rider, jumping to his feet right away, could get his head kicked in by the flying hooves of a still-bucking horse. Yes, it was as plain as the nose on a man's face that this boy knew horses and that he also knew how to ride. Murranji Bill admired that. And he especially admired a rider who had no interest in punishing a horse with spurs and whip. Of course, there were those that did. But mostly it was because, underneath, they were scared of horses.

After catching his breath, Calum slowly rose to his feet. He spat out sand and brushed it off his shirt and pants. Picking up the reins, he leaned against the bay's shoulder. For a moment he rested his forehead against its wet neck and was conscious of the smell of green grass, salty sweat and oiled leather. He told the bay that it wasn't behaving very well and not to think that it'd won because he was determined to ride it. But he wouldn't be holding any grudges just because it'd bucked him off.

"Stubborn young bugger, isn't he?" Les Jackson remarked, nodding to himself.

"I kinda like a kid who doesn't give up."

"I'll lay odds when he comes off again, he'll give up."

"I wouldn't bet on it, Boss."

Calum mounted again with the same easy motion. And again the bay exploded. This time, it reared up on its hind legs, and for a moment Calum, low along its neck and with its mane wrapped around his face, thought that it was going to topple over backward. A vivid picture of crippled Herbie Oliver flashed into his mind. These days Herbie went to the Pakenham races in his wheelchair. All the regulars knew him. He'd been a top jockey till his foot had caught in his stirrup iron and a fractious, two-year-old filly had fallen over on top of him. Her weight had broken his back and had crushed his pelvis. Calum hastily freed his feet from the stirrup irons and readied himself for a clearing vault; but catlike, the bay managed to land on its feet.

Calum thought that he could feel it tiring, but it was just gathering itself for another series of spiteful, gut-wrenching bucks. Then it revealed a new trick, and the moment that it leaped high into the air, all four feet off the ground, Calum knew what was coming. He didn't believe that there was a rider, anywhere, that wouldn't be heavily thrown when a horse pulled this one. While in midair, the bay twisted violently and simultaneously kicked both, back heels upward with explosive force. Calum felt as if his stomach had been left behind and momentarily thought that he'd vomit. The bay had generated so much force that it seemed as if a gigantic, steel spring beneath him had uncoiled and hurled him upward. This time Calum landed like a sack of seed potatoes, dumped off the back of a truck.

"Jesus!" Les Jackson exclaimed. "What if he gets hurt?"

"Nobody forced him to get on that horse, Boss," Hank answered. "And sand *is* soft."

Les Jackson held out an arm toward Calum. "That'll do, boy!"

Prostrate on the ground, Calum glanced over at Hank Nelson. The Head Stockman's face was expressionless. After a long moment, Calum sat up. He was badly winded and hurting. He gingerly stretched out his legs, and again, he and the bay considered each other.

Calum was drenched with perspiration and could feel it dripping down his back and running into his eyes. It was making them sting. Flies were buzzing on his sweat before settling on his face. He brushed them off. The hot sun was burning into him through his wet shirt, and his whole body seemed to be aching. Slowly, he got to his feet. Breathing heavily and feeling pain in his chest, he moved unsteadily toward the gelding, which was now blowing hard.

"That'll do, mate," Murranji Bill called out. "You've already shown these grinning bastards you can sit a horse. You've done well, young feller."

"Hank, *you* tell him to turn it up," Les Jackson ordered.

"He'll be okay, Boss. For him, this is personal. You see, he's decided this is between him an' me, and I'd kinda like to let him have his win. Okay?"

"You're both as mad as cut snakes. He's shown he can ride. Jesus, isn't that enough?"

"It is for me. But not for him."

Some of the other spectators started to call out. Theirs was a mixed chorus of congratulations and suggestions.

"Yer done enough, kid."

"Fuck the boss. That'll do!"

"Good on yer, mate."

"You got him beat. Finish him off."

Calum ignored their yells. He slowly got to his feet and went to the gelding. Gathering the reins, he leaned against its lathered-up wither for a brief minute. He was conscious of the bunched, twitching muscles under its wet, silky skin and that its near-front leg had started to quiver. The youth spoke quietly, and it listened. He asked the horse why it kept on fighting. He told it that he was going to persevere till it let him ride it. And that he wanted it for his own horse. He patted its dripping neck, shortened the left rein, put his foot in the stirrup iron and slowly swung himself into the saddle. He knew that he wouldn't be able to remount if it threw him again, and what an old stockman had once said to him flashed through his mind: "There's never a horse what can't be rode, young feller. And there's never a man what can't be throwed."

He began to wonder if he was good enough to ride this bay. Would it be his will that prevailed? *Keep concentrating*, he told himself. *It's all about balance and anticipation. That's all you have. That's all any rider has.* Under him, he could feel the gelding gather itself. He waited apprehensively. Then it gave a couple of pig roots, which were so half-hearted its back legs barely cleared the ground. It stood stock-still and started to tremble. It was spent. Quickly, Calum dismounted, stood at its head, and allowed it to reach out its nose and sniff his chest. He gently stroked its face. He was so absorbed that he was oblivious of the reaction around him. In any case, it was a subdued one.

"He's just a puppy dog, mate."

"Good on yer, kid."

"Yer bored it up the boss, fer sure!"

It was over. Thankfulness flooded through Calum, anaesthetizing his aches and dispatching his exhaustion. His thoughts turned to Hank Nelson. He wondered whether the man could be trusted to give him a job as agreed. Or had he just been used to provide some passing entertainment? He resolved that his voice wouldn't reveal his desperation. He led the gelding toward Hank Nelson and then stood stony-faced before him.

"Do I get a job, Mr. Nelson?"

"Sure, kid."

Relief washed over him like cool water on a hot day. He looked at the Head Stockman. "Mr. Nelson?"

"Yep."

"I'm not a kid. I'm seventeen, and my name's Calum."

"Tell you what, ringer. You call me Hank, and I'll call you Calum."

"I'm going to take this bay back and give him a drink, Hank. Then I'll ride him at a walk, till he cools down."

"Makes sense."

On the way back to the stockyard, Murranji Bill joined Calum. "Well, young feller," he asked with a smile, "do you think you won?"

"I don't know. So long as Hank Nelson didn't. That's what matters."

"Right," Murranji Bill said with an amused, half smile.

At the stockyard, Hank watched his new ringer mount. He saw that the bay was still blowing hard and watched Calum touch his heels to it and move off, at a walk, toward the trough. He saw that Calum had the gelding nicely gathered under him and that he sat very straight in the saddle. He noted that the bay was responding well to its rider and also noted its keen interest in cattle. How it constantly asserted its supremacy over those in its way. How it pushed through them to get to the trough and showed its low regard, for them, by putting its ears back and biting those, which didn't move away quickly enough.

Les Jackson nodded to Hank. "At least he's sitting that horse same as a ringer."

"Yep."

"Looks like you'll also get a fair stock horse to go with your new ringer."

"I liked the way he kept talking to that bay. It wouldn't surprise me if he turned out to be one of those people that horses follow around like dogs. I've only come across one or two in my time."

"Yeah? See yer, Hank."

"Right, Boss."

Les Jackson moved off. *Silly young bastard*, he thought. *He wouldn't have a clue what he was letting himself in for.* God! How he'd come to hate this life. All it offered was damn heat and dust and the stink of cattle and horse shit. This was no life for a man who appreciated good company, the bright lights and good food.

He felt a stab of envy as he thought about his younger brother, in Adelaide. *Yeah*, he thought, *that young bugger's never short of a good time! And he's never dressed in clothes that stink of cattle. And he always has a good-looking, white girl on his arm. And I bet he's never fucked a bit of black velvet that stinks of wood smoke, earth and sweat.* Les Jackson smiled wryly to himself. Some of these Long Creek gins, though, weren't half bad. They could really put their backs into it when they had a mind to. He wondered whether there were any black whores in Adelaide. Yeah, black sheilas knew how to wriggle all right.

And the only bloody thing that was stopping him from taking off for Adelaide, right now, was a job there, which would support the lifestyle that he craved.

CHAPTER 3

DOREEN

Hank had grown to love his new country. In many ways it reminded him of his Texas. It offered similar, sweeping vistas and innumerable, Shorthorn cattle and ringers that weren't all that different from cowboys. And more and more, he'd found that Murranji Bill was proving to be a never-ending source of information that was teaching him much about the Northern Territory's culture, institutions and wildlife.

The two had taken a brief break from the hot, branding fire and also from branding foals. They were enjoying a cigarette and were chatting amicably.

"Yeah," Murranji told Hank, while wiping his sweating brow with an arm. "Those mission stations have been around for as long as folks can remember."

"That right?"

"And most of the whites, in them, do an all right job. Of course they also do their best to bring Christianity and Western civilization to all the Murries in nearby camps."

"Of course," Hank said, and couldn't help grinning.

"I know. I know. But give 'em their due because they also look after the sick and start up mission schools."

"Yeah?" Hank raised his eyebrows in surprise.

"Sure. And they must have a ton of Faith, because they don't hesitate to look after Murri lepers, as well as all those Murries who've caught syphilis, the poor buggers."

Hank shook his head in amazement.

"Of course," Murranji informed him, while exhaling twin runnels of cigarette smoke. "Not all mission stations are squeaky clean."

"No?"

"Well, according to the Murri grapevine the one at Cord River isn't real good," Murranji offered cautiously.

"I suppose you'll always get the odd, bad apple."

"Most likely."

"And where's Cord River?"

"It's about eighty miles east of here, Hank."

It was too soon, in their budding relationship, for Murranji to discuss with Hank the extreme disquiet that he felt about those mission stations, which accommodated mixed-descent children. Or that he found it impossible to come to terms with the fact that the Federal Government subsidized those Churches that took on the responsibility of rearing and assimilating, in their orphanages and mission stations, mixed-descent children, which had been forcibly removed from their Aboriginal mothers. And that their mothers were never told to which orphanage or mission station their children had been taken. Or that those little girls, who were taken to Cord River, were told that their mothers had given them away but that, from now on, they would be loved by Jesus.

****

About a fortnight before Perce had come across Calum McNicol, an attractive, going-on-fifteen mixed-descent girl, named Doreen Shillingsworth, was cowering in a small, linen room inside the Cord River mission station. She sat on a urine-stained, old, straw mattress with her knees drawn up and her arms and head resting on them. The small room didn't have any furniture, and because it only had one, small skylight, it was hot and stuffy.

Running through the frightened, angry and confused girl's mind was the curt ultimatum that Sister Rose had given her before locking her inside this room.

"And this is where you'll stay, Doreen Shillingsworth, till you confess you lied. Till then, the only time you'll leave this room will be to go and kneel before the altar, to pray for forgiveness." Sister Rose had regarded her scornfully. "And because you've been such a silly, little girl, you can also use a potty. There's one in the corner over there."

Doreen thought about Sister Rose and realized it'd been a mistake to tell her. Heavens, all the girls knew, from bitter experience, how careful they had to be with Sister Rose. Doreen wondered if there were many others in Edinburgh, like the tiny sister, because that's where she came from. She reminded Doreen of a bright, little bird in the way that she flitted around the mission, her constant, pious smile hiding a dark side. Doreen wondered why Sister Rose was so down on fibs, even little ones, when she told such whoppers herself. Then, if she took a liking to a girl, as had happened to her, you got favoured. And she was always putting her arm around your waist. But heaven help you if you forgot to crawl to her, because then you got promptly punished. Doreen sighed and closed her eyes. She wished and wished that all this wasn't happening to her.

Apart from Sister Rose, who was the senior sister, Doreen had soon learnt that other sisters were in charge of Cord River's surgery, school, dining room, sewing room, dormitories, and bakery and that all had female Aboriginal helpers. One person, though, exercised overall control. He was the man that the girls referred to as the Big Father. But what Doreen only half suspected was that he relished his power and ruled the mission as if it was his personal fiefdom.

Doreen and the older girls had soon become very aware that Cord River boasted a small jail, colloquially called "the boob." And that mostly it was used to house, temporarily, campsite dwellers that had caused trouble, given that Cord River was also an Aboriginal settlement. And that explained the array of *humpies* that had sprung up not far from the mission. The female, Aboriginal helpers, within the mission, tended to be gossips. And it was from them that the older girls had learned that most of the jailed campies had found themselves being punished, by the Big Father, following violent, domestic disputes. And that this was mostly due to the fact that the settlement women significantly outnumbered the men and that the men took advantage of this. Indeed, some men had as many as three women, and this often led to violent confrontations.

But the older girls had soon learned that the Big Father had found another use for his boob. It was to there that he led those unfortunate girls who warranted a beating. Doreen became terrified of being thrashed by him because, once, she'd been ordered to wash its floor after a girl had been beaten. It'd been Ruby O'Hare who'd been thrashed for stealing food, while working in the ration store. Later, Doreen advised her close friend, Susie, that what Ruby and others had told them was totally correct. Susie and Doreen may have differed in appearance, but emotionally, they were close, and they always strongly supported each other. Susie was towheaded, had a darker complexion than Doreen, and wasn't as pretty.

"It's all true, Susie," Doreen had confirmed. "I saw and smelled the wee myself. Like Ruby said, he keeps on thrashing you till you've weed all over the floor."

"Oh jeez! Dor, I couldn't take that," Susie had responded fearfully.

"Me neither. I'm sure I'd faint."

There was minimal happiness and precious little laughter at the mission. But there *was* plenty of work for the girls. Indeed, Sister Rose had told Doreen, with one of her "I know everything" smirks, that the Big Father strongly believed that a girl with idle hands was both slothful and sinful.

The girls often complained, among themselves, that the food that was served was very poor quality. Indeed, initially for weeks, following her arrival seven years ago, Doreen had had an ongoing craving for Brushtail Possum and Echidna. Breakfast now consisted of semolina or (rarely) porridge, a cup of tea, and a slice of bread with dripping. And at dinnertime, the girls were given vegetable soup, bread, and tea. Doreen tolerated the soup because it had decent-sized pieces of goat or beef in it.

Sister Mary was in charge of the dining room. She always carried a long ruler, and the girls had soon learned that if she caught any of them speaking in language, she'd whack them with it.

"Why do yer reckon they won't let us talk in language, Dor?" always curious, petite Brenda Johnson had wondered.

"Well, once they get us to forget our own language, Bren, we're well on the way to being *in the white,* aren't we?" Doreen had grimly replied.

Some young men worked in the main compound. They did those jobs that required manual labor or heavy lifting. And being teenage girls, much discussion centred on these young men. Young Paddy, a "campie," who worked in the ration store, was particularly admired because of his slim, white feller-shaped nose. But Doreen, who had never come into contact socially with boys, remained rather nervous when around them. That wasn't the case with Ruby O'Hare. She'd become totally infatuated with Young Paddy.

"My Gawd, Dor," she'd whispered fervently, "ain't he pretty? An' he's half-carse too, jus' like me!"

Sometimes disagreements between the girls led to the odd, quite savage fight. But the only serious fight that Doreen got into was over Young Paddy, after she'd been ordered to go and help weigh out the campie rations. As soon as she'd returned to the dormitory, Ruby had accosted her.

"You been lookin' at my feller, slut!" she'd yelled.

"No, I haven't, Ruby; I was told to help out there by Sister Rose."

"I never hear that."

"It's true," Doreen had stated placatingly.

"Shurrup, slut."

With that, Ruby had suddenly attacked Doreen with her fists. Doreen had been getting the worst of it till Susie and Brenda had piled in to help. Later, Ruby and Doreen had made up, and Ruby had confided to Doreen that she was desperate to get herself pregnant by Young Paddy.

"Dor, I needs a bub real bad to love alla time," she'd said longingly.

"Ruby, they'll take it from you when it's three or four. You do know that, don't you?"

"Yeah, but it'll be mine till then. An' I'll get ter live in the mums' place."

"How old are you, Ruby?"

"Close-up fifteen, I t'ink."

The girls were aware that the main residence at Cord River had a number of wings. And that one, small one, was where the mothers lived. Gossip had it that these were some of the girls who, on reaching sixteen, had been put to work in the local township where, unfortunately, they'd been impregnated. Being pregnant and with nowhere to go, they'd had no option but to throw themselves on the mercy of the mission. The female, Aboriginal helpers often gossiped that many of these girls were permanently depressed because they lacked the support of their communities. As well, they knew that sooner or later, without warning, their child would be taken from them and sent to another mission station.

Not surprisingly, all the sisters made a point of constantly warning the bigger girls about the risks of pregnancy. And Doreen, like the other girls, had had it drummed into her that boys couldn't be trusted because, unlike girls, they couldn't control themselves. And that this could lead to girls being overpowered and impregnated, even by so-called nice Christian boys. Besides, it was every girl's duty to keep herself "nice" for her future husband.

"Yer don' talk much about fellers, Dor," Susie had remarked one evening. "But maybe I'm different ter you 'cause I come here when I was eleven."

"What do you mean, Susie?"

"I reckon yer gettin' the same as a white sheila."

"How come?"

Susie had laughed. "Me mum said the white missus she worked fer, on the home station, was shocked 'cause me mum was so open 'bout fuckin'. It seems if a white missus admits, open like, she enjoys fuckin', then other whites reckon she has ter be a whore. But you take us. Crise, fuckin' is no big deal. Heck, we see it as bein' no different ter enjoyin' a good feed."

"Oh."

Once she'd turned fourteen, Doreen had found that she was assigned to work in the sewing room after school. She quite liked it. Sister Josephine was in charge, and she was a kindly, old sister. The first time that Doreen had presented herself, she'd been given the same advice that Sister Jo, as the girls called her, always gave.

"We must look after our machines, Doreen, because we use them to make all the clothes our lovely mission needs. Now, I'm happy to help all I can, dear. And one day I hope you'll find yourself happily married with a family. And wouldn't you be a wonderful wife if you could make all the clothes your family needed?"

Like many older girls, Doreen also had to do her spell in the spacious quarters where the sisters and the Big Father lived. There, she spent time in the kitchen learning how to cook under the watchful eye of Aunty Sally, the stout, middle-aged, Aboriginal woman who was the permanent cook. Doreen couldn't believe how well the white, mission workers ate.

"I tell you, Susie," she'd confided wide-eyed. "They stuff themselves on roasts and beef pies and curries. And they get puddings like rice pudding or even cakes for afters."

"Did you eat any of that posh food, Dor?"

"No way."

"So what's going to happen after you learn to cook, Dor?"

"Then I get my cap 'n' apron training, and I also learn how to iron."

Susie had nodded knowingly. "Yes," she'd said. "They must reckon you'll do good at bein' a maid *Down Below* in some posh house."

"I reckon."

Doreen often wondered why Sister Rose never stood up to the Big Father. Of course, he *was* in charge of everyone. But it was like she was scared of him, she decided, because she was always bowing and scraping to him. And he never said much back to her, though that wasn't surprising. All the girls knew that he never spoke much to anyone. He just walked around with his big-man, heavy tread and with that practiced smile on his face. But if you looked past his smile, you saw that his eyes weren't smiling.

Everyone, and especially the older girls, was frightened of him, particularly when he came into the dormitory, just after lights out, to tell them a Bible story. Because, by then, they were only dressed in their chemises, and he always made sure that when he lay down on a girl's bed, he lay right beside her. And when he came into the dorm, everyone stayed real nervous till he'd chosen a bed. Then when he'd left, there was always a chorus of urgent whispers, with everyone asking the same question.

"What'd he do? What'd he do?"

Susie, Doreen remembered, had sounded real relieved and flippant. But then Susie always spoke bold when she was uptight.

"By Joves," Susie had said. "He put his hand under me shimmy all right. But, thank Crise, he on'y put it on me tits. Blutty hell, I reckon I can cop that."

But Brenda had been in tears. She hadn't answered them, and Doreen had heard her sobbing quietly into her pillow. In the morning, Brenda had confided.

"He left his hand on *it* all the time. I was dead scared he'd stick his fingers inside. I've washed meself lots of times. But I keep on wantin' to wash meself again and again."

Doreen had wondered, aloud, whether or not Brenda should complain to Sister Rose.

"No blutty way," Brenda had said scornfully. "Who'd believe the word of a creamy like me?"

"He's a pig!" Doreen had cried.

"Ssh! You mustn't talk like that about someone God's chosen ter do *his* work here, on earth!"

"Yes."

"But I don' know why he *never* lies on your bed, Dor. Blutty hell, yer the prettiest girl here, by far!"

"I'm sure my turn'll come, Bren," Doreen had declared anxiously.

"And yer also the cleverest by a long shot. Course yer've always got yer nose in a library book. Or else yer studyin', aren't you?"

"Bren," Doreen had replied determinedly. "I don't know any other way to take me away from this place. Even if it's only for a little while."

"Dor," Brenda had asked, "do yer really think Sister Daph meant it, when she said you were clever enough to go ter Adelaide University?"

"It doesn't matter, Bren," Doreen had replied dismissively. "Blutty hell, a university is only for rich whites who can afford the fees. Anyway, I wish Sister Daph would teach us about our own people, instead of ol' Cromwell and the king who got his head chopped off."

"Don't you want to be like whites are, Dor?"

"I just want to be me." Then she'd brightened and had smiled at Brenda. "Know something, Bren? Today, I looked at an English magazine someone had left in the library." Her eyes had gone all dreamy. "And it had some photos of a ballet called *Giselle*. It looked like a fairy tale. Fair dinkum. So different from this crook place."

Now, locked in the linen room, Doreen wondered if Sister Rose was carrying out the Big Father's bidding. Crise, that Sister really knew how to crawl to him. As well, she was always telling the girls to cover themselves up except, of course, for the girl that she now favoured. Suddenly, panic-stricken, sweating profusely and with her heart thumping, what had just happened to her came flooding back. It had all started so normally—just the usual meeting in the Big Father's study, to continue her preparation for Confirmation. But this time he'd seemed different, preoccupied even. Next thing she knew, he'd grabbed her and had forced her, facedown, over his large desk. Horrified, struck dumb and paralyzed with fear, she'd felt him pull down her knickers and lift his black cassock. Suddenly, he was trying to shove his stiff *darra* into her. But it wouldn't go, and it'd been hurting her. Then he'd grabbed her breasts, through her tunic, and was squeezing them harder and harder. Then the hurting abruptly stopped. She'd become aware that he'd gone soft, and then she'd felt his stuff running down the backs of her legs. Fearfully, she'd looked around. He'd been looking at her, as if nothing had happened.

"We must continue with your preparation tomorrow," he'd said dispassionately while opening his study door.

Hastily pulling up her knickers, Doreen had fled.

Later, sitting rigidly in the big, footed bath in her dormitory's bathroom, Doreen tried to come to terms with what had just happened. She became aware that Sister Rose had entered, pulled up a stool and was sitting next to her. She liked it when Sister Rose put an arm across her shoulders because, right then, she really needed somebody to hug her and to reassure her that it hadn't been her fault. And she also liked it when Sister Rose started to soap her, just like her mother used to do. And she closed her eyes and enjoyed the lovely feeling that came when Sister Rose took her time, when soaping and then washing her breasts. Then suddenly, she became aware that Sister Rose had reached down and was touching her.

"No!" Then she screamed shrilly, "The Big Father tried to stick his thing in me."

"That's the worst lie I've ever heard," Sister Rose said coldly and calmly. "Get dressed immediately, while I decide what to do with you."

That had been this morning. Now the sound of the key being turned, in the lock, caught Doreen's attention. She looked up when Sister Rose opened it.

"Come with me, Doreen Shillingsworth," Sister Rose curtly demanded. "It's time you prayed again for forgiveness and guidance."

Doreen followed her along the wide passageway till they came to a well-furnished room that'd been turned into a tiny, decorative chapel. She assumed that this was where the white staff came to pray when they wanted privacy.

"Kneel in front of the altar, Doreen Shillingsworth, and pray till I come back."

Doreen didn't pray. *Why should she,* she asked herself, *after what had happened?* Instead, she thought about her mother. She remembered clearly the distress on her shocked mum's face when the white policeman had led her away. Doreen reminded herself, yet again, that the story they'd told her, about her mum giving her away, was nonsense. No, that was what they told all the girls, and she had yet to meet a girl who said that her mum *hadn't* been real upset and crying. Doreen thought that she was lucky because some of the other girls had been taken so young, they couldn't remember what their mothers looked like—but not her. She could even remember the sound of her mum's voice and how it felt to be cuddled in her mum's soft arms.

When Sister Rose took her back to the linen room and locked her inside, with her bread and soup and tea, it was starting to get dark. She ate hurriedly and lay down and looked at the peeling, paint patterns, on the ceiling, till it became too dark to see.

After six days, Doreen felt totally overwhelmed. She knew that she couldn't take any more. She felt cowed and drained, and when Sister Rose next came to take her to pray, she made sure that she kept her voice humble.

"I told God I was sorry I told a lie, Sister. And I asked him to forgive me."

"And so he shall," Sister Rose replied brightly. "Our Lord God always forgives!"

"And I'm sorry for the trouble I've caused."

"Yes, you have caused trouble. And we've decided that from tomorrow, you can start work in the laundry. It won't do you any harm. Besides, cleanliness is next to godliness, and it'll be good training for the job we're going to find you."

"Job?" Doreen numbly asked.

"Of course." Sister Rose smiled enigmatically. "We think you're now old enough to leave Cord River. The Church has taken care of you quite long enough. It's time you stood on your own two feet."

"Oh."

"But don't worry." Sister Rose narrowed her eyes. "We'll find you work as a maid. Or as a kitchen hand on some cattle run."

"Yes."

Doreen's heart lurched. Her shoulders slumped, and unbidden tears came to her eyes. She turned her head away so that Sister Rose wouldn't see. Suddenly she felt very alone. Even though living at Cord River was horrid, it'd been the only home that she'd known for the past seven years. And now Sister Rose and the Big Father were throwing her out. And all because she'd told the truth. Heaven alone knew what the future could hold for her. But she was determined that Sister Rose wouldn't see her cry and that she wouldn't cry properly till after lights out when she'd be in her bed. Then, after the rest of the girls were asleep, she'd be able to hide her face in her pillow and have a good cry for as long as she liked.

Chapter 4

Ringers

It was piccaninny dawn on Calum's second day. Sleepily, he left his *swag* and headed for the stock trough to slosh his face and clean his teeth. The night had been crisp, and the day promised to break clear and sharp. As he threaded his way through drowsy cattle, he enjoyed the smell of their sweet-smelling breath as they chewed the cud in the fresh, false dawn. And once he'd put on his shirt and trousers, he sat with his blanket over his shoulders and waited for the others to rise.

There was a light in the kitchen, and the sociable smell of wood smoke, coming from the flue above the stove, together with the sound of banging pots, told him that Charlie had started to prepare breakfast.

The breeze that chilled his face carried with it the escalating din of cows that were urgently summoning their calves to come and relieve bags that were stretched tight with milk. And from the dark shape of the *mangan* tree came the frantic-sounding, harsh, territorial cackling of a Blue-winged Kookaburra, which, apart from being a particularly noisy bird, was distinctively coloured, being uniformly flecked brown, except for its sky-blue wings and tail.

Calum felt a sense of anticipation. He'd been told that today, they'd be getting everything ready to leave for their first, bullock-mustering cattle camp. And that Mr. Jackson was getting impatient because the other three, Long Creek cattle camps were already hard at it.

Calum cast his mind back to the previous day, when he'd joined the rest of Hank's white ringers for the late-afternoon meal. The kitchen table had been laden with fried steaks, ox tails swimming in gravy and thick slices of freshly-baked white bread. Dessert had been canned peaches and evaporated milk. And, as Calum was to learn later, Long Creek was one of the few cattle runs that provided dessert for its ringers when they were at the home station. Also, Calum couldn't help noticing that the atmosphere around this kitchen table, unlike home, was warm with plenty of easy banter.

"I dunno why yer don't say much, George!"

That comment had been offered by a cheerful, red-haired, freckled-faced ringer nicknamed Talkin' Blue, who looked to be about nineteen. Blue's eyes had twinkled mischievously. "I reckon, George, yer don't like ter waste yer breath," he'd continued. "D'yer reckon it'll be worth two shillings a lung full one day, mate?"

George, seated opposite Blue, had continued to eat. Finally, he'd condescended to notice Blue. "Yer a bloody yapper, Blue," he'd pronounced disdainfully. "Yer worse 'n a terrier what's spotted a possum up a small tree."

George was lean and taciturn. He'd started his working life as a boundary rider and was typical of those who've spent long periods alone in the bush. He scornfully dismissed anyone as "not bein' the arse end of a bushman" unless that person could "hear what the *bush* is sayin'." He regarded Blue as a poor bushman.

Blue had continued unabashed and had continued grinning his disarming, gap-toothed grin. "Now what if yer finds yerself," he'd chided, "sittin' next to our King George over a feed? Yer can't jus' sit chewin' an' starin' at him."

"When would I ever get to sit next to the King, yer yapper?" George'd asked scornfully.

Blue had ignored George's question. "Because," he'd continued loftily, "the King'd think all us ringers was ignorant and must be kep' away from. Your ignorance, mate, could cost me from bein' invited to some posh function to meet the King."

George had shaken his head in bewilderment and disbelief. "Can't yer just shut up fer five minutes?" he'd asked mildly. "Your yackin' is stoppin' me from fully appreciatin' Charlie's tasty tucker."

"That's what I'm sayin', George. We need ter talk as well as eat. We got ter be adaptable."

"I'm already adaptable, Blue! Hell, I can eat an' listen ter you, can't I?" Blue had continued his chattering unabashed. He'd indicated the wiry, blond ringer seated next him. "Now, Calum, yer haven't met me mate, Nugget. He's got ter be the best ringer in the Territory, next ter yours truly, of course." He'd given Nugget a nudge and had winked at Calum. "Like that one, Nugg?"

Nugget had offered a slow smile and had then nodded to Calum. "Not a bad ride this arvo, mate," he'd offered. "Seen worse an' I seen better."

"That's what I also reckon," Blue had chirped.

Blue and his mum had been evacuated to a Gulf Country, cattle run when Darwin had been bombed by the Japanese in 1942. He'd been fourteen and had never ridden a horse. But he'd taken to cattle run life, like a spaniel to water, and had never wanted to return to Darwin. His mother, though, had hated her job as a home station cook.

"Bugger the Japs," she'd told him angrily. "I'm off back to Darwin because these men don't respect a lady. They're even *worse* than your always-grabbing father."

Blue and Nugget were good mates, and Nugget let Blue do all the talking, except when it came to horses or cattle. Nugget had been born in his drover father's wagon but, at fifteen, had opted for work on a cattle run. It meant, he'd reasoned, that you weren't saddled with the daily responsibility of finding sufficient feed and water for the thousand-odd *fats* that you were droving.

He'd met Blue when they'd both been working on the Vestey-owned, Wave Hill run. They'd hit it off immediately and had been good mates ever since. Nugget feared that someone might ambush and shoot him due to his reputation as a knife fighter. That was why he tried to avoid confrontations. His reputation had been gained accidentally, but the passage of time and exaggeration by others had grown it. It'd all started in the pearling town of Broome during the 1941 Wet. He'd been having a few drinks in the pub with a couple of Japanese pearl divers. Their yarns about big Tiger sharks, sudden *Cockeye Bobs* and the bends had fascinated a young ringer who was seeing the sea for the first time.

"But they'd have ter be the strangest coves I ever met, mate," he'd told Blue, his voice puzzled. "Real polite an' always bowin' ter yer. But they change abrupt, after a few grogs. Then they get rude an' become real dirty on a man. One of 'em went ter hit me, fer no reason, with his chair. I dunno ter this day how I upset 'im. Anyway, I had me clasp knife on me belt, o' course. Lucky fer me, the *Beak* seen it my way. His verdict was self-defence, but the ol' bugger give me a real talkin'-to. Tol' me that fightin' with knives was un-Australian. Said it was the dago way."

That had been the most that Blue had ever heard Nugget speak in one hit, and he'd promptly assured Nugget that he'd be the one who fronted in future disputes. To date, it hadn't quite worked out that way. It was always Nugget who did the fronting.

Calum now thought about how Blue had sat up in his chair and had looked expansive. Clearly, he delighted in having an audience. He'd nodded toward the light-coloured, young part-Aborigine seated next to Calum.

"Now, Calum, yer've met yeller feller Brian, o' course," he'd announced. "But yer wasn't told he's the best tracker in the Territory. Got a bonzer-lookin' sister too, who's here on holiday right now. Course, any ringer what sniffs around her'll probably get that spear-in-the-leg bijnitch. That right, mate?"

Brian had grinned at Blue and had regarded him with steady, brown eyes. "For sure! "he'd agreed. "Except fer you, Blue. You cop it differently because you're such a yappin' *kuttabah*. With you, a *Kaditje* man gets to cut off your *darra* using a stone knife, an' I get to watch. I've never seen a freckled one before, you know."

"It's not freckled," Blue had strongly averred.

"I don't see why it wouldn't be."

Blue had looked alarmed. Having that sort of operation inflicted on him was apparently something too fearful even to contemplate. "Fer Crissake!" he'd protested. "Our mob only *mark* bull calves, an' they is not even human!"

"Oh, did you want that done to you as well?" Brian had asked.

"Mate, I'm going ter look the other way every time I pass yer mum's place. An', I've also decided, no way is yer sister good-lookin'!"

"I wouldn't trust that yacker, Brian," Charlie'd warned. "An', I'd pay big money ter have 'im marked. At least we'd be hearin' a new voice!"

"How much'd you pay, Charlie?" Brian had asked, pretending to smile eagerly. "I sharpened my knife this afternoon. It'll do a good job, no worries."

Murranji Bill and Hank had arrived later. Neither had said much; they were too busy eating. It was only when Charlie had spoken, somewhat sanctimoniously, that Murranji had looked up from his plate.

"I see yer've got yer manners, young Calum," Charlie'd said. "By the way, yer hold yer knife an' fork. Now, jus' shoe yer horses proper termorrer an' stay away from the gins. Else yer'll be called a *combo*. An' that's the las' thing any white feller'd want."

Murranji Bill had immediately grimaced, smacked the table hard with his open hand and had glared at Charlie. "For Crissake, Charlie!" he'd admonished. "You might be a damn good cook, but you do talk some terrible bullshit." He'd nodded at Calum. "Let's cover the shoeing first an' get that out of the way. Up here, we shoe 'em so they're up on their toes. Know what that means?"

"No."

"Well, I'll show you tomorrow. It makes your horse better-footed so, with a bit of luck, it won't go down on you. Nothing worse than your horse taking a tumble in rough country. That's how a man gets his neck broken."

"Oh."

Murranji Bill had nodded at Hank. "You know, this yakking about staying away from the *lubras* pisses me right off," he'd said indignantly. "It's fuckin' hypocritical because I reckon nine out of ten fellers up here go with lubras. So it's against the law? But we all know 'necessity is the mother of invention an' the father of all half-castes.'"

There'd been a palpable silence. Everybody, except Hank, had been taken aback by Murranji's bluntness. Hank had pushed the subject further.

"Were the early days any different, Murranji?" he'd asked.

"No different at all, except most cattlemen didn't think it was wrong going with lubras. An' why was that?" Murranji had scanned their faces.

"Anyone want to guess how many white *sheilas* were in the Territory, just thirty-odd years ago, when I started droving?"

"You tell us." Hank'd grinned.

"Yeah, well, there was only two-hundred-an'-seventy-one of 'em that were over nineteen. An' most were married!"

"Ah." Hank'd nodded. "That explains a lot."

"You know," Murranji had continued, looking at Calum, "when I was a youngster, most drovers an' cattlemen had their black 'boy' or drover's 'boy'! They depended on them, an' not just for fucking. Hell, a lubra was great company for a lonely, white feller. An' lubras were good with horses an' good at droving an' were great at finding water. An', of course, nobody was better at tracking the horses come morning. Also, his woman saved many a white feller from copping a spear."

"Interesting," Hank'd remarked.

"Anyway," Murranji'd continued and had stared challengingly round the table, "how much has really changed? Hell, we all know that what white sheilas there are live mostly in towns like Darwin. And now, black sheilas aren't even allowed to wear trousers in town." He'd scornfully scoffed.

"But what about these names white fellers are now called?" Hank'd asked.

Murranji's voice had sounded as exasperated as he'd looked. "Bloody names like combo, gin jockey, an' *black velvet* rider are just hypocritical bullshit. They're used by whites who want to be seen as keeping up bullshit white standards. An' fair dinkum, it's also crystal bloody clear why we've got a law that bans white fellers from fucking lubras, who are seen as being degenerate."

"I don't know why," Hank had admitted.

"Well, I'll tell you." Murranji had laughed mockingly. "The Government's shit scared the number of half-castes up here will get outta control an' swamp the whites. Hell, this is a white man's country, an' the government's hell-bent on keeping it that way." He'd grinned widely. "Bugger the fucking government! Yeah, I break that bloody law. An' when my sheila's uncle asked her to go with me, she said, 'S'pose Murranji like … me try 'im.' Just like that. An' no bullshit modesty either."

Murranji had abruptly risen from his chair.

"You're off, Murranji?" Hank had asked.

"Yeah, I'm goin' to see my woman." Murranji had paused at the door. "An' I reckon half the trouble we've got up here is 'cause a ton of whites Down Below still want to believe that black sheilas can't stop fucking an' that they corrupt an' disease every white feller that goes with them."

"And what do you believe, Murranji?" Hank had asked, smiling.

"All I know is that a black sheila, except for the colour of her skin, is built no different to any other woman in Australia."

"Well, that's one thing we can agree on."

After Murranji had departed, all the ringers had been unnaturally quiet, and Calum had thought that Charlie had looked as if he'd got the sulks.

Murranji Bill's comments had also caused Calum to think about Aborigines. There were lots up here, though very few could speak English properly. They spoke Creole. And come to think about it, he couldn't understand why most whites looked down on them. He thought that they were the happiest people he'd ever seen. They were always smiling and laughing and joking, unlike his mother's people who had a melancholic streak running through them.

****

Calum was startled out of his reverie by the sound of Brian's voice. He hadn't heard the other's light approach.

"You coming in for breakfast, mate?" Brian asked.

"Too right," Calum said and immediately rose to his feet.

When they entered the kitchen, those already there nodded their greetings. Brian immediately walked over and put an arm across Charlie's shoulders. He winked at Calum.

"Charlie." He grinned. "You make the best brekky in the Territory. Now how about three eggs, eh?"

"Siddown, yer bullshit artist."

But when Charlie gave Brian his plate, Calum saw that there were three eggs on it. Breakfast comprised sturdy portions of fried steak topped with eggs, thick-cut bread and steaming mugs of black tea.

Blue, on seeing Brian's favoured treatment, screwed up his freckled face to feign massive indignation. "How come *I* never got no three eggs?" he demanded. "I thought the eagles had took all the chooks, an' you was rationin' the last of the eggs. But oh no! Just 'cause I don't crawl ter yer, I get punished. Well, I'll jus' have ter sing yer favourite song."

Charlie instantly became enraged. "Get out o' me, bloody kitchen!" he yelled. "Get to work yer mongrel. Jeez! You won't be getting no lunch, and yer can bet London ter a brick on that. Get out. Get out!"

Blue retreated to the door. His blue eyes were sparkling above his grin. "Hooroo, you ol' Bait Layer!" he called. "Anyway, I'd need binoculars ter even notice yer tiny lunch rations."

Through the open, kitchen window, Calum then heard Blue's light baritone singing the words of an anonymous and oft-quoted ringer's poem to the tune of *The Wild Colonial Boy*.

A mob of travellin' stock,
And the days was fuckin' dusty,
An' the nights was fuckin' hot,
The cattle they was rushin',
The horses fuckin' pore,
The boss he was a bastard,
And the cook a fuckin' whore,
AND THE COOK A FUCKIN' WHORE.

It was the shouted repetition of the last line that made Charlie turn apoplectic. Beneath the brim of his always-worn, grey Fedora, his eyes narrowed, his face grew a mottled red and he spoke through gritted teeth.

"I'm goin' to put rat poison in the next plate o' stew that I give that irritatin' bastard," he fumed. "I'd enjoy seein' him with a gutache so bad, it kills him!"

Brian grinned, amused at Calum's look of alarm. "Relax, mate," he said. "I've been waiting two years for Charlie to give Blue that killer gutache!"

Following breakfast and while heading off to join Hank at a holding yard, Calum heard a Spotted Nightjar, grey-brown with grey-black and yellowish streaks, loudly chastising the dawn with its distinctive *caw-caw gobble-gobble*.

"What was that?" he asked Brian.

Brian grinned. "Just a damn noisy bird that's probably been up all night."

Hank was with two, Aboriginal horse tailers. He appeared to be quite jovial. "Okay, you guys, this is the deal," he explained. "Murranji is checkin' out the horse gear. Jalyerri and Jacky Jacky here are coming with me to muster the breeding paddock. There are some foals that need branding. Now, you two can start mustering the Number 1 horse paddock, and I'll join you when I can. And, Brian, I want more than fifty good ones. Also, night horses and packhorses. Okay?"

"Yeah."

Jacky Jacky cheekingly grinned at Brian and then rolled his eyes. "That Talkin' Blue, he make my lug hole knock up," he chirped.

"You're no different from the rest of us, mate," Brian agreed with a smile, before he and Calum turned and headed for the horse paddock.

"I've never met anyone before called Murranji," Calum mentioned conversationally.

"The Murranji Track's a stock route running from stations like the Big Run to Newcastle Waters," Brian explained. "It's not a worry now 'cause there are Government bores every twenty miles. But when Murranji was doing droving, the hundred-an'-twenty-five miles between Top Springs and the Bucket Water Hole was often dry."

"And?"

"When he was sixteen, Murranji signed on to help drove seven-hundred fats down it. The boss drover got speared, an' he took over. They say he never lost a horse or bullock. Maybe he was that good. Who's to say?"

"Have you been along the Murranji Track, Brian?"

Brian grimaced. "Just once. I didn't like it!"

"Oh?"

Brian raised his eyebrows. "Mate, it's spooky. Scrub so thick you can't see a horse if it's thirty yards away. An' it's real dark. An' there's poisonous Ironwood all over. Strange, but I never saw any white cockatoos, only black ones. Dinkum spooky, mate."

Calum made a mental note to avoid the Murranji Track. He'd inherited his mother's apprehension about anything that could belong to the spirit world.

Hank had left Long Creek's old Bedford truck at the number 1 horse paddock. It contained the saddles, bridles and ropes that'd be needed. Calum studied one of the *green hide* ropes. It'd been made from three strands of neatly plaited, one-inch hide and looked strong enough to hold even the *cheekiest* bull.

"Put that rope on a horse you like," Brian said. "Oh hell!"

Calum followed his gaze. A pretty, grey mare, not far from the fence, stood on three legs. She held her head low and was moving it slowly from side to side. A small trickle of blood had dried on each cheek, under the empty sockets, which had once held soft, brown eyes.

Brian swore angrily. "Bloody crows! They give me the shits!"

"Crows?"

"She can't move 'cause she's got that broken, back fetlock, so the bastards've eaten her eyes."

"Christ!"

Calum knew that the mare would have to be put down. He also knew that a close-up rifle shot could spook the entire mob. He watched Brian duck through the fence, walk up to the mare and speak to her reassuringly. Then he held her by the mane, up behind her ears, while he quickly cut her throat high up, with his clasp knife. As he stepped back to avoid her pumping blood, she tried ineffectually to plunge on three legs before slowly sinking to the ground. Brian didn't stay to watch. On his way to the truck, he called over his shoulder.

"Hold open the gate for me, mate. And don't let any of her mates get out. They're jumpy now, 'cause they're smelling blood."

Brian drove to the dead mare. He secured one end of a green hide rope to a back leg and the other end to the truck's tow bar before starting the motor and dragging the body through the open gate. Calum shut the gate, climbed in and Brian drove off. The truck rattled for six-hundred yards along the rutted, dirt track before Brian swung it out onto the open plain. He didn't go far before he stopped, jumped out, undid the rope and threw it in the back.

"We're not going to leave her there, are we?" Calum asked when he climbed back into the truck.

"Mate, dingo an' wild pigs'll clean up most of her during the night, an' birds an' Beef Ants'll pick her bones clean tomorrow."

Calum again realized that he needed to come to grips with the rawness of Territory life. Pondering what he'd just seen, he noticed that the sky had changed. The rose-gold gilding had disappeared, and it was now a cloudless, brassy hot-blue, which seemed to go up and up forever.

Brian glanced across at him. "I've never been *Inside,* you know," he said. "Not like you. Me? I'll be stayin' *Outback.* It doesn't worry me if I never see Adelaide or Brisbane."

"I'm also staying here."

"Yeah? Well, you'll need to know our ways then."

"Yes?"

"Like when you're visiting, you don't climb off your horse till you're invited. An' you don't turn up at meal times. An' you never complain about their water. An' you don't go to their holdin' yards unless you're invited. Things like that."

"Why do you stay away from holding yards?" Calum asked, puzzled.

"Well, you don't know what brands are there, do you?"

Calum wasn't sure how you went about calling on your neighbours when you were slap bang in the middle of an eighty-five-hundred-square-mile cattle run. He decided, though, not to show his ignorance.

Others soon arrived to help them muster the sixty square miles horse paddock. And when, at long last, Hank was satisfied, he allocated three mounts to each ringer.

"Everybody gets three horses," he told Calum. "Because a horse has two days' rest after it's been worked." He indicated the two horses that Jalyerri was holding. "You've got Quiet As already. That liver chestnut is Meg, and the grey gelding is Stupid. Relax." He smiled. "He got his name because he tried to suck from another mare when he was a foal. And watch Meg. She'll probably buck."

"Hank?"

"Yep."

"I want to buy Quiet As. He'd be in the horse book as 'can't be broken,' wouldn't he?"

"I think I can talk Mr. Jackson into selling. Can you afford four pounds?"

"Yes. And I'm calling him Socks."

Calum's horses didn't give him any trouble while being shod. And Murranji had duly appeared to show him how to shoe his horses the

Long Creek way. Hank stopped by, a couple of hours later, to check on his progress. Calum had nearly finished.

"Where did you learn to shoe?" he asked.

"Down south," Calum answered dismissively.

"You don't give an inch, do you?"

"What do you mean?" Calum asked aggressively.

"I'm talking about relaxing and being friendly. Hell, you won't even sleep in the ringers' hut with the rest of us."

"I don't like doors," Calum replied scornfully, with a curled upper lip. "My father used to lock me inside."

Hank gave him a sharp look but decided against following up the opening. He thought that Calum appeared to be too prickly. "Well, you're in the right place," he said with a friendly grin. "Here, you have to spell SPACE with letters that're so big you can't get your arms round them!" He changed the subject and smiled. "Looks like Brian's really got his hands full with one of his horses."

Indeed, Brian *was* having trouble with a powerful, brown mare. He'd already been kicked once, as well as bitten. And despite having a mouthful of shoeing nails, a back leg under his left arm, a horse shoe in his left hand and a shoeing hammer in his right hand, he was still able to describe her ancestry in a less-than-flattering way.

"You're a bloody slut an' a dirty, rotten bitch. Doesn't surprise me, 'cause your pa was a bloody pimp, and your ma was a bloody whore. An' from now on, I'm calling you Bitch!"

Blue walked past Calum. He was limping noticeably and looked grumpy. At first, he didn't want to talk about it and then, after being prodded, grudgingly informed Calum that he had come off a temperamental, black gelding called Bombproof and had landed awkwardly on his ankle.

"I don' know why they give horses such lyin' names," he complained bitterly. "That bloody mongrel shoulda bin called Gotcha!"

Blue didn't have anything else to say, which was quite out of character. Obviously his pride was hurting as much as his ankle.

Calum went off to get his saddle and bridle. He noticed that Hank, Nugget and Murranji were in a group. They were quietly talking to one another, and their faces looked set and hard. He walked over to them.

Hank nodded to him. "George just got snakebit," he informed Calum. "A Browny got him on the wrist. Now we just have to wait and see if he pulls through."

"Jeez."

"Yeah," Hank continued sombrely. "George left his saddle in that bit of shade, there. And when he reached to pick it up, he got bitten, right on the vein. The bastard must've slid underneath it to get out of the sun."

"Can we do anything for him?" Calum anxiously asked.

"I guess not," Hank said, shaking his head. "You can't cut a big vein. Anyway, I don't believe that cutting the flesh, sucking out the poison and then using Condy's crystals ever works. And there's no point in calling the Flying Doctor. There's nothing he could do."

"What sort of snake was it, again?" Calum asked.

"An Eastern Brown and they're bad," Hank replied. "Now, it's up to George." He looked at their gloomy faces. "We'd better move it, fellers. We've got work to do. I'll be back when I've asked Brian's mum to stay with George."

Hank could've asked one of the others to go, but he wanted to see Jan, Brian's sister. She'd recently been transferred to the Commonwealth Bank's, Catriona branch and was holidaying with her mum, Alice, for a few days till she took up her new position. Alice was grey-haired, plump and motherly, and lived in a tiny cottage nearby. She was Les Jackson's housekeeper and cook.

She answered Hank's knock on her door. "G'day, Hank. Goin' all right, mate?" she asked with a warm smile.

"Yes, thanks, Alice. But we've got a problem. Unfortunately, George's been bitten by a Browny. He's in bed. Is there any chance you could sit with him?"

Deep concern showed on Alice's face. "Too right I can. I'll head fer the ringers' hut right now."

Just then, Jan came to the front door. She'd heard everything. "Can I help, Mum?" she asked.

"No, love. It'd be best if it's just me," Alice replied before hurrying off.

Hank smiled at Jan, and she met his gaze. Jan was two years older than Brian, and her skin, like his, was a creamy brown; sort of like someone who spends all their time in the sun. She was wearing a colourful, floral-print dress and possessed the type of full figure that had always attracted Hank. Her shoulder-length black hair was tied back with a navy ribbon and her dark-brown eyes were steady and friendly. Hank thought that she had the calmest manner of any person he'd met. In fact, she was so serene that he could literally feel it. It made him feel settled and comfortable. She was a practicing Catholic, was secure in her faith and could be disconcertingly direct at times.

"Have you time for a cuppa, Hank?" she asked with a pleasant smile.

"Not really. I just wanted to say I'd like to see more of you."

Both were well aware that relationships, on cattle runs, needed to be cemented quickly because ringers spent so many months, miles away in cattle camps.

"Hank," she told him gently, "I know where you're headed, mate, but I also know we could never marry. Look, I think you're lovely, but honestly, I'm just not ready to be any man's mistress."

"I'll get a couple of days off when we finish mustering fats. Can I come and see you in Catriona then?" he persisted.

"I'm owed more holidays, so I'll probably be back staying with Mum when you've finished mustering. Besides, you wouldn't enjoy the way townies behave when they see a white man with a half-caste girl."

"Oh. Is that it then?" he asked.

"Don't look so disappointed, please," she pleaded. "Why don't you come round this evening, after you've eaten, and then we can go for another walk?"

"You betcha. I'd sure like that," he said, brightening.

"Bye, Hank."

"Right. See you this evening, Jan."

"And relax about George. I'm sure that Mum's watched over someone before who's been bitten by a snake."

"Of course."

Jan was right. It certainly wasn't the first time that Alice had watched over a snakebite victim. Her people, of course, knew that the symptoms suffered by the victim depended on the type of snake that had done the biting. And Alice knew what to expect with an Eastern Brown.

The initial effects were evident within an hour. First, George experienced a severe headache and then bad stomach pains, followed by nausea, and vomiting. Beads of sweat covered his face. Alice held a bucket with water in its bottom, for him, when he vomited. He was too sick to feel embarrassed.

"Yer got ter hang in there, George. Keep holdin' on, mate," Alice encouraged. "Look, it's all up ter you. Jus' hang in, awright?"

"I know," George answered, ashen faced. "An' I'm doin' me best."

"Good on yer, mate."

Alice watched as George lost consciousness. She knew that that would be temporary and that the worst was yet to come. She looked round when Hank entered the room and saw that worry lines were creasing his forehead.

"Oh God!" he exclaimed. "He's unconscious already."

"He'll come roun', fer sure," Alice reassured him. "It's the nex' hours we got ter worry about, mate."

"Please tell me his chances are good, Alice," he begged. "George is a fine man."

"Yeah? Well, he's doin' awright so far."

"Great. I'll be back soon. Okay?"

"No worries. See yer, mate."

Just as Alice had predicted, George did regain consciousness. He gave Alice a wan smile, and when he spoke, his voice was weak. "Am I goin' ter make it, Alice?" he asked resignedly.

Alice's face mirrored her concern, and as was her way, she answered truthfully. "I wish I could tell yer yes. But it's too early ter know, mate."

"What a bastard," he groaned. "I never thought a bushy like me would get snakebit."

"It can happen ter a Murri too, mate. I seen it."

"Did he live?"

Alice didn't answer.

Within a couple of hours, what she'd feared most did happen. George's eyelids started to droop, and shortly afterward, he complained of double vision. Then his voice changed, and before long, he lapsed into a coma. Alice knew that he was slipping away.

"Well, mate," she murmured, "if you was one of us, yer'd soon be a *tjooloo*, an' in the Dreamin' Place." She reflected on the prolonged grief that all white folks seemed to experience when a loved one died. *Our way is better*, she decided, *'cause we know they'll be comin' back.* But that depended, of course, when a tjooloo decided to leave the Dreamin' Place after first having found a father with the right Skin.

George passed away some four hours after he'd been bitten. Alice knew that the venom had eventually thickened his blood, so much that no heart could pump it.

When Hank re-entered the room, Alice had closed George's eyelids and had covered him with a sheet.

"Sweet Jesus!" Hank groaned. "I'm so sorry. He was a real fine workmate."

"Yes," she said matter-of-factly. "An' remember, he won't keep long in this heat."

****

Both Meg and Stupid watched Calum as he approached. He didn't think that he'd have any trouble with Stupid, who nickered at his approach.

"I don't know why you're pleased to see me," he told the big, rangy grey. "You don't even know me yet." He went to the liver chestnut mare. "You're first, Meg. I can see you have a nice, kind eye. And because you're a lady, I don't think we'll have any trouble."

He continued to speak to both horses, while he put his open-face bridle with its ring-jointed, Tom Thumb snaffle bit on her. He told them how much he needed this job and that he was going to work hard to hold his own. And because Meg'd relaxed, he didn't think that she'd surprise him by getting nasty. After he'd saddled her, he quickly mounted. She promptly gave a couple of perfunctory bucks. He sat them easily, with a boyish grin.

"Meg, you're a pussy cat. That wasn't even fierce."

She settled quickly. He gathered her, gave her rein and then touched her sides with his heels. He was still upset by what had happened to George and needed space to be on his own.

They passed the homestead's tiny graveyard and the small, nearby billabong. He thought that the sky seemed bigger than the one down south. And the descending sun had painted a broad, golden slash across the billabong's surface.

Ahead, stretched the apparently endless, grass plain. The strong mare between his knees felt good, and so did the smell of horse, green grass and oiled leather. There wasn't another human being in sight, and he experienced a feeling of boundless freedom. Meg wanted to run, and he had to hold her firmly. She kept dancing forward, against the bit, with her head and neck held to one side.

When they came to a track, indented with cattle pads, he turned her onto it and gave her rein. She leaped straight into a gallop. The fresh wind buffeted his face and stung his eyes, making them water. Meg pounded forward with her neck outstretched and her ears back. It felt exhilarating, and he knew that floating feeling that comes when horse and rider are one. He gave her more rein. She lengthened stride, and her wind-whipped mane stung his face and the backs of his hands. He felt as if she was about to take flight and that, like some great Flying Fish, she would bear him aloft as she skimmed over this wide, green sea. When she slowed, Calum held her to a walk. He felt so free that he couldn't resist the urge to shout at the plain ahead.

"I've got a job!"

Meg shifted under him skittishly and then settled down as if that sort of behaviour, by a rider, was only to be expected. She was more concerned when a Gould's Goanna, about four feet long, scuttled from her path. She made a point of snorting and jumping and staring after the big lizard, with her ears pricked. Calum interestedly watched the fast-departing, dark-grey monitor with its cross bands of yellowish flecks. He stroked Meg's neck and spoke reassuringly.

"Now, that's not the first goanna you've seen, girl, is it? Are you testing me, or did one of those give you a bad fright when you were growing up?"

He waited for Meg to calm down and then turned her toward the homestead.

When he got back, Brian told him that George had died and had already been buried. He was shocked by what he perceived as Brian's matter-of-fact manner. Then, over the late-afternoon meal, he was again shocked by the casual way in which George's death was discussed. Outwardly, nobody showed emotion. Calum decided that they were heartless. He had hardly known George, but they'd known him well. He'd been their mate, had lived in camp with them and had shared their lives. It was as if they were thinking, "Poor old George. What lousy luck. But snakes are always around, and it was too bad if you got bitten. Then either you lived or you didn't. End of story."

Murranji said very little. He merely pointed out that Australia had more than its share of venomous snakes. "Yeah," he said. "Out of the ten, most poisonous snakes in the world, we're stuck with nine."

Hank even seemed to be more interested in trying to get Murranji to talk about the old days. He wanted to know whether or not there'd been major conflict between the early cattlemen and those Aborigines on whose traditional lands cattle had been released.

"I'd like to know if it was anything like the ongoing struggle between Texas settlers and Comanche," he explained.

"Not tonight, mate," Murranji Bill said, excusing himself. "I'm off to see my woman. But maybe around a campfire, over a mug of rum, I'll tell you about those days." He paused. "I'll also tell you about how, when I was a boy, a helluva lot of cattlemen believed they could cure their syphilis if they fucked a virgin. So they used to ride down and then rape eleven- and twelve-year-old, Murri girls." Murranji Bill shook his head as if to himself. "See you tomorrow, fellers."

"See you, Murranji."

Hank promptly left the kitchen when he'd finished his meal. He found that he was really looking forward to seeing Jan. He felt a strong need to be near her calmness, because he was feeling so churned up about George's death.

CHAPTER 5

PEG

Peg Shillingsworth, Doreen's mother, had always been very stubborn and very patient. Ever since Doreen's abduction, all those years ago, she'd never wavered in her resolve to regain her daughter. Initially, she'd sought out those who'd been institutionalized and had asked a lot of questions. She knew that she must learn everything that she could about this white feller bijnitch of stealing mixed-descent children.

Peg was half-caste and thirty-six. And being a perceptive person, she'd also long realized that it didn't pay to rock the boat. Indeed, the sensible thing to do was to merge into the background. That way you wouldn't be noticed. Other things too, like getting known as someone who never drank grog, and knowing that a good way to avoid the bullying, sexual attentions of whites was to pretend that you were a real churchie. So for years, Peg had made a point of regularly going to Mass and Confession and, during Confession, saying the things that her Confessor liked to hear. *Yes, the Church's protection,* she'd dryly concluded, *was infinitely preferable to the sand, which some half-caste Tennant Creek women put in their vagina entrances to discourage the sexual advances of drunken miners.* Lately, though, Peg had come to rely more and more on her Church. It was always there, and it never changed. And unlike some other mums, she never blamed it for keeping mixed-descent children on its mission stations. No, she blamed the

Government for that and believed that the Churches were only doing what the Government had demanded of them.

She often thought about her daughter's father. She'd met him when the cattle run, on which her people lived, had offered her work in one of its cattle camps. They'd expected, of course, that she'd be no different from the other Aboriginal women that worked in cattle camps. And that she also would routinely use sexual favours to barter with their white ringers.

One particular ringer had constantly badgered her to have sex with him. He'd kept offering her the usual tobacco, rum or calico, even though she'd made it clear that she had no intention of accommodating him. She'd heard that he was unacceptably rough. And when she'd continued to refuse him, he'd forced himself on her after having followed her when she'd left camp to collect firewood. She'd tried to resist, but that had only excited him. He'd laughed as he'd pulled up her dress. Then he'd knelt between her legs and had forced her thighs apart. She'd watched in disgust as he'd stared greedily at the outline where her arched mound was deeply bisected. Laughing some more, he'd placed two of his fingers in his mouth, covered them liberally with saliva and then thrust them roughly inside her. She had cried out with pain. Then had lain there and had watched, in revulsion, as he'd released his erection from his *moleskins*. She'd closed her eyes and had willed herself to relax. That was when the ringer, who would become Doreen's father, had unexpectedly appeared and had intervened. He'd grabbed the man by the collar and had hauled him off her. Then he'd stood there, with his jaunty smile and with his rifle nonchalantly held in his left hand.

"Leave her be, Tom," he'd grimly warned. "An' turn your mind to a woman who wants you."

"An' if I bloody don't?"

"Well then, it'll be on for young an' old, won't it!"

"Yer fuckin' bastard! What's got inter yer?"

"That's my woman, Tom." He'd grinned mischievously and had winked at her. "So long as that's all right with you, Peg?"

Later that night, she'd gone to him.

His eyes had laughed in the moonlight. "You do know you don't have to stay, Peg, unless you want to?"

She'd regarded him carefully. "I'll stay," she'd said slowly. "Fer ternight, anyways."

He'd really surprised her. He hadn't just shoved his darra in and then kept ramming it into her till he'd come. No, he'd been thoughtful, had even kissed her and had enjoyed her breasts and had caressed her *kumara*. Despite herself, she'd become aroused, and once he'd gently entered her, she'd willingly thrust in unison with him. He'd made sure that she'd climaxed before he did, and afterward, she'd been surprised to find that, suddenly, she'd wanted him to come inside her. And she'd gripped his darra, with her inner muscles, till she'd felt him spurt and spurt deep inside her. And all the while, she'd clasped his rigid body tightly to hers.

After that, she'd only slept with this one smiling ringer. He'd never treated her badly, and she'd been very content. She'd even ridden alongside him when he'd been out mustering, and had been surprised to discover that she couldn't keep her eyes off him. And when he'd left to start work on the Big Run, she'd accompanied him because she'd been so totally and passionately in love. But then, for reasons of her own and despite enormous anguish, she'd left him. Mostly it had to do with pride. And later, she'd heard that he'd looked for her for a long time. But again her pride and stubbornness wouldn't let him find her. She'd been quite certain back then that he'd deliberately demeaned her, though now she wasn't so sure.

Down the years she'd had a couple of short-lived relationships, but neither had met either her emotional or physical needs. And nowadays, if she happened to wake at night and confront herself, with a 3:00 AM hard-edged honesty, she would have to admit that she was still totally in love with this man.

****

By chance, a former inmate of Cord River had confirmed to her that there was a Doreen Shillingsworth at the mission. And the answers that Peg had been given had convinced her that this Doreen must be her daughter. Peg had immediately moved to the township because, luckily, she'd had distant relatives there. On arrival, she'd found that because she was a churchie, she'd had little difficulty in landing two, menial jobs. So far, she'd been in Cord River for seven months but was no closer to having a plan about how to get her daughter out of the mission, than on the day that she'd arrived. She constantly worried that Doreen had forgotten her or that maybe she was now *in the white*. Heavens, she had the skin colour and the features too that could possibly favour assimilation into a white community. And if that was what Doreen desired, she certainly wouldn't want a dark-skinned mother suddenly turning up.

During the day, Peg worked as one of the cleaners in the township's hotel and after work there went to the bank, and cleaned it till it was spotless. That was what Mr. Brady, the Manager, had demanded when he'd given her the job.

"Peg," he'd said. "It's got to be spotless. You got that straight?"

"Yes, Mr. Brady."

"You better, Peg. Otherwise, you're bloody out!"

Peg had held down both jobs without complaint. Mr. Brady had even allowed her to open a passbook savings account and, right now, its balance was fifty-three pounds.

Peg had been introduced to Mr. Brady by Mary, the half-caste, who'd been the Bradys' servant for some years. Mary was one of Peg's distant relatives. She knew a lot about the Bradys' and their domestic arrangements: information that she'd had no hesitation in passing on to Peg.

Peg had been told that Mr. Brady was in his late fifties. And that as soon as their children had left home, Mrs. Brady had moved him into a vacant bedroom. She was a very strong-willed woman and had told Mary that she had no intention of being pestered any more by her husband's sexual demands.

"I've done my duty by the Church, Mary. So I've earned my bit of peace at night."

Eventually, Mr. Brady had managed to overcome his scruples about skin colour and had offered Mary money in order to satisfy his sexual urges. Mary had happily agreed; money was very important to her. Now, according to Mary, Mr. Brady blamed his wife for this ongoing expense and, bankerlike, apparently regarded the payments to Mary as being unnecessarily wasteful. Hence, it hadn't taken him long to develop petty and parsimonious habits about the housekeeping money that he gave his wife. And it didn't bother him that the meals that were put in front of him continued to diminish in both size and appeal.

When Peg had first asked Mr. Brady to be permitted to open a bank account, he'd closed the door of his office and had put an arm around her waist.

"What if I come back tonight, Peg?" he'd suggested. "You're not a bad-lookin' sheila, and I'll bring a bottle of rum. Then we two can enjoy a quiet drink in my office, okay?"

Peg had looked the slight, bespectacled Bank Manager right in the eye. She'd feigned horror. "I'm sorry, Mr. Brady," she'd said prissily. "I don't drink, and I'm off ter Confession ternight."

Mr. Brady had looked surprised and confused, and he'd quickly taken his arm from her waist. He hadn't realized that Peg was Catholic and then couldn't help wondering why Father Ahearn allowed blacks to use the same Confessional as whites.

"I hope you didn't take me the wrong way, Peg," he'd simpered. "I know yer not allowed ter buy grog, and I was just offerin' a little treat."

"That's the exac' way I took it, Mr. Brady," she'd said with a prim smile. "I know you is kind, but I'm a law-abidin' woman, so I never drink."

"Now, you be certain to tell Father Ahearn that I said you were doin' a good job, you hear?"

"Yer extra kind, Mr. Brady. Thanks."

"See yer, Peg. An' keep up the good work, eh."

"Ta ta now, Mr. Brady."

****

As ordered, Doreen duly started work in the mission's laundry. She already knew, by sight, the four women working there. One of them, Nellie, was stout, middle aged and had an infectious laugh.

"Goo' day!" she cheerfully greeted Doreen. "You watch first, then gibbit a try."

It was a straightforward operation. Roper Billy, the old Murri gardener, brought the firewood by cart and pony, and everybody helped unload it. Fires were then lit under a row of round, copper tubs that'd been two-thirds filled with water. And once the water had boiled, dirty washing was tossed in and boiled till it was clean. It was then hooked out with bleached, wooden slats, placed in double-handled tin baths, rinsed, mangled and then pegged out on the clotheslines.

Doreen soon found herself carrying pails of water and stoking the fires under the brick-supported coppers. This was very different from sitting in the relative cool of the sewing room. The fierce heat from the fires, boiling water and hot sun was exhausting. Soon Doreen was bathed in perspiration and literally panting. Nellie indicated the shade of a nearby acacia.

"You chit down lil while," she kindly suggested.

Doreen headed gratefully for the shade and collapsed onto the ground. She still felt nervous and unsettled because she couldn't get it out of her head that they were going to ship her off. The only thing that'd made Cord River bearable was the strong ties that she'd forged with girls like Susie Milligan and Brenda Johnson. They were now almost like family. And whenever she thought of being separated from them, she got this nervous pain in her tummy. And for Crissake, Sister Rose could send her anywhere. Heavens, she'd heard frightening stories, from the Murri women, about the way some white fellers treated girls like her. Mostly, she'd heard that they worked you hard and then came to your bed and forced themselves on you. Doreen shuddered. If other white fellers were like the Big Father, then all those stories were probably true. And she felt so helpless and fearful that, once again, tears came to her eyes.

Late in the afternoon, when she and Nellie were unpegging the last lot of dry linen, Nellie abruptly turned to her, with stern eyes.

"You say nutching!" she strongly warned Doreen. "'Cause your mumma waitin' close by!"

Doreen's heart gave a sudden lurch. "Where?" she gasped.

"Roper Billy take you. You wait! Say nutching!"

Nellie refused to elaborate, and when pressed by Doreen, she turned her back on her. All the time, on her walk to the dormitory, Doreen's breath kept coming in little gasps. Her mum was nearby, and after all this time.

Susie greeted her when she entered the dormitory. "How was it, Dor?"

"Bloody hard and bloody hot!"

Doreen tried to concentrate on Susie, but it wasn't easy. All she could think about was seeing her mum again. But how could that be possible? She noticed the concerned look on Susie's face.

"You better lie down, Dor. You look like the sun's hit you."

"I'm all right. I'll just sit."

I have to keep my mouth shut, Doreen warned herself. *I can't even tell Susie*. She willed herself to act naturally and then made herself lie down on her bed.

On her third morning, after Roper Billy's firewood had been unloaded, Nellie ordered her to get into the empty cart and to lie down.

"You be quiet!" Nellie hissed.

Roper Billy covered her with a square of canvas and then led the pony to a pile of garden clippings and cuttings, which he loaded on top of Doreen. Following that, he led the pony toward the mission's front gate. Suddenly, Doreen heard the Big Father's commanding voice and immediately lay panic-stricken and scarcely able to breathe.

"Hey, Billy! You hang on."

Doreen could tell from the sound of his voice that the Big Father was now beside the cart. Then she felt the cart move slightly as he leaned heavily against it. Certain that she was about to be discovered, she lay completely rigid, as if paralyzed. Suddenly, she felt some of the cuttings on top of her shift before settling. She became convinced that her left ankle was now exposed. Petrified, she didn't dare move it, in case the movement attracted the Big Father's attention.

"Billy," she heard the Big Father order, "you go find two, three other fellers and make veggie garden more big. Awright?"

"Yu-ai."

"And don't forget!"

Doreen felt the cart move off and breathed a huge sigh of relief. Soon, she felt the old cart jolt and creak its way along a rough bush track. Her heart began thumping again, and her thoughts fluctuated wildly. What if Sister Rose had been watching all the time? What if she was waiting for them with her gloating "you didn't get away with it" smile? Was her mum truly waiting? Why hadn't Nellie told her more? Then the tension became too much, and Doreen started to shake and sob silently. And she didn't know why she couldn't stop crying.

She felt the cart halt and became aware that the rubbish on top of her was being moved. She hadn't heard any voices. Oh Christ! She panicked, felt very weak and was sure that Sister Rose was standing there, smiling and not saying a word. She closed her eyes tight. She didn't want to see Sister Rose's look of triumph. Then she felt a gentle hand take hold of her arm, but she kept her eyes pressed shut and stayed rigidly curled up on the cart's floorboards.

"Aren't yer goin' ter give me a hug, love?" her mum's voice asked.

Doreen opened her eyes wide and found herself gazing up into her mother's concerned dark eyes. She saw the attractive, much-loved face that she'd never forgotten, except there were lines on it now that hadn't been there before. And her mum's shiny, black hair now contained the odd grey streak. Doreen's breath seemed to have got caught in her chest. Wonderful feelings of relief and excitement and love flooded through her. She jumped up and leaped from the cart, down into her mother's arms. She felt her mother's comforting arms hold her tight and her mother's lips kiss the top of her head again and again. Uncontrollable tears kept pouring down Doreen's cheeks, and she couldn't stop sobbing.

"Yer don't have ter cry no more, love," said her mother's gentle voice. "I'm here, an' I'm goin' ter look after yer. Now, we's goin' ter have ter move. We've got a long walk, through the bush, comin' up. That way we'll avoid white fellers. Uncle Henry here will be with us all the time. An' he'll look after us."

Doreen pulled back and looked up into her mother's face. "Oh yes, Mum," she pleaded. "Let's start walking now. We've got to get far way from here. This is a bad place."

Her mother took her hand. "Yes, love," she said. "An' I'll tell yer everythin' as we is walking."

"Please, Mum, let's leave now."

"Course, love. An' I'm so happy I've got my beautiful girl back at last."

They watched Roper Billy turn the pony around. He smiled at them and then started back toward the mission.

Doreen held her mother's hand tightly. "Oh, Mum. I never thought I'd see you again!"

"I wasn't about ter give up, love," Peg said fiercely. "No blutty way!"

CHAPTER 6

FATEFUL ENCOUNTERS

It was a crisp, first light, and the area around Calum bustled with activity as the last of the packing up was completed. Large, leather pack bags had been hooked onto the trees on each side of pack saddles, and swags were then strapped on top. A full pack bag weighed around one-hundred pounds, so Hank personally checked that the load on each side of a packhorse was balanced. He was clearly impatient to start the three-and-a-half-day, one-hundred-and-twenty-five-mile journey down, off the Tablelands, and well into the Gulf Country, where they'd make their first camp.

Charlie was running around like a chicken without its head. He was convinced that he'd forgotten the yeast.

Hank yelled at him, "Stop your goddamn clicking, Charlie, and get some more. We can't waste time sifting through your pack bags!"

Calum saddled Socks and mounted. The bay had a pair of green hide hobbles fastened to a strap around his upper neck. A canvas, water bag hung from a wither, and a saddlebag was strapped to the near-side saddle Ds, while a folding-handles, mug-lid, quart pot was strapped to the offside Ds. Calum's rifle was in a scabbard in front of his right leg and, like the others, he was dressed in a long-sleeved, khaki shirt, moleskins and concertina, leather leggings. His seven-foot, twelve-strand, plaited, 'roo-hide, stock whip with its half-plaited, cane handle hung over his right shoulder, with the handle against his chest.

Hank, mounted on a big, raw-boned black, pulled it to a stop next him. "Show me your hooks," he demanded.

With a derisive look skyward, Calum took a boot from its stirrup iron and held it up to show his angle-heel, Wave Hill spur with its short, goose neck and modest rowel.

Hank didn't miss Calum's look. "Okay, they're short enough. At least you're not a horse-killing, young show-off," he grunted before turning the black. "Right!" he yelled. "Let's move it."

He moved off at a steady walk to lead the small caravan northwest, across the waving grass plain. Murranji Bill rode beside him, and behind them rode Charlie, with his grey Fedora firmly jammed onto his head. After Charlie came the packhorses and spares and the new, Aboriginal horse tailers, Edward and Tarpot. Jalyerri and Jacky Jacky, promoted to ringers, brought up the rear. Blue and Nugget were on the right flank and Brian and Calum on the left.

Jalyerri was rather pleased that he'd been promoted. He made a point of emphasizing to Tarpot and Edward that he and Jacky Jacky used to be horse tailers. "Us, two feller bin horse tailer. Now ringer," he insisted with a white-toothed grin.

But it didn't matter either way to Jacky Jacky. He always went along with everything, even with the name that a ridiculing Head Stockman had bestowed upon him.

The freshly spelled horses exuded power and urgency. Muscles rippled, ears were pricked and necks arched. Often they danced a few steps forward before strong hands and calming voices brought them back to a walk. Time in a spelling paddock plus a full belly of green grass, with its abundant green seeds, had a northern, stock horse reefing at its bit just as strongly as any southern cousin that was feeling its oats.

Riding along, Hank's mind was on Jan. Moonlight had lit the last part of their walk. And when they'd said good night at her mum's front door, he'd kissed her. She'd willingly come into his arms before pulling away. He'd been surprised by the look of confusion and then vulnerability, which had suffused her face.

"No, no, please," she'd cried. "I'm not ready. Really."

Now, he could hardly wait to see her again.

He surveyed the peaceful, wide-open space ahead and couldn't help thanking his lucky stars that First Northern had given him a job, some twelve months back. He recalled the chain of events. The American Consul in Sydney, where he'd spent a delightful and lazy, eight months, had given him a letter of introduction to the General Manager, in Brisbane, of First Northern. The kindly-looking, greying executive had studied him from across his desk.

"Yes," he'd said. "I'll give you a go, son; no worries. If it hadn't been for your mob, winning the Battle of the Coral Sea, God knows what would've happened to us up here. You see, our Government was only prepared to defend what lay south of Brisbane."

"No kidding!"

"I see you were foreman on your father's ranch. Also, you ran Shorthorns, so we'll start you off as a Head Stockman. Will the Territory be all right with you?"

"That'd be great!"

Hank had departed, thrilled. A Head Stockman. Wow. And it wasn't till he got to Long Creek that he discovered that he'd be one of its four Head Stockmen. And thankfully, the Station Manager had been told to make sure that he had an experienced ringer in his crew. That ringer had turned out to be Murranji Bill.

And for Calum, this was the start of a huge, new adventure. A lightly perspiring and sure-footed Socks was between his knees, and the soft creak of newly oiled leather was in his ears. He was chock-full of adrenaline.

The infant season was advertising its March vigour with plump scuttling Ground Goannas, fat cattle and dense flocks of waterfowl that crowded the waterholes. These included grey-brown Grey Teal, Pacific Black Duck, fast-flying, mahogany-brown Hardhead ducks and Plumed Whistling-Duck with their long, white, pinion plumes. While stately, tall Brolgas, clad in subdued grey, seemed through choice to hold their distinctive, bald, red heads disdainfully above the noisy throng with which they shared the billabongs. And loose flocks of very large, brown-backed Plain Turkeys, with their black-and-white-chequered, wing shoulders, gorged unhurriedly on transparent-winged grasshoppers. Brian pointed at a flock.

"Our mob reckons they're good tucker." He smiled. "But so do your lot, so I reckon they'll soon be getting scarce."

"I don't know anything about Plain Turkeys," Calum said mildly. "You see, I come from a small town that's not far from Melbourne."

"No wonder you're so ignorant," Brian responded with a wide grin. "But I don't mind teaching you a few things, because I reckon you're different from lots of white fellers."

Brian was his usual relaxed self. Nothing ever really bothered him because he'd decided long ago that, notwithstanding his mixed blood, he'd been born lucky. For starters, he'd missed out on being taken from his mum to be assimilated. And he was real lucky that he hadn't been born thirty-odd years earlier. In those days, many of the *Old People* had regarded half-caste babies as evil, white creatures that'd been sent to the tribe by bad spirits, and many had been killed quick smart. He reflected now on the fact that a lot of the Old People still believed that babies made themselves. And it puzzled him why they thought that sleeping with a woman had nothing to do with conception. But that conception probably occurred when the Baby Spirit entered the mother with the tucker that the man brought to her. And what's more, they even believed it was their duty to lend their women to people they trusted. They called it "changing sweat" because it also meant swapping clothes that were full of sweat. That way neither of the fellers could use the other's sweat to make harmful magic. He doubted, when married, that he could lend his wife to another. That meant that he'd be labelled a "badhead" or jealous bugger.

He reflected that he was neither one thing nor the other, neither white nor black. But he had to watch his step with whites. Mostly, though, they were all right provided he kept his mouth shut. But that didn't apply to Hank and Murranji Bill. They'd never given even a hint that he was looked down on. And it was the same with young Calum. He'd noticed Calum with Jalyerri and Jacky Jacky. They enjoyed teasing him by pretending that they didn't understand all that he was saying, but actually, they were encouraging him to learn Creole. And already Jalyerri, particularly, was showing signs of being protective toward him.

A small mob of Red Kangaroos bounded away from the horses. Calum watched them. They were the biggest kangaroos that he'd ever seen, and he was impressed by their attractive brick-red colouring, mule-shaped heads and long, pointed ears.

Brian indicated them. "They make great tucker, especially the tail. And Murranji told me that they're our biggest marsupials. But you've got to watch the big males because they can get nasty."

"Right."

"And, I've got the same Skin as the 'roo, you know."

"Yeah," Calum replied doubtfully.

"We call it Skin," Brian informed him. "White fellers'd call it totem. My clan Skin is 'roo, so I can only fuck a woman whose Skin isn't related to me. And you know, the Old People believe I've got the same flesh as the 'roo. An' it's the 'roo that also gives me my language an' food an' waterholes. Also, there are parts of a 'roo I can't eat, like the front an' back legs." Brian grinned widely. "I reckon I'm lucky my Skin isn't File Snake 'cause all those body parts look the same to me!"

"Why can't you marry someone with your Skin?"

"Mate, it'd be like marrying my sister."

"Oh."

They rode in silence, with Calum digesting what he'd been told. He stroked Socks's silky, sun-hot neck and told him that he was a fine horse. The bay responded by moving its ears back.

"That horse likes you," Brian remarked.

"Socks is a good horse," Calum replied. "But he's got some unlearning to do. And I think unlearning is hard for a horse, because it's got such a good memory." He changed the subject. "That was good of your mum to look after George."

"Yeah, she's all right," Brian agreed. "But you know, my old man's a bastard. He's off with his white wife and kids, managing an outstation on one of the biggest runs in Western Australia. And he doesn't give a brass razoo about me or my sister."

"You don't have to have a half-caste mum for your old man to treat you like shit," Calum said quietly.

"You know," Brian said, without rancour, "I'm called names like boong, nigger, half-caste or yeller feller. An' my sister's called a creamy or a creamy piece. An' a ton of whites'd expect a woman, like her, to become a whore."

"You're joking, aren't you?"

"Well, a lot of 'em do, you know," Brian continued. "They don't seem to want to marry Murries an' white fellers won't marry 'em." He thought for a moment. "It's like Murranji said. Lots of white fellers now have half-caste or Murri sheilas, but we say they're only mixin' blankets 'cause they're not married. An' there's only one thing that's changed from the old days, I reckon."

"What's that?"

"Nowadays, a Murri or a half-caste is looked down on, worse than before."

Calum saw that incomprehension and frustration had spread, like a stain, over Brian's face.

"Why did things get worse?" he asked, his voice sympathetic.

Brian thought for a minute before answering. "According to my mum," he said, "things changed when more an' more white sheilas came up here. They had different standards, an' were shit scared of all the syphilis that was going around. And they were also dead set against white fellers abducting Murri sheilas. Next thing, it became dirty an' sinful for a white feller to have a Murri sheila. An' if he lived with her, nobody talked to him." Brian shook his head slowly in disbelief. "Then all these names came about, like combo an' gin jockey an' black velvet rider. An' people reckoned some white fellers had to have it like it was opium!"

"Jeez. You know, I'd never heard of these names till I came up here," Calum said.

"Yeah? Well, after my sister was born, my mum said a mate of my dad gave him a cork that'd been half burned away."

"What for?"

"Because my sister was proof he was a combo."

"So?"

"Giving a burned cork is like telling a white feller he can't fuck a white sheila till he's gone and blacked her face with it."

"Good heavens."

"An' my mum said the shame of being called a combo finally got to be too much. My dad couldn't take it, an' that's why he pissed off."

A whistle from Hank interrupted them. He beckoned, and Brian cantered over to him. When he returned, he had Hank's Winchester rifle.

"There's a cleanskin bull in that little mob of cattle over there," he said, pointing. "Hank wants it shot now. Save doing it when we're drafting off fats." He saw Calum's questioning look. "Lots of those bulls get to be ten or twelve without ever seeing a human being. Often, if you're on foot, they'll charge straight away." Brian grinned engagingly. "Hank reckons I need shooting practice. Come on," he enjoined. "I need you to hold my horse. I don't want it taking off an' that big bastard coming at me if it's not been knocked over by the first shot."

They rode to within fifty yards of the mob before dismounting. Calum took Brian's reins and watched Brian crawl, on his hands and knees, till he was forty yards from the solid, brown bull. The bull was at the face of the mob. It was obvious that it was more edgy than the other cattle. It'd smelled the approaching riders. Its ears were forward and its nostrils were flaring, and it was snorting loudly. It had its eyes wide and was slinging its head about to focus on the nearest horses. And it was constantly pawing the black earth with a front hoof. Calum watched Brian sit up, rest his elbows on his knees, cushion his cheek against the rifle's stock, aim and fire. He saw a small puff of dust rise from the bull's kidney region. The *whump* of the striking bullet carried clearly. The rifle's sharp *crack* startled both horses and also scattered the small mob with the bull. Calum struggled to hold the horses, which were jerking their heads back strongly. When they were under control, he returned his attention to Brian. The bull was on its haunches attempting to rise. He saw Brian aim again and saw another puff of dust rise from the bull's kidney area. By the time that Calum had settled both horses again, the bull had collapsed onto its side. And its four legs were in tremors while straightening right out.

Brian took the reins of his horse. "Thanks, mate," he said, breathing out audibly. "I'll just take this rifle back to Hank."

When he returned, Calum spoke supportively. "Nothing wrong with that shooting," he enthused, needing to settle Socks after yet another, danced shy at nothing at all.

Brian grinned at him. "And your folks down south are dinkum Aussie, are they?"

"Yes, except for my mum. She comes from Skye, an island in Scotland, where they have their own language."

"You serious?"

"Yes. It's called Gaelic."

Calum needed to settle Socks again. The bay had suddenly leaped diametrically sideways, and a lesser rider would've found himself sitting in midair with no mount under him.

"I've been watching your bay," Brian remarked. "He's looking for things to shy at."

"I know. He's testing me. But I'll work on him, and he'll come good."

They saw that Hank had stopped for lunch, beside a billabong that was fringed with Coolibahs. They watered the horses before squatting on their haunches to watch expectantly as Charlie made a fire and began to fry steaks.

"Don't expect a cooked lunch every day," Brian warned Calum. "When we're working, you'll be eating while you're on the back of your horse!"

Charlie surveyed the waiting ringers with some irritation. "Enjoy these while yer can," he grunted testily. "This is the end of the fresh meat till Hank says we can have a killer. An' the *only* reason I'm workin' while you bludgers is sittin' around is because this steak'll be 'off' by this afternoon."

"Yer better enjoy this, Calum," Blue advised with a grin. "Because we'll all be eatin' shit beetles soon."

"Charlie does a fine job, Blue," Hank remonstrated. He nodded to Calum. "We kill a fat cow once a week and salt the cuts to stop 'em from going off. That way, Charlie's got corned beef for his stews and curries and battered steak."

Blue, as usual, didn't need an excuse to hold forth. And apparently, the behaviour of Dung Beetles was a subject that was close to his heart.

"I know the corned beef is stacked on a table in camp," he said. "An' green branches is kept lit under the table, 'cause smoke is supposed ter keep the Blowflies and shit beetles away." He looked at Calum and waved a forefinger for emphasis. "But it don't! An' after a couple of days, maggots and shit beetles has got inter the meat. Of course, when Charlie builds up that fire, most of them maggots gets fried up, and he brushes what's left of 'em off. But them shit beetles burrow right inter the meat."

Hank attempted to divert Blue. "Charlie always soaks the meat before cooking it, and most of 'em get drowned and float to the surface. And he does a fine job in conditions that'd test *any* cook."

Blue refused to be diverted. "I refuse ter argue with yer, Hank. Anyway, I was only goin' ter educate our young mate here on the evolutionin' of shit beetles." He paused before adding grandly, "I was taught 'bout Mr. Darwin, yer know."

Hank shook his head, exasperated.

"Now, Calum," Blue said, pausing theatrically, "these beetles live in cow shit; eat it even. But why do they compete with us, fer our corned beef? Well, Mr. Darwin has found the answer." Blue raised his voice in triumph. "They prefer beef. So they're evolutionin' an' startin' to grow hooks on their legs so they can grab on ter passin' cattle and burrow inter 'em. And yer know what that means?" Blue raised his voice and turned his head to look triumphantly at the other ringers. "It means we're goin' ter have to dip the fats twice. Once fer ticks an' once fer shit beetles."

Nugget pricked up his ears. "Are yer dinkum sure, mate?" he asked.

"Course I am, Nugg. I brained it out, didn't I?"

Brian caught Calum's eye. "I'm off to wash my hands. Coming, mate?"

While they washed their hands, Brian explained why it was imperative to have clean hands before a meal. "Out in camp Charlie'll put a slab of corned beef on the table so we can help ourselves. And another thing," Brian said, "out here, there's no toilet paper, so don't go picking up a stick to stir your tea."

"What do you mean?"

"When you're in timber country, you'll use a smooth stick to wipe your bum. Here on the plains, if there are no trees, you'll use the smooth, round, gidgee stones about the size of a cricket ball."

"Oh."

Following lunch, they started their descent down into the Gulf Country. Calum had been told that they'd be descending some twelve-hundred feet.

Below, the landscape that they rode through was markedly different. Trees were abundant, especially those widespread twenty-foot-high, bushy-looking Mulga acacias while sixty-foot mottled-trunked River Reds and ethereal-looking Ghost Gums grew beside creeks and billabongs.

Calum found himself liking and opening up to Brian. He sensed that Brian liked him too.

"You know," he said. "I just can't come at English people."

Brian shook his head, and his face registered resignation. "Here, it was the English mostly; we call 'em poms that gave the Old People bacca, grog, and syphilis. Course, if white fellers now reckon there are too many Murries hanging around, like in Darwin, the coppers round them up an' take 'em to the harbour. Then a ship takes them to Garden Point on Melville Island. An' that's where they stay."

"Heavens above. Your mum's people must hate whites."

"What good would that do? Would holding on to their anger keep 'em warm at night?"

Calum didn't answer.

Brian changed the subject. "Are your folks still down south?" he asked.

"My mum's dead. A stallion killed her."

"Bad bijnitch."

"What does that mean?"

"Like *Sunday bijnitch* means 'sacred stuff.' An' *wrong-side bijnitch* means 'against the law.'"

"Oh."

"Now, do you know what I'm going to do one day that's against the law?" Brian said, grinning.

"No."

"I'm going to start my own run. I'll lease Crown land next to a big station, an' my breeders'll be their cleanskin cows an' calves an' heifers that I'll put my own brand on." He studied Calum's face. "Like I said, you're different."

"Because I come from Down Below?"

"No, 'cause you don't see the colour of my skin. I notice things like that."

Calum didn't know what to say.

"I don't have a partner for my run, know what I mean?" Brian told him. "And I was wondering if you'd be interested. Of course, we'd be starting from nothing, with nothing but hard work."

He grinned at Calum and proffered his right hand. Calum met his eyes and then reached across and grasped Brian's hand, secure in the knowledge that he could trust him.

"Partners!" he affirmed and then grinned mischievously. "And I'll help you steal all the cattle we need. I think I'm quite good at stealing."

"Partners," Brian agreed with a grin. "But I hope you don't keep on hating every pom you come across. There's too many of them. Besides, we've all got to bend with the wind, mate."

****

They reached their campsite on the third day, in the heat of the early afternoon. It was on a bank of a wide, Charles Creek billabong, and the surrounding countryside offered typical, Gulf Country diversity. Areas of low, eucalypt woodland were common, and there were Bloodwood stands and clumps of Lancewood scrub with a Spear Grass ground cover. And vivid-green Native Currant bushes stood out like viridescent, signal lamps against the bushy, drab-looking Mulga acacias among which they grew. Ghost Gums graced the billabongs, and the earth was a strong red.

The arrival of sixty-odd, thirsty horses, at the billabong caused a dense, mixed throng of waterfowl to smack the water with their wings as they laboured up into the air. Dappled light, sparkling on the disturbed, brown water, flashed into the riders' eyes, and the sound of the hammering wings provided a background beat to a cacophony of protesting *quarks*. A large goanna with a browny-grey back, yellow belly and yellow-striped tail exited speedily up a Ghost Gum, and the feisty, small, black-and-white Willie Wagtail that it disturbed, wagged its tail and scolded it with an indignant *kirri-kirri-kirrikijirrit*.

Back from the billabong stood a large stockyard. It was one of many that'd been built on permanent water, which dotted the Long Creek countryside. This one's sturdy bronco panel was temporarily festooned with *screeching*, yellow-crested Sulphur-crested Cockatoos that shone shimmery white in the afternoon's hard sunlight.

Calum eyed a young brown cow, which seemed to be determined to stand its ground. It was some fifteen yards from Hank's horse. Hank and Murranji Bill were seemingly discussing the merits of setting up camp here and didn't seem to have noticed her. She continued to stand her ground with her ears forward and with her wide eyes fixed on Hank's black horse. Her flickering ears showed that she was listening to their voices. Calum wondered if Hank's horse was between her and her calf.

"I reckon that young cow's got a calf hidden," he remarked casually to Brian.

Calum looked all around. He couldn't see the calf, but that wasn't surprising. Young calves slept hidden, in long grass, for much of the day, and their mothers' grazing could take them forty yards from where they lay. He was conscious too that there wasn't a horse in the Territory, which could beat a wild cow over the first fifteen or so yards. He was about to yell a warning to Hank when she suddenly lowered her head and charged. And when she swept in, head down, she caught the black gelding on its offside flank. The impact of her charge slewed the gelding around. Blood immediately started to run from the nasty-looking hole in its flank.

"Jesus!" Hank yelled.

He leaped from the black and ruefully looked after the young cow. She'd reached her calf, got it to its feet and was now trotting off, bag swinging, with her calf beside her. She left without so much as a backward glance at the damage that she'd wrought.

The black had been badly horned. Blood was now running freely down his quivering leg. He was standing still, with his weight on his three, sound legs. He held his ears wide and low, and his eyes were dull.

"Will you guys take his gear off?" Hank asked. "I'll get Charlie. Looks like he's setting up already."

When Hank and Charlie returned, four ringers quickly pulled the black's legs from under him. In a trice, the struggling horse was flat on its side. Brian sat on the ground and clamped the black's neck, just below its head, firmly between his thighs. Nugget tightly looped a stirrup leather around the gored leg's fetlock and pulled on it to stop any movement.

"You okay, Brian?" Hank asked.

"Yeah, I've got his head held real tight. There's no way he can get up."

"And, Nugg, you hold fast. We don't want Charlie's head kicked in because he's the only one who can cook, remember!" Hank emphasized.

"So long as he remembers to cook good," piped up Blue, "he should be safe. But if I was you, Charlie, I'd swear on the Bible, my standards wasn't goin' ter slip."

Charlie cast a disdainful look in Blue's direction but managed to keep his mouth shut. He put down the pot of clean water and the container of tar that he'd brought. First, he carefully cleaned the wound with a wet cloth and then held it against the hole to stem the flow of blood. Calum could see that the black was hurting. Charlie then threaded a flat, curved needle with catgut and methodically began to stitch the wound. Watching Charlie's stitching was unsettling, and the pain for the black must've been hell. When Charlie'd finished, his stitching was the neatest that Calum'd ever seen, and that included stitching by racehorse vets.

Hank liberally covered the whole area with Stockholm Tar. "That's it, fellers," he said. "You can let him go now."

The black swung his head up, stuck out his front legs and then pushed himself up with the back ones. The tar and stitching held, and there was no bleeding. Calum slowly led him away. He was limping badly.

"We could've done with that sort of stitching during the war, Charlie," Hank remarked.

Charlie stuck out his chest, like a puffed-up Bantam rooster, and looked disdainfully at the others and at Blue in particular. "Course a man's got ter know what he's doing," he replied immodestly.

"Don't say another word to him, Hank," Murranji Bill cautioned. "Otherwise, he'll be looking down his nose at the rest of us for the next couple of days!"

Once the camp had been set up, Hank sought out Brian and Calum. "Why don't you take Calum for a ride, Brian?" he suggested. "And show him the country round here and teach him a few things. We haven't the time to go looking for somebody who gets himself lost."

"And if he did get bushed," Brian replied, "you wouldn't need to worry. I'd just go right out and find him."

Hank's blue eyes showed amusement. "I see we have an alliance here." He started to turn away. "Do me a favour anyway, Brian, and show Calum around."

Hank watched the two walk off and grinned to himself. Ringers were so damn transparent. But the same couldn't be said about Billy Jack, his accountant brother, who was just downright shifty—and always had been. And, Hank decided that he was lucky that he wasn't practicing psychology for a living. Better by far an outdoor life, alongside people who were as straight as they come. And they needed to be because sometimes your life could depend on them.

Calum saddled his grey gelding, and Brian saddled the mare that he'd nicknamed Bitch. Once the others had seen what a determined biter she was, nobody disagreed with him.

They mounted and headed toward a distant clump of sixty-foot high Bloodwood eucalypts— that were renowned for their distinctive, blood-red sap.

Groups of Shorthorns were dotted along the way. Some were lying on the ground with their legs tucked under them, chewing the cud. Others grazed desultorily or stared at the horses with curious, big eyes. There was no urgency to their grazing and little haste about the way in which they moved from the horses' path.

"They've got full bellies," remarked Brian. "But it's different when we've got a drought. Then they're too weak to move fast 'cause all they have to eat is Mulga leaves an' such."

"Yes."

"Too right. Drought, an' they all gather round the bores. Now," he said and indicated with a sweep of his arm, "with all this water an' good feed, the bastards are scattered hell, west an' crooked."

"Right."

"Now, you better get used to being in the saddle," Brian said, "because we'll be going seven days a week an' ten hours a day. Plus a two-hour shift on a night horse, every night." He started laughing. "We get paid for sitting on horses, an' here's us with a couple that're called Stupid and Bitch."

Calum grinned widely because nobody would dream of calling a racehorse Stupid. Racehorses' names often reflected their breeding or else the dreams of their owners. Here, people didn't dream of winning a Melbourne Cup, Australia's richest horse race. No, there weren't all that many dreams about, just the reality that no hard rain meant drought. And your horse was a hardworking, stock horse that carried you through long hours of mustering. Your bed was a swag that you rolled out beside a creek or a bore, and your pillow was the padded underside of your saddle's sweat flap. And you went to sleep hearing the *wark wark* croaking of green frogs and the dovelike *coo-coo* of their spotted-brown brethren. Cleanskin bulls bellowed throughout the night, and dingoes howled and squabbled in the distant darkness. But as far as Calum was concerned, he'd found the peace of mind plus the freedom and space for which he'd always yearned.

Increasingly, since leaving the home station, Calum had become all too aware of his inexperience. He'd paid attention when Brian had taught him how to use his watch as a compass.

"Okay, let's hop off our horses," Brian now told him and then pointed to Stupid's hoofprints. "See how his hooves cut deeper into the earth when you're on his back? Now remember what your horse's tracks look like, 'cause all horses have different tracks. That way you can track your way back to camp."

"I see."

"Now, I'm still talking about getting bushed," Brian continued.

"Yes."

"First thing, if you're not certain where the camp is, don't panic. Just give your horse its head. It knows where water is better than you. Give it its head, an' it'll take you to water."

"Yes. And could you tell me what you look for when you're tracking?" Calum asked.

Brian threw his head back and roared with laughter.

"What's up?" Calum demanded suspiciously.

"Mate, you want to learn everything at once. You're like a kid with a box of chocolates who wants to eat the lot at one hit."

"I'm not a kid. I'm seventeen," Calum spat out.

Brian's expression immediately softened. "Mate, I didn't plan to offend you. Now, you wanted to know about tracking?" he asked, humouring Calum.

"Yes."

"Okay," Brian said, squatting and pointing. "Every animal or bird has got different tracks, an' these are a big 'roo's. Now, see this grass that's been pushed over? It's pointing in the direction the animal is moving. An' little stones like this one that've been moved from its place are always pushed backward from the way the animal is running."

"Gee."

"I'll teach you, but remember, it'll take time."

They mounted, and without warning, Bitch took it into her head to put her ears back, reach over and bite Stupid on the neck. Not surprisingly he leaped sideways and watched her suspiciously. She really did have a dirty disposition.

"Crise!" exclaimed Brian. "And he wasn't even crowding her. I tell you, I gave this mare the right name."

"She probably needs a run to let off steam. She's too full of herself." Calum thought for a moment. "Where does Mr. Jackson get his stallions?" he asked.

"He buys 'em when their racing days are over. Those that're not good enough to stand at stud."

"I see. Do you think Bitch can move?"

"Yeah. She'd be up there with most stock horses."

"This cattle track is straight," Calum said. "I'll give you forty yards start. I've a feeling about this grey. Let's see if Stupid can catch her."

He took his feet from his stirrup irons and started to shorten his leathers.

"What're you doing?"

"I'm going to balance my weight up front."

"Jeez, you're sitting just like a jockey."

"You can start any time you like, you know."

Brian loosened his reins and dug his spurs into Bitch. Within a couple of strides, she was galloping fast and as straight as a gun barrel. She'd stretched out her neck and had pinned back her ears. Calum held Stupid back, balanced him, let him go and then gave him a quick rake with his spurs. Stupid leaped forward and was quickly into his stride. Calum concentrated on riding him hands and heels.

It was the first time that Calum had galloped him, and he was astounded by his action. Like some of the better Thoroughbreds that he'd ridden, Stupid had a low-to-the-ground, classic, daisy-cutter action, and his giant stride was longer than that of any Thoroughbred that Calum'd ever ridden. Calum was excited. Crouched low over the big grey's neck, he felt the rushing wind in his eyes, with Stupid's long mane whipping hard, against his face and stinging it. It was a smooth, rocking ride that was every bit as kind as a rocking horse's.

Stupid caught Bitch and went past her as if she was a lumbering cold blood and, true to form, she tried to savage him as he swept by.

When they pulled up, Calum turned to Brian exultantly. He spoke between deep breaths. "We've got ourselves a racehorse here, for sure."

"Crise, did he ever go past Bitch. And she was moving."

"Are there any picnic races held around here?"

Brian thought for a minute. His dark eyes were wide with excitement, and his chest was heaving from the exertion. "Jan used to work in Tennant Creek. She told me celebrations, including picnic races, were planned there before the Wet."

"Celebrations?"

"Something to do with mining, because they had a really big, gold rush there, ten or twelve years ago. An' there's still gold mining being done. Fair dinkum," Brian added, "she's a wild, old place on Saturday nights, with drunken miners picking bad fights over Murri sheilas."

"I don't have any time for drunks. My old man was a drunk. He used to hit my mum."

"You're joking. Any man that hits a woman or a kid is piss-weak an' should be put away, permanently."

"Yeah. He never appreciated what he had," Calum said quietly. "And Mum always helped in the stables."

"Is that where you learned about racehorses?"

"Yes."

"Lots of men don't appreciate what they've got, mate. You take my mum. Yeah, she's darker than me. So what?" Brian said. "She looked after me an' my sister real good. Sent us to the Catholic school too. An' she looked after my old man for four months after he broke his hip coming off a horse."

"You said your mum's dad wasn't a Murri, didn't you?"

"That's right," Brian said. "He had a good bit of Irish in him, so that probably makes me somewhere between quarter and half-caste. But don't ask me where."

"Oh."

Brian suddenly put a forefinger to his lips and indicated. "Can you shoot those two dingoes?" he whispered.

Calum passed his reins to Brian and grabbed his rifle. The dingoes had just emerged from a stand of Bloodwoods. The range was ninety yards, but the space between the two shots was hardly more than the time it took Calum to lever another cartridge into the Winchester's breech. He remounted, and they cantered to the dead dingoes.

"Now that's real shooting," Brian marvelled.

"Well, I've hunted foxes a lot, on neighbouring properties near my old man's stables. They kill a heap of lambs. Also they'll take the teats off a cow when she goes down to calve. And often they'll eat away half of where her calf's going to come out."

"Bloody hell. Course, there are no foxes where you've got the dogs, 'cause the dogs kill 'em."

When he reached the dead dingoes, Brian dismounted and quickly scalped both with his clasp knife.

"Why're you doing that?" Calum asked.

"Government pays five shillings for every dingo scalp you bring in. Cross the border into Western Australia, and you'll be paid two pounds. But they've got sheep there."

Brian wrapped the scalps in plenty of green grass before putting them in his saddlebag. The horses were jumpy. They could smell the combination of blood and dingo. They were snorting and starting. Brian noticed the swollen dugs on the dead female.

"Hang on to this, Bitch," he said. "I want to check around for pups."

Brian searched among the Bloodwoods. He picked up a stick, and Calum saw him poke it down the end of a hollow log that'd been eaten out by termites. Then he watched Brian use his knife to cut away a square of bark.

"What're you doing?"

"I'm not going to stick my arm down that log. I want to keep my fingers."

Calum watched him pause above the hole he'd cut and then thrust down quickly. He withdrew his arm, holding a chubby, yellow, squirming puppy by the scruff of its neck.

"Hey, look. A little *warrigal*," he called.

He brought it over to the horses and waited for Calum to dismount before passing it to him. Both horses showed a lot of interest in the pup. They pricked their ears, flared their nostrils, snorted and stretched out their necks to try and sniff it close up.

"Nosey buggers," remarked Brian.

Calum held the pup against his chest, but when he moved to stroke it, it sank its sharp milk teeth into the base of his thumb. He uttered a startled ouch and opened the pup's mouth with his other hand. When the pup again tried to bite, it received a firm tap on its sensitive nose. It blinked its eyes and continued to watch him closely, and when it again tried to bite, it received another firm tap on its nose and another firm command.

"No, pup. No!"

Once more the pup tried to bite Calum, and again, it received a tap on its nose. After this last tap, it allowed Calum to rest his fingers on its head. It lay still but kept its little, oval eyes fixed on his face. And it listened while he talked to it.

"You're a fat little thing. Looks like your mum fed you real well. But you haven't got her now, and you've got to learn not to bite. I know you're trying to stand up for yourself, but your teeth hurt." He looked at the large drops of blood that had formed on his hand. "Little bugger."

"Breathe onto his nose," Brian suggested. "That way he'll get used to you quicker."

Calum did as Brian suggested. The pup wrinkled its small, black nose but kept its eyes fixed on his face. Calum glanced across at his friend.

"You sure there are no more pups in that log?"

"Yeah. I checked real good. I reckon the others could've got killed."

"How?"

"Cattle maybe. If they caught the pups in the open, there's no way the male could protect 'em."

"You know about dingoes, don't you?" Calum asked.

Brian put his forefinger under the rim of his hat and pushed it back while he collected his thoughts. "Yeah," he said, "there are always tame dingoes in Murri camps. You know, they don't stink like other dogs. White fellers reckon they don't bark, but that's bullshit. When there's danger, they'll give three or four short, rough-sounding barks that end in a screeching yowl. An' when they're real content, they sort of purr like a cat, an' you can see their lips shivering."

Calum watched Brian shorten his reins and then mount. He wondered what his friend intended to do with the pup. He wanted to keep it.

"What're we going to do with this little fellow?" he asked.

"Either kill him or keep him. You can't leave him on his own."

"Let's keep him."

"He's yours, mate," Brian said. "I'm giving him to you."

"Really?"

"No worries." Brian grinned. "See how you go with Hank. Like most cattlemen, he doesn't have much time for the dogs."

"I don't know about Hank. He lied to me on my first day at Long Creek."

"Hank's all right," Brian stated. "I reckon he's straight, an' you've got to remember anybody that's new'll get tested. This is hard country, an' people have got to hold their own. Give him a go." Brian laughed. "Murranji's got him bluffed though. Hank hasn't worked out it's the Aussie way to take the boss down a peg or two. Stop him from getting too big for his boots."

"Yeah?"

Calum tucked his shirt securely into his moleskins and tightened his belt another notch. Then he undid three buttons on his shirt and put the pup inside it. The pup stayed there with its head poking out. It felt soft and warm against his body, and it didn't move or make a sound. And it didn't try to bite him. It just kept looking around, taking everything in.

On the way back, they rode into a lowering sun. High above, a pair of Wedge-tailed Eagles lazily twirled through the sky, and the cattle that they passed were grazing industriously before darkness descended. The breeze had strengthened, and high in a flowering Woolly Butt, among its stunning rich-orange blossoms, a mob of Red-tailed Black-Cockatoos screeched and squabbled over roosting places.

"Peaceful little pup, isn't he?" Brian remarked.

"Stupid's gait is sending him to sleep." Calum looked down. "Is the dingo bitch a good mother, Brian?"

"For sure. An' both of 'em look after the pups. An' when the pups are old enough to eat solid food, both the male an' the bitch fill themselves with meat. An' then come back an' spew up this half-digested food for the pups to eat."

"Oh."

They were negotiating a broken stand of Mulgas when unexpectedly they came upon an unobtrusive campsite. The three occupants stood and silently watched them. They'd been spotted long before they'd seen the camp. The woman looked to be in her midthirties. She appeared, to Calum, to be half-caste. What surprised him, though, was the dress that she was wearing. It wasn't the sort of dress that a woman would wear when she went walkabout. The middle-aged Murri with her regarded them with cold eyes. His only clothing was a red cockrag. The final member of the trio was a light-coloured girl of about fifteen. She wore what looked like a school-uniform-type tunic. Terror showed on her face. It was the sort of grabbing terror that could root someone within a snake's striking radius. Brian started talking to the man in Creole. Calum looked at the girl and smiled and saw the fear leave her face. And for a moment, he saw confusion register on her face, but that quickly turned to surprise. She held his eyes, and he saw that hers had changed. Now they were gentle and full of wonder. Unaccountably, his heart started to beat faster, and goose pimples made his skin tingle. Then, for him, it was as if rain clouds are suddenly stripped away and summer's sun shines through, and everything looks light and bright, and gold and magical. He held her eyes, and it struck him, with great clarity that all his dreams lay within their wide, dark depths. And he knew that not only in his brain but also in his heart and in his gut. He was also quite certain that he was looking at the girl he'd marry one day.

When she returned his smile, she found herself looking into the bluest eyes that she'd ever seen. She was taken by the concern that she saw within them. Then suddenly and surprisingly, the space between them seemed to come alive, and she felt herself being drawn to this youth. And for her came the sudden realization that she was looking at a boy who was right beside her and, for the first time in her life, she wasn't nervous; in fact, being near him made her feel safe. And she was aware that her heart was now beating against her ribs.

Stupid shifted away from Bitch, and the spell was broken.

"Let's go," Brian said.

"Looks like this is good-bye," Calum murmured.

"Good-bye," she answered with a small smile.

He nodded and smiled, and she smiled back before they turned their horses and rode off.

"They're on the run, mate," Brian said. "I'm going to forget I've seen 'em."

"I can't forget her. She's too pretty."

"Yeah? Well, if you want to keep her safe, you won't tell anyone you've seen 'em."

"Yes."

On the ride to camp, Calum couldn't get her face out of his mind. Why had she been so scared? And why were they on the run? But heck, wasn't she pretty! And he wasn't wrong there. Her skin was a soft olive brown. A small splash of freckles adorned her straight nose and high cheekbones. Expressive, big, dark eyes looked out from above full lips and a determined chin. And, already, her body's shape pushed against her shapeless tunic.

The horses had barely passed the little camp's concealing Mulgas when the girl collapsed onto the ground. She lay curled up in a foetal position. Her rigid body was shaking, and her eyes stared straight ahead. Watching her was like watching a delicate piece of lead crystal that's inexorably quivering toward its breaking point. But because this was the second occasion on which this had happened, Peg was less alarmed. She sat on the ground beside her daughter and gently stroked her hair and cheek.

"It's all right, love. It's all right," she crooned. "An' I'm real sorry I couldn't think how ter get yer out sooner. Oh Crise, I can see you is hurtin' real bad. But fair dinkum, I was stuck till I met Roper Billy and Nellie. Course, I'd enough money, so they wouldn't say no."

In a little while, Doreen's shuddering diminished and finally ceased. She sat up and clutched her mother. Peg cradled her daughter in her arms.

"Was it seein' those ringers, love? Yer do know yer don' have ter worry, 'cause one of 'em is the same as us?"

"That white boy is hurting too. I saw the hurt behind his eyes, till he hid it."

"What is it then, love?"

"When I was in Cord River, I was holding myself together all the time. Now, 'cause I'm out of there, that strength has left me."

"Give it time, love."

"I can't go back, Mum. It'd kill me. It's such a bad place."

"Yer *never* goin' back. Yer got ter believe that."

"I get so frightened. It comes all of a sudden, and it's like I panic and can't move."

"Give it time, love. Give it time an' slowly yer'll come good."

"Are you sure, Mum?"

"Yes!" her mother answered fiercely. "Now, jus' lie back an' rest. I'm goin' ter make us a cuppa."

Doreen rested and thought about the boy with the blue eyes. She also thought about his pup. It'd looked so safe inside his shirt. All that'd been showing was its head and neck, and it'd kept swivelling its head around so that it didn't miss anything. Doreen felt certain that the boy was gentle and kind. She wondered again at what had passed between them. It'd been like a lightning bolt, and she could still feel it. She knew that the boy had also felt it because she'd seen it in his eyes. She decided that he looked about eighteen, and she wondered what his name was. She turned to her mother.

"Mum?"

"Yes, love?"

"I'll be seeing that boy again."

"What?"

"The one with blue eyes."

"Why?"

"I know he's going to ask me to be his girlfriend."

"What!"

"And I'll say yes."

"Blutty hell. But yer said yer wanted nothin ter do with white fellers?"

"He's different, Mum. Very different."

****

Brian kept glancing across at Calum, who remained quiet and seemed lost in his own thoughts.

"You look like a stunned Pop-eyed Mullet," Brian remarked.

"I was thinking about that girl. She's beautiful."

"She's only a sheila you saw for a couple of minutes."

"No, she's not. She's special, and I need to find out where they're going so I can see her again."

"You've got lots o' time, mate. You're not even eighteen."

"I soon will be!" Calum flashed. "And I'm sure that girl also likes me."

"What's that sayin' you use a lot? The one in your mum's language."

"Chi sinn? Which means 'we'll see'?"

"Yeah. Chi sinn," Brian said.

Brian saw that Calum might as well have been a thousand miles away. He thought about the girl. *Yes*, he concluded, *she's pretty, but Calum looks like he's in a daze. An' it's plain crazy because the last thing anyone up here needs is to get rapt in a girl who's on the run.*

It was very late in the afternoon when they reached camp. The tropical sun was setting fast. A giant, blood-red blush permeated the few, stepped clouds that hung motionless and low in the western sky. Above, the sky had darkened, and already some of the bolder stars had come out and were bravely trying to twinkle.

On reaching camp, Calum noticed tied horses that he hadn't seen before. He looked questioningly at Brian.

"Those are Ed Smith's, mate. He's a pommy, dog stiffener."

"A what?"

"He makes a living poisoning the dogs," Brian explained. "An' he's welcome on any run 'cause he keeps the dogs down. The only people who don't want him are the Old People."

"Why?"

"The bastard gets carried away when he's fucking an' hurts the woman. I heard he hurt one, in Queensland, so bad she died a week later. Now, he always stays this side of the border."

"Jeez, his saddlebags smell bad," Calum complained. "That stink'd bend six-inch nails."

"He's too lazy to dry his scalps properly."

They rode their horses over to Tarpot, unsaddled them and left them with him.

"Lil warrigal," Tarpot exclaimed, beaming whitely. "Him good lil bugger."

"Yu-ai," Brian agreed and asked Tarpot if he'd mind giving the pup a midday feed when they were mustering.

"Da's awright. Get him plenty tucker."

"Thanks, mate."

Charlie was in the process of putting out still-warm bread, a slab of hot corned beef and a large bowl of mustard-flavoured, white sauce. He glared at them. "I held back this meal for you buggers. This isn't some bloody Adelaide hotel, yer know."

"We galloped all the way back, just so we wouldn't hold you up," Brian fibbed.

"Bloody liar."

"Calum, this is Ed Smith," Hank said. "He's thinning out the dogs for us." He noticed the pup. "Don't tell me you've got some future work, for Ed?"

"Not if Calum brings him up properly," Murranji Bill observed, grinning.

Hank gave Murranji Bill a hard look. Murranji promptly grinned back at him. "An', if Calum doesn't want him," he said, "I'll be happy to take him."

This time Hank gave Murranji an exasperated look.

Calum could smell Ed Smith's pungent odour from where he was standing. Clearly, the man hadn't bathed in months. Even his black, beard stubble couldn't hide the ingrained dirt. Ed Smith's expressionless black eyes stayed fixed on Calum, and when he spoke, his mouth remained in a leer.

"Best thing you can do, boy," he told Calum, "is hold it by the back legs an' knock its head against that tree there."

Calum didn't answer.

"What do you say, boy? Can't you speak?"

Calum could feel the sudden tension between them. He looked at Ed Smith and saw the cruelty behind the man's eyes. He thought about Brian's remark that Ed Smith enjoyed hurting women when he was having sex. Then it hit him. It was causing pain that excited Smith.

"He's my pup," Calum said quietly.

"Better let me kill him, boy. Or are you goin' to grow him for me? So I'll get a couple of quid for his scalp?" Ed Smith laughed a high-pitched laugh and continued to laugh as if he'd said something very funny. "Don't you have the guts, boy?" he asked. "Want me to do it for you, right now?"

Alarmed, Calum saw Ed Smith start to rise. He quickly passed his pup to Brian and nervously steeled himself for a fight, which he knew he couldn't win. Suddenly, Nugget had his clasp knife in his right hand. Ed Smith saw it and quickly sat down, fear whitening his face. Before Calum realized Nugget's intentions, the tip of the pup's left ear had been sliced off. A thin line of red droplets started to ooze from the cut. The pup didn't make a sound. It just shook its head a couple of times and continued to look at the fire and the squatting figures around it.

Nugget winked at Calum before speaking. "I don't see no bloody dingo, Smith. All I see is a Long Creek mate an' his pup."

"You're fuckin' blind."

The knuckles on Nugget's knife hand went white. His light-coloured eyes stayed expressionless. "My earmark on that pup's as good as a brand," he said quietly. "An' if he goes missin', an' I hear a dog stiffener's collectin' on a scalp what's earmarked, well, I'll go lookin' fer that feller."

"Think you're smart, don't you?" Ed Smith said.

"Anybody what killed Long Creek stock wouldn't be real bright," Nugget observed grimly.

Hank immediately picked up the quickly increasing tension and nodded at Calum and Brian. "Charlie'll give you fellers some meat. Why don't you two see if you can get some food into the pup?" He paused. "You never know, it might turn out all right." He glanced at the dog poisoner. "I think the rest of us should enjoy the meal Charlie's prepared. Funny isn't it, Ed," he continued conversationally, "how kids and pups go together? Always have, I guess. But enjoy our hospitality, please. Charlie's a fine cook."

Blue, though, had decided that he wouldn't let things rest. He started to grin wickedly and then turned to Nugget. "I forgot, Nugg," he said, "so you best remind me."

"About what?"

"Was it two or three Japs you killed in that knife fight?" He continued speaking before Nugget could answer. "Now, I remember. Yeah, it was three. An' the coppers reckoned they never seen so much blood. It was even runnin' onto the verandah of that Roebuck Bay hotel."

Ed Smith was looking increasingly uncomfortable.

Hank tried to sound reassuring. "Like I said, Charlie's a fine cook. You'll sure enjoy the meal, Ed."

"I'll eat your cook's meat," Ed Smith told Hank. "But I'll be sleepin' in my own camp. This has been a poor way to treat a guest."

Ed Smith ate his meal in silence. When he'd finished, he stood up and headed straight for his horses without saying a word.

"Now look what yer done, yer little yapper. You upset a guest," Charlie complained.

"He's a bludger, not a guest, Charlie. Now, Nugg," Blue said, turning to Nugget and grinning, "yer did say it was three Japs, didn't you?"

"Yer a bastard, Blue, an' you knows it," Nugget said, shaking his head in frustration. "I tol' yer previous ter stop puttin' me weights up."

"You sure you told me that, Nugg?" Blue questioned, smiling naughtily. "But if you say so, I won't argue, mate. You could well be right."

After feeding the pup, Brian and Calum put it beside Calum's swag. Calum still felt uneasy. There was something about Ed Smith that really disturbed him, and it wasn't superstition either. It was an extremely strong foreboding. And it was so strong that he could almost feel it.

"Would Nugget really've gone for him?" Calum asked, trying to banish his foreboding.

"Hank was worried. That's why he told us to move. Anyway, you're going to have to watch Ed. He's gone troppo, I reckon."

"Troppo?"

"The heat an' the dust an' the loneliness make some white fellers go real strange."

"Oh."

"An' I reckon that's only half his problem."

With Ed Smith gone, they returned to the fire. The pup waddled along determinedly behind them. Calum sat with his back to a tree stump and sipped his tea. The pup stayed with him. It turned and lay down, with its tummy to the fire, and promptly fell asleep. Calum felt totally relaxed. These wide-open sweeping spaces made him feel strangely secure. *It's funny*, he thought, *how they had the opposite effect on others. Like all those people who needed to walk on comforting, crowded pavements.* He stared into the fire and watched its red coals crack and break up before burning fiercely. Their sparks rose among the wispy, white smoke that spiralled upward and then got lost in the blue-black sky. And from the billabong, more and more frogs added their voices to a chorus that continued to swell till it reached a croaking crescendo. And just beyond the circle of firelight, he could hear the sound of Hank's black cropping grass. *Horses were like dogs,* he thought. *This one chose to stay close to him, despite having had to endure the pain of Charlie's stitching.* Then each time that he looked into the red coals, he saw her face looking back at him. And again he saw her breeze-touched, black hair and her half smile and the look of wonder in her wide, dark eyes.

Around the campfire rum was being drunk. And conversation and arguments and laughter were sometimes passionate. Recurring flashes of humour lit up faces, almost as much as the firelight that danced on them. After a long day in the saddle, the ringers found that humour not only enlivened this, their principal forum, but together with a stiff rum also acted as a balm that soothed aching insteps.

Hank turned to Murranji Bill. "Remember, you said you needed a rum and a campfire before you'd talk about the early cattlemen and the Murries. You've got both now, my friend."

Murranji smiled and nodded his agreement. He took a swallow from his mug, looked into the fire, and spoke matter-of-factly. "According to my grandpa, first up the Murries were pleased to be given knives an' matches. But it didn't last."

"No?"

"No. Too many settlers reckoned, 'cause they were white, they were superior. They called the Murries niggers an' didn't give a shit about 'em. An' trouble really started when they began abducting Murri women an' taking over the waterholes. As you know, those are meeting places, an' lots are sacred. That's when the thieving an' spearing really got going. The shout when Murries were sprung near holding yards was always, 'Niggers in!'" Murranji Bill paused. "Of course, the Murries soon got addicted to bacca, an' they thieved it from storehouses. That got stopped by setting a bear trap outside the storehouse. An' if a Murri was found in the trap next mornin', he was clubbed to death. They reckoned it wasn't worth wasting a bullet. An' often the feller they'd clubbed was hung from a tree, with a twist of bacca sticking from his mouth."

"Jesus! A human scarecrow!" Hank exclaimed in revulsion.

Murranji Bill coughed and cleared his throat. He rolled himself a cigarette and passed his makings to Hank, who then lit both with his Twenty-ninth Infantry Division Zippo.

"Did things improve, Murranji?" he asked.

"No, they got worse 'cause native, police units were formed. An' those native police were proper bastards."

"I suppose they joined up for the power?" Hank suggested.

"Too right. A native policeman got a uniform, horse, carbine, pistol an' grog." Murranji Bill drew on his cigarette. "Queensland was the worst. Its native police were supported by a couple of hundred, white volunteers, and the standing order was 'disperse the natives.' Course, whites can't track real well, so the native police were used where there were no tribal ties. The poor Murries didn't stand a chance. Horses were the difference. Christ, what Murri can outrun a horse?"

The others were shocked into silence.

"What exactly did 'dispersing the natives' mean?" Hank asked, frowning.

"It meant having native police track a mob of Murries, surprise them an' open fire, an' murder the lot: men, women, and children. Then dump the bodies in a *dry gully.*"

"Oh sweet Jesus," Hank exclaimed, sickened.

"An' it wasn't crash hot here either," Murranji continued. "Of course, it was before 1911, an' the Territory was still being administered by Adelaide. The officer in charge of the coppers here was a Mounted

Constable William Willshire. His boss was based in Port Augusta, so that feller couldn't have had a clue what was happening here. I remember one old Murri telling me that after cattle were speared on the Big Run, this copper, Willshire, an' his trackers an' white volunteers trapped a good-sized mob of Murries. It was in a gorge on the Wickham River. Then they shot the hell outta them except for a few women an' kids. There was a good-lookin' lubra captured, an' Willshire reckoned she was a bit of all right."

Hank shook his head in disgust. "But it wasn't as bad here as it was in Queensland surely?" he asked.

"Too right, it was damn bad here. From what I heard, Willshire an' his white volunteers murdered a ton of Murries from around the Daly Waters an' Roper River areas. An' he got away with it, despite being finally charged with murder. You see, his trial was abandoned because nobody'd serve on the jury. Yeah, Willshire was a big hero to all the whites."

Hank was visibly stunned. *Christ,* he thought, *this was sure different from Texas.* Sure, his grandfather always asserted that "the only good Comanche is a dead one" and that it was the Comanche who'd committed the worst atrocities. But they'd had horses and were better horsemen than most whites. And latterly, they'd had rifles and revolvers. But whites here, on horseback, had banded together and pursued people who were afoot and armed only with spears and boomerangs. And then wantonly murdered the lot. That was monstrous. The only parallel that came to mind was the Sand Creek massacre. Yes, that was one helluva shameful episode in American history. Colonel Chivington and his Colorado volunteers had descended on peaceful, sleeping Cheyenne. And to think that formerly, Chivington had been a Methodist minister. Well, he and his soldiers had ended up butchering and mutilating one-hundred-and-five women and children alone, and they'd been totally depraved. Hell, Chivington's troops had even cut out the private parts of women, stretched them over their saddle bows and had then worn them round their hats!

Hank drew deeply on his cigarette. God, he thought, why had colonists always behaved so abominably toward indigenes? And it didn't matter whether it was the Portuguese in Goa, the Belgians in the Congo or the Dutch in the Cape. It was always the same. He looked beyond the firelight. *Hell, but it's peaceful right here,* he thought, *what with that slight breeze whispering through the grass and tiny moonbeams dancing on the gently rustling leaves of that Ghost Gum.* He shivered involuntarily and wondered if he could sense the peripatetic spirits of murdered Murries moving restlessly beyond the circle of firelight. He was deeply dismayed to know that the whites in his new country had treated its indigenes so barbarously. And he couldn't help wondering whether it was Australia or his own country that had treated its native peoples worse.

Murranji Bill continued to speak matter-of-factly at the fire, and his voice now sounded liturgical. It was almost as if he was invoking a higher power, possibly to seek forgiveness on behalf of his own kind?

"It stayed bad up here till twenty-odd years ago, you know. Volunteer, white fellers used to go on nigger-hunting expeditions. I can swear to that. The big, company-owned runs were the worst. But maybe it was only their ringers, an' the bosses didn't have a clue what was going on. Who knows? Only a few stations, far as I know, wanted no part of it. Folks like the Macdonalds of Big River. I can still remember Iain Mac saying, as if it was yesterday, 'I won't shoot here. An' don' you come and shoot here.' Iain was talking to twenty-three whites an' two trackers that'd ridden over to his homestead. And I heard one of his Murries say to Iain, 'Why white feller want shootem black feller? Why no wantem my colour? Why want finishem up?' An' another old Murri that I met years later told me, 'That Iain saved the blutty mob, yer know. Maybe hundreds, and hundreds.'"

"And you were there?" Hank asked, astonished.

Murranji Bill didn't answer for a long moment. He kept staring into the fire. Finally he spoke in that same matter-of-fact voice. "I'm ashamed to say, mate, I *was* there. An' I wasn't working for the Macs, either. Yeah, it's something I have to live with."

Chapter 7

Mustering Fats

Calum wasn't certain whether it was the sound of Blue's laughter or the invasive, territorial screeches of those striking-looking, pale-pink and white Major Mitchell's Cockatoos, with their long pink-and-yellow banded crests that woke him. He'd been happily dreaming about the freckle-faced girl and, in his dream, she agreed to be his girlfriend. He couldn't believe his luck.

Still half asleep, he remembered that Jacky Jacky had cautioned him against suddenly waking anybody because that person's *Shade*, which roved at length during sleep, needed time to return. And if it wasn't given sufficient time, permanent separation from the body was likely. And if that occurred, the Shade was permanently *on the wallaby* as it searched for another body. And the person who'd been separated from their Shade? There was no question about that. He or she became an imbecile. Calum found himself hoping that his Shade had been given ample time to get back. Some of the things that the Old People believed in were very spooky. In fact, just as spooky as the things that his mum and her people believed. It was all right during the day because it wasn't dark. Also he was always flat-out. Indeed, it'd been only yesterday that Hank had had a friendly expression on his face when he'd spoken to him.

"I'm kinda gratified by the way you're shaping up," he'd said. "And as far as I'm concerned, you don't have to prove yourself to anybody here. Unless it's to yourself."

Calum decided that one of the things that irritated him about Hank was that he was fair. And that made it hard to keep on disliking him. And he was determined to keep on disliking him. Hell, hadn't Hank put him on a horse that he'd known would throw him and in front of everybody as well?

When he was certain that he hadn't hastened to be awake, he focused on the source of the loud laughter. Blue and Nugget were visible in the half-light. They were squatting at the camp fire, and both were laughing and looking in his direction. Still lying down, he looked about him. All he could see was Socks. But that wasn't unusual, because if he happened to be riding Socks that day, Edward invariably let him loose knowing that he'd head for Calum. And Calum'd become used to being awakened by the feel of Socks's soft whiskers and warm breath on his face. He could see Socks standing close; the bay's head was low to the ground, and his ears were pricked.

Puzzled, Calum sat up. That was when he saw the dingo pup. The noses of the horse and the puppy were twelve inches apart, and the pup was standing his ground. His little, chubby legs were firmly set, and his back was rigid, and he'd determinedly thrust out his small head. But he kept glancing back at Calum, as if to say, "Hurry up and help, won't you?"

Calum put on his boots, rose, and scooped up the pup in his left hand, and as he did so, he remembered Ed Smith. Thinking about Ed Smith made him think of his mother for some reason. And how soft her bosom had felt when she'd cuddled him to her. And hatred for his father once again welled up inside him.

He continued to hold the pup in his left hand while he splashed cool, billabong water onto his face. Then he put on his shirt and joined the others who were also making their way to the fire.

"Got a few guts, that pup," Blue observed with a cheerful grin.

Calum felt the pride of ownership and stroked his pup. *Blue was right*, he thought, *the pup had shown guts, despite being only a little tacker.* His thoughts were interrupted by Brian's arrival.

Brian opened and shut his eyes sleepily as he squatted next to Calum. "For a dinkum grog eater," he yawned, "that dog stiffener doesn't have any trouble getting up early. When'd the bastard leave anyway?"

"When it was still dark," replied a newly-arrived Hank. "He said he'd be back for the pup's scalp when it was worth two pounds."

"I'll also be older," Calum said with a frown.

Hank suspected that Calum had said that largely for his own benefit and he reflected that it hadn't taken long for the men to start showing an interest in the pup. Yep, they were no damn different from Texas cowboys, tough as old leather on the outside but suckers when it came to children, foals and puppies. This kid, though, was different. There was obviously nothing special about him, yet everyone had time for him. Nugget had taken his side against Ed Smith so fast that he, Hank, had been taken by surprise. And the Murries liked the kid too. Murranji had told him that Jalyerri had decided that the kid's unusually coloured eyes must be a sign of colour blindness. The kid smiled, but he didn't laugh much. But one thing on which they didn't differ was that horses liked him. Hell, now his gored black had started to follow Calum around, while Bitch had never tried to bite him. Both he and Murranji had concluded that they'd yet to meet a person that a horse couldn't see through. He remembered that his father had had an expression to describe people like this kid. As far as his father had been concerned, they'd been "born blond." And that's how he'd continued to see them, no matter what colour hair they had.

"How's he where I earmarked him, mate?" Nugget enquired drowsily.

"Pretty much healed already, Nugg."

Nugget nodded his head and rubbed his eyes with the back of a hand. "Watch out fer that dog stiffener," he said. "He seems ter get badder every year."

"He's a mean son-of-a-bitch, all right," Hank agreed. "But you know, I like to extend the hand of friendship to fellers like him. I kinda think they appreciate it."

"That's where you an' me are different, mate," Murranji Bill said tersely. "I take a stock whip to 'em."

"I like to think I'm civilized, Murranji."

"Civilization is what you've got in all those towns Down Below. An' just maybe it's slowly coming to towns like Catriona an' Katherine. But out here, mate, all we've got is the Never-Never."

"Never-Never?"

"Yeah, it's a land that's far away from the real Australia. You see, the real Australia is all those cities and towns down the east coast."

"Oh."

Brian grinned at Murranji. "I'm with you, mate," he said. "In fact, that dog stiffener's is the only neck I've ever felt like sticking a fork into."

Murranji Bill burst out laughing. "What," he chuckled. "That's got to be a laugh, Brian. You're about the easiest goin' feller I've ever come across."

"I don't why you're laughing," Brian complained mildly. "I can be real fierce when I want to be."

"Just let me know when you're havin' one of your fierce days," Murranji begged. "I wouldn't want to miss it."

Jalyerri arrived to get the food to take back to the Murri fire. Charlie handed him a pot of stew that was identical to the one that he'd put out for the white ringers. That was Hank's doing. Hank demanded that his Murries be offered the same food that he ate. Charlie'd been surprised the first time that he'd been given the order, because he'd worked with many a head stockman who couldn't have cared less. After all, Murries could always go out and get bush tucker, couldn't they?

Jalyerri greeted them with his usual flash of white teeth. "No goot goona bugger dat feller," he observed, referring to Ed Smith.

"What's goona?" Calum asked Brian.

"Shit."

"An' what're yer goin' to call yer pup?" Charlie asked, glaring and daring anyone to comment on his hatless head. "Not that it'll make any difference 'cause, when he's older, he'll rip off yer hand."

Calum's pause before giving Charlie an answer suggested indecision. In fact, it was silence borne of ongoing amazement because he'd never before seen Charlie, even when indoors, without his Fedora, with its wide, black hatband: that caused Blue to utter, not infrequently, out of the side of his mouth and to nobody in particular, a well-known slight.

"Bloody thick as Dick's hatband *he* is."

And Charlie would whip round glaring, to see whether or not Blue was looking at him. Blue never was, of course.

But right now, Calum needed to get used to the fact that Charlie's head was completely bald. Not a single hair sprouted from its shiny, white-pink surface.

"Anyway, pups are always pissing and shitting," Charlie grumbled.

"And they often do things," Hank offered, "that suggest a good name for 'em."

"I'm going to call him Curaidh," Calum said quietly.

"Does that mean anything?"

"It means 'warrior' in my mum's language."

"How about that? Now, that's a fine name. Tell me, what's the language?"

"Gaelic."

"Do you know that that's the first time you've given me a direct answer? We must be making progress."

"Well, you're not making much progress with me," Murranji quipped.

Hank ignored Murranji and poured himself the last of the coffee from a blackened pot that'd seen better days. Nobody else drank coffee, and he hated to leave any in the pot. He stood up and complimented Charlie.

"That was a fine meal, Charlie," he said. "You know, most cooks only know how to make damper, but you bake fine bread that lines a man's stomach real good." He nodded to the others. "Let's move it, fellers. We've got some mustering to do."

At Hank's compliment, Charlie's face glowed, and he contrived to grow at least four inches. He stayed that way till everyone had left his fire.

Calum and Brian had built a small shelter for the pup beside Calum's swag. Three short logs formed three walls of a rectangle. The roof was a slab of stone, and an unwashed shirt of Calum's provided the floor. Calum placed a full pan of water beside the entrance before he put the pup inside its shelter.

"It won't move," Brian said. "The bitch's taught it to stay put till she calls."

"Yeah?"

"Let's go."

They headed for their horses with their knee-pad saddles and saddle blankets over their right shoulders and with their bridles in their left hands.

****

Hank led them north at a brisk walk. Behind their right shoulders, the eastern sky was being streaked a tropical rose-gold by the swelling sun. Its slender, golden fingers touched the dewdrops that embroidered the grass and transformed them into spectrums of shimmering colour; while small spiderwebs in the grass, decorated with tiny dewdrops, shone glittery white in the slanting shafts of radiance.

Above, a powerful, almost-white Little Eagle flew in tight circles as it diligently scrutinized the ground beneath it. The broad, diagonal white bars on its darker underwings were clearly visible.

Leather creaked, and the horses pulled and vied competitively for the lead, as fit horses will when in a group.

Hank had been thinking about Brian's claim that Stupid was as fast as a racehorse. He was aware that Les Jackson was a determined punter and decided that he'd tell him about the grey. He also knew that Les Jackson had had enough of Long Creek, so he'd made a point of ingratiating himself with his boss. He wanted Les Jackson, when he did leave, to recommend him for his job. He dropped back till he was riding alongside Calum.

"So you think your grey is fast enough to win a race?" he asked.

"I'm sure of it."

"Could you train a racehorse? Get it ready for a particular race?"

"Yes."

"I need to know that Stupid is much faster than the big chestnut I ride. We'll have a quick race when we finish work tomorrow. Okay?"

"Yes."

"That's when Mr. Jackson'll be here," Hank said. "He's dropping by to see how we're going."

"Oh."

Hank touched his heels to his horse and cantered back to the front. As was his habit, he looked around and pointed at the pair of ringers that he wanted to peel off. And today, the first pair to which he signalled was Brian and Calum.

"All right, mate," explained Brian. "We're going to make a sweep of about six miles an' muster the beasts we find into one mob, and then we'll drove 'em back to camp. An' the more fats we have, the better."

"What then?"

"We join up our mob with those the others've mustered. Then, this afternoon, we draft off the fats. Or if we get back too late, we draft 'em off tomorrow. An' so on. An' so on."

It wasn't hard riding. They rounded up small pockets of cattle along the way and combined them into one mob. Socks soon showed that he was going to be an excellent stock horse. From the outset, he watched the Shorthorns the way a sheepdog watches its sheep. Soon he was able to sense when a beast was about to make a break from the mob, even before Calum. And he'd be after it as keenly as a dingo that chances upon a feral piglet, which has become separated from the sow. And Socks proved to be as sure-footed as a cat. Calum's respect for him continued to grow throughout the morning.

Dark-brown Black Kites, with their distinctive, long, forked tails, swooped on the large grasshoppers, which whirred into the air after having been disturbed by the horses. Brian indicated them.

"You ought to see those fellers during 'time b'long burnem grass,'" he said.

"What's that?"

"During June, when there are heavy dews, to damp out fires, the Old People that're on Crown land set fire to the thick, old grass. It makes it easier for walking through an' hunting. An' when the grass is burning, there are hundreds of those little, black fellers hovering above an' divin' through the smoke to get the 'hoppers an' other bugs that are escaping the fire. An' soon fresh, green grass has shot up an' the 'roos have got full bellies an' are growin' fat. That's when the Old People concentrate on huntin' 'em. It's the time they call 'time b'long kangaroo.'"

"Oh."

Out in the open, the horses took over, twisting and turning to head off any breakaways. And the crack of a stock whip was all the inducement needed to keep the mob moving. Mostly, Brian and Calum rode behind the mob, one on each side. Often they briefly came together to chat.

"This mob's moving slowly, Brian," Calum complained.

"Be patient, mate. Haven't you learned yet that the speed of any mob's the same as its slowest beast?" Brian pointed with his stock whip. "There's a cow, new dead, over there. Probably got snakebit. You watch this lot, an' I'll go an' kill the calf."

Calum looked in the direction indicated by Brian. A tiny, brown calf was standing, forlorn and slightly humpbacked, beside the inert form of its mother. It was standing with its head down. And it'd only be a matter of time before pig or crows or a dingo found it.

"Do you want me to shoot it, Brian?"

"No, be a waste of a bullet. There'll be a lump of wood near that creek. I'll hit it over the head with that."

Calum watched Brian ride up to the calf and looked away as his mate dispatched it. Up here, it was certainly different from those Pakenham farms, which were next to his father's place. There, if they had an orphan calf, they bucket-reared it. And if they found a cow with a dead calf, they'd skin the calf and tie its hide, using hay band, onto a calf that they'd bought from a dairy farmer. The new calf then smelled familiar, and the cow usually accepted it within a day. Then you removed the dead calf's skin, and life for that cow and calf then went on as normal. Here, the calf joined its dead mother. He watched Brian canter back.

"That Murranji doesn't miss a trick, you know," Brian remarked. "He's noticed the way you move between the Murri fire an' Charlie's one. He told me he admires that."

"You also do that. But why do we have to have separate fires?"

"It's always been like that. An' if I was darker, I'd be expected to stay at the Murri fire."

"Murranji or Hank wouldn't expect that."

"No. But Charlie an' Blue would."

"Oh." Calum paused before asking. "And who are those three girls that Edward and Tarpot brought with them?"

"Those sheilas help Charlie by collecting firewood an' washing his pots an' pans. An' they'll also look after any feller that wants to be looked after at night."

"Bloody hell."

"Course it costs, you know."

"What do they charge?" Calum asked, very curious.

"Depends how much they like you, so you need to bargain. And what they're really after is bacca an' calico."

"They look so young."

"Yeah? Well, that's Murri sheilas for you." He glanced at Calum. "I was just thinking," he said, changing the subject. "You don't want to pay too much attention to the superstitions of the Old People. I notice they stay on your mind."

Calum was silent. Then he spoke a shade defensively. "My mum was superstitious, like all her people," he admitted. "In fact, Gaels are very superstitious. But I don't see anything wrong with that."

"In what way is her mob superstitious, mate?"

Calum thought for a moment before answering. "In lots of ways. For example," he said, "the old folk, particularly, believe that Water Horses live in lots of the lakes, which they call lochs."

"What the hell's a Water Horse?"

"It's half man and half horse. And people are terrified of them, because they reckon they ambush passersby, mostly at night, and eat them."

"For Crissake! Do they really believe that?"

"Too right."

"Amazing."

"Anyway," Calum said, "I'm not going to call Jalyerri crazy just 'cause he believes *Debuldebuls* are real. And I'm not going to say people, like my mum's mob, are silly. Maybe these sorts of things do exist."

"By Crise!" Brian exclaimed. "Your mum's mob sounds just as bad as the Old People here."

"I reckon." Calum grinned and wheeled Socks toward another small group of Shorthorns. Socks quickly mustered them.

"We've got enough now," Brian shouted across to him. "There's two-fifty here. Let's turn 'em and head for camp."

They hadn't gone far when Calum saw his first feral pig. The big reddish-black boar wasn't concerned in the slightest by the horses. It just watched for a moment before dropping its head and continuing to feed on the remains of a nocturnal Northern Nailtail Wallaby. At first glance, the boar looked to Calum, as if it was all head and shoulders because of its relatively small rump and hind legs. A short, sparse, bristling mane ran along its back. Long tusks, below small, round eyes, grew out and up from its lower jaw, and its straight shortish tail hung over large bulbous testicles. He thought that it had a real don't-mess-with-me look.

"Don't mess with those fellers when you're on your own, mate," Brian warned. "That's four-hundred pounds of real cheeky pig when it's wounded."

"Yeah?"

"My word."

They'd been droving for a couple of hours when Brian signalled to Calum with a raised hand.

"What's up?" Calum called.

"I need a piss. Watch this mob an' keep them away from that patch of Lancewood there, okay? That Lancewood scrub is so thick we could easily lose some of these beasts in it."

"Yes."

Brian dismounted, walked to the end of his held reins, and undid his fly. He'd no sooner started to piss when an old, brown, and very cantankerous, cleanskin bull with long, curving horns broke from the face of the mob and lined him up. Its irritation at being pushed along had apparently festered into a frothy fury. Or maybe a couple of ants, inside its penile sheath, were driving it mad? Either way, it'd obviously decided to vent its fury on the human being, which now stood before it. It snorted and huffed, put its head down, cocked its ears and raised its tail. It was clearly overflowing with murderous intent. Then it went for Brian at full gallop. Massive alarm instantly registered on his face.

"Crise!" he yelled.

He didn't hesitate and didn't bother to do up his fly either. Still dribbling, he ran to his horse and leaped onto it faster than Calum'd ever seen anyone mount a horse. The bull halted abruptly and began to sling its head from side to side, as it sought the human being that'd magically disappeared. It didn't appear to be able to make the connection between horse and rider. After a minute, it stopped throwing its head about and turned around. Then, with scrotum swinging, it trotted back to the mob. Once it was safely out of the way, Brian let fly with a nonstop torrent of abuse and threats. He was livid.

"You bloody, cheeky, old bastard. I'll kill you. You've made me wet my bloody pants! You're dead. You're gone. D'ya hear me?"

He noticed that Calum was unsuccessfully trying to stop grinning.

"What's wrong with you?" he demanded angrily. "Why didn't you shoot?"

"I couldn't. I was laughing."

"You're a piss-weak mate," he accused. "And if you tell anyone I wet my pants, we're finished. I'll never hear the end of it from that damn Blue."

"I didn't see anything," Calum said solemnly. "I never even *saw* a cleanskin bull." He started giggling again. "Or you wetting your pants. And have you put it away yet? Or are you still hanging it out to dry?"

"You mongrel mate. You were useless. I could've been hurt bad. An' all you can do is laugh."

Brian looked straight ahead and ignored Calum, so Calum spoke to Socks. He told the bay that he'd need to get used to the dingo pup. And he'd need to be careful where he put his feet because, knowing pups, it'd be running in and out between them without a thought.

Brian eventually calmed down and decided that he was prepared to talk to Calum again. "That bay you've got is coming on," he said. "He's going to be a one-man horse, though."

"I know."

Calum studied the position, within the mob, of the cranky bull. "Do you think we'll have a rush if I fire my rifle?" Calum asked.

"No. They've got used to the cracking of whips, an' they're tired. But make certain you don't crowd the bastard 'cause it's an evil mongrel."

Calum took out his rifle and eased Socks into the mob. He picked out the bull, rode up behind it, moved to one side, steadied Socks and shot it in the head. And Brian was right. Only those cattle immediately around it jumped away and showed alarm. But they didn't start to rush.

They reached camp without further incident and saw that the others had already arrived. And when Calum and Brian went to get a mug of tea, Calum cadged some meat from Charlie for his pup. Curaidh immediately rushed from his shelter to greet him. He dropped his ears, wagged his little tail furiously, and stood on his chubby back legs and tried to clasp Calum's shin with his front paws. Calum picked him up and held him at arm's length. Being at eye level increased Curaidh's excitement. He squirmed and wriggled and stuck out his pink tongue and his neck as far as he could in an effort to lick Calum's face.

"Hey, that's a great welcome you're giving me, but I reckon you must be hungry, so I've brought some tucker."

He was amused to see just how quickly Curaidh bolted down the chopped-up pieces of beef. The pup managed to keep his front legs out of the pan, but he kept moving his back legs outside and forward of his front ones. In his eagerness, he kept moving them farther forward till he lost balance and landed on his nose in the pan. And all the time his tummy was getting rounder and rounder. Eventually, alarmed, Calum picked up the pan, removed the remaining meat, and filled it from his water bottle. He pushed it toward Curaidh.

"Have a drink, little mate. I bet that salt's made you thirsty." He watched his pup lap thirstily. "That's it, pup. You go back to your kennel now. I'm off to see what I've got to do next. But I'll be back for you when Charlie calls us to eat."

****

They spent next day drafting off the fats. Calum's impressions of that first day would be forever etched into his mind. He would recall a burning sun and a brilliant-blue sky; quick-footed sweating horses and well over a thousand milling Shorthorns, with the acrid smell of their fear and sweat sharply contrasting with the dry, earth smell of the red ground; the churning hooves that sent billowing clouds of red dust up into the air to coat horses and riders with its powdery, choking fineness; and a throat that became so parched that he found it hard to swallow. He'd always remember the constant, rifle-shot *cracks* of stock whips; plus the sound of ringers constantly yelling and cursing and seeing those same riders superbly balanced on twisting, turning, propping mounts; and the din made by so many frightened and confused and bawling beasts, which kept ringing in his ears. He'd remember too, being impressed when strong, clever Meg, without being urged, cleverly shouldered a darting breakaway. And constantly seeing, before him, a moving sea of wild-eyed Shorthorns with their plunging heads and forest of arcing horns, which loudly clicked against one another while thrashing about like storm-tossed branches.

Separating the fats from the mob was done by Hank and Murranji Bill. They were the ones riding the trained camp horses. So, while the others kept the thousand-odd head in a compact mob, Hank and Murranji Bill rode into it, and each chose the bullock that they wanted with a flick of a stock whip. Then their camp horses took over, pushing and shouldering till the reluctant fat was forced to the face of the mob. Two of the ringers then rode up and herded the wide-eyed bullock, which was still desperately trying to escape, into the stockyard.

By late afternoon, well over a hundred fats had been drafted off and yarded. The rest of the mob was then released to drift off over the countryside.

One of Long Creek's old trucks, chugging and snorting and trailing clouds of grey-black smoke, signalled the arrival of Mr. Jackson. That didn't interest Calum. He was intent on getting a bone from Charlie.

"That bone's far too big fer the little bugger, Calum," Charlie said.

Just then Blue turned up. He handed Charlie his Fedora and grinned wickedly. "Look what I found, Charlie. I reckon I'm flamin' brilliant. The wind must've blowed it away durin' the night."

Charlie was so furious that his face immediately turned a mottled red. "The bloody wind be buggered! You stole my hat while I was bloody well sleeping. You're a lyin', thieving, little mongrel."

"Now, mate, is that any way to treat someone who thinks so much of yer fine cookin', he's walked all the way over here ter give you yer hat?" Blue started to sound indignant. "Jus' think, I've saved you a most terrible sunburn. Mate, you woulda looked real strange with poxy-lookin' blisters all over yer bare skull."

Calum left them to it. He was more interested in the lesson that he planned to teach Curaidh. When he sat down next to Curaidh, the pup initially couldn't work out how to handle the bone. He only knew that it now belonged to him, and he started to make fierce little proprietary growls.

"Now, pup you have to learn to let me take food from you without biting my hand. I'm not worried about now. But when you're big, if you really have a go, you could take off half my hand."

Calum slowly reached toward the bone. Curaidh didn't hesitate. He turned his head, as quick as a striking snake, and sank his teeth into the extended hand and then held on grimly.

"Ouch. You little bugger. You can move quicker 'n' a cut cat."

Ignoring his stinging hand, Calum gave Curaidh's nose a firm tap and, at the same time, gave him an equally firm command. "Drop it, Curaidh!"

The pup ignored Calum's command and hung on. Calum was amazed that something so small could be so determined.

"You rotten, little beggar!"

This time Calum gave the same order while simultaneously prying open the pup's mouth with his other hand. Curaidh returned his attention to the bone. Calum glanced at his hand. Oozing blood was forming large drops over the pup's teeth marks. He considered his small adversary. The pup was having a great time with the bone, gnawing at a small outcrop.

Again Calum reached for the bone, but this time, he anticipated his pup and tapped him on the nose before he could latch on. Once again Calum reached for the bone. This time Curaidh just looked at him, occasionally wagged his tail, and made no attempt to bite. Calum stroked him and praised him.

"You're a good little pup. And you're a quick learner too."

Calum looked up at the sound of Brian's whistle. Brian was holding a saddled Stupid and beckoned to Calum to join him.

"I'll be back soon, little mate. I've got to go now."

Curaidh was so absorbed with his bone that he didn't notice that Calum was leaving.

"Hank and Mr. Jackson want to see whether Stupid's faster than Hank's big chestnut," Brian said.

Calum checked the girth, took the reins from Brian and mounted quickly.

"Who would you have your money on?" he asked.

"You." Brian grinned. "But only 'cause you're my mate."

As soon as they began to race, Calum tucked Stupid in behind Hank's chestnut. And all the while that both horses were pounding along the cattle track, Stupid fought for his head. Some of the grass-green froth, from his mouth, blew back and settled momentarily on

Calum's face, before the wind blew it away. And often, the hooves of Hank's big chestnut flung back red dirt that hit Calum in the face and stung.

It wasn't a contest. Stupid had the big chestnut covered all the way, and a hundred-and-thirty yards from the finish, Calum gave him a quick jab with his spurs. Stupid shot forward and won, easing down by three lengths.

Immediately after the race, Les Jackson headed for the truck. He was meeting some First Northern people in Catriona and wanted to make the most of the remaining daylight. He was excited because he was convinced that the grey, which he'd just seen run, was his ticket to Adelaide. Anyway he'd know for sure, when Hank used the stopwatch that he'd given him, to write down the training times. But that big grey had certainly looked the part.

****

That night, squatting round their campfire, the ringers debated just how much money they'd be able to raise for bets. Calum was half-listening to them, while tracing patterns in the ash with the large stick that he was holding.

"What d'ya reckon, Calum?" Brian asked.

"If he's fit, I'll put everything I have on him."

"And if Calum's going to put everything he has on Stupid, that's just what I'm also going to do," Brian stated.

"Don' expect me ter shout yer both beers," Blue warned. "When yer've turned yerselves inter broke, thirsty punters."

"I always knew that bloody yapper was all talk an' no action," Charlie mocked. "Hell, he'd stand by and watch a mate die fer a beer. What a mongrel."

"No, I'm not," Blue protested. "I jus' forgot fer a moment, they was Long Creek mates."

Suddenly, Calum yelled, "Ouch!" He dropped his stick as if it was a red-hot coal.

"What's up, mate?" Murranji asked.

"I've been stung. It was a small insect with a tail that curled up over its back."

Murranji got to his feet, held Calum's hand toward the firelight, and examined it. "Was it small with a greenish-grey an' brown marbled sort of look?" he asked.

"Yes."

Murranji frowned, nodded his head sagely, but said nothing. He went over to his swag and returned with an unopened bottle of rum. "I'm sorry, mate," he said to Calum, "but this has to be for us only. It'll only get your blood racing an' move that poison—you've now got inside you—to your heart real quick."

Calum's hand had started to throb painfully. What Murranji had just said frightened the hell out of him, but he was determined that nobody would see his fear. He saw Murranji Bill look at him, shake his head and pour rum into the quart pot mugs that were held out before him. Then Murranji raised his.

"Here's to Calum, fellers," he said cheerfully. "An' we hope the pain doesn't get too unbearable before he moves on to that better place yonder."

"That's bloody well it," announced a concerned Brian. "This joke's gone far enough." He touched Calum's shoulder. "You were stung by a scorpion, mate. You won't get any sleep tonight 'cause your hand'll give you hell. But I can tell you, for certain, you'll be alive come morning."

Calum got to his feet. The huge relief that he felt was followed by a determination to keep his face expressionless. He pretended that he didn't notice the grinning faces that were looking at him.

"Where'd it come from?" he casually asked Brian.

"Most likely from under the bark, on the stick, you were playing with. You don't often see 'em because they come out mostly at night."

"Oh." Calum nodded briefly to Murranji. "You got your laugh Murranji, didn't you?" He said mildly. "Anyway, I'm going to hit my swag, so I'll see all you jokers tomorrow."

"Good on you, Calum. See you, mate."

When Calum was out of earshot, Murranji nodded to Hank. "What do you make of that young bugger? He didn't even get cranky."

"He was making sure you didn't get any satisfaction, Murranji," Brian said. "I liked that."

"Is that right?"

Brian stood up and yawned. He frowned at Murranji. "How's Calum supposed to know when you're joking, Murranji? Have you forgotten he's new up here?"

"He's going to have to put up with a lot more than that if he's goin' to make it."

"Oh, he'll make it all right. He's got me backing him."

"An' me."

"Yeah?"

"Yeah."

Chapter 8

The Big River Run

During the week following Calum's painful experience with the scorpion, two of the three people chanced upon by he and Brian had reached an old homestead. It was situated atop a steep rise, which overlooked the Big River. It'd been built seventy years ago, and its stunning outlook took in a sweeping meander of that broad, tree-lined, coffee-coloured stretch of water.

Peg Shillingsworth and her daughter were seated on the homestead's verandah and were conversing with the run's retired lessees, Alasdair and Iain Macdonald. Both brothers were freckled, wiry old-timers in their late sixties, with thinning, ginger hair and sun-faded, blue eyes.

Alasdair, whose ever-increasing irascibility continued to outpace the measured passing of his months, held the opinion that the stinking law that caused this sort of terror was just plain bloody shithouse. Hell, these poor folk had just appeared out of the bush, and he'd watched as they'd wearily trudged up the slope toward the house. He'd known immediately that they were on the run—probably from Cord River— by the way the girl was dressed. Well, they'd come to the right place all right, because there was no bloody way that anybody here would hand 'em over to the cops; and hell, if anyone even as much as thought of doing that, it'd cost 'em their knackers.

Alasdair now reflected on the pact that their dear, old mother had made with Jawoyn, an elder of his people. Poor Jawoyn, he'd kept his side of the bargain all right, but those bastards, over on that damn, Eastern and African Cold Storage run had shot him down like a dog. Of course, he'd been foolish to go over there. And after Jawoyn's murder, both he and Iain had promised their mother that when she was gone, the pact that she'd made with his people would always be honoured. And it *had* been honoured. It'd even been widened.

Yes, over the years, the Big River run or Big Riba, as the Murries called it, had become known as the place to go if you somehow got caught up in white feller, wrong-side bijnitch. There'd always be tucker there, and you could rest up. Then, some fourteen years ago, Big Riba had become a haven where mixed-descent children and their mothers could stay, till the coppers had forgotten about them. And that'd started following a conversation that the brothers had had in Katherine with a Protector of Aborigines. He'd had the gall to say that this Government policy was for the good of half-caste kids. And then he'd held forth in that superior tone of his.

"Of course," he'd pompously announced. "The Government knows that blacks are woeful mothers."

"You're a fuckin' crock o' shit," Alasdair had angrily retorted. "An' don't you spoil me rum by makin' that sort o' stink near me glass. Now piss off."

It was Iain who'd raised the subject in their hotel room that night. "Listen, mate," he'd said. "What's wrong with those kids an' their mums hiding out with us? All right by you?"

Alasdair very much regretted that nowadays, there wasn't much call for their help. The cops and their trackers had become too efficient. Those mongrels sifted the camps without warning, grabbed the kids and that was that. Now, he felt pleased that he could be useful again. Yes, he thought, it'd perk up his day real good because lately, he'd started to feel that yet another damned day had ebbed out of his life. And he'd even begun to have a recurring fear about picking green bananas from his tree, as if, by Christ, he might not be around to eat them when they'd ripened.

Peg gained his attention by touching his arm. She spoke uncertainly. "Years ago, a frien' o' mine, Murranji Bill, tol' me people wasn't turned away from here."

"He didn't lie," Alasdair answered.

"We jus' need ter rest up a bit. We come a fair way, like. An' we is headed north 'cause I don' reckon the coppers'll bother lookin' up there."

"You said yer daughter had escaped from Cord River?" Alasdair asked gently.

"Yes."

Alasdair looked at his brother, and Iain nodded his assent.

"Well," Alasdair said, "we reckon yer'd best stay *here* for a good spell. Till they've given up lookin'. Yer see, if a girl did manage ter get away from Cord River, it'd reflect terrible bad on the people runnin' the place. An' it'd show their bosses they is failing in their job of assimilating. An' yer girl? Well, if she got caught, they'd make an example of her." He concluded, "No, yer'd best stay, an' we'll make it our business ter keep yer safe."

Peg looked away for a moment and sniffed. A lump had come into her throat. She'd also been worrying and then steeling herself about what she could offer them. And she felt very vulnerable because not much money remained. Most of what she'd possessed had gone to Roper Billy, Nellie and Cord River's tracker.

"I didn' expec' yer to be so kind," she murmured.

"Peg," Alasdair said, "I reckon we're just bein' ordinary, Christian, human beings. Now, where's yer uncle Henry?"

"He's back trackin' ter see if we is bein' followed. I paid the mission tracker ter lose our tracks, but we need ter be sure."

"An' if you are bein' followed?"

"Uncle Henry'll stop the tracker." Peg's face hardened. "Nobody should cheat on their own mob. It's not right."

"Yes," Alasdair agreed. He winked at Doreen. "Now, young lady, you can cheer up, yer hear! An' tell me, are yer hungry or jus' tired?"

"Both." She smiled. "But I'm not too bad right now."

Alasdair looked at Peg, and his face now showed concern. "Did anyone see yer while you were travellin'?" he asked.

"Yes, a coupla ringers. The yeller one tol' Uncle Henry they'd say nothin'."

"An' the other?"

"He was jus' a boy. His eyes was a differen' blue."

"That'd be young Calum McNicol from Long Creek."

Doreen sat up, raised her chin and spoke out. "That boy won't say anything," she stated.

"Now, what makes you so certain, young lady?" Iain asked with an amused twinkle in his eye.

"I just know."

Her mother smiled at her tolerantly. "But yer never seen 'im before, love," she said.

Doreen turned to her mother. She spoke matter-of-factly, and her tone suggested that there was nothing unusual about what she said. "Mum, I told you he'll be coming for me one day." She glanced at Iain. "He likes me, and he knows I like him."

"Jus' like that," Iain said, astonished. "Isn't that a bit sudden?"

"I don't think so."

"I see," Iain said doubtfully. He rose to his feet and smiled down at Doreen. "Come on, young lady," he said kindly, "and I'll show you yer room."

"Yes, go with Iain, love. I won' be long."

When they'd gone inside, Peg gave Alasdair a quick glance. She didn't believe that anything in this world was for free, not from white fellers at any rate. *Besides,* she told herself, *she would feel more secure if she paid her way.*

"I don' have much money ter pay yer," she said uncertainly.

"I don't remember me or me brother talkin' money," Alasdair said. He indicated the grazing Shorthorns that dotted the grassy slope below them. "We've enough to share," he said gently. "An' when yer leave, your tucker bags'll be full."

Peg swallowed hard and looked away. She wiped her eyes with a hand. Alasdair appeared not to notice. Peg didn't know whether or not to believe him, so she decided to take the bull by the horns and offer the one thing that she could. She met Alasdair's eyes and spoke hesitantly after sitting up straight and putting her shoulders back.

"There is a way I can pay, but it's only me what pays," she said. "Not my girl."

She noticed Alasdair briefly appraising her body and told herself, *You'll be able ter do it awright, because you'll be doin' it fer yer girl. And you'll be able ter do it jus' as often as yer have to, an' with both if need be. Crise, woman, all yer have ter do is lie back, look at the ceiling an' think about yer girl, till the old buggers are done. An' also think about how lucky yer are ter have her back.* She saw that Alasdair was now looking out across the river's wide sweep.

"Now, Peg," he said, "I am flattered because you're young an' good-lookin'. And we're jus' a coupla wore-out, ol' fellers. But age has taught me the difference between givin' an' takin'. We're givin', Peg. I reckon that's the Christian way. So I'm sayin' again, I'm real flattered but no thanks." He smiled. "An' we'll be paid good, mate, if yer send a message sayin' yer've arrived safe at where yer headed. An' mind too, yer'll always be welcome here 'cause there's always room in *this* inn." He paused. "Besides, we enjoy company. Yer see, we don't work long hours anymore, so it gets lonely, an' the days can drag somethin' terrible."

Again Peg had to wipe her eyes, and she found that she needed to swallow a couple of times before she could speak. "That'd be real good, Alasdair," she murmured. "Up north, we'll be stayin' with the Old People, but I don' want Doreen ter forget her white feller ways. This country's changin', know what I mean? Since the war, more an' more white fellers is comin' here."

"That makes sense." He changed the subject. "Doreen's a lovely girl. Any man'd be proud ter have a daughter like her."

"Her dad don' know 'bout her," Peg said quietly.

Alasdair waited for Peg to continue. She appeared to think hard before speaking. "It were a long time ago, yer know," she said hesitantly. "I met Murranji when we was workin' on the same run. An' then I were his woman fer eight months. It were a happy time. That year he took me ter the Catriona Races, but afterward, we both went our own ways. An' that were my doin', not his."

"I have ter say, Peg, if I was Doreen's father, I'd be proud ter show the world she was mine."

"You sure 'bout that? Murranji's a white feller, remember."

"Too right I'm sure. An' if I were you, I'd give Murranji a chance. He's a good man." Alasdair met her eyes. "And have yer thought yer also deprivin' yer girl of a father who'd love her? Hell, Peg," he said and shrugged his shoulders, "what've yer got ter lose, mate?"

Peg nervously nibbled at a fingernail. "I'll think on it," she said cautiously. "Course, he's probably married now with his own, white children."

"No, Peg. I know fer certain Murranji never married." Alasdair got to his feet. He stretched his shoulders and glanced up at the sun. "That sun looks like it's low enough, Peg. Will yer join us in a glass of rum?"

"I'll settle fer a cuppa."

"Come on then, an' I'll show yer the kitchen an' introduce yer to our cook, Mr. Ah Lee. I want ter know what he's plannin' ter feed us 'cause I'm getting' hungry. Course, he probably won't tell me. Yer see, he's an awful independent cook."

****

Doreen went to her bedroom after they'd eaten. She was tired, but sleep wouldn't come. She lay in bed feeling very secure and listened to the sounds that came to her: her room's windowpanes being rattled by the wind, the distant brassy neigh of a stallion, and right outside, the metallic flapping of a loose piece of corrugated iron. She thought about the blue-eyed ringer. Well, now she knew his name: Calum McNicol. But where did the Calum come from? That was a new one on her. Anyway, importantly, she now knew where he worked. And she also knew that he wouldn't tell anyone about her. She remembered how blue his eyes were. And most vivid of all, she remembered that tingling feeling when something sort of like electricity had passed between them. She just knew that when they were together, she'd be as calm and as relaxed as his puppy had been. She wondered if she'd be his first girlfriend. And she wondered what his lips would feel like when they kissed. It was exciting to know that she now had her own boyfriend, and she suddenly experienced a new feeling about boys, about this one anyway. It was a feeling of ownership.

She heard a gentle knock on her door and knew that it was her mum.

"Come in, Mum."

Her mother entered the room and sat on the edge of the bed. Doreen saw the concern and love on her face.

"I'm really happy, Mum," she said. "This is a good place. I can *feel* it."

"And you is real safe here, love."

Peg put her arms around her daughter and hugged her. "I can't tell yer how rapt I am now I've got yer back, love," she murmured.

117

"I'm happy too, Mum. But let's not rush off from here, please."

"We won't. An' termorrer Iain's goin' ter show yer the mare he's picked out fer yer. He reckons it's near as pretty as you are."

"I'm being spoiled."

"We both are. Are yer tired, Dor?"

"Yes."

"I'll leave yer to it then. Good night, darl, an' sleep tight."

"Good night, Mum. And, Mum?"

"What is it?"

"Never ask me about what happened at Cord. All right?"

"I don't understand."

"I want to bury it deep down and forget it ever happened."

"I see," Peg said, concerned. "I hope that's wise."

When her mum left, Doreen fell asleep almost immediately. She dreamed of Calum McNicol and his blue eyes and his little, soft puppy. They were happy, warm dreams because they were full of gentleness and laughter. They were the dreams that only a teenage girl who's fallen in love, for the first time, can dream.

****

At around midmorning, the next day, Perce arrived with the mail. He and Alasdair had what could be described, at best, as an intermittent relationship. Perce thought Alasdair was a dangerous, old coot. And Alasdair knew that.

Doreen was relaxing on the verandah with Alasdair when Perce waddled up with the mail.

"G'day, Alasdair," he called.

"G'day. An', Perce, yer better forget yer ever seen this young lady here. Yer got that?"

"Hell, Alasdair, I thought that was a statue yer bought ter decorate yer verandah. I'm shortsighted, yer know."

Alasdair glared, rose from his chair and literally ran inside. When he returned, he had a three-inch nail and a rifle cartridge. Iain followed him out onto the verandah.

"Now, what's yer brother up ter, Iain?" Perce asked, wide-eyed.

"He's scratchin' yer name onto a cartridge, 'cause he hates people with good memories."

"Yer jokin', aren't yer?" Perce said, looking as if he was about to wet his pants. Then he stupidly blurted out, "Course, His Majesty's mail contractors should get danger money, 'cause they have ter put up with short-tempered, ol' coots as well as *myall* blacks."

Alasdair immediately turned and rushed inside. When he returned, he had his rifle. He'd gone very red in the face. He stood and glared at Perce.

"I'll show you danger money," he roared. "I'm going ter shoot yer back tyres when yer drive off. You forgot I'm Scottish as well as Australian. And I don' give a damn about yer His Bloody Majesty Pommy King!"

Perce almost stood to attention and looked as if he was about to sing *God Save the King.* "Ugh," he cried. "If they had a Tower of London in Catriona, you'd be locked up for treason."

Alasdair's face grew even redder, and his veins stood out. Abruptly, he cocked his rifle. Immediately, Perce turned and, waddling faster than a speeding duck, headed for the sanctuary of his truck. He leaped in, revved the motor, and drove off as fast as his truck would let him, leaving behind a huge and smelly, oily-black smokescreen that hung in the air. Alasdair raised his rifle and fired.

"Bugger," he swore. "I couldn't see the tyres for smoke, but I reckon I got the bloody back mudguard."

"What if he stops delivering our mail, Alasdair?" Iain inquired, unperturbed.

"He can't; otherwise, he'd lose his contract. That means I can shoot at his truck as often as I like."

Peg, who had been watching this little drama wide-eyed, from the doorway, suddenly burst out laughing and couldn't stop.

"What is it, Peg?" Iain asked.

"Iain," she managed to gasp, "I feel real safe now. Fair dinkum."

CHAPTER 9

A BAD RUSH

It was late afternoon, and Calum was leaning against a River Red's trunk. His attention alternated between Curaidh and some Shorthorns at a not-too-distant stand of twenty-foot-high Whitewoods, which was another tree that helped sustain cattle during drought. Some were tearing off the waxy, grey-green leaves while others were rubbing their shoulders and sides quite vigorously against the grey, flaky-bark trunks. Curaidh's interest was his tail. He was intent on catching it, but once he had the end of it, in his mouth, he seemed to be uncertain about what to do next, except to hold on. Then, Calum found himself wondering whether Murranji had reached Big River. Like the others, he was puzzled why the Macs had urgently summoned him, via one of the Big River Murries.

Drafting off the last of the fats had finished before lunch today. They now had their final mob of thirteen hundred, and Hank had informed them that as far as he was concerned, this year's bullock muster was over.

Calum grimaced as he remembered that Hank had told him that he'd be taking the first watch tonight. Riding a night horse for two hours while it walked around the perimeter of a mob of sleeping fats wasn't anyone's favourite job. But now that the mob was being held in the open, because its number had outgrown the stockyard, it meant that they had no choice. And Calum had found that he couldn't even ride

Socks. Certainly Socks was as sure-footed as a dingo and had excellent night vision, but the temperament wasn't there. There was no way that he could be relied upon to find his way calmly around the sleeping mob during a pitch-black night. After their first, abortive attempt, Calum'd felt compelled to chide Socks, even though he'd known that his horse hadn't a clue where he was coming from.

"I love you, Socks, but you were plain hopeless. And it's not as if you don't like my singing. Besides, Hank says singing relaxes the fats and stops 'em from taking fright when a horse and rider suddenly loom up on a night that's as 'goddamn black as a widow's shawl!'"

Calum looked down at Curaidh. He supposed that his pup was now more than six months old. The puppy fat had been replaced by a gangly, uncoordinated look. There'd also been a perceptible change in Curaidh's colour. He was now more reddish-yellow than yellow. And sometimes, in the early-morning sun, Calum could detect golden glints in the ruff on his neck and shoulders.

"But the only thing that's *not* handsome about you right now," he told him, "is your teething. When are you going to stop chewing green hide ropes?"

Curaidh sat up at the sound of Calum's voice and looked at his master. His ears dropped, and his intelligent, oval eyes stayed fixed on Calum's face. Every now and then his tail brushed the ground in a half wag. He was fully alert and wanted to play. Calum had learned that Curaidh's games were part of his instinctive preparation for survival in the bush. And that during their walks, one of his favourite games involved stalking Calum.

And it fascinated Calum that Curaidh instinctively knew what was dangerous and what wasn't. He'd always see a snake long before Calum did and would give it a wide berth. But that wasn't so when it came to Frill-neck Lizards. The one that they'd come across during their walk after lunch had adopted its usual stance when facing a possible aggressor. It'd stayed still on all fours, mouth agape and with its brick-red body culminating in its fully extended fiery-orange-red-and-yellow frill. Then as soon as Curaidh had seen the small dragon, he'd boldly bounced toward it. Immediately, it'd stood up on its back legs, frill still extended, and had turned and fled. From behind it'd resembled a small, bandy-legged runner. Calum had admonished Curaidh.

"Now, why do you want to terrorize somebody, pup, who's still being punished?" he'd asked. "Maybe I'd better tell you what Tarpot told me about those. Now, do you know why they walk on all fours but run like a human? Well, during the Dreamtime, there was this one feller who went to a sacred ceremony but wouldn't listen. The Old People warned him that he was breaking the law and told him he'd be punished. But he still didn't listen, so the Old People lost patience. And when they punished him, they didn't muck around, mate. Not only was he made to walk forever on all fours, but his children and their children and their children were also condemned to walk on all fours. And on top of that, he was turned into a skinny, bandy-legged, little person."

Because of the now-abundant grass, Red Kangaroos were numerous, and large mobs weren't uncommon. Calum had shot a young male today, shortly after he and Curaidh had encountered the Frill-neck. He wanted to take back a haunch for Jalyerri and the others.

Returning to camp, Curaidh had begun to lag behind, and Calum'd realized that he'd need to give the pup a rest. They'd settled in the shade of an eighty-five-foot-high Woolly Butt eucalypt. Calum had leaned back against its fibrous, yellowish-bark trunk. Curaidh had instantly fallen asleep. A nearby Willie Wagtail had wagged its tail at them and had called out its *kirrikijirrit*. Then Calum'd started to feel uneasy because Jalyerri had warned him that he'd only be safe from a *Debuldebul* if he was on horseback or beside a fire or if he was carrying a fire stick. Only Jalyerri had called it "faya stik."

He'd been so uneasy that he'd thought about lighting a fire but then had told himself that he was being silly. Instead, he'd decided to keep talking to his sleeping pup. And he'd hoped that the sound of his voice would be enough to keep away any Debuldebul. He'd taken a deep breath and had looked carefully all around before speaking.

"I can't spot anything, mate," he'd said. "Now, pup, you know Sally in camp? Well, she's the towheaded one with the nice smile. And Brian says she's been asking him why I don't go to her. And he's even offered to give me the calico to pay her." Calum paused and grimaced. "But you see, I've never done it, and I'm really worried I'll make a fool of myself. And then Sally'll tell the others. And then that Blue'll never let it rest." Calum paused again and then changed the subject. "Do you know what the Old People think a *kirrikijirrit* is saying, pup? They reckon it's calling out, 'Sweet, sweet, wrong-side love.' And they reckon a kirrikijirrit can always spot a wrong-side love, and then it goes and tells everyone, because falling in love is mostly wrong-side. You see, it's *tjarada*, and they reckon that the only people who know all about that are *kwee-ais* or lubras. So a feller's got to be real careful when he's around them. And did you know a *kwee-ai* is only allowed to marry the feller her mum's brother tells her to? That's it, and no argument. Now, do you see why tjarada is so dangerous?" Again, Calum had warily looked all around before he'd relaxed. A faraway look had come into his eyes. "Gee, that freckle-faced girl is pretty," he'd said. "Heck, if a feller had her for his girl, there'd be no way he'd ever look at another girl. And you know something else? If she did practice her tjarada on me, then I'm real glad she did!"

He'd continued at length to think about the freckle-faced girl. But then he often thought about her. Finally, he'd sighed. "Come on," he'd said and had risen to his feet. "You can manage the rest of the way. And you know, pup, I reckon you're great company because since we've been together, I haven't felt lonely. Not even once."

****

Hank noticed that Calum was by himself. He decided that he'd try to overcome Calum's obvious distrust of him. He walked up to him and smiled cheerfully. "I'm glad I've got this chance to talk to you," he said.

Calum turned at the sound of Hank's voice. "G'day Hank," he said carefully.

"That sure was a nice thought to bring back the 'roo meat for Jacky Jacky and the others."

Calum smiled slightly. "They diced up a piece for Curaidh," he said, "and he choked because he gobbled it so fast."

Hank grinned, coughed, rolled himself a smoke and lit it. He drew deeply on his cigarette and then slowly exhaled. Wreaths of grey smoke swirled around his face.

"And tell me," he asked, "are you enjoying your job out here?"

"Too right."

"I'm sure glad to hear that. And don't worry about your pup. Ed Smith won't be allowed to touch it." Hank smiled warmly. "Besides I'm kinda interested in this outcome. It seems a long time ago now, but I studied Clinical Psychology. And here I have a Nature-versus-Nurture experiment happening right before my eyes."

"What do you mean?"

"What'll win? Genes or upbringing?" Hank looked around him. "You know," he continued in a friendly voice that contained a hint of awe. "I still can't get over the size of this country. Hell, it's as big as the States, but it's only got five percent of America's population."

"It won't get crowded here, will it?"

"If it does, it'll take a while. But, already, Australia is taking thousands and thousands of migrants from Europe. And most only have to pay five pounds toward their fare! The Government pays the rest."

"Yeah?" Calum gave Hank a quick glance. "Murranji said that you fought in Europe, Hank?"

Hank didn't answer straight away. Calum saw that a distant look had come into his eyes, which had narrowed.

"Yep," he drawled slowly. "I sure did. I was based in England, and I was one of those poor grunts who landed on Omaha Beach. I was also one of the first to enter Belsen." He paused. "And you know, I sure didn't like England or the Limeys."

"No?"

"You see, the English needed us, but I figure they didn't like us. I guess they thought that we were too brash." Hank paused and frowned. "And whenever I think of Belsen, I remember it was England that invented Concentration Camps."

"You're having me on, aren't you?"

"No, I'm not." Hank grimaced. "Hell, it was only around forty years ago that well over twenty-thousand Boer women and children died in English Concentration Camps from starvation and disease."

"I wasn't taught about that at school."

"That's no surprise." Hank smiled sardonically. "Most nations, as well as the Churches, find it convenient to bury their uglier moments. You know, when I was in Germany, I didn't come across anyone who admitted to being a Nazi. Most said they were only carrying out orders." Hank stood up straight, stretched his shoulders and ground his cigarette butt under a boot heel. "I'm off," he said. "Early start tomorrow, don't forget." He smiled at Calum and started to move off. Then he turned and looked over his shoulder. "Say," he drawled with a grin, "are we friends yet? Like, have you kinda forgiven me for testing you out on Socks?"

Calum reddened. "I don't know what you're talking about. Course, we're friends."

"I hope so because that was our first real chat. And I surely enjoyed it."

Calum didn't know what to say and changed the subject quickly. "Hank?"

"Yep."

"How would I find a girl if I didn't know her name or where she lived?"

"Ask around. Though if she's interested in finding out about you, she'll soon learn you're from Long Creek, won't she?"

Calum saw that Brian and a burly newcomer were approaching. He noted the stranger's polished, revolver belt and holster. His Wide-Awake hat had a large, blue-and-silver badge in its pleated, brown-and-white, puggaree band.

"Looks like it's our one and only Mounted Constable Sean Fitzpatrick," Hank remarked dryly.

Fitzpatrick gave Hank a cheery wave. "G'day, Hank," he shouted. "I'm callin' at stations an' camps on my way back ter Cord River. I don't suppose yer've come across a young creamy 'bout-fifteen, and travellin' with a couple o' blacks?"

"No, Sean, I sure haven't."

"An' how about you, young feller?" he asked as he neared them. "See anybody while you was out musterin'?"

"What did the girl do?"

"She made a bloody nuisance of herself by getting born."

"Nothing wrong with being born," Brian remarked and turned away.

Fitzpatrick's manner immediately changed. "Hey you, yeller feller," he shouted. "What the hell'd you say?"

Hank quickly moved between them and blocked Fitzpatrick's view. "That ringer's hearin' is kinda bad," he said. "He was kicked in the head."

"By a white feller, I hope. He's nothin' but an arrogant, boong nigger."

"A rough horse kicked him. Maybe that's why he's not stone deaf."

"Well, he soon will be if I get 'im in a police cell. Yeah, I'll put the boot in good. Christ, he's one arrogant nigger awright. But when we get niggers like that back ter the station, we know how to fix 'em."

Calum looked calm, but underneath he was really worried. Christ, what if this disgusting copper caught the freckle-faced girl? What could he do to her? Hell, almost anything from the way he spoke about Brian. He forced himself to think calmly.

"Mr. Policeman," he said, speaking up. "I'm sure it would've been them I came across."

"Boy," Constable Fitzpatrick demanded, "tell me what you saw. And if you're right, your blood'll be worth bottling. And you'll be officially thanked for assisting the Law, no worries."

"Well, it *was* a fair way south of here. There was a Murri, a woman and a girl in a school uniform."

"South? You sure, boy?"

"I'm positive."

"You beauty," Constable Fitzpatrick enthused. "Now I get it. They were heading north, but that was only to throw us off their trail. And they have to go south, probably to Tennant Creek, because that half-caste woman always gets cleaning jobs in hotels and banks." He clapped Calum on his shoulder. "Thank you, son. Hell, won't the bastards get a shock when I catch up with 'em!"

Hank gave Calum a conspiratorial smile and nod.

"How about a feed and a pot of tea, Sean?" he suggested. "You know, before you head after 'em?" He put his hand on Fitzpatrick's elbow and turned him in the direction of Charlie's fire. "Are you hungry?" he asked. "Because Charlie baked today, and his bread will sure be fresh."

"Fair dinkum bread, eh? Good-oh, I won't knock that back."

****

His increasing concern regarding the freckle-faced girl caused Calum to sleep poorly that night. He was wide-awake just as dawn was breaking. He looked across the billabong. The trees, on the other side, appeared as feathery silhouettes through the thin, dawn mist that hovered just above its brown surface. And, already, a pair of glossy-looking Black Swans, not often seen this far north, with their yellow-tipped, red beaks and the small, white bar on their wings were gliding gracefully and silently across the billabong's still surface; while a large, white, stork-like Royal Spoonbill, with its spoon-shaped bill and long black legs, was already sweeping its beak distinctively from side to side as it fished the shallows.

Soon, the camp was alive with the after-breakfast bustle of the final pack up. Curaidh found himself in a canvas bag that'd been secured to saddle Ds and Socks's girth. The only part of him showing was his head. He constantly turned it to observe everything that was going on around him. His bearer, Socks, sleepily stood with his eyes closed and ears back and with the tip of one, back hoof just touching the ground. He'd become used to carrying Curaidh.

It was well past dawn when they started droving the fats toward the distant, concrete, dipping tank. Each fat had had the lower half of its tail tassle cut off to show that it was a road bullock.

Calum was forward, on the right flank, with only Blue ahead of him. And when Hank swept up beside him, he could see that the Head Stockman was in a jovial mood. Obviously, he was pleased that they were on their way. He winked at Calum engagingly.

"And tell me," he asked, "what good will your Gaelic do you in our new Australia?"

"I'll tell you what my mum once said to an Englishman."

"Fire away."

"It's not here that matters. It's when we reach the Pearly Gates."

"And?"

"Because Saint Peter, when he sees a Gael, always opens the Gates with a flourish and calls out loudly, 'Thig a-steach, a' charaid!' which means, 'Welcome, friend!'"

"Ah yes, Hank observed. "But what if the Gael is down *below*, and he's facing Satan?"

"That wouldn't be a problem. You see, we Gaels also speak English!"

Hank was still grinning when he touched his heels to his chestnut and cantered off.

****

They'd been droving for four days. Today was the start of the fifth, and the home station wasn't more than six hours away. Calum was enjoying the ride. The fats were moving nicely and, as usual, were being led by the big, roan bullock that they'd christened Ol' Roany. Ol' Roany had capably defended his position, and now the mob had accepted him as its natural leader. The ringers had come to regard him with some affection.

"I reckon we don't hand him over to the drover," Blue had suggested last evening, at their camp fire. "We should keep him and give him the job next year."

"Yeah," Charlie had agreed. "An' tell him that if he don' keep up his standards, he'll end up bein' our first killer."

"Charlie," Blue had protested, "yer don't show no loyalty."

"Neither will you, yapper," Charlie had sniffed, "when yer lays yer eyes on the juicy rump steaks, we'll get off him!"

"Charlie," Blue had complained as he put another log on their fire, "I reckon it wouldn't take much ter turn yer inter a cannibal. Yer showin' all the signs awready!"

"Cannibal be buggered. Piss off, yer little shit!"

Now, as he rode alongside their mob of fats, Calum recalled Brian's thoughtfulness on the first day that the fats had to be held in the open because their number had outgrown the stockyard.

"Now, listen carefully, mate," Brian had advised. "As Hank'd say, this is now a different ball game. You see, we don't have that built-up fire between the mob an' our swags for nothing. So if you hear a noise that sounds like bullocks running, you head for the fire quick smart. An' you stand behind it. Because if there's a rush, that fire'll split the fats, an' those standing directly behind it won't be run over."

"Oh."

"Yeah, you get run over by a mob of fats, an' what's left of you can be slid under a door real easy!"

"Bloody hell. And what about you?" Calum had asked.

"First up, I'll make damn sure I won't be causing any Chinaman Laning." He'd noticed Calum's blank look. "That's where you get ringers on both sides of the mob by mistake, 'cause they can't see each other," he'd explained. "Then, instead of gettin' ringed, the mob runs faster an' faster an' dead straight. That's not real good. You see, ringing a mob can easily take up to two miles. But when a mob is Laning, you could have a disaster on yer hands. An' it's happened. Fats right out of control an' going over a gorge."

"Jeez."

Calum now decided that he'd better stop thinking about rushes in case he put the mockers on them and brought one on. He saw that they were now crossing one of those wide, ridge areas with red grass, Bloodwoods, Snapping Gums, red earth and dark-red, ant beds. Abruptly the light suddenly worsened. Big, black clouds appeared, rolled over the sky, and blotted out the sun. Calum looked skyward. *Surely,* he thought, *there couldn't be hard rain at this time of the year.* Then jagged flashes of lightning rent the clouds, and resounding thunderclaps boomed and echoed all around them. Suddenly, it happened without warning. He heard the sound that every ringer fears, which grips the guts of even the most experienced ones with a chill dread. Calum hadn't heard it before. At first, it sounded like far-off rolling thunder. He looked at the mob and, for a moment, couldn't believe his eyes. It was as if all thirteen-hundred bullocks had exploded. Those at the rear were milling and clambering onto the backs of those in front before breaking into a gallop as soon as they'd gained the room to run. Now the entire mob was rushing. Those in front were galloping faster and faster as they found themselves being pushed forward by those behind.

He took in the scene at a glance and saw wide, staring eyes, mouths that were open, nostrils that were flared, cloven hooves that were cutting into the red earth and great muscles that were powerfully driving the heavy bodies onward. Soon, the entire mob was moving as one. A vast, rising cloud of red dust enveloped everything. Calum could feel the ground under Socks vibrating. This was the rolling thunder that was being generated by five-thousand pounding hooves, and it was growing louder and louder. Through the red dust, Calum could see rocking heads and fixed eyes. A long train of convulsively thrashing, curved horns glinted in the sun and dust-tinged, pink and white, foam spumes dangled from gaping mouths.

Calum's initial rush of adrenaline blocked any fear. He stroked Socks's neck. "I'm trusting you to keep your feet, mate," he whispered.

But what in the hell had caused the rush? Of course, it had to be those jagged bolts of lightning, followed by the resounding thunderclaps.

And instantly panic had spread. Now, as one, the mob wheeled and began to gallop straight toward him and Blue. Instinctively, he hauled Socks back on his haunches and swivelled him round. Now, he could pick out Hank and Nugget through the dust. They were pushing their horses hard but were still some way behind.

Socks was parallel with the mob and galloping flat-out. He was catching the leaders. Ahead, Calum saw Blue. Blue was up with the leaders and was flailing and cracking his whip. Calum spurred Socks.

Already the panic-crazed mob had galloped for over a mile. Calum became aware that behind him, Hank, Brian and Nugget were frantically spurring their flagging horses and were catching up. But how the hell had Brian come from the other side? Had he crossed through, for Crissake? Now Calum was right behind Blue, and he began flailing and cracking at the leaders with his stock whip.

Were they starting to turn? Just then Hank appeared on his inside, with his big revolver pointing skyward. Loud reports started to crash out. Bullocks were moving away from the gunshots. Yes! They were definitely turning. Suddenly, to Calum's horror, he saw Blue's brown mare stumble badly. And he watched, shocked, as Blue was pitched straight over her neck and into the path of the leading scrum. He saw the mare turn and gallop off with her reins dangling and with her stirrups flapping. Calum felt numb. *Why in the hell were they called Shorthorns,* he *wondered, when they had such lethal horns? Poor Blue. It wouldn't have been their horns though.*

The mob was slowing right down. Now it'd stopped to a walk, and the dust was settling. Calum could see through it. Trails of red spume dangled from open mouths and dust-caked, red bodies heaved for air. He himself was gasping for breath. He felt numb inside. His throat was dry, and his nostrils were filled with the smell of red dust and hot, sweating bullocks. Under him, he could feel Socks blowing hard. He rode back to Nugget and Hank. They'd dismounted. He saw Hank take a sheet of canvas from Jalyerri and place it over Blue's broken body. And he saw that Hank's face was tight and drawn.

After they'd roped Blue's canvas-wrapped body to a packhorse, Nugget came over to Calum. He looked toward the horizon with unseeing eyes.

"Yer done good, mate," he told Calum. "It was jus' one o' those things what can happen ter any ringer."

Then they heard Charlie's voice call out, "Gimme the lead rope. This'll be the little yapper's last ride, an' I'll take it with him."

CHAPTER 10

REUNITED

Murranji broke camp while it was still dark. He'd woken far too early and hadn't been able to get back to sleep. Alasdair's cryptic message puzzled him, and it'd stayed on his mind. When he mounted, he estimated that he was about four hours' ride from Big River. The light from a white-yellow moon lit his surroundings, and the blue-black sky twinkled with the stars that he needed to guide him.

During those still hours, he rode past sleeping groups of Shorthorns: heavy, dark humps lying in the dewy grass, with their legs tucked under them and with their big, arching horns glinting in the moonlight. Grazing Red Kangaroos and the odd, largely nocturnal Euro, a shaggy, pale-looking, grey-brown kangaroo, moved out of his horses' path with exaggerated, slow-motion hops. Their unfazed eyes reflected the moonlight and switched on and off, like little, signal lamps, as they watched his progress before again lowering their heads to feed. While the shadowy outline of a hunting dingo stopped and stayed motionless beneath a feathery-looking, Mimosa acacia till Murranji's horses were well past it.

He rode by a spectral-looking Ghost Gum and decided that it was only by moonlight that one could fully appreciate its fitting name. In daylight, the near-white trunk and branches shone through its glossy-green foliage like sun-bleached bones. But if the night was right, its foliage became lost against the night sky, and only the spectral trunk and limbs were visible. Then, from December, white flowers would frame those ghostly limbs and would seem to hang, unattached and ethereal-looking, in the night sky.

He saw the Big River homestead standing stark against the skyline long before he reached it. It was midmorning when he finally arrived. Alasdair met him, helped him to wash down his horses and then turn them out. Afterward, they leaned against the stockyard's rails and talked.

"The ride awright, was it?" Alasdair asked.

"Preferable to droving fats, I reckon."

Alasdair nodded and looked about him with his faded, blue eyes.

"Your message said you needed help, mate," Murranji said. "So of course I came."

Alasdair took his time in answering. Like many old-timers, it didn't pay to push him. "I see that," he said. "An' it's appreciated." He frowned. "Do yer know if Fitzpatrick's lookin' for a girl and her mother?" he asked.

"Some Murries I met said young McNicol told Fitzo he'd seen 'em heading south."

"That McNicol's awright, is he?"

"I reckon."

"Well, mate, they're here. An' me an' Iain reckon they're real nice people." Alasdair rubbed his eyes and then looked at Murranji. "I believe the mother's someone yer used to know," he offered cautiously.

"Yeah?"

"Does the name Peg Shillingsworth ring a bell?" Alasdair asked.

"Most definitely. That's if it's the Peg Shillingsworth I'm thinking of."

Alasdair looked back toward the homestead. He indicated with a nod of his head. "Well, yer'll soon know, Murranji," he said. "Because this is her comin' now."

As Peg approached, Murranji saw her eyes widen in recognition. And he felt his guts suddenly tighten. Then he smiled and moved toward her. "G'day, Peg. I recognized you immediately. An' I have to say, you've worn much better than I have."

Peg nervously brushed a grey-streaked lock back behind her ear. *He's hardly changed*, she thought. *No added pounds and just a bit o' salt an' pepper in his hair.* She couldn't help hoping that he wouldn't notice the slight thickening around her waist and hips.

"Is that right?" She smiled, trying to appear calm. "An' I see yer still the charmer."

Alasdair grinned. He put an arm around Peg's shoulders and gave her a brief hug. "I reckon I'll leave yer both to it," he said. "An' how's Dor getting on with Mr. Ah Lee, Peg?"

"He's showin' her how ter make what she calls dim sims, an' he's insistin' is called dim sum. Neither was givin' ground when I left."

"See yer later," Alasdair said, laughing. "Now, Murranji, you remember I said Peg's a real nice lady, awright?"

"I wouldn't argue with that."

Alasdair moved off. He was thinking that since Peg and Doreen had come into his life, things had brightened up a treat. Like, whenever he and Peg went for a wander, she'd always take his arm. And it was the same when she accompanied Iain. He supposed that this is how it would've been had he been lucky enough to have had a daughter. And wasn't Doreen a bright young spark? She could add up a column of figures faster than anyone else he'd come across. As well, she was steadily working her way through his late mother's small library, and right now, she'd about finished *Wuthering Heights.* Also, she and her mare, Lady, had bonded well, and her riding was really coming on. And lately, she'd started giving him and Iain a brief peck on the cheek before she went to bed. *Yeah,* he thought, *the poor, little tacker wouldn't have found much affection at Cord River.*

Murranji Bill gave Peg a slow smile that started at his eyes and then gradually extended till it lit up his face. He couldn't help noticing that her body had barely changed. It was her shape that'd first made him notice her, all those years ago. And, bloody hell, now it was already causing him to have those same, damn stirrings.

"Now, that I'm here, Peg Shillingsworth," he said, "maybe you can tell me how I can help?"

Peg suddenly started to feel apprehensive. What if he got cranky because she hadn't told him before? At the time, it'd been pure agony to leave Catriona without saying good-bye. But she was sure that he was about to dump her for that white sheila, who'd been all over him like a rash. And it'd been her pride, by Jove, which'd forced her to take off. But how was she supposed to know that she'd been pregnant? Of course, it'd always been her pride, especially where white fellers were concerned. Because all they'd ever wanted from her was the fuck they couldn't get from white sheilas.

"I been thinkin' long an' hard on it," she said carefully. "An' I don' want yer to feel yer gotta help. Or that you is obliged, in any way."

"Peg, if I can help, I will. You know that."

"Well, there's no easy way ter say this." Peg took a deep breath and met his eyes. "I know I didn't look real hard fer you after I took off. But the plain fact is my daughter is *our* girl."

She thought that Murranji looked as if he'd just been kicked by a particularly peevish mule. Her next words came tumbling out. "Look, she don' know, an' she don't have ter. An' you don' have no responsibility here. I'm not askin' fer anything. I hope you is not cranky …" her voice trailed off.

Murranji Bill was frowning, not from annoyance but because he was thinking hard. He was also thinking about all the implications that were inherent in what Peg'd just said. It was like somebody throwing a stone into a billabong because the ripples that were caused just kept on spreading wider and wider. Finally, he did manage to say something.

"What if she doesn't want me as her dad? She mightn't like how I look."

Peg couldn't help herself. She burst out laughing. Wasn't that just the sort of thing that this man would say? "You should see yer face, mate," she managed to say. "Yer look like you is in shock. Crise, an' I'm the one who has ter explain why I never tol' her about her dad."

Murranji grinned his wide grin and shook his head. "I'll be darned," he said. "Come on, I reckon I'm game if you are."

"We'll both need ter be as game as they come, I reckon. But you wait here, Murranji, an' I'll go an' fetch her."

Murranji looked down toward the river, thinking hard. His thoughts were abruptly disturbed by a rat's frantic squealing. He looked in the direction of the squealing. His keen eyes spotted a Northern Quoll. Brown with large, white spots, the ferocious little carnivore, about the size of a very large kitten, was some thirty yards away. It'd cornered a big rat against a log. And it didn't take it long to kill the squealing rodent. Murranji nodded his head in approval; he couldn't abide rats.

His thoughts quickly returned to what Peg had told him. *I'll be jiggered,* he thought. *Now, this has got to be a real, once-in-a-lifetime shock. Bloody hell, a brand-new, grown-up daughter! Fair dinkum, a man wouldn't read about this sort of out-of-the-blue surprise. But what if she doesn't want anything to do with me?* That thought made him feel a bit sick in the stomach, sort of like when he'd drunk too much rum. He turned at the sound of Peg's voice.

"Doreen, love, this here's Murranji Bill Taylor. He'll help us any way he can."

Murranji found himself looking into curious, big, dark eyes. They were staring at him from above a small splash of freckles. *Christ,* he thought, *those're my eyes, an' that's my willful chin.* Suddenly he felt the strongest urge to hold his daughter in his arms. To tell her that everything would be all right. That he'd always be there to protect her. *You silly old bugger,* he chided himself, *you'd frighten a year's growth out of her.* Instead, he slowly took her slim hand in his, shook it carefully and tried to sound reassuring.

"I'm told you've had a rough time." He paused. "I was real sorry to hear that. But you've got to believe it's over now. An' that's the Gospel truth."

"Mr. Taylor," she asked, with wide eyes, "were you there when the policeman asked that boy about me?"

"No. But same as you, I heard he sent Fitzo south."

"Mm," Doreen murmured and smiled to herself.

Murranji quickly looked at Peg before he spoke, but what he said next wasn't planned. It just seemed to slip out before he could stop it. "How would you feel, Doreen," he asked, "if your dad happened to turn up one day? You know, sort of unexpected, like?"

"I don't know. And I don't know if he's alive, even."

"Would it matter very much, love," Murranji continued, swallowing hard, "if he sort of looked a bit like me?"

Doreen gasped. Understanding crossed her face and her eyes opened wide. She turned to her mother. "Mum?"

Peg held her daughter's gaze and gave a small nod. Doreen looked back at Murranji, and her eyes grew even bigger. She tentatively reached out a hand, and her father took her small hand in both of his. He held it as if it was the most precious thing that he'd ever held.

"If you can put up with having me as your dad," he said, blinking his eyes, "I would be real proud to call you my daughter."

Doreen hesitantly moved forward half a step. Murranji held out his arms. Next minute, he was holding her, and her face was buried against his chest. He could feel that she was crying, and he found himself feeling very churned up. He looked at Peg. Peg was sniffling unashamedly, and tears were running down her cheeks. Murranji met her gaze and nodded his head. He kept swallowing, and Peg was surprised to see that his eyes were moist.

Later, after the brothers and Doreen had gone to bed, Peg and Murranji sat on the moonlit verandah. And in the stillness of a balmy night, they nursed mugs of tea. They were conversing comfortably. It was a bit like the old days, she thought. But then talking to Murranji had always been easy. In fact, it was the first thing about him that'd attracted her.

He glanced at her. "You said when things've settled, you'll be staying here for spells. I reckon that'll suit me," he said. "It'll give me the chance to nick over an' get to know my girl properly."

"Yeah. It'd be good if yer could do that, Murranji."

"Peg, I won't have any trouble finding the time," he said earnestly.

"Is that right?" She smiled.

"An' you know, she asked me to tell young Calum that her name was Doreen. But I said I'd go one better if her mum agreed."

Peg looked at him questioningly. "Agreed ter what?"

"To me taking you both to meet all the fellers. They're my mates, an' I want them to know Doreen's my daughter. It'd mean more people looking out for her. I also said the first person I'd introduce her to was young Calum. An' she could tell him what her name was herself."

"What did she say?" Peg asked, showing interest.

"Nothing. She just went a bit red."

"Now, that don't surprise me!" She grinned. "An', mate, I don' have a single worry 'bout goin' ter Long Creek."

"Then it's settled. We'll likely get there, by the time they've dipped that last mob of fats. An' I've also been thinking about if somehow, Doreen was caught an' got taken back to Cord."

"Crise, I pray not."

They were quiet. Then Peg looked at him. "How come yer never got married?" she quietly asked.

"If I was forced to be honest, I'd have to say it was maybe 'cause I never met another Peg Shillingsworth."

"Oh."

"An' you?"

"I never wanted any man in me bed, permanent." A glint came into her eyes. "But it wasn't awful hard fer me. Course, I reckon it'd be harder fer a man. What dya reckon?"

He looked away and didn't answer. He stayed pensive as he stared out into the darkness. Above, the moon was a large, white crescent that looked as if it was about to be swamped by myriads of big, tropical stars.

It was good being with Peg, he thought. Course, she'd always been real easy to be with. And still, the thought that'd stayed at the back of his mind wouldn't leave him. He started to speak and chose his words carefully.

"Of course, there *is* one way Doreen'd be safe," he said.

"Yeah? What's that?"

"Well," he said slowly, "we could always get married."

"Yer *got* ter be jokin', by Jove." Peg looked shocked. "No way, Murranji. No way at all."

He laughed out loud at the shocked look that'd stayed on her face. "I don't mean living together, Peg. Or me making husband demands on you. Besides, I'll have you know, mate, I'm not desperate."

"Well, that's a helluva compliment ter pay a woman yer haven't seen in fifteen years," she shot back.

"Come off it, Peg." He grinned. "I know you're not thin-skinned."

"Yer right, I'm not thin-skinned." She hesitated before speaking. "An' now I've caught me breath, I want ter say straight out that what yer offered is mos' thoughtful fer our girl."

"Will you think about it, then?"

"Yes, I will."

Peg's eyes clouded. Then she felt annoyed. It griped her that after all these years, Murranji could still have this effect on her. She wondered if, *maybe, that was another reason why she'd left him, because she'd never wanted to be emotionally dependent on any man.* Specially, not a white feller who'd dump you for the first white sheila who let him put a hand up her skirt. *Maybe, it was 'cause there were so few white sheilas in the Territory, but fair dinkum,* she thought, *white fellers had 'em up on pedestals like they was all blutty Lana Turners or Rita Hayworths.* Now, damn him, Murranji was forcin' her ter realize he was different from other white fellers. Well, she'd always known that, but when he'd started flirtin' with that white sheila, it'd just become all too much. She'd known that she could never compete. And now, by Crise, she found herself wanting him, just like she had way back then. It was if the years had suddenly been rolled back. Sort of like clouds that the wind blew away after the rain, to let the sun shine out of a brand-new, shiny-blue sky.

"Yer a decent man, Murranji," she finally said. "Fair dinkum you is. I s'pose I never realized jus' how decent. An' that's no credit ter me, o' course."

"You reckon so, do you?" he said, and his expression softened.

She looked away, not wishing to meet his eyes. "An' I reckon now 'cause I'm older," she slowly admitted, "I shouldn't have run off like I did, know what I mean?"

"It was all my fault, Peg," he quickly said. "I didn't show you proper respect. I'm still ashamed about that. An' you know, I didn't appreciate just what I'd lost till you were gone." He paused. "Of course, I looked for you, but couldn't find you."

"Maybe I didn't want ter be found."

"I wanted to find you real bad, Peg. 'Cause I wanted you for my woman—for always."

"Yeah?" Her eyes turned soft. She was conscious that her heart was now hammering against her shirt. Unbidden, her eyes began to sparkle. "Maybe," she cautiously murmured, "I need ter give some thought on whether I still like yer, like before."

"I do know it's been a real long time, Peg."

"'Course, I never even thought ter take up with another feller permanent, yer know."

"How come?"

"Could be, some things don't change," she said quietly.

His eyes widened, and he looked at her carefully. "You're not just saying that, Peg?"

She didn't answer. After a long moment, she rose to her feet, nervously looked down at him and then slowly held out her hand. He saw that her hand was trembling.

"I don' know if yer have any plans fer ternight, mate," she said uncertainly. "But if you *is* free, I'd be real pleased if yer thought ter keep me company."

He stood up, met her eyes, and took her outstretched hand. "Peg," he told her earnestly, "I would've been free any night durin' these past fifteen years. You only would've had to say what you said just now."

"Oh, mate."

CHAPTER 11

A Pleasant Picnic

Two, imposing, Bloodwood gum trees shaded the small graveyard behind Long Creek's homestead. They always flowered by Christmas, and their fragile, bunched blossoms then offered a vibrant, massed-scarlet tribute to those buried below. Today, one was sheltering half a dozen of those impressive-looking Red-winged Parrots. The males—with their green heads and underparts, black backs, purple-and-yellow rumps, long, green tails and broad, scarlet, wing stripes —were noisily screeching their almost-metallic-sounding *crilling, crilling.*

And bordering, Grevillea shrubs were now in bloom. They were playing host to little Friarbirds. These pale-brown birds, blue-grey around the eyes, were thrusting slender, nectar-seeking beaks into the delicate, orange blossoms.

The men bowed their heads and stood around the open grave. Blue's body, wrapped in canvas and secured by a green hide rope, was lowered into the grave by Hank and Nugget. Nugget said the words that he'd been mentally rehearsing all morning.

"Now, Blue, this is all what comes ter mind, so it'll have ter do, awright?

"There is a green hill far away, without a city wall,

"Where the dear Lord was crucified; he died ter save us all.

Amen."

The grave was then filled in, and Nugget put in place the heavy rock that would serve as a headstone. He'd chiselled this inscription into it:

JOHN (BLUEY) WHITE

A Good Mate

Killed by a Rush

JUNE **18, 1947**

The ringers then put on their hats and left the tiny graveyard. Hank briefly put an arm across Nugget's shoulders and told him that he'd done Blue proud. And, also, that it was goddamn inconsiderate of Les Jackson to have left for Katherine before Blue's funeral.

Wondering if he should write to Blue's English father caused Hank to think of the time that he'd spent in England and how appalled he'd been to discover that so many Limeys were as racist as all hell, although they were subtler about it than Texans. And that wasn't damn hypocrisy coming from a Southerner either. No, he'd started to question the whole business of segregation when he'd been in college. And the war had ensured that he'd made a total U-turn once he'd got to know and admire as human beings the black American GIs. He'd particularly admired the sergeant who'd saved his life. And God alone knew that Elijah Brown had many reasons to dislike whites. But he hadn't hesitated when he'd seen that Hank was alone and under fire from an enemy, machine gun.

And later, when Hank had been appointed to Eisenhower's personal staff, he'd accompanied the Supreme Commander when he'd been shown over the newly liberated Belsen. Unimaginable horror! A dreadful abomination that'd damn well been created by barbaric and depraved racists. It still caused him to have appalling nightmares. And Belsen had been liberated during April '45, over two years ago, for Crissake.

Hank sighed and made a mental note to buy enough rum from Perce to last him through the months of branding. He'd found that when tiredness was pulling him to his swag, a stiff rum stopped him from thinking about Donna and Belsen and all the other goddamn "awfuls" that prevented him from getting to sleep.

Then he brightened because, now, he could look forward happily to seeing Jan tonight. Alice had told him that Perce would be bringing her from Catriona this afternoon.

****

Calum still felt down in the dumps, and he had to tell himself that burying Blue was bound to leave anybody feeling crook. He sat down under a sturdy, bushy tree with Curaidh between his knees and leaned against its trunk. He thought about Blue. It'd been so sudden, just like his mum. In the morning, she'd given him his breakfast and had teased him about his too-hasty efforts at washing up. Then, before lunch, a highly strung Thoroughbred stallion had grabbed her by the shoulder and had flung her like a rag doll against its stable wall before kicking her to death. Calum still couldn't understand why she'd gone into its stall. Certainly, she'd cuddled and petted it when it'd been a foal, but she also knew that you never trusted bulls or stallions.

He forced himself to stop thinking about his mum and pondered on how to train Curaidh to ignore the home station chickens. It wouldn't be easy, given that Curaidh had already killed one impertinent hen that'd stupidly stuck her head into his dish while he'd been wolfing down his meat. The damn hen had nearly gone the way of Curaidh's meat and would have, but for the fact that he'd grabbed it, praying that some life might still remain within its rumpled feathers. And he'd considered it prudent not to tell Charlie what had happened. He'd learned that Charlie had a way of constantly bringing up certain things.

Riding up the track leading to the homestead, he noticed a ringer on a good-looking buckskin, leading a packhorse. Up here, he reminded himself, Palominos and buckskins were called creamies.

The rider halted opposite him and reached for his makings. He was wiry, blue eyed and had a greying moustache that drooped in cow-horn curves past the corners of his mouth. Calum guessed that he was in his midforties.

"G'day, young feller," the man called in greeting. "The name's Jack Kelly."

Calum rose to his feet and held up his outstretched hand. "Calum McNicol."

"That pup looks like he's around seven or eight months?"

"I think that's right."

"Best dog I ever had was a dingo," the other observed a mite wistfully. "Thing is you get attached to dogs."

"A bit like horses, I suppose."

"That'd be right, young feller. 'Cept a man can't do without a horse in this country." He briefly appraised the tree under which Calum was sitting and then glanced at Calum's swag. "Yer not plannin' ter sleep under that tree are yer, young feller?"

"Yes, I was."

"It's a *Kumbitji*, and there'd be plenty of folks who'd give it a miss," Jack Kelly gently observed.

"I don't understand."

"Accordin' ter the Murries, anyone who sleeps under a Kumbitji, exceptin' a Kaditje man, don't wake up in the morning. Then again," he continued, "there's whites who'll say that all that sort o' stuff is bullshit."

"Would you sleep under one, Mr. Kelly?"

"No."

Jack Kelly shortened his reins, gave Calum a nod, and touched his heels to his buckskin. Calum watched him ride toward the ringer's hut. He sat straight in the saddle.

Brian, who'd been with his mum, joined Calum. He had a grass stem between his teeth and, as usual, his face reflected his sunny personality. "How're you going? All right, mate?" he said with a smile. "I thought Nugg did well. What dya reckon?"

"Too right."

Brian squatted down and stroked Curaidh. "Do you know who you were talking to?" he asked.

"His name's Jack Kelly."

Brian's voice evinced admiration. "Yeah," he said. "But that's *the* Jack Kelly, mate."

"So?"

"He's a legend up here, and he's been everywhere. They reckon he knows every billabong between the Kimberley and Rockhampton.

Funny thing, though, he never stays on any run more than three months. Been that way ever since his wife died, after being bitten by a snake. And that'd be twenty years ago. Murranji reckons he's looking for someone. He an' Jack Kelly are good mates."

Calum still had that bad feeling in his stomach about Blue. He looked out over the rolling vastness toward the lowering sun. It was colouring the sky on each side of it, a hot vermilion.

Sensing that Calum wanted to be alone, Brian stood up. "Now I really came," he said, "to tell you to come an' eat at my mum's tonight. My sister'll be there too."

"Yeah?"

Brian yawned and stretched. "Come round in an hour," he said. "Mum an' Jan are looking forward to meeting you." He grinned. "I even told 'em you were an all right feller!"

"Well, I am." Calum smiled. "And I'm looking forward to a good feed."

"Well, you'll get *that* all right, 'cause Mum's a beaut cook. Hooroo, mate."

"See you later."

****

Calum rose, clapped his thigh to gain Curaidh's attention and headed for a tap to wash him. Then he saw Murranji walking toward him. At first glance, he thought that the slim figure with Murranji—dressed in a loose-fitting shirt, baggy moleskins, and floppy old hat—was a boy, but the walk was unmistakably girlish. He wondered if this could be Murranji's friend from the Murri camp. As he headed toward them, he took care to look only at Murranji so that he wouldn't appear inquisitive.

"G'day, Murranji," he called out. "I thought you were still over at the River."

"Yeah? How're you going, young feller?"

"Good."

"Actually, I came back with my daughter an' her mum for a couple of days."

Calum turned to the girl, very surprised by what Murranji Bill had said. He started to speak before he looked beneath her floppy, stock hat.

"I'm pleased to ..." He stopped speaking, and his heart lurched wildly. Astonishment covered his face. The girl had taken off her hat and was looking up at him, with an impish smile. He found himself gazing once again into those same, wide, dark eyes that he remembered so clearly. They looked at each other without speaking. Murranji was still grinning when he broke the silence.

"Doreen wants to thank you, young Calum, for what you told Fitzo. I'll leave you both to it, 'cause I need to catch up with Hank."

They continued to look at each other. Calum was conscious that his heart was now hammering within his chest. Doreen was the first to speak.

"Thank you for what you did," she murmured.

Calum's mind started to race, and he tried to control his breathing. "I didn't know Murranji was your dad," he said.

"Dad and me are still getting to know each other. Mum's over at Alice's cottage. They've met before, and they're having a good old chat."

The way they'd started to talk, as if they'd known each other for ages, surprised him. And she was even prettier than he'd remembered. And her voice was easy to listen to as well.

Doreen smiled. "I don't even know how old you are," she said.

"I'm going on eighteen."

"I'm fifteen."

"And are you living at the River now?" he asked.

"For a while, till we head up north." She saw the look of disappointment on his face, smiled, touched his arm and spoke reassuringly. "We'll be back when the branding's over. Will you come and visit me when we get back?"

"My very word," he vowed.

"Promise?"

He looked down into her eyes. They were soft and questioning.

"Nothing'll stop me from coming," he assured her.

"I needed you to say that." She noticed that her father was waving to her. "That's Dad giving me a wave. I think he wants me to join him."

"Doreen?"

"Yes."

"I don't have a girlfriend, you know."

She smiled and a look of wonder came into her eyes. "Are you just telling me that?" She asked. "Or are you asking me to be your girl?"

"I want you to be my girl."

"Do you want me to say I'm your girl?"

"Yes."

"I think you know I've been your girlfriend from when we met." She smiled. "And I've already told Mum we're going together."

She reached toward him and rested a slim hand on his arm. He kept looking at her and couldn't take his eyes off her face. He'd never felt this happy before. She smiled again, and what she did next seemed very natural. She moved forward, put her arms around him and hugged him. Her shirt smelled of lavender, and her skin smelled of the bush. He was conscious that her bosom was soft against his chest. He wished that they could stay like this for a very long time. Finally, she pulled back and looked up at him.

"That's Dad calling again," she murmured. "I really have to go."

"Yes."

"But we'll see each other again tonight at Alice's? You are coming?"

"Oh, my word."

She turned away, and he stood and watched her walk toward her father. Then he headed toward a tap with Curaidh. There was more purpose in the way he strode out. He had his shoulders back, and he held his head high.

****

Calum arrived at Alice's cottage promptly within the hour. He'd washed and had put on a clean shirt. He put his swag down on the cottage verandah, told Curaidh to stay with it, and as was customary, removed his boots before knocking. He hoped that nobody would notice the hole in the heel of his right sock. A plumpish woman with black hair, greying markedly, opened the door. She was wearing a bright floral dress, and on seeing Calum, her full lips broke into a wide smile. She held out her hand.

"You must be Calum. I'm Brian's mum. Come on in, love, an' take the weight off yer feet. The others is already here."

Calum followed her into the room. Hank, Brian, Murranji and Doreen and her mum were all seated there. They looked around when he walked in. Murranji rose and indicated Peg.

"Now, you haven't met Doreen's mum, Peg, have you, Calum?"

Peg flashed him a smile that offered warmth and friendship. "How are yer, Calum?" she asked. "I've heard so much about yer, I reckon I jus' about know yer already!"

"Hello, Peg. Hello, Doreen."

Calum took an instant liking to Peg. She had direct eyes that seemed to sparkle with a laughter that promised to arrive and touch her lips at any moment. He saw that she made no attempt to hide the bond that existed between herself and Murranji. It was obvious in their every gesture, word, look and smile.

"You come an' sit on this chair next ter Doreen, mate," she told him. "We've bin savin' it for yer."

Brian looked across at Calum. "You haven't met my sister, mate. This is Jan."

Jan was two years older than her brother. Like Alice, she was barefoot and was also wearing a floral-print frock. Her shoulder-length, dark hair was tied back with a ribbon, and her brown eyes were calm and friendly. Calum thought that she was very pretty. And as he'd learn, in time, her Faith never stopped her from acting like one of the boys. Neither did it prevent her from laughing heartily at risqué jokes. She moved toward him, smiling.

"So you're the ringer who's going to win the big race at Tennant Creek," she said.

Calum noted that she'd called him ringer rather than boy. He liked that. "Well, I hope so," he replied.

"And I hope you like beefsteak pie, Calum?" she said with a smile.

"My word."

"Like Mum said, it won't be long. So I'd better go and check how things are going in the kitchen and see if I can help."

"Yes."

Calum sat down beside Doreen. They smiled at each other, and she rested her hand briefly on his arm. "I'm glad you came," she said.

"Me too. And you look real nice tonight."

"Do you really think so?"

"For sure."

Calum looked around him. The room was neat and had been simply furnished. The floor consisted of crushed-up, ant beds that'd been pounded down till it'd set like cement. The chairs and sofa had been made from sapling-sized wood and broad lengths of cowhide. The red cushions on them brightened the room. Framed photographs of Brian and Jan hung on the wall near the only window, and two, roan-coloured, bullock skins served as floor rugs. A scrubbed, wooden, trestle table, without a tablecloth, stood at the far end of the room. On it were place settings, tin mugs, salt and a bottle of tomato sauce.

Alice returned from the kitchen. "What's Nugget up ter tonight, son?" she asked Brian.

"Told me he'd some drinkin' to do," Brian answered. "It wouldn't surprise me if he went on a bender. He did that when his old man died."

"And Charlie?"

"Charlie can have some funny ideas at times."

"Oh."

Alice moved next to Calum. She rested her hand lightly on his shoulder. "Not long now," she told him. "An', son, you make sure yer sleep on the verandah here if yer don' want ter sleep in the ringer's hut, all right? An' yer'd better keep away from Kumbitji trees." She grinned down at him. "An' yer'd also better keep away from Mangan trees."

Calum saw that Peg and Murranji Bill were smiling.

"Why?" he asked.

"Because Mangans'll put a magic spell on young lovers what makes 'em stay stuck in the one spot. That's one way wrong-side lovers can be easy caught. An' I already heard, a tow-headed kwee-ai, at the camp, has got her eye on yer. She thinks you was gentle with that horse what kept tippin' yer off."

"Best you don't keep reminding him how often he came off, Mum," Brian said, grinning. "An' there's no way Calum'll be looking in *her* direction."

Alice looked at Doreen and Calum. Understanding dawned, and she laughed at herself. "Well aren't I a silly ol' woman! I'm sorry, Doreen, love. Yeah, looks like my place has got ter be the kitchen, fer sure."

Peg and Murranji exchanged quick glances. He'd raised the subject of Doreen and Calum with her. He could remind Calum, he'd suggested, that Doreen was younger than he was. But Peg had shaken her head.

"No way, mate," she'd told him. "Cord River made her much older 'n her years. Jus' leave things be. If we interfere, it'll on'y make her more determined. Besides, she's too sensible ter have a child an' get it taken away. No, mate, we make Calum feel welcome. After all, she's come right out an' tol' us he's her feller, hasn't she?"

Calum felt comfortable, though he and Doreen didn't talk much. Peg thought they appeared to be a little self-conscious in the company of others. But she noticed that they frequently looked at each other, held hands and exchanged little smiles.

Jan returned from the kitchen, smiling. Everybody looked at her and stopped talking.

"The pies'll be ready in a couple of minutes," she announced, "and they do look delicious."

So far, Hank and Jan had barely spoken to each other, though Jan was aware that he often looked at her. And Alice soon noticed that whenever Hank spoke, Jan's eyes stayed on him.

"I suppose yer lookin' forward ter goin' home one day," she said to him. "Yer must miss yer family an' friends somethin' terrible?"

But when Hank answered her, Alice knew that he was really talking to Jan.

"The Territory's my home now, Alice."

"I've heard that where yer come from, blacks and whites is separated like here?"

"Yes, that's right," Hank agreed frankly. "But it's something that some white GIs who fought alongside black Americans don't agree with." He glanced at Jan and added quietly. "I owe my life to a black sergeant."

Brian caught Murranji's attention. "Hank's like my mate here, isn't he, Murranji?" he said. "Skin colour doesn't seem to worry him at all?"

Murranji Bill grinned and nodded his agreement. "Too right. An' mine's the only skin he's usually after. I reckon he thinks I don't pull my weight."

"Know something, Peg?" Hank said. "I believe the score between your man and me is pretty even. I've finally worked out, every time he thinks I'm behaving like an army sergeant, he starts calling me Boss."

"Just as well you don't know what I call you behind your back, my friend." Murranji looked at Alice and grinned. "Just bribe me with some pie, Alice, an' I'll tell you the most frightening stories about this feller. Fair dinkum, I never knew Yanks were such terrible people."

"Cut it out, Murranji, please," Hank protested. "You'll get me thrown out before I've had a chance to enjoy Alice's pie."

"Just you relax, Hank." Jan smiled. "I'm on *your* side, and I'll make sure you don't leave hungry."

Hank looked at her quickly. The smile that she gave him was direct and conspiratorial. Alice looked at Murranji and winked at him, before she left the room to check on her pies. She reappeared a minute or two later.

"All right, you mob." She grinned. "I'm ready ter serve up, so yer better find a seat at the table."

As one, they rose from their chairs. Hank poured the beer while Alice divided two, large, beefsteak pies into steaming quadrants.

"I'd rather a man drank beer instead of rum," Jan said quietly.

"I see." Hank's eyes crinkled. "You are a straightforward person, aren't you?"

Jan reddened slightly, but she met his eyes and held them. "I don't see the point of not being honest," she said.

"Me neither, Jan," he agreed sincerely.

Brian hungrily eyed his quarter of pie made from prime, Long Creek beef and kidneys. Then he eyed the big, steaming bowl of roast potatoes that Jan had placed on the table.

"This looks great, Mum," he said. "I'll never knock back any tucker that you cook."

"An' how could I forget that, son?"

Hank rose to his feet. "I'd like to propose a toast," he said. "So would you, please, raise your glasses? To absent friends," he toasted. "And especially our mate, Blue. May he rest in peace."

"God bless," responded Alice.

Calum thought that it was a fine meal. The beefsteak pie was delicious, and the apple pie that followed reminded him of the ones that his mother used to make. Around the table the conversation flowed, and happy laughter rang out.

When all of Hank's beer had been drunk, Jan got up and made a big pot of tea. And for ringers who were used to rising every day before first light, the odd, stifled yawn was becoming increasingly apparent.

Finally, Hank stood up and held out his hand to Alice. "That was a wonderful meal, Alice," he said. "Thank you."

Jan turned to Hank. "Tell me," she asked, "if I made the effort to pack a nice, picnic basket, would you have the time to go on a picnic tomorrow?"

Hank smiled broadly. "You betcha," he said. "And Murranji needs time off, because he has to take Peg and Doreen to Big River. And the boss is in Katherine, so what he doesn't know can't hurt him."

"Well, maybe you'd better sit down," Jan said, smiling. "So you can tell me what you like to eat on picnics."

Doreen was smiling too, when she looked at Calum. "This is great," she said. "Now you'll have the time to go for a ride with me tomorrow and show me around."

Calum's face lit up. He promptly decided that tomorrow couldn't come fast enough. "Early tomorrow morning would be good," he said. "Is that all right with you, Peg?"

"You can make it as early as yer like, mate," Peg said with an understanding smile. "My Dor's an early bird, an' she'll be here. That'll save you from havin' ter come to our camp."

When Doreen left, it seemed to Calum that a lot of the light in the room followed along after her. He and Brian left shortly afterward.

"You know, Brian," Calum said. "I don't know what to call your mum. I can't call her Alice because I'm too young."

"If you were my colour, you'd call her Aunty Alice."

"Yeah? Well, I'm burned pretty brown by the sun, so if she doesn't mind, that's what I'll do."

"She won't mind. In fact, she'll be pleased you're showing her respect."

When Hank finally left, Jan saw him to the front door and then, very naturally, came into his arms. They kissed and then, very passionately, kissed again. Both were breathing heavily when they finally said good night.

Walking through the crisp, starry night to the ringer's hut, Hank's thoughts were on Jan. He thought that she was lovely, though her sex appeal was somehow at odds with her serenity because, he decided, it felt a bit like wanting to go to bed with a nun.

Then he began to think about his parents. Of course, had they still been alive and known that he was attracted to Jan, they would've been horrified. Very simply, Jan wasn't white, and she wasn't a Texan. They could've accepted, albeit reluctantly, a non-Texan— but a coloured girl? Definitely not. And if he'd persisted with the relationship, they'd have made it clear to him that he was no longer their son. They would've been quite incapable of seeing that Jan had qualities that Donna would never have, like self-esteem, honesty and strength of character.

Yes, a man got the feeling that Jan was rock solid, he told himself. *And you also got the feeling that once she'd committed herself to somebody, that'd be it.* He knew that he wanted to have a continuing physical relationship with her, but after that, things got a bit hazy. He wondered if her Catholicism would get in the way. Then, of course, most white Territorians were as damn racist as Limeys or Texans. *He knew that he could deal with that but,* he wondered, *if Jan would be able to cope.* For a moment, he felt quite lofty, while he pondered whether or not it'd be fair to have a relationship with her. Then he ruefully smiled to himself. *You're not that goddamn full of principle,* he told himself. *Get real.*

****

Doreen was already waiting for him on the verandah of Alice's cottage. She looked very pretty, and he felt his senses heighten. Suddenly, the sunlight seemed to be a lot brighter and the sky a deeper shade of blue. He was aware of Lady, her mare, standing nearby swishing her tail. Lady had already been saddled.

Doreen came off the verandah, reached out, and touched his arm lightly. "It's real good to see you," she said softly.

"I thought we could also go for a picnic," he suggested. "I've made roast beef sandwiches with fresh bread."

Her face brightened. She left her hand on his arm. "That's beaut. I love picnics. I'll just go and tell Mum we're off."

He watched her walk indoors. She was dressed, as usual, in her floppy, old hat, oversize shirt and trousers. The ache that he now felt inside was a wonderful ache that didn't hurt at all.

When Doreen returned, she came to him, stood on tiptoe and pecked him on the cheek. She grinned impishly. "That's because you're my boyfriend," she said.

He felt tempted to touch his cheek where she'd kissed him. Instead, he stood by Lady's head while she mounted.

They slowly rode toward a little creek that he'd thought would be a nice place to picnic. He was struck by how shiny and bubbly she appeared. *Being with her is nice*, he thought, *because she looks like she's happy just to be with me.*

Doreen looked down at Curaidh. "Your dog's a nice-looking dingo," she said. "And he's always looking up at you."

"He's a fine dog, and we suit each other. Charlie keeps telling me he'll take off my hand when he's older, but Brian doesn't reckon that'll happen. And Brian thinks he's going to be a good, tucker dog too."

"I'm sure Brian'd know best."

Calum grinned. "Brian's been trying to teach me to track, but he gets impatient. He says he can't understand why I don't see things like he does."

"You and Brian get along well, don't you?"

"Too right. He's a true mate, and he's taught me most of what I've learned since I've been up here."

"You know," she said. "I can relax with you because you're always yourself. You don't show off."

He raised his eyebrows and smiled. "I like being with you too," he said. "You act a lot older than you are, you know."

"We all had to grow up quick where I was. Yeah, real quick," she said, frowning.

He sensed that she didn't want to talk about the past.

The spot that he'd chosen gave them a commanding view back, toward the homestead. They tethered the horses side by side and head to tail so that they could swish the flies off each others' faces and then sat down beneath a Coolibah to eat their sandwiches.

Behind them, a little creek tinkled. High above, small, white clouds sped over the blue sky like yacht sails scudding over a wide, blue sea. Birds sang, butterflies fluttered and a frog croaked. And above them, in the Coolibah, a white-collared, green-and-yellow Sacred Kingfisher thoughtfully scrutinized the creek and its banks as it searched for small lizards and fish.

Calum offered Curaidh his last half of a sandwich. It was delicately accepted before being swallowed in one gulp. They both laughed at Curaidh's indecent haste.

"I'd made up my mind to start looking for you after the branding, you know," Calum confessed.

She smiled mischievously. "I'm not patient like you. I couldn't wait that long."

"You're teasing me."

"Only 'cause I like you. If I didn't, I wouldn't bother." She laughed and patted her tummy. "I'm so full," she said. "I couldn't eat another thing."

"That billy's boiling," he said. "I'll get us a mug of tea."

He handed her a steaming mug.

"Ta," she said. "Now, if you sit with your back against this Coolibah, I'll have you to lean against."

She leaned against him and left a hand on his knee. He put his mug on the ground and rested his cheek lightly against the top of her head. "You smell nice," he said.

"It must be all that sugar-'n'-spice stuff," she said. "I thought, seeing as you're my boyfriend, I didn't want to sit miles away from you." She leaned back against his chest. "Mm, you feel comfy."

"You know," he said, "Brian mentioned we'll have to put up with whites who'll give us a hard time."

He felt her stiffen. "Does he think it'd be better if you had a white girlfriend?"

"No way! He was only warning me that going together could make it difficult for both of us. Does that worry you? And will your mum's people give you a bad time?"

"No. And Mum said if they like you, they'll treat you as one of them." She paused. "But if you do ever change your mind about me, you will tell me, won't you?"

"I'll never change. I just hope you don't change your mind about me."

"I won't. I'm like my mum. Once I make up my mind, that's it."

She turned her head and drew his gently down to hers. She kissed him on the cheek and then relaxed again against his chest. "It's funny," she said, changing the subject, "but I felt like giving you a hug that first time I saw you."

"Yeah? Now, that would've given everyone a real shock."

"And just for a moment you didn't hide your eyes, and I saw hurt in them."

"I thought you looked scared. And I wanted to put my arm round your shoulders and tell you not to be frightened."

"When I saw your hurt, I remembered my own. That's what scared me." She giggled. "I wish you had put your arm around me. I would've left it there."

"Was it bad for you at Cord River?"

"Yes. But I never want to talk about it, because I need to forget."

"Your mum told me to be gentle if you got a sudden, fright attack," he said.

"I won't, because I feel safe when I'm with you."

"Mm. But when you're up north, you'll be far away, won't you?"

"Put your arms round my waist so I can hold your hands," she told him. "That's better." Her voice grew definite. "Now, you listen to me, Calum McNicol. I knew I was going to be your girl on that first day. And I knew you wanted me for your girl, so as far as I'm concerned, we've been going together ever since. And I'll be coming down often to stay with the Macs. So you'd better learn to find your way there, 'cause I'll be expecting you to come over whenever I'm down."

"Course I'll come. And are the Macs nice?" he asked.

"They've been lovely."

Calum thought about her living with her mum's people. And he thought that he wouldn't mind living with people like Jalyerri and learning their ways of hunting and fishing and also learning about the bush. Indeed, that very morning, Jalyerri had told him that 'roos could smell water from twelve miles away. Hell, cattle couldn't even smell water in a trough if they were away from it.

"What is it?" she gently asked. "You've gone quiet."

"I was wondering if you'd have to marry someone up there if an uncle told you to?"

"Yes."

"Oh."

She laughed and her eyes danced. She stopped giggling, and her face grew serious. "Don't you dare think about that because it can't happen. You see, Mum never *promise-married* me to anyone." She giggled. "And I swear I'll wait for you to be a man."

"Heck, what do you mean by that?"

She began to chuckle. "Well, I'll stay fifteen so I'll be the right age for you when you reach twenty-one. That's about the age the Old People marry, you know."

"You're teasing me again."

"I know. But I like teasing you, 'cause you get so serious."

"I'll soon be eighteen, you know!"

"You told me that yesterday," she reminded him with a smile.

"You're younger than me, but sometimes, I think you're cleverer than I am."

"Don't think that, please," she said quickly. "You're just right for me, I promise."

"I'm glad you're my girlfriend."

She let go of his hand and unbuttoned her shirt. Then she took his hands and put them inside her shirt and held them against her bare bosom. He didn't think that she was fast, and he was happy just to sit and hold her.

"I'm only doing this 'cause you're my boyfriend, and we'll be apart soon," she told him. "I wouldn't do it if you weren't my boyfriend."

"I know."

She felt round and soft and warm, and the scent of her hair filled his nostrils. He didn't want this to end. And he knew that she'd believed him when he'd told her that having her for his girl was all that mattered.

"What're you thinking about now?" she murmured.

"That I'm happy. And I won't have to wonder any more what your bosom feels like."

"Oh." She paused. "When were you wondering that?"

"In camp. Mostly, before I went to sleep."

"Oh." She was quiet for a moment. "Would you also like to look at me?" she murmured.

He didn't know what to say. He found it hard to admit out loud that he would like to look at her. She sensed his difficulty, got to her knees and slowly turned around. Then she sat back on her calves and slipped her shirt from her shoulders. She stayed motionless like that for some time.

"Now, you also know what I look like," she said shyly. "So you won't have to wonder about that, either."

"You're beautiful, Dor."

"Do you really mean that?"

"Oh, too right."

She smiled mischievously, but her eyes remained soft. "Is it all right if I do up my shirt now?" she asked.

He didn't answer, and they smiled at each other. Finally, she got to her feet.

"I think we should go," she said. "I don't want Mum to worry."

"Yes." He paused. "And I'd like to kiss you again, Dor."

"I also want that. And you never have to ask, you know. 'Cause I want you to kiss me whenever you feel like it."

"Yes."

Their lips met in a long kiss, and he felt a little giddy. They kissed again and held each other tight. And when they finally moved apart, she made no effort to conceal her breasts. It seemed very natural. And he thought that from now on, he'd be able to tell her anything that he'd been thinking about. He looked at her breasts again, and he was very glad that she was his girl.

They picked up their quart pot mugs and put out the fire. As she mounted Lady, Doreen couldn't help thinking about how different he was to her. How he'd got so much pleasure from holding her bosom and looking at it. She giggled to herself. Heck, she couldn't have cared less about what his darra looked like. All she'd wanted was to have his arms around her.

They were within a mile of the homestead when Calum recognized the approaching rider. He slid his Winchester from its sheath and held it in his right hand. When he spoke, he made his voice sound casual.

"See this feller coming? I want to keep Socks between Lady and him. All right?"

"What's wrong?"

"Nothing. I'm just being careful because this feller's real strange."

"Oh."

Ed Smith halted his horse in front of them. He was leering and trying to see past Calum to look at Doreen. He had a pair of war surplus, navy binoculars hanging around his neck. Calum watchfully kept his rifle resting on Socks's neck. He could smell Ed Smith's foul odour and noticed that Ed Smith kept on leering. Then Smith tapped his binoculars before putting his hand in his shirt pocket and withdrawing a bundle of one pound and five pound notes.

"I seen you from me camp," he said. "And I'll give yer four pounds ter hire yer creamy fer ten minutes."

Calum felt rage spread right through his body. He quickly levered a shell into the rifle's breach. "No way, you filthy animal. Turn your horse and ride in front of me. Now!"

"Why're you carryin' on? Shit, she's only a bloody creamy, an' I'm offerin' you four quid. Hell, you should throw in your dog's scalp as well, because four quid's a lot of money. Course, your slut probably wouldn't be worth it, but I'm feelin' generous."

Calum didn't hesitate. He raised the Winchester and fired, without appearing to aim. Ed Smith's hat flew off his head. His look of astonishment quickly turned to one of alarm.

"You're bloody crazy," he cried. "Hang on now. And don't do anythin' else what's stupid, McNicol."

Doreen had been shocked by Ed Smith's smell and then by the dirty way that he'd looked at her. What he'd asked had made her cringe inwardly. God, was this what white men thought of girls like her? But she wasn't frightened. She'd seen how all expression had left Calum's eyes and how his face had turned hard. *He* wasn't frightened. But she couldn't say the same about this horrible man. When his hat had been shot off, fear had chased the colour from his face, and it'd gone grey. He obviously had no idea what Calum would do next, and that frightened him.

"You can see the homestead from here, Smith," Calum coldly said. "Just head for it."

"I need my hat," Ed Smith whined.

"To hell with your hat."

"You're crazy. You could've killed me. You'd 've been charged with murder, you madman."

Emboldened by the thought that he'd given Calum reason to be cautious, he lewdly blew Doreen a kiss. "We'll meet again, girl, an' you'll love it. All your lot do. Yeah, girl, so long as it's a white feller your lot can't get enough."

Calum immediately fired again, and the bullet sang past Ed Smith's right ear. The *crack* of the rifle right behind Smith's horse startled it, and he struggled to bring it under control.

Then Doreen thought about his binoculars. Oh no. This disgusting man was managing to turn something that'd been lovely into something dirty. Tears came to her eyes. Then she tightened her lips. *And* she told herself *that there was no way that she'd let anyone spoil the wonder that she'd seen on Calum's face when he'd looked at her breasts.*

They rode in silence. Now and again, Calum glanced at her and gave her a reassuring smile. But mostly he kept his eyes fixed on Ed Smith's back. When they reached the homestead, Calum spoke briefly.

"Turn your horse, Smith, and go. I'll stay and watch till you're well gone."

He sat on Socks and watched the man put his horse into a canter and head off over the grassy vastness. Ed Smith neither said a word nor gave a backward glance.

Calum didn't tell Doreen, now that Smith had gone, that he'd started to shake inside. And that he needed time to regain his composure. "Dor," he fibbed. "I just want to sit here till he's out of sight. You go on in."

"Don't be too long, please."

"I won't. I promise."

When she'd gone, Calum sat quietly, watching and also willing his breathing to return to normal. Soon the sound of Ed Smith's horse grew faint. Finally, he couldn't see horse and rider any more.

The sound of a horse's hooves behind him made him look over his shoulder. It was Murranji, and his face was set and hard.

"How are you, Murranji?"

"Good. My daughter just told me," Murranji said in a hard voice. "I want a word with that piece of scum. Which way did he head?"

Calum pointed, and Murranji Bill nodded to him. "Are you coming?" He asked. "I don't mind company."

Calum nodded. They turned their horses onto Ed Smith's trail and then put them into a fast canter. At first, Curaidh kept up with them, and then he tired. He dropped back but followed by keeping his nose just above Socks's hoofprints.

"When we come up on Ed Smith, you stay out of it. All right?"

"Yes."

"An' you're smarter than I gave you credit for. I like the way you made that mongrel ride in front of you. You're starting to think fast. That's what'll keep a man alive up here."

"Is Dor all right?"

"Yeah. It's you she was thinking of. She was worried you might shoot the mongrel, but I told her you weren't that stupid."

"I think Dor's special."

"I know you do, son. An' tonight, Peg an' me want you to come an' eat at our campfire." Murranji smiled. "I heard Dor tell her mum when she's with you she forgets about Cord River. And that's good."

"Oh."

"So you'll come tonight?"

"My word."

They spotted Ed Smith's camp half a mile ahead. It wasn't all that far from where Calum and Doreen had picnicked. The area was treeless, save for a couple of straggly-looking, Gidgee acacias. He hadn't heard them. They'd approached with the wind in their faces so that it blew away the sound of their horses' hoofbeats. When they were fifty yards from his camp, they saw him sit up. He'd been resting in his swag. He spotted them and became agitated. Abruptly, Murranji spurred his horse. Ed Smith immediately jumped to his feet and started to run. He kept glancing over his shoulder, but before he could reach the rifle on his still-saddled horse, Murranji had caught up. He took his right boot from its stirrup iron, raised it and kept his leg rigid. Then grasped his saddle, with his right hand, to brace himself against the impending shock. The speed of the running horse caused his boot to slam into the small of Ed Smith's back with such force that Smith was hurled sprawling. Murranji pulled his black gelding back on its haunches and leaped from it. He reached Ed Smith just as he was beginning to rise. Calum was shocked to see Murranji draw his boot back and kick Smith viciously in the face. Ed Smith screamed and covered his face with his hands. Murranji swore at him angrily.

"Fuck you! You're getting yours now, you mongrel bastard!"

Calum saw that Ed Smith had doubled himself up into a ball. He was still holding his face. Murranji kicked him hard again in his side. And Calum heard the dull, bony-sounding crunch of ribs breaking.

Ed Smith screamed shrilly. "You bastard. You've broke my nose and teeth. Stop. Stop."

"I haven't finished. That was *my* girl with McNicol, you filthy pig."

"How was I to know? Stop!"

Murranji grabbed his stock whip from his saddle. Then he began brutally and methodically to whip the screaming dog stiffener across his shoulders and back. Calum saw Smith's cotton shirt rip and come apart. Ugly raised red welts on Ed Smith's bare shoulders and back seemed to grow before his eyes.

"Maybe," Murranji ground out, "this'll help you remember. *Never* go near my girl again. If you even look at her, just once, I'll come after you. And I'll *gut* you like a pig. And you won't be the bloody first. And that's the Gospel bloody truth."

Murranji abruptly stopped whipping Ed Smith. He went to his horse and mounted, without a backward glance. Calum saw that Ed Smith had taken his shaking hands from his face. Blood was pouring from a nose that'd been squashed sideways. Blood also covered his broken front teeth and smashed lips. He began to whimper continuously.

"You bastard," he whimpered. "You'd no right. You bastard."

"I had the right. She's *my* daughter."

Calum was stunned. Murranji had said that he only wanted to have words with Smith, and he'd believed him. He'd thought that Murranji would just warn Smith to stay away from Doreen. Then Calum was filled with a grim foreboding. He was totally certain that Murranji had just started something that'd rebound badly on Long Creek. And what his mother used to prophesy, in Gaelic, came to him and wouldn't leave him. "What goes round, comes round," she'd often warned. And it wasn't just superstition talking either. It was common sense.

They turned their horses and headed for the homestead. Murranji nodded at Calum. "That'll teach the mongrel," he said curtly. "And let that be a lesson to you. If you're going to start something, make sure you get in first with a good one."

"Yes.'

Calum was quiet. He was still stunned by the ferocity of the other's attack. And he was still filled with foreboding.

They saw Curaidh before he saw them. He had his nose to the ground and was following Socks's trail. He wagged his tail and dropped his ears when he recognized them.

"You're a good pup," Calum said. "Just tuck in there beside Socks. We're heading back to see Dor."

He looked across at Murranji. Murranji held his eyes while he spoke. "An' don't you tell Doreen what I did. All right?"

"I understand."

"An', tonight, Dor's cooking something special for you. So make a fuss of her cooking, all right?"

"Yes."

"An' bring your swag. You can have a grog with me an' stay the night."

"Yes."

CHAPTER 12

BRANDING

Before Murranji headed for Big River with Peg and Doreen, he assured Hank that he'd be at their first, branding camp by the time everyone else arrived.

Calum and Doreen were very aware that they wouldn't be seeing each other for the next four months. And before she mounted Lady to catch up with Murranji and her mum, she and Calum held each other tightly and kept kissing passionately.

"Tell me again I'm your girl," Doreen implored.

"You'll always be my girl."

"Tell me again you love me."

"Dor, I've loved you from the moment I first saw you."

"That was when I fell in love with you too."

This was the first occasion on which they had declared their love.

When they finally parted, Doreen openly sobbed. Calum silently stayed beside Lady's head while she tearfully mounted. He stood and watched as she rode toward her parents. Watching her ride away from him, felt like a kick in the guts

****

Murranji and Peg had purposely ridden on ahead so that Doreen and Calum could say their good-byes in private. He grinned at Peg and then spoke in response to her questioning look.

"They put me in mind of a couple of lost souls that've finally found each other," he said, "an' now they have to part."

"Yer've hit it in one, mate," she agreed. "That's jus' what they are. An' yer know, I reckon they is good fer each other."

Murranji smiled at her. Their eyes held, and he saw in them the deep love that she had for him. It was as obvious as the magnificent, mauve profusion offered by a Jacaranda tree when in full bloom.

"I wish I'd really appreciated all those years ago what you were offering me," he said. "But I was like blind Freddie an' never saw it. And I'd be lying if I said I wasn't rapt we're together again."

"Yer know, many's the time I wisht I'd hung aroun' back then," she said. "But I was certain you was after that white sheila, with the red hair, what was always flirtin' with yer."

"Yeah? Well, let me tell you, Peg Shillingsworth, since getting back with you, I'm all of a sudden smiling a lot. It's good just being with you, Peg. An' even better when I'm holding you." He paused. "Did I ever tell you, you're one helluva, good-looking sheila?"

Her eyes widened, and her crow's-feet deepened. "Only the once or twice," she said, smiling. "An' what we has now is real good fer me too, love. An' yer know, you can still shake me up inside, somethin' fierce, when we hit the swag."

He took a deep breath, considered her, and exhaled slowly. "An' I do want to marry you, you know," he declared.

"I'm real flattered, darl. An' I am thinkin' 'bout it."

"About what are you thinking, for Crissake?" he demanded.

"About whether it's fair ter yer? An' how yer'll manage when all them other whites has given yer the brush-off? An' how many bad fights yer'll get inter over me?" She considered him. "Yer do know yer have got me whether we is married or not, don't yer?"

"Oh hell," he groaned. "You're not still fussing about those sorts of things, are you?"

"Darl, these is all-important matters."

"The only important thing to me is having you for my wife an' giving our girl parents who are married." He winked an exaggerated wink. "I've never been married before, so you'd be getting a brand-new husband with *no* miles on the clock."

She grinned back at him. "Don't you go tryin' ter get round me."

"Well, please don't take too long, Peg. I'm starting to worry you'll disappear on me again."

"Yer not *that* lucky, darl!"

"Well, you have done it once, you know," he told her grumpily. "So I do worry."

She regarded him and saw that his face had grown utterly miserable. And all the love for him that so filled her rose up within her. She found it hard to breathe.

"How come yer always get round me?" she said feeling choked up. "Awright, darl," she continued, swallowing. "If it means that much, I will marry you, right after the brandin'. So long as you get the permission we need from Native Affairs."

"I'll write them when we get to the River. Now you're not just saying that to shut me up?"

"No, darl, I'll be your wife when yer get back."

"Promise?" he asked earnestly.

"Cross my heart, darl." She looked at him steadily. "An' have yer tol' yer sheila in the camp, at the Creek, it's over?"

"Yes, I have, Peg. An' her uncle too."

"Good."

****

Hank had decided that it was sensible to start mustering the northwest boundary that Long Creek shared with Big River. As convention dictated, he sent a message advising the Big River Head Stockman of his plans so that a joint muster could be arranged. This courtesy was designed to ensure that all boundary, cleanskin cows and calves, in this land without fences, would be equally divided.

Both Murranji and Jack Kelly, who had signed on for the branding, knew Johnno Morris. Johnno, Big River's Head Stockman, was a spare-looking, longtime Territorian who'd been working for the Macdonalds on and off for twenty-five years. And of course, Jack Kelly had been doing all the breaking at Big River for as long as Johnno could remember. They greeted each other warmly.

"When are we goin' ter see yer, Jack?" Johnno asked. "There's a fair few colts what need breakin'."

"I reckon them colts'll keep till after the brandin', eh?"

"I reckon. An' I'll pass on ter the Macs, what yer said."

'How're they goin'?" Jack Kelly asked.

"Slowin' down some. But I wouldn't tell 'em that."

"No?"

Johnno shook his head. "Definitely not," he said, with feeling. "Last time that damn Alasdair give me a payout, I reckon he just about stood on me toes so I couldn't get away."

"That'd be Alasdair." Jack Kelly nodded his head and frowned. "The problem with Alasdair," he ventured, "is he's bored nowadays. And, I reckon, he's started his second childhood."

"That so?" Johnno said, raising his eyebrows. "Then he's turned inter a quick-tempered kid, awright."

"Yeah? Though Murranji reckons now he's bin lookin' after Peg an' her girl, he's bein' less naughty."

"I don' know nothin' 'bout any women at the homestead," Johnno said hastily. He changed the subject. "Tell yer what, Jack," he suggested, "why don' you an' Murranji come over ter my camp, ternight? An' bring that Yank with yer. Yer'll get a good feed, an' we'll have a bit of a natter 'bout the old days. Jeez, but it's getting' borin' now. I tell yer, this country has now got civilized an' dull. Not even any big cattle duffing!"

"Yer on, Johnno," Jack Kelly said. "I'll bring a bottle, an' we'll educate young Hank on how ter drink, Territory style."

Next morning, Hank was suffering from a near-debilitating rum hangover. His head felt as if a small jackhammer was pounding away inside it, and he was as dehydrated as the heat-struck foal of a mare whose milk had run dry. And to top it off, he was enduring the embarrassment of uncontrollable, dry retches. Jack Kelly, by contrast, was maintaining such a cheerful demeanour that Hank sourly thought that there was absolutely no goddamn justice in the world. And to top things off, that damn Murranji was looking as if all he'd to drink all night was lemonade. Hank continued to regard Murranji sourly because he didn't think that Murranji's was an entirely solicitous grin.

"Put rum in your coffee, Hank," Murranji cheerily suggested. "Some hair of the dog'll get you feeling better in no time."

"God no," Hank groaned. "I'd rather feel *worse*."

Following breakfast, they commenced the routine that they'd follow for the next four months. By then, the Wet would be on them, and as well, the calves would've lost so much condition that they couldn't take the shock of being branded.

Branding, on this particular day, was proving to be productive because their mob contained a larger-than-usual number of breeders and cleanskin calves. Hank, Murranji and Jack Kelly were on the bronco horses. The others were around a branding fire that'd been lit near the short, fence-type structure made from solid, bush timber called a bronco panel. The gear on a bronco horse intrigued Calum. It comprised a wide, leather breastplate that was firmly attached to the saddle and girth, plus a fifteen-foot, green hide rope, which was securely buckled on. And which was used to drag roped calves to the bronco panel.

They were managing to get through forty-odd calves an hour. The day's temperature was around ninety degrees, though it was much hotter next to the branding fire. And the heat-blurred day distorted the figures of the ringers and the outlines of the wheeling, milling, bawling mob of Shorthorns. And, always, there was the unmistakable smell of distressed cattle, coupled with the cloying odour of the excrement that'd run down the back legs of those beasts, which'd been so unnerved that they'd involuntarily voided their bowels. And the air was filled with the hiss and smell and smoke from burned hair and hide, plus the bawling of cattle. And through it all, the odd yet-to-be-branded, small calf, concerned only with its own pressing hunger, jerked at a teat and butted its mother's bag to tell her to let her milk down.

Jalyerri tried to convince Calum that scuttling through the fence was not the best way to avoid the cow angrily charging the ringer that was nearest to her bawling calf.

"Chit down and chuckim dirt," he smilingly advised. "More better 'n jumpin' through fence."

Calum wasn't convinced. It was one thing to watch Jalyerri squat down, when charged, till the *coola* bugger was a couple of yards away. And then throw handfuls of dirt in its eyes to make it veer right or left. But he wasn't overly keen to try it himself. And whenever he heard

Jacky Jacky yell, "Cutchacutchera," he'd be through the fence like a startled rabbit. When he'd returned to the fire the first time, he'd looked enquiringly at Brian.

"I know cutchacutchera means 'move quick smart,' but what else was he saying?" Calum unashamedly asked.

"He was just saying you can move quicker 'n a cut cat."

"Oh."

The day was getting hotter. Hank, on his lathered-up bronco horse, Boy, dragged up another bull calf. It was quickly dropped on its side. Calum bent its left foreleg double from the knee, held it in place with a shin, put a foot on the right leg and slit its right ear. Brian dragged the left, hind leg back and forced the right one up and forward with his foot. Jalyerri quickly castrated and then branded it.

Jack Kelly's horse dragged up a struggling cow and, in the process, created a bigger-than-usual, dust cloud. "Here's a 'lumpy,' fellers," he spat out through dust-caked lips.

Calum and Jalyerri leg-roped and threw her. She had a large abscess growing on the underside of her jaw. Brian expertly knifed it, waited for the mixture of blood and pus to stop oozing and then liberally covered the incision with tar.

"You'd think," Brian observed, "that some of the really bad 'lumpies' weren't going to make it, but they do. Amazing."

Shortly afterward, Murranji dragged up a cow with an in-growing horn, which, if not straightened, would soon curl right round and start embedding itself in her cheek. Calum'd been told about such beasts. Indeed, Brian'd said that he'd once seen a bullock with a horn curled round, so much that the horn was beginning to grow into its brain. Jalyerri didn't muck around. He picked up the iron bar, lying next to the bronco panel, and levered the offending horn well away from the cow's cheek. He grinned widely at Calum.

"Me feller fix 'im. Prop-er-lee."

Calum had been watching Jalyerri and Jacky Jacky eagerly grab the castrated testicles and then toss them onto the branding fire. When they were cooked, they were quickly devoured. He couldn't contain his curiosity.

"Why you fellers eatem balls?" he asked Jacky Jacky.

"Oh yeah. Eatem balls make me feller strong, awright."

Brian bent down and, while putting a branding iron into the fire, gave a brief guffaw. "That's bullshit," he stated. "They reckon it's going to give 'em strength in one place only. An' I reckon Jacky Jacky's the one that needs it most, 'cause he's got two wives and Jalyerri's only got one." He turned to Jalyerri with a grin. "What for you feller eatem balls? Only one missus belong you."

Jalyerri looked at Jacky Jacky and started laughing. Soon, both were convulsed with mirth. Finally, Jalyerri managed an answer. "My missus beat any two b'long him feller!"

Following that pronouncement, both Jalyerri and Jacky Jacky again dissolved into laughter.

"There's one thing you've got to admit about Murries," Brian said. "They're always happy an' laughing. An' I've never seen one going around with a long face, like so many white fellers."

"Do you really think that eating calf balls will turn you into a better husband?" Calum asked.

"It's best you don't know, mate," Brian teased.

"Come on, Brian, can calf balls help?" Calum asked impatiently.

"Look, mate," Brian grinned. "I hope you haven't got any bad thoughts about Murranji's daughter!"

"No way!" Calum protested. "She's not that sort of girl."

Brian grinned to himself. He often found Calum's naïveté amusing. "I suppose it's all right then," he stated solemnly, "to go ahead an' tell you. An' I'm pleased to say I haven't sprung you scoffing any balls on the quiet."

"Shut up, Brian," Calum admonished. "That's not nice."

Brian grinned at Calum, and his deepening crows'-feet cracked the layer of red dust around his eyes. "If the person eating them really believed they'd improve his fucking, then I reckon they'd work well," he said.

"Bloody hell!"

"But just you remember," Brian warned, "if I catch you eating even *one*, I'll be honour bound to tell Murranji what you've been up to."

"Brian!"

****

During their brief lunch break, Jack Kelly was his usual affable self. "I tol' yer I had a dingo once," he told Calum conversationally. "An' he was smarter 'n' any station dog I ever come across. An' he picked up quick when I wasn't bein' fair. Then he'd go an' lay under a bush an' sulk. Now you be sure ter teach yours proper. He'll learn good, an' one day, if he has ter, he'll give his life for you. Mine did."

"Are you telling it dinkum, Jack?" Calum asked.

"Too right. An' I'll also tell yer one more thing, Calum."

"Yeah?"

"A dingo's not a house pet. I learned that the hard way."

"What happened?"

"Years ago, me an' me wife, God rest her soul, stayed a spell with me parents in Darwin. Anyways, I thought me dog'd be awright in the back garden at night. I knew I couldn't have 'im in the house 'cause he'd o' felt trapped an' would o' wrecked it."

"And?" Calum asked.

"First, he chewed all the cowhide strips on their garden chairs. Then he killed their terrier. An' he moved so sudden, I never had the chance ter grab him. I reckon he must o' got tired of its yappin'."

"For Crissake!"

"Too bloody right." Jack Kelly took a large gulp of tea. He considered Calum thoughtfully. "An' take my advice, young feller. Make the time ter learn from Jalyerri," he said. "I've watched him, an' he likes yer. He'll teach yer how ter merge in an' belong in this country. An' ter appreciate what *Kunapipi* created."

"Who's Kunapipi?" Calum asked.

"She's the ol' lady who walked outta the sea in the nor'east, young feller. She had a dingo with her, called Wanjin, that was her scout an' protector. Us whites call Wanjin the Dog Star. An' over her shoulder, Kunapipi carried a special *dilly* bag."

"Yes?"

Jack Kelly paused and lit the cigarette that he'd been rolling. He inhaled deeply, exhaled slim steams of smoke, and tossed his makings over to Hank. "And in it," he continued, "she carried all the Shades that she needed to create all the good things yer'll find in this country. Like honey, yams, and Barramundi fish. An' Paperbark trees what yer can use ter make everythin', from rafts ter bandages, ter babies' shawls. But whatever's bad, like snakes, mosquitoes, floods an' droughts was created by somebody else."

"Who?" Calum asked, very interested.

Jack Kelly grinned, reached over and briefly placed his hand on Calum's shoulder.

"Somebody else can fill yer in on that, young feller." He got to his feet. "Anyway, it's time I earned me keep."

"You like the Aborigines, Jack, don't you?" Hank said.

"Yeah, an' I respect 'em plenty. Enough even ter marry a dark, half-caste lady. An' I was real proud ter call her me wife an' take her home ter meet me parents. I'm sorry ter say, they couldn't take ter her. But that was their loss."

"I see. All right, fellers," Hank said, tossing out his mug's coffee dregs, "you've had your nose bags on. Let's go and brand some calves."

****

That evening, Calum leaned back against a tree stump. He was content and relaxed, despite it being a sticky tropical evening. Charlie's battered steak, with fresh bread, had been delicious. Now, he idly watched the camp fire flames dance, and its coals grow ever redder till they cracked and broke up in a small shower of sparks before burning up fiercely. And he listened to the flow of conversation around him. This was the one time that they were all together though, right now, Nugget was with Johnno Morris, ensuring an even division of cleanskins. The evening fire was always their principal forum, and Calum never tired of listening and learning.

"Jack," he asked, "which star is Kunapipi?"

"See that small group of seven stars shaped like an' ol' woman?" Jack Kelly replied, pointing. "An' right behind her is the dilly bag she's draggin'. It's the sort of triangle that's followin' her." Jack Kelly paused and then added for Calum's benefit, "Kunapipi's group is the cluster we whites call the Seven Sisters. And the lot that's her dilly bag is the one we call Taurus."

Jack Kelly turned to Hank. "I'm curious, Hank. What on earth made yer decide ter come all the way ter the Territory?"

"I'd had enough of the States, and I don't like Europe. Too crowded. Hell, I couldn't even enjoy a swim. It felt like I was swimming in people, not water!"

"Now, don' yer go swimmin' in the Big River, Hank, or a gator'll grab yer," Jack Kelly warned.

"Are there alligators in it?" Hank asked incredulously.

"We call 'em gators, but they're really saltwater crocs, mate. They come up the rivers an' creeks ter breed. An' they also go across the floodplains durin' the wet. Then, when the plains dry out, they get trapped in the billabongs. They'll take a bullock or a horse, no worries. Yeah, they'll even come out at night an' grab a sleepin' Murri who's forty yards from a riverbank."

"For Crissake," Hank swore, alarmed.

"Yer jus' need ter respect 'em," Jack Kelly said. "Know yer bein' watched all the time. An' don't get inter habits like cleanin' fish at the same place every day. 'Cause a gator'll have seen that, an' one time yer do it, he'll grab yer!" Jack Kelly lit himself another cigarette. "Yeah," he said reflectively, "them bloody gators'll *still* be here long after we humans are gone from the face o' this earth."

"What makes you say that, Jack?" Hank asked.

"Because they is amazin', damn lizards. They can stay underwater fer five hours, without breathin'. They can go more'n a year without a feed. They see at night, better 'n a cat, an' they can sniff out tucker from three mile away."

"Unbelievable!" Hank exclaimed.

"You know, Murranji," Jack Kelly said, glancing at his friend and then giving Hank and Calum a quick look. "I reckon the odd, new chum who gets attracted to a nice, half-caste, Territory girl doesn't have a clue about what he's letting himself in for. What d'yer reckon, Murranji? Should we enlighten 'em or leave 'em ter their ignorance?"

Hank tossed his makings to Murranji. "If you're going to enlighten us," he suggested, "you better get a bottle, or else it'll be a goddamn, dry argument."

"I'll get us a grog," Jack Kelly said, "but only 'cause yer need the drinkin' practice, Hank."

"Just piss-off and get a bottle or two, Jack."

Hank found himself thinking, yet again, about Jan. He couldn't help comparing her to Donna. Hell, when Donna had kissed him and had moved her body against his, he'd known, from the start, that she viewed her body as a currency to be exchanged for favours; or, more usually, extra money with which to go shopping, in San Antonio, for "mah *fem-in-ine* bits and pieces, dahlin'." But Jan was different. When they'd kissed good-bye she'd freely responded to his increasingly passionate kiss, and had held her body against him as though she'd enjoyed the feel of his. He doubted if the word *artifice* existed in her vocabulary.

More and more green frogs, in the billabong, had begun to croak. And the low, harsh cry of a dumpy-looking, cinnamon-coloured, yellow-legged Nankeen Night Heron on the other side echoed across the water. While above, numerous, furry, red-brown Little Red Flying-foxes were silently winging their way toward the eucalypt forest, where these little bats'd find eucalypt honey. It was also where they'd roost.

Hank held out his quart pot mug and watched the rum being poured.

"But you know, Jack," Murranji abruptly complained. "It's the damn Churches that give me the shits. Fair dinkum, right from the start, they've been calculating buggers. An' they're supposed to be the conscience of the country. Instead, they've been as cunning as shit house rats in the way they connive among themselves an' help the Government in its stinking treatment of black mums and their yeller kids!"

"Hang on," Hank remonstrated, holding up his hand. "I spent some months in Sydney, and nobody talked about that sort of thing. And it was never in the newspapers or on the radio. Look," he continued, "I know Jan and Brian were never taken to a mission, but Doreen was. So what?"

They were quiet while Murranji topped up their mugs. Then Jack Kelly, remembering the son that he'd never been able to find, grew angry and resentful.

"You tell 'em, Murranji," he ground out. "You tell 'em how these righteous, bloody Churches have been quicker 'n rats up a drainpipe in helpin' the Government steal heaps an' heaps o' yeller kids. Shit, it's enough ter make a man puke."

"Are you kidding?" Hank asked. "Like I said, no one in Sydney even mentioned it."

Murranji took another big swallow from his mug and thought *that it was just as well that Peg wasn't watching him.* He made himself think clearly, and then he spoke matter-of-factly.

"You see, Hank," he explained, "the Federal Government decided, about fifteen years ago, to grab yeller kids and assimilate them. An' it's supposed to take about five generations to breed out all that degenerate, black blood. And after that, there won't be any yeller kids around, 'cause everyone'll be snowy white." He paused. "An' that's the main reason we've got a law that says it's illegal for a white feller to fuck a Murri woman."

"You're joshing me, aren't you?" Hank asked, stunned.

"You reckon, eh?" Murranji smiled sardonically. "Well, how come the Methodists rushed off when the Government asked them seven years ago to build a Croker Island Mission? An' the Catholics built Garden Point on Melville Island that same year? An' then the Anglicans went and made their Groote Eylandt one much, much bigger?"

"I have no idea why."

"Well, I'll tell yer why," Murranji angrily spat out. "'Cause more 'n' more, the coppers were sifting the camps an' grabbing four-an' five-year-olds, as well as older, yeller kids from their mums. An' taking them ter these mission stations. An' also, to orphanages an' other places, in Darwin an' Alice Springs."

"Jesus!"

"And He hasn't been much help," Murranji grimly said. "An' when these kids are let out, they're grown up, they're in the white an' they've forgotten their culture. An' even where they used to live."

"Christ, is that why I never see any older, coloured kids in Long Creek camps?" Hank queried, the penny dropping.

"Now, you're catching on," Murranji said, grimacing. "An' of course, brothers and sisters are separated. The boys are taken to Alice Springs an' Darwin. To places like the Bungalow an' Kahlin. An' the girls are taken to places like Groote Eylandt an' the Roper River Mission. Of course, when they're grown up, they won't marry anyone who's been taken, in case they marry their brother or sister."

Hank became agitated. He'd always been affected whenever he'd witnessed or had heard about cruelty to children or to animals. He stood up and walked a few paces out into the night before he returned. He silently held out his mug to Jack Kelly. Then he sat down, sipped his rum, and retreated into his own thoughts. *Christ*, he thought, *was this really the world that I fought for? Where an unfeeling Government and its Christian allies are clinically removing kids from their mothers? And are engaging in some sort of despicable, biological-engineering experiment?*

"Obviously," he sighed, "because the churches are backing the Government, ordinary citizens must think that this assimilation business is perfectly acceptable."

Murranji Bill laughed derisively. "The Churches aren't just backing the Government, mate," he said. "The Government couldn't bloody well have this policy, unless they could count on the Churches to run the missions an' orphanages."

"Sweet Jesus," Hank exclaimed. "I feel desperately sorry for these kids. Not only have they been stolen, but they're also at the mercy of every warped being, who worms his or her way into these institutions."

"I don't follow you," Murranji said.

"I'm talking about a certain type of people who worm their way into positions where they have authority over children. They seek these positions for one reason only, and that's to abuse or sexually molest the kids in their care."

"For God's sake," Murranji exclaimed. Then he groaned, "Oh hell. Please, no."

"What is it, Murranji?" Hank asked.

"Nothing," Murranji said fiercely. "Nothing at all."

"Those poor, poor kids," Hank lamented. "They've got about as much hope as lambs in a slaughterhouse. You know," he mused, "the day will come when people will want to know why every cleric in every church didn't preach against this abomination. And didn't preach against it every week from *every* goddamn pulpit in the land!"

Calum stood up. His head was reeling. "I'm tired," he said tersely, "from listening and trying to understand everything that's been said. I'm off. See you in the morning."

"See yer, Calum!"

"And," Hank called after him, "tomorrow's the last day we muster breeders and calves before we give it away and head back to the home station."

"Yes."

****

Next morning, they left to commence their final muster. Curaidh was now old enough to accompany them. And once Brian and Calum had dropped off to start their sweep, he'd learned to fall back some thirty yards so that he wouldn't spook the Shorthorns that were being mustered.

Brian was riding Bitch. As usual, she'd tried to bite him when he'd been doing up her girth. But now, when he knew that he'd be riding her, he carried a large needle that he'd threaded into his shirt. And when he was going to be near her head, he held it in his left hand. Then, as soon as she swung her head around to bite, he'd jab her in the lip. She'd always start and toss her head. Invariably, Calum would see bafflement in her long-lashed brown eyes. To date, she'd bluffed every ringer who'd ridden her and being jabbed didn't stop her from wanting to take a piece out of Brian.

"I think you're making progress with her, Brian," Calum observed, while stroking Socks's neck. "But it'll take time. She's one dinkum, dedicated biter."

"Don't I know it! By Jove, but she's caught me a couple of bad ones."

"Who told you about that needle trick?"

"Jack Kelly suggested a thorn. What that man doesn't know about horses would fit onto the back of a postage stamp."

"I've been doing some thinking about last night," Calum said. "And when we get our run, I don't want any coppers or ministers anywhere near the place."

"Are you having a be-kind-to-black-fellers day, mate?"

"Maybe. But yeller fellers *aren't* included."

"Shit, what've I done?" Brian removed his hat to let what little breeze there was cool his head. "She's a warm one, all right," he remarked.

"Yeah. And it's just as well we're turning it up tomorrow, because all the horses are losing condition fast. There must be twenty that can't be ridden 'cause they're girth-chafed."

"I've seen 'em," Brian said.

"Listen, mate," Calum asked, "could you tell me the quickest way to Big River?"

Brian glanced across at Calum. He had a twinkle in his eye. "Are you riding or walking?" he slyly asked.

"Riding, of course!"

"Well, *that's* got to be the quickest, hasn't it?"

"Brian!"

They'd been the final pair to begin mustering their arc. Brian decided to complain about it, not that it would do any good, except make him feel better.

"Damn it! We'll be the last ones back. And on the last day too."

"I'm not worried about that. But it means we'll be mustering that Bay of Biscay country, with all the gorges and ravines that the cattle love going into. I reckon there'd be a ton of myall blacks living there, who could easily throw spears," Calum said apprehensively

"Are you dinkum worried?"

"My word."

"Well, stuff the beasts that have gone into those gorges. We'll leave 'em. What Mr. Jackson doesn't know won't hurt him," Brian asserted.

"That'll do me!" Calum uttered thankfully.

They mustered for the rest of the morning. It was now well into October, and the parched countryside had long surrendered any moisture. It was as dry as a sun-struck bone, and the soil appeared to have shrivelled up from the heat. Even from Socks's back, Calum could smell its dryness. The red dust was now merciless, in the way that it dried and clogged throats and nasal passages. And in the final lead-up to the Wet, the land would only become drier and dustier.

It'd passed noon, and Calum was coming out of a shallow ravine when he felt Socks stumble and immediately start to limp. He jumped off, gave Socks's head a quick cuddle, and then picked up the problem front hoof. A stone was wedged between shoe and frog. He pried it loose with his clasp knife, but when he walked Socks, he saw that his horse was limping badly. Brian cantered over.

"What's up, mate?"

"Stone bruise. I can't ride him."

"Bloody hell."

"You know the billabong back there?" Calum said. "The one with the big, old Ghost Gum?"

"Yeah."

"I'll camp there. Maybe tomorrow, you can bring me another horse and keep me company till my mate here can walk back to the home station, providing he doesn't have to carry me."

"Yeah, but before I go, check to see you've plenty of bullets an' matches, mate."

Calum checked one of the leather pouches on his belt. Like any ringer, in addition to a pouch containing his clasp knife, he wore one containing matches plus another that held his watch. Satisfied that he'd plenty of matches, he checked his saddlebag to make sure that he had enough cartridges.

"I'm okay," he said. "And don't forget to bring flour, baking soda, and that other stuff so we can make damper."

"Yeah. All right, I'll be off. I better see how many of this mob I can get back on my own."

"See you, Brian."

"Hooroo, mate."

Calum watched as Brian swung Bitch around and headed back to the mob of cattle. Then he turned to Socks, gave him another cuddle, took off his bridle, and put a lead rope on him.

"Come on, pup," he said to Curaidh. "Let's go and check out this billabong."

CHAPTER 13

THE KADITJE MAN

Calum walked slowly, mindful of Socks. The air was hot and sticky, and the red earth released puffs of powdery dust every time a boot or hoof made contact with it. He had a quick look skyward. The cloudless void wasn't offering even a hint of compassion. Ahead, the billabong's margins shivered and shimmered behind a heat haze. Calum began to look forward to a swim.

"I reckon we're spending time here, fellers," he remarked conversationally. "And it's a pity I don't have a fishing line because there'd be some big Catfish in this waterhole."

On arrival, he became aware that the billabong was communicating a strong feeling of serenity and wondered whether it could be a sacred waterhole. He studied his surroundings. The still surface of the jade-green water mirrored the red-gold tones of the high sandstone face on the other side. And at its base, he noticed a heavily built Yellow-Spotted Monitor, which was sunning itself in the open. The five-foot-long lizard, reddish-brown on top, and with bands of large, black spots interlaid with bands of dark-edged, pale-yellow spots, soon smelled Curaidh. Alarmed, it promptly scuttled off and disappeared in among the sandstone.

On Calum's side was a huge Ghost Gum. And above the billabong, he noticed a Frangipani and some majestic-looking, tall Paperbarks, with their wide-spreading, leafy branches; also, some markedly green

Pandanus trees, which, as usual, displayed their distinctive, flopped-over frondage. And peacefully basking on a log that protruded above the waterline, Calum noticed a Mertens' Water Monitor. The yard long lizard had a dark-brown back, *which looked,* he thought, *as if it'd been daubed with a profusion of yellow spots.* It was sunning itself, and Calum knew that if disturbed, it'd drop into the water and would remain submerged till it was satisfied that any danger had long gone.

He unsaddled Socks, stroked his neck, and then turned him loose. "You're a good mate, Socks," he said. "And how come you still like me, when I ride you over such stony ground?"

Socks briefly nuzzled Calum's cheek before turning and lowering his head to graze on some tufts of dried grass. Calum looked at Curaidh, who was lying, stomach-down, with his head resting on his front paws.

"I don't know about you, pup, but I'm going to have a swim and wash my clothes," he said, shedding his boots and clothes. "Come on, you also need a wash. And we don't have to worry about gators 'cause we're too far from any river. Could be freshies here, though. But Brian reckons these freshwater crocs only grow to about eight feet. And they won't bite you unless you annoy 'em."

The shallow water around the edge of the billabong had been warmed by the sun, but the deeper water, farther in, was refreshingly cool. Calum took his time rinsing out his clothes. Curaidh, after a splashing frolic with his master, now lay near its edge. Calum relaxed.

"This is the life, pup. Honestly, the sweating I do in that bronco yard, wrestling calves next to a hot, branding fire, is real hard work. This," he said, floating on his back, "is my idea of how to spend a hot day while being paid."

Gentle *coos* came from some tumbled-down sandstone on the opposite side. It was a pair of newly arrived Spinifex Pigeons. Calum thought that they were attractive-looking birds, with their black-barred wings, sandy-rufous breasts and backs, and pointed, vertical crests. He watched them drink and then depart as suddenly as they'd come, leaving the three of them in possession of this serene, small oasis that Kunapipi had tucked away in one tiny corner of her vast, dusty and burnt-brown land.

Finally, Calum left the water, wrung out his clothes, and spread them over sun-hot rocks. Completely naked, save for his hat, he collected his rifle and found a smooth, shady rock on which to sit while his clothes dried. He was enjoying the sensuous feel of a tiny breeze on his naked body when he heard the grunting of feral pig. He immediately levered a cartridge into the rifle's breech.

Across the billabong a half-grown, ears-flopping, black sow was snuffling at the ground with her mobile nose, while she moved toward the water. He aimed and squeezed the trigger. The rifle's *crack* agitated a following sow with her brood of piglets. Calum rested a hand on Curaidh's shoulder and watched the sow's reactions. She apparently decided that she was sufficiently unsettled to seek another waterhole. He yelled at her and waved his arms to accelerate her departure. He had no intention of going near the pig that he'd shot till she was well gone. He knew that feral sows, with piglets, were very aggressive. After putting on his boots, he took his clasp knife from its pouch and crossed the creek above the billabong. The half-grown sow lay dead in her rapidly drying blood. Already, flies were buzzing on blood, still oozing from her mouth and head wound. Quickly, he slit the carcass from its jawline to well into its chest cavity to bleed it. Then he gutted it and covered it with leafy branches before collecting wood for the fire that he'd light later.

After washing his hands and then dressing, he and Curaidh briefly reconnoitered their surroundings. Up creek, on the way back, he noticed a deposit of healing pipe clay and rubbed some on a cut that Curaidh had on his flank. He also took some with him.

When the day had cooled, he butchered the pig into portions that'd roast quickly, carried them to his lit fire and started cooking. The air became filled with the rich aroma of roasting pork, the smell of wood smoke and the sizzle of pig fat. Calum saw that Curaidh had started to salivate and that his eyes were fixed on the roasting meat. He grinned at him.

"Not long now, pup. Just be patient. Pork meat needs to be well cooked, you know."

Calum started involuntarily, when his dog suddenly leaped to its feet. He was alarmed to see that the hackles all along Curaidh's neck and back were fully erect and that he had drawn his lips right back in a silent snarl. Calum forced himself to breathe right out, while he slowly reached for his rifle. He knew that he needed to appear calm, so he tried to look nonchalantly in the direction indicated by Curaidh. At first, he didn't see the stationary figure, and when he did, he continued to check the surroundings to see whether or not this apparition was alone. He couldn't see anybody else, and Curaidh was only concerned with this one, motionless figure. Putting down his rifle, Calum indicated the roasting meat and beckoned. After some hesitation, the figure began limping toward him.

Calum had never seen an old man like this one. Grey, body hair and copious, red dust coated his skeletally thin frame. His matted, long, white hair hung loose and was also covered in dust. The whites of his eyes were red-veined, and the slit septum of his nose, which held a bone, nose peg, dangled weirdly below wide nostrils. But it was the old man's body that really caught Calum's attention. It bore numerous scars, but they weren't the usual ritualistic ones. These were the result of intricate brandings and knife work into which warm ashes had been rubbed to produce the raised, patterned ridges and entangled motifs. The man's only clothing was a wide, black, belly band, woven from human hair, and a near-knee-length *narga*. His belly band held a quartz knife, fire-making equipment and boomerangs. In his right hand, the old man held a woomera, and in his left were spears, none of which had modern, steel heads.

Instinctively, Calum knew that his visitor wouldn't speak Creole. He indicated that the old man should seat himself. There was hesitation before his visitor limped forward and sat down. And when the old man fixed his eyes on Calum's, Calum had the strangest feeling that the old man was looking into every corner of his soul.

Then the ancient one moved his hand and lightly rested it on Calum's arm, and Calum felt himself beginning to relax. Soon his body felt weightless, and every sense seemed to have sharpened. Then, like pus draining from a wound, the fear and loathing that he felt for his father drained away. He felt lighter, but his senses remained heightened, and he became much more aware of his surroundings. He could easily smell the clean, dry smell of the earth and also the individual smell of every eucalypt and acacia around him. Everything was distinct and quite separate. Even he was apart and despite the presence of the old man, Curaidh and an interested Socks, Calum felt that he was now on a completely different plane. He realized, with a start, that he'd become as one with his surroundings and that the burden of his past had slipped from his shoulders and would never again tug him backward. That only his future with Doreen now beckoned.

The pork was cooked. Calum blinked his eyes once or twice and then placed three nice pieces on a strip of paperbark and passed them to his visitor. He felt genuine warmth toward the old man. He fed Curaidh. Then, in an effort to convey feelings of friendship, he rose and went to his saddlebag and returned with matches and twists of tobacco. He sat down next to the old man and offered them to him. Again the red-veined eyes opened wide, and a faint smile appeared and stayed on the old man's lips while he carefully placed them in his dilly bag.

Calum returned his attention to his own unfinished pork. He ate it and, about five minutes later, began to feel very drowsy. The last thing that he remembered was his visitor supporting his head and then gently resting it on the inside of a saddle flap.

****

It was midmorning when Calum awoke. He felt groggy and immediately saw that Curaidh also wasn't himself. He forced himself to sit up. There was no sign of the old man. It was only then that he became conscious of the stinging that was coming from the inside of his left forearm. Pipe clay had been smeared there, across a three-square-inch area. He walked to the water, washed it off, and was astonished to see what appeared to be the raised, outline tattoo of a snake's head. No wonder it was stinging, he thought. He gently washed his forearm and then reapplied pipe clay to the incisions.

He still felt groggy, so he lay down next to Curaidh and tried to sleep. He hoped that his headache would go away even if he couldn't get to sleep.

Brian's loud "coo-ee" rudely awakened him. Brian was riding Bitch and had Stupid on a lead rope. Socks stopped grazing, threw up his head and gave a loud whinny. Brian raised his right hand.

"I see you're still living," he called. "Did you get anything to eat last night?"

"A young pig."

Brian indicated Socks. "How is he?"

"Hardly limping this morning. The bruise isn't as bad as I first thought, but he'll need another couple of days before he can walk any distance."

"I'm in no hurry," Brian said.

Calum watched Brian unsaddle Bitch. He was amused to see that, though she eyed him sourly, she made no attempt to bite. He got to his feet and walked over to Socks to stroke him. The bay nickered at his approach and then rubbed his head hard enough against Calum's chest to unbalance him.

"Haven't I told you not to do that," Calum scolded. "Using me to fix your itches is bad manners."

He grabbed Socks's head, held it firmly and rubbed his face for him. Socks then stood placidly with his head at rest against Calum's chest.

Brian looked up at the cloudless sky. "Bit muggy today," he said. "Are you coming in for a dip?"

"Yeah, why not. I'm feeling crook, and a swim might help."

"You probably didn't cook the pig meat enough," Brian admonished. "Haven't I always told you to cook it right through, an' then some?"

"Yeah, yeah."

Calum joined Brian in the water. It washed the pipe clay from his forearm. Brian noticed the tattoo and frowned.

"What's that thing on your arm?" he asked.

Calum showed him the incisions and recounted the events of the previous evening. Brian closely studied the tattoo before standing up and heading for the shore.

"Shit! I've got to have a look around," he said.

Calum watched his naked friend carefully study the ground all around the campsite. He was envious that Brian, when in bare feet, never seemed to stand on anything that hurt.

"Well?" Calum asked impatiently.

"Had to be that Kaditje man. I saw where he sat when watching over you an' your dog. An' I saw where he was sitting when he was working on your arm."

"And?"

"Jalyerri told me there was one hanging around. They took tucker outside the camp for him. He watched you spend time at their fire an' wanted to know about you. Him being around, even for one night, made our mob real nervous."

"Thanks for telling me."

"Now, mate, don't go getting your knickers in a knot. I'm like Jalyerri, an' I never talk about those fellers unless I have to."

"Anyway, why did he do this to me?" Calum grumpily asked.

"I'll think on it." Brian glanced at his friend. "But you've got nothing to worry about. If that Kaditje man'd meant to harm you, you wouldn't be alive now. Just put it out of your mind."

"But what did he give me and Curaidh that knocked us out?"

"How the hell would I know? The Old People know lots of things white fellers wouldn't have a clue about. An' Kaditje men have all kinds of magic that the Old People couldn't even dream of."

"What sort of things do the Old People know that whites don't?" Calum demanded irritably.

"Oh, like they'll get sap from a Freshwater Mangrove that poisons fish in a river so they float on their sides and are easy to catch. And Bauhinia bark that's soaked in water is good for a fever. An' Spinifex grass soaked in water gets rid of colds. Even little things like breast milk that's squirted into a baby's eyes'll clear up the soreness. But Crise, nobody has any clue about the magic a Kaditje man's got. Like I said, forget it for now."

"Shit."

"Come on, mate, brighten up. An' enjoy your swimming for Gawd's sake."

Calum looked at Brian, frowning. "Tell me," he demanded. "Is this waterhole sacred?"

"I heard tell it is," Brian admitted.

"Jesus! Why don't you tell me these things? That Kaditje man probably hangs around here a lot."

"I didn't bother, 'cause I didn't think it'd matter to you."

"Well, it does. I don't want to explain, but this waterhole is now sort of special for *me*."

"All right, all right." Brian studied his friend thoughtfully. "I don't know everything that happened last night," he said hesitantly. "But you seem different from what you were yesterday."

"How?"

"You sort of seem more grown up."

"I *am* eighteen, you know."

"Of course, mate. Of course."

****

A couple of days later, when they judged that Socks could walk without undue discomfort, they packed up and headed for the home station. As they rode, Brian stayed quiet and seemed to be deep in thought.

"What is it, mate?" Calum asked.

"I think I better start at the beginning." Brian took a deep breath. "Now, you remember how Kunapipi made this land into a paradise?"

"Yes."

"Well, soon after, the paradise got wrecked and turned into the country we now live in. It was a huge snake, called *Tchinek-tchinek*, that wrecked it. You've seen him often, all different colours and leaning over the sky and looking down and threatening us. So how did he wreck Kunapipi's paradise? Well, he sneaked in and used his powerful magic to bring in shit insects like mosquitoes an' ticks. Then he called in his poisonous, little mates like Death Adders and, of course, Fierce Snakes, which are the most poisonous of all. An' then he made droughts an' floods. An' not forgetting the lightning, which causes bad bushfires."

"But where does my tattoo fit in?"

Brian grinned widely and shook his head. "You are just *so* impatient. I'm trying to teach you, mate. Just listen or you might end up like the Frill-neck."

"All right, all right."

"Now where was I? Oh yeah. The old people reckon there are Kaditje men that're close ter Tchinek-tchinek. And that he's given them some of his bad magic. These are old Kaditje men that live alone. An' they are always on walkabout, an' everyone is shit scared of 'em. They are dangerous 'cause they're always working some sort of magic. But you weren't frightened. You even invited one to share your tucker."

"For Crissake. I didn't know who he was. Anyway, he was quiet, and he seemed to make everything around him peaceful."

"He knew you weren't scared. An' the important thing is he appears to have adopted you." Brian laughed. "God knows why. It stands out he doesn't know you like I do."

"Oh, shut up, Brian. And finish what you're telling me."

"Okay, I'll be serious. Now, that tattoo you've got warns everybody that you are not to be harmed. An' any person that does harm you will bring down on their head the most terrible magic from *on top*. That's where Tchinek-tchinek lives."

"Jeez."

"An' I reckon he picked you 'cause you don't look at a person's skin."

"He had these amazing scars on his body."

"Yeah, mate, but the scars were all you could see." Brian shook his head in bewilderment. He grinned at Calum. "You've got me tossed, fair dinkum. Horses follow you around like dogs. Your dingo wants to eat anyone that goes near you. Now this. Every Murri around will want to get a look at you. They'll want to make sure you don't get into any strife that they could get blamed for."

"What sort of bad things could happen to them?"

"Every Murri knows a Kaditje man can get a gator to take 'em or make a snake kill 'em. But most of all, they're shit scared of sickness. You see, Murries are dead certain all sickness is caused by magic. An' a Kaditje man's got more of that than you can poke a stick at."

"Bloody hell."

Brian now began to speak airily, and banter had crept into his voice. "Course, all this has big advantages for you," he said with a wink.

"Yeah?"

"Like, I don't reckon any kwee-ai is going to say no, if you want to fuck her."

Calum looked away. He pretended to look at something on Socks's neck.

"Haven't you been with a kwee-ai very often, mate?" Brian gently asked.

"I'm not as old as you, you know," Calum replied defensively.

"Strewth. When you an' Dor finally get together, it'll be the blind leading the blind! Hell, looks like I need to teach you everything."

Calum was feeling uncomfortable, but he knew that Brian really was the only person that he could ask about these sorts of things. "Well, if it ever does happen," he asked, "how will I know exactly where to put it?"

"Now you *are* getting ahead of yourself."

"What do you mean?"

"That's not where it starts. That's where it ends."

Now Calum was really confused. "You better tell me, Brian. I don't want to look like an idiot if it does happen with Dor. It'd spoil everything."

"I tell you what," Brian said. "It's about time you really grew up, so I reckon I need to be like a big brother."

"And?"

"Now, there's a sheila in the camp called Maudy. She'd be ten years older than you, and her husband an' his other wife are real old. I don't reckon I'll have any trouble fixing it, with him, to let Maudy break you in. Anyway, it's always best when an older sheila breaks in a young feller."

"Why?"

"All sorts of reasons." Brian smiled. "She teaches him not to take himself too seriously and that fucking is fun. An' it's not the end of the world if he can't get it up one time."

Calum stayed quiet. "I wouldn't want to do the wrong thing by Dor," he finally said.

"You won't be. In fact, you'll probably be doing her a favour."

Calum's eyes were now as round as tennis balls. "How will it happen?" he asked.

"Well, I'll give you a box of rubbers an' take you over the first time to meet Maudy an' her husband."

"And *he* won't worry?"

"He's not a badhead. Besides, he's probably past it by now."

"And then?"

"Maudy'll take you out into the scrub an' start to break you in. Nothing to it."

"But I ..."

"Now, don't start lathering up on me. I tell you, you've got no worries. Maudy is kind. She'll take account of your feelings, an' she won't go gossiping about you." Brian grinned. "Not even about how you're built."

"That's it. I'm not going."

"For Crissake, I was only teasing."

"Anyway, how long will it take?"

"About ten days should see you saddle broke." Brian tried to hide a grin. "Course with that cutting you've got, Maudy might want to put in a bit of extra time. An' make sure you're properly gentled an' can even be halter ridden."

"Brian!"

"All right. All right."

Calum was beginning to think that everything was happening very fast. First, there was Doreen and then the Kaditje man. And now Maudy. And yes, he did want to be introduced to Maudy. There was no way that he wanted Doreen to think that he was ignorant. But he couldn't help hoping that Maudy would be kind.

Finally, they reached the home station and rode toward the horse paddock. At least with only three horses, Calum thought, the dust stayed low instead of rising up and choking you.

They rode to a stock trough, watered the horses, unsaddled them, and rinsed their backs before turning them loose.

Hank and Nugget were squatting in the shade of the kitchen verandah, with their backs against the wall. Curaidh immediately retreated to a patch of shade and collapsed on his side. He continued to pant, and his long, pink tongue lolled a long way out of his mouth.

Brian indicated Calum's tattoo. "I tell you, my mate here has got it made." He grinned. "Calum's going to have every Murri in the country looking out for him."

"All I did was share my pig."

Hank and Nugget listened while Brian provided a full account of all that'd happened. Finally, Hank shook his head before speaking.

"You sure as hell were born blond, Calum. That's all I can say. Just make sure none of this bad magic comes my way."

"Don't worry me," Nugget said. "I don' put much store in that sort 'o stuff. More important, you fellers've come at the right time. Perce is already inside, butterin' up Charlie an' eatin' lots o' bread I'll bet, while we is hungry fer our tucker."

"Did Jack Kelly move on?" Brian asked Hank.

"No, he's gone with Murranji." Hank gave a broad grin, and his voice grew animated. "Hey, I've got some great news. Murranji and Peg are off to be married by that little Irish priest in Catriona. Jack, Alice and Jan will be there, and when they get back to the River, there'll be drinks and feasting, courtesy of the Macs."

"Jeez, that *is* good news," Brian enthused.

Calum face suddenly sported the widest of smiles. This was marvellous. It meant that Doreen was already back from up north, so he'd soon be seeing her. Excitement coursed through his whole body. He felt like riding off to Big River that very instant.

Charlie appeared at the kitchen door and pushed back the brim of his Fedora with a supercilious gesture. "Come on, yer bludgers," he intoned. "Better get yer nose bags on."

Perce was already seated. He'd managed to put on more weight and quite overflowed his chair. He had a half-eaten piece of bread in his hand, and some flour was sticking to his top lip. He greeted them as effusively as a salesman who can't remember the last time that he took a worthwhile order.

"G'day, fellers. Good ter see yer. I saved some bottles o' beer fer yer. I tell yer it wasn't easy, but I jus' kep' rememberin' you."

"I don't know, Perce. Mr. Jackson's been told to keep a bigger stock of liquor for employees," Hank fibbed. "And at good prices too."

Perce's chin dropped. He looked around at the others. "But yer'll still buy from me, won't you? Yer won't ferget how loyal I been down the years?"

"It all depends on your prices," Hank informed him loftily. He grinned nonchalantly. "And whether you're prepared to run the risk of being shot at if we find out you're a rip-off merchant."

Perce paled. "My prices won't change," he said hastily. "An' I don' know, I'm sure, why you cattlemen are so quick to grab yer rifles."

"Because rum salesman, as well as wild cattle, can be goddamn dangerous," Hank told him.

Perce quickly took an envelope from his shirt pocket. He handed it to Calum. "Here's a letter fer you, mate, from the River."

"How come only Calum got a letter?" Brian complained. "Hell, nobody ever writes to me. I don't reckon people even know I'm alive."

"Maybe, all the people you know can't write," Nugget suggested.

"Yeah? Well, I know you, don't I?" Brian said mildly. "An' I've got to say I've never seen you writing anything."

"Course, yer never see me writin'. Hell, I always keep that side o' me hid."

Calum looked at the feminine handwriting on the front of the envelope before putting it in his pocket.

"And," Hank advised, "we'd better head for the River pretty much right away. Murranji said the Macs'd lend him their truck, so we'll need to move it 'cause we'll be riding."

Just then Les Jackson poked his head around the kitchen door. "G'day, fellers," he said. "Don't let me disturb you, but there's been a change of plans. Tennant Creek's out. You see, Catriona's Races Week was delayed. Now it'll be on in a fortnight, so that's where we'll be taking the grey. All right?"

"Catriona it is," Hank said.

"See yer, fellers."

"Yes, Boss."

When he'd finished lunch, Calum went and collected Curaidh. They sat in the shade of the Bloodwoods so that Calum could read Doreen's letter in peace. It was short.

> Dear Calum,
>
> Mum and me are now back from up north. The Macs are always good to us. They are kind people. How did the branding go? It seems so long since I saw you, and I've missed you so much. As you probably heard, Mum and Dad are getting married in Catriona. We all think it's best if I stay here till they're well and truly married. Please come for the celebration afterward.
>
> Are you still my boyfriend?
> I love you,
> Doreen.

He felt his heart start to hammer. He wondered how long it'd take to get to Big River. So much anticipation brimmed within him that he felt like an overfull glass of water. He hoped that Doreen would let him look at her breasts again, but he made himself stop thinking about that because when he did, he got so bothered that he needed to do something about it.

****

Jan and her mum were in Jan's rented cottage in Catriona. They were discussing the forthcoming, Big River festivities.

"I won't be goin', love," Alice said. "Your aunty Lil's too sick. I can't leave her."

"And I can't go, Mum. I can't get the time off work. It's so disappointing. I was looking forward to seeing Hank."

"Well, at least we've bin able ter give Peg some comfort. 'Cause that Jack Kelly's bin a real bugger. Did yer know he an' Murranji drank themselves stupid after the weddin' ceremony? An' Jack never once tried ter tell Murranji that enough was enough. Poor Peg. She tol' me it took a couple o' days before Murranji came good."

"Men!"

Accordingly, Peg, Murranji, and Jack duly reached Big River just half a day prior to the arrival of Hank, Nugget, Brian and Calum.

Doreen was the first to see the Long Creek four riding up the dirt track. She ran to meet them excitedly, and as soon as Calum had dismounted, she threw herself into his arms. Neither spoke. They just hugged, kissed and held each other.

After Calum had been introduced to the Macs, Alasdair eyed him truculently.

"Now, young man," he warned. "Doreen is like me own granddaughter. You lead her astray, and I'll shoot yer bloody balls off with me rifle."

Calum blanched, gulped and hastily excused himself. He didn't feel at all brave and immediately headed for the familiar security offered by Brian and Nugget, who were relaxing on the verandah.

Soon the festivities were going full bore. Rum and beer were being drunk as if there was no tomorrow. And Mr. Ah Lee kept on trotting out plate upon plate of Chinese delicacies, while loudly proclaiming, "Yum cha. Yum cha. Velly good!"

Peg took a sheet of paper from her pocket and passed it to Hank. "It's Jan's address in Catriona, Hank. She hopes you can come and see her during Races Week. She's always home by five."

"Thanks, Peg. And I sure will."

Murranji had obtained a copy of Doreen's Birth Extract. It named him as her father, and he constantly waved it at everyone and anyone.

Jack grew impatient and gave him a real serve. "Bloody hell, Murranji," he said. "I didn't think yer'd any lead in yer pencil in them days. I thought all what come out was *rum*."

Peg watched patiently as her husband consumed more than a few rums. "It's me, darl, yer new wife," she finally said, tapping him on the shoulder. "An' ternight's the wedding night we shoulda had two days back. And I expect you ter do the right thing. Awright?"

"But, love, you took so long to marry me I reckon I've unlearned *how*."

"An' that coming from a man who insisted on startin' his honeymoon the night *before* he got married," she scoffed.

Doreen overheard her mum and visibly reddened. "Mum!"

"Now you is older, love," Peg told her, "yer'll need ter learn ter put up with yer parents. 'Cause the older children get, it seems, ter me, the more they is embarrassed by what their parents say an' do."

"But, Mum, everyone heard what you said to Dad."

Peg studied her daughter and smiled gently. "Jus' be happy yer dad an' me enjoy each other that way. 'Cause there's lots our age what is already bored with each other. An' when you two gets ter our age, I hope yer'll have what me an' yer dad have got. 'Cause, I honest couldn't wish yer both more happiness 'n that."

"Oh, Mum."

"Now, off yer go an' rescue Calum, love. Look, there's Alasdair bendin' the poor boy's ear again."

CHAPTER 14

AN ODD WEDDING

Calum was having trouble getting Stupid to go into the horse float. Socks was already inside. He was there to help settle Stupid who tended to get agitated and, true to form, Stupid was playing up. It'd started when Calum was leading him up the float's tailgate. He'd suddenly taken fright, flung his head up and had cracked it against the float's roof. Now he was resisting every effort to get him to enter it.

The ringers had been eagerly looking forward to the entertainment that was part and parcel of Catriona Races Week. Now, growing frustration was rapidly souring their anticipation. Nugget and Brian weren't backward about telling the big grey what they thought of him.

Even Hank finally lost patience. "You silly, Goddamn animal," he swore. "You must have a couple of fused wires in your brain!"

It was getting hot. Calum was sweating freely and becoming annoyed. It showed.

"That's it," he said tersely. "Could somebody pass that green hide rope to Brian, please? Thanks. Now, mate, you and Nugg each take an end and have it halfway between his hocks and his bum. Then, when I start to lead him up the tailgate, both of you start sawing. And do it quickly enough to give him a bit of rope burn. Ready?"

When they started sawing, Stupid forgot all about the float's roof and pounded up the tailgate so fast that Calum had to jump aside and duck under Socks to avoid being bowled over. Brian and Nugget swung the tailgate up and had it closed and fastened before Stupid could back out. Calum came out from beneath Socks's belly and chest and quickly tied Stupid's lead rope to a wall bracket.

He gently patted Socks. "You're a good boy, mate," he said. "I reckon if it'd been another horse, I could've copped a nasty, cow kick."

Meanwhile, Les Jackson had been sitting in the driver's seat, impatiently watching proceedings in the side mirror. "Thank Christ for that," he exclaimed.

Hank climbed into the passenger's seat. He stuck his head out of the window. "Everyone in the back *now* who's coming," he yelled.

Piled into the back of the truck were Nugget, Brian, Jalyerri, Calum, and Curaidh. Charlie, who detested being in any place that even remotely resembled a town, had elected to stay behind. Alice was already in Catriona. She was staying with Jan, in the small cottage that Jan was renting.

Les Jackson drove without speaking. He was excited and thought again about the letter that his brother had written.

Les,

If those bloody training times are anywheres near accurate, buy that horse now. And book me into O'Hara's. When I see you, I'll tell you how we'll both clean up big.

Mate, yer won't be working up there much longer. And that's a fact.

Hooroo,
Dave.

The drive along the dusty and rutted dirt road to Catriona was uneventful.

Nugget accurately summed it up. "Too bloody hot and too bloody dusty. And too bloody thirsty!"

When they reached Catriona, Les Jackson headed for the camping sites on the river's eastern bank. The small township boasted a white population of three-hundred-and-twenty-two and had first been surveyed twenty years earlier. It now took pride in the fact that it possessed not only a bank but also a school for its eighteen white pupils, a bush hospital, a general store, an airstrip, a public hall, a railway station and a racecourse. O'Hara's "Famous Top End Pub" was the only other building of note.

Brian had a unique relationship with O'Hara's, as he'd explained to Calum. "I've got to watch it, mate. Seems the busier they get, the darker my skin looks."

"How come?"

"If there are just one or two regulars in the bar, they're happy to serve me. Course, when the bar's full, they reckon I'm an Abo."

"Bastards."

Catriona was a cattle town. Its livelihood was largely derived from servicing the needs of surrounding cattle runs. And it was to Catriona that many ringers headed to forget temporarily the unremitting hardship and loneliness of their working lives. Here, they could find female company. Either with those mixed-descent ladies who were happy to act as dance partners at the Saturday dance in the public hall. Or with those few who waited, heavily made up, outside the dance to accommodate any ringer who sought a different type of embrace. If a ringer was seen heading off with one of these ladies, the standard comment that was passed was always a heartfelt one.

"There goes another poor sod headin' fer the long grass. Hope all he manages ter catch is a cold in the bum."

During his only previous visit, Calum had been impressed by O'Hara's. Now, as they passed it, Nugget thirstily eyed the two-storied hotel, with its corrugated iron walls and upstairs verandah, onto which each bedroom door opened.

"I don' know 'bout you fellers, but I'm hotter 'n a 'roo what's been burned in a grass fire," he said.

"You mean you could go a cold beer?" Brian said.

"Well, maybe jus' five or six."

"Everything comes to him who is patient," Calum teased.

"So long as I don' have ter wait too much longer, mate. I never died o' thirst before, yer know."

The Long Creek party, with the exception of Les Jackson, decided to set up camp down river from the white's camping area. They piled out of the truck, unloaded everything, unhooked the horse float and watched Les Jackson drive off back to O'Hara's. Hank looked upriver, grimacing at the camping area that'd been reserved for whites. It was dotted with tents and tent flies.

"If we camp here," he remarked, "it means Jalyerri can stay with us."

"Stop yappin'," Nugget complained. "I tell yer, I've bin bloody short of a good time lately."

"Will you stay with the horses, Calum?" Hank asked.

"Yes."

"And set up camp?"

"Yes."

"I'll stay with my mate," Brian said. "But don't forget to bring back some beer for us an' Jalyerri too."

"I thought jockeys had to stay sober," said Hank, smiling.

"It'll be okay, Hank," Brian said. "I'll drink Calum's."

"Thanks a heap, mate," Calum sarcastically complained.

"Well, I'd better be going," Hank said, his mind on his impending date with Jan. "I told the boss I'd call into O'Hara's and get the truck's keys from him."

Just as he'd written that he would, Hank headed for Jan's small cottage to make certain that he'd arrive precisely five o'clock. While she waited, Jan thought about the chat that she'd had with her mother.

"I get the feelin' yer a bit keen on Hank?" Alice had offered.

"It's more than that, Mum."

"Yeah?"

"You see, he's the only man who's *ever* treated me as an equal. And I'm in love with him."

Unaccountably, tears came to Jan's eyes.

"Now, why're yer cryin', love? Lovin' someone should be a happy time, shouldn't it?"

"Yes. But I know I can't hope for marriage."

"Yes. But yer've known that ever since yer ol' man took off. Everyone knows white fellers don' marry our kind."

"I know. But that doesn't make it any easier, does it? And I know I'd make him such a good wife too."

Her mum had given her a big hug and then had sat down on the sofa next to her. "Are yer sure it's wise ter see Hank, love?" she'd asked.

"Yes, Mum." Jan'd paused and had met her mother's eyes. "I've thought about it, and I'm going to be his mistress."

"Oh, love."

"I know."

Jan heard Hank's knock on her front door. It was exactly five o'clock. She opened the door. He was standing there with a smile on his face, and her heart jumped. He saw that she was wearing the same floral dress that she'd had on during their last evening, following the picnic. He thought that she looked radiant. She smiled the same, warm smile that he'd remembered every day since then.

"I thought this dress might remind you of our last evening at Long Creek," she said.

"I didn't forget anything about you. Not the way you look or how your voice sounds."

She smiled shyly and led the way into the small lounge room that she'd furnished simply. Photographs of Alice and Brian were on a shelf on each side of an old, chiming clock. Jan was conscious that her heart was still racing. He was so self-assured and seemed so different from lots of Territory men who found it hard to accept that she had a responsible job in the bank. Often they were awkward or overbearing, but not Hank. He was just nice to be with.

"Where's your mum?" he asked.

"She's at my aunty Lil's place. I don't know when she'll be back."

They stood looking at each other.

Finally she broke the silence. "Would you like a cup of coffee or tea?"

"No, thanks."

"Do you want anything?"

He didn't answer immediately. *God*, he thought, *she really is lovely! And there's character there. Any man could see that. Yes, and importantly, she knows what living up here is all about.* And unlike Donna, he'd never have to worry about what she got up to while he was away in camp. No, this was a woman for the long haul. And he'd bet everything that he had on that. He spoke gently.

"I'd like very much to hold you, Jan."

She searched his eyes. It was as if she was seeking the answer to some unspoken question of her own. Then she moved to him and stood still, her body against his. He put his arms around her and was very conscious of the softness and fragrance of her hair against his cheek. His body responded, and his desire kept rising.

"I wanted this when I first saw you at Long Creek," he murmured.

"Yes."

Her arms went around his neck. He held her closer, and he felt her whole body, soft and giving, through her thin cotton frock. He knew that she could feel him pressing into her.

"You know that I want you, don't you?" he murmured.

"Yes."

He held her bare breasts and was surprised by their weight and firmness. He kissed her tenderly and then more passionately. Abruptly she pulled away. She was breathing heavily, and he saw a vulnerable look in her eyes. She reached for his hand and led him to her bedroom. The vulnerable look remained. She rested her cheek against his chest. And then it hit him, the way that first flash of lightning lights up the whole bush around you so that you can see everything with total clarity. His mind started to race. *Hell*, he told himself, *this isn't the way our first time needs to be, because it's really shortchanging her. And it's shabby. You're the one who's pushing it, and she's going along because it's what you want. But what about her, Goddamnit? This is one woman who'll stand alongside you come hell or high water. Come on, you're not gutless, and you don't worry about the rednecks of this world. So what's stopping you? Are you blind? Can't you see how much she loves you?*

He felt his desire lessen.

He reached down and gently raised the front of her dress till it covered her breasts. She slipped her arms through the straps, and he saw that her confusion had been replaced by hurt.

"I don't have very long in Catriona," he said.

"I know."

"If I move too fast, Jan, please stop me."

"I just don't know what you want."

He took her face in his hands and tenderly kissed her. "I want to marry you," he said. "And please don't take too long to say yes."

Shock replaced the hurt on her face. Then she searched his eyes and clutched his arms. "You didn't have to say that. I'm a big girl, and I wasn't expecting marriage."

He continued to hold her face gently. "I know *exactly* what I'm saying. I'm asking you to be my wife. And I'll sure be gratified if you're able to say yes."

Tears came to her eyes, and she started to cry. Then she was in his arms, holding him tightly, her face hidden against his chest. "Yes, I want to. But you haven't known me very long," she sniffled. "And you're from Texas, and I'm not white."

"Before the War, that would've mattered. Now, honestly, I don't give a damn."

"Please say you mean it?"

"I wouldn't propose to you unless I meant it." He smiled ruefully. "Though, if my parents were still alive, they'd be mortified."

"And you couldn't take me to Texas, could you?"

"It'd be hard. Anyway, my home is here now."

"Tell me again," she murmured, "that you want to marry me. And please don't say it unless you mean it."

"I do want to marry you, Jan. And for the *best* of reasons. Very simply, I'm in love with you." He paused. "And unless I'm making a grave mistake, I think you're also in love with me. And truly, I don't give a damn that you're not white. Or that your family's not white." He paused. "I'm not Catholic, but if you can put up with that, I promise to respect your Faith. And I'll work hard to make our marriage a good one."

"Is it because I'm Catholic that you want us to get married?"

"That's only one consideration. I just want to do what's best for us."

Jan was finding it hard to believe that this man could be so caring. All the white men that she'd met, since leaving school, had only wanted one thing from her. And they'd been none too subtle about seeking it.

"Are you sure you're not doing this because you're lonely?" she asked softly.

"No, I'm not," he answered. "I want to spend the rest of my life with you." He ruefully looked down at his half erection and grinned. "Though that doesn't back me up, does it?"

She half smiled to herself. *He's not at all self-conscious,* she thought. *And that probably means that we'll have a pretty healthy, sex life.* She watched him button his shirt and do up his moleskins. It surprised her that she already regarded him as being hers.

He looked at her. "Jan, who's your local priest?"

"Father Edward. But he's usually drunk by now. Anyway, we need to see the Protector of Aborigines first."

"I would like to see Father Edward," he said. "Do you mind?"

"Now?" she asked.

"Yes."

It interested him to hear that her priest was a drunk. He wondered if this was a situation that could be manipulated because, if it could be, he'd have no compunction about doing just that.

Jan quickly looked in the wall mirror to check how she looked, and when they walked out into the early evening, she took his left arm. *That feels good*, he thought. *Her hand kinda belongs there.*

The air was warm and still, and the evening sky was studded with bright stars.

A middle-aged white couple walking toward them looked at them in disgust. And as they passed, the woman glowered at Jan and yelled at her.

"Yer dirty, yeller slut! Leave white fellers alone and go with your own mob."

Jan immediately grasped Hank's arm in both hands and tugged to prevent him from stopping. "Please," she entreated, "don't let her spoil our night."

When they reached the Catholic presbytery, Hank knocked firmly against the heavy, wooden door and gave Jan a reassuring smile.

"I love you," he told her.

"And I also love you," she whispered shyly.

Father Edward opened the door himself. He'd been drinking. *Rum, by the smell of it*, Hank thought. Father Edward was Irish, a little leprechaun of a man, with a shock of white hair, thick glasses and a pronounced brogue.

"And what is it you're both wantin' at this hour?" he asked, squinting up at them.

"We want to get married," Hank answered.

"Now, that tis a serious matter. 'Twould be best if you came by in the mornin'."

"We can't wait," Hank said. "It's become urgent."

Father Edward cast a quick glance at Jan's stomach. "Well, if tis terrible urgent, you'd best be comin' in. Though I've not long at all."

They followed Father Edward into an untidy study. The little priest sat down abruptly, in a threadbare armchair. He fixed his gaze on Jan. "I know you, girl. Have you not started comin' to Mass?"

"Yes. I used to live in Tennant Creek."

Father Edward frowned at Hank. He was endeavouring to look uncompromising. Instead, he appeared a little owlish as he tried to focus his eyes. He flicked one hand impatiently. "And I suppose you expect to be married right away? Just like that?" he asked.

"Yes."

"Well, tis not the way it works. My Bishop will need to give his permission. Then there's the Protector of Aborigines. You'll be needin' to see him, and he'll have to inform the Department of Native Affairs and get their permission."

"But I have to return to the run on Sunday," Hank protested.

Jan's heart sank, and disappointment drained through her body. *Heavens*, she thought, *all we want is to get married and live a decent Christian life.*

"And were you born into our Church?" Father Edward asked Hank.

"No. But I do respect Jan's Faith."

"Then, after you get Native Affairs' approval," Father Edward continued in a dull monotone, "you'll be needin' to come to me for instruction in our Faith. And you'll be needin' to sign our legal document, statin' your children will be brought up in their mother's Faith."

"But how can we do all that when I'm stuck in cattle camps for months on end?" Hank asked.

"So I suppose you'll be livin' in sin if you don't get married?" Father Edward asked scornfully.

"Is there any other choice?"

Father Edward's eyes blinked wearily. He ran his tongue over his dry lips. He pulled himself to his feet and went to his desk. He rummaged around and then thrust two sheets of paper at Hank before collapsing in his armchair.

"One's the form for the children," he said. "And the other tis a Marriage Certificate. Now, you'll start off by fillin' in and signing both. I'll be back in a trice."

"Why am I filling in these if we can't get married?"

"The Church must protect your unborn child. What if, bein' so far away, you don't get married? This child must be brought up in its mother's Faith." He looked at Jan sternly. "And you'll be needin' to come to Confession. You have sinned."

"Yes," she said in a small voice.

Father Edward placed his hands on the arms of his armchair and pushed himself up. Hank thought that he looked like a man trying to stand in a small boat that'd just turned side-on in choppy water. He continued to sway alarmingly as he departed.

Jan looked at Hank. Disappointment had dulled her eyes. "He won't marry us tonight," she said in a low voice.

"Have faith in the power of rum, sweetheart."

"I don't understand."

"I intend to leave here with a Marriage Certificate and, also, with the wife that I love."

Father Edward swayed his way back into the room. He peered at Jan and slurred his words. Clearly, he'd just drunk more rum. "And how hash Native Affairs classified you, girl?" he asked.

"As a Quadroon, I believe."

"I'm shurprised. I took you for an Octoroon."

Hank winced inwardly, reached over and squeezed Jan's hand.

"I don't understand why we need permission from Native Affairs," Hank stated flatly. "Surely, the Church is the sole arbiter when it comes to deciding who can and who can't get married?"

"Quite so. Quite sho. Of course, the Church ish the real authority."

Hank's eyes lit up when Father Edward said that. He settled back in his chair, and when he spoke, his voice dripped empathy. "I have all the time in the world," he said. "Please start at the beginning, Father. And explain to me why the true Church defers to the bureaucracy when it comes to marrying people."

Father Edward bridled visibly. "Of course, the Church has the shreal responsibility. And I can tell by your shpeech you're American."

"Yes, I am. I'm a new arrival, and I'm confused. Here I'm confronted with a situation where a man who represents God on earth is not allowed to marry me. I'm absolutely staggered."

Father Edward pushed himself to his feet. "I never shaid I couldn't marry you," he said. "I'll be back shoon. Now, you fill out thosesh forms. Especially the one for your children."

. When the little priest returned, Hank could see that he was well on the way to being drunk. Though now he appeared to be quite aggressive. It never ceased to amaze Hank how so many people changed so much when they were inebriated.

"You're quite shright," the little priest angrily insisted. "I alone do God'sh work in this forsaken, heathen parish. And if it wasn't for me, heathens'd overrun thish whole parish. So if I decide to marry you, thatsh God's will, because his authority is vested in *me* alone."

Hank grinned to himself. Father Edward now held his clenched fist against his chest. "I alone have God'sh authority!" he self-righteously trumpeted.

"I respect that," Hank said. "And I am most humbly asking you to do his will before an illegitimate child has the misfortune to be brought into the world. I'm thinking only of the child, of course."

"And sho am I. And Godsh'll grant your wish. I like your shtyle, my son. Are you shure you're not of the true Faith?"

"Not yet, Father. But please give it time."

Jan sat open-mouthed. She couldn't believe what she was hearing.

"I can see that you're a true and devout man of the cloth, Father," Hank gushed. "And much more worthy of your calling than many from my Church."

"Not many possessh your clarity of vishion, my son," slurred the little priest. "Not many a' tall."

Hank stood up quickly. Father Edward steadied himself by grasping Hank's arm. He continued to hold on to Hank's arm.

"Come with me, my shon."

Father Edward led the way into the church. And still grasping Hank's arm, he took up a position well to the side of the altar. Then, without looking at them, he started to intone their Nuptial Mass in Latin. Jan looked at a depiction of the Virgin Mary on the near wall, and it seemed to her that the Holy Mother's small smile was being directed at her. Suddenly, it was unimportant that she was being married away from the altar. And that a truncated and disjointed Nuptial Mass was being celebrated by a rum-soaked priest, who was rushing his words because he was desperate to get back to his bottle. She looked again at the picture of the Virgin Mary.

"Oh, Holy Mary, Mother of God," she invoked silently, "you are witness to my marriage. I thank you for allowing it to be blessed in your church. Hank's a good man, and I'm going to make him the best wife that I can."

When Father Edward had finished, he thrust the already-signed Marriage Certificate at a starry-eyed Jan before hustling them out of a side door.

"Now, shremember your children belongsh to the Chursh!" he warned Hank before abruptly closing the door in their faces.

They found themselves alone in the warm night. Hank wondered how the little priest would manage to negotiate his way, without help, back to his bottle.

He smiled down at Jan. "It seems Father Edward has converts who haven't been conceived yet," he said.

"Do you mind?" Jan asked softly.

He put his arm round her shoulders and hugged her and kissed the top of her head. "No, I don't mind. I guess if we keep on respecting each other's beliefs, then, I'm sure, our marriage'll be a happy one. You know, I didn't think I could ever trust again," he murmured. "You've shown me that I can." His eyes clouded momentarily. "I never told you that I've been married before. Is that a problem?"

"No. Besides, how were you to know, I was waiting round the corner?" She took his arm, hugged it against her and looked up into his face. Her dark eyes were shining. "I do love my new husband."

"Am I allowed to take my wife to bed yet?"

"I also want that. But can we tell Mum first? Aunty Lil lives in the next street, and Mum'll be there."

"Great! Just lead the way, beautiful wife."

Alice was very emotional and excited, as was Jan's aunty Lil. Alice alternated between smiles and tears. And if Alice was disappointed that she'd missed their wedding, she hid it well. They stayed just long enough to allow Alice and Lil to toast their future happiness with a cuppa. Then Alice removed the plain, gold band, which she'd bought cheaply years ago, and placed it on Jan's wedding finger. Tears came to her eyes again.

"Wear it always, love," she implored.

"Oh, Mum!"

Hank kissed Alice on the cheek. "Thank you for having such a lovely daughter, Alice. I know I'm very lucky."

"An' I reckon my daughter's got herself a real man," she replied. "An' yer know somethin', mate? I was wrong about you. An' I'm ashamed o' that."

"Don't be, Alice." Hank smiled. "Because, for a while there, I had reason to doubt myself."

Jan kissed them both good-bye.

"An' don' worry," Alice told Jan. "I'll go ter the river termorrer mornin' an' tell Brian an' the fellers yer good news. An' I'll also tell 'em ter give yer both some peace."

"Thanks, Mum."

Jan and Hank walked out into the warm moonlit night. They had their arms around each other while they walked the short distance to Jan's cottage. Once inside the front door, Hank held his wife tenderly.

"God, I want you so much."

"Please, Mary, you always will."

Chapter 15

Races Week

Cup Day, their second day in Catriona, dawned. The just-emerging sun was already shooting streaks of sunlight across the brown river, and the air was warm and lifeless. On the far side, a forest of impressive-looking, tall Paperbarks were growing in such close proximity that the widespread branches of many were intertwined with those of their neighbours.

Calum, not yet fully awake, idly watched three, long-legged Glossy Ibis that were stalking along the shallows beside the opposite, sloping bank. The water, in which they waded, wouldn't have been more than five inches deep. These large, iridescent, purple-brown waders were seemingly unfazed by the noise that was coming from the opposite bank as they diligently searched for small fish, frogs, freshwater shrimps and small, aquatic animals.

Calum was feeling stressed now that the race was so close. It'd hit him hard last night, because everybody had acted as if the race was already won and had been animatedly discussing how they planned to spend their winnings.

Jalyerri was up, had already fed and watered the horses, and had started to groom Socks. Noticing Calum, Jalyerri flashed him a wide white grin.

"Goot day! Crise, we drink too much, eh? S'pose you take these two feller geldin'?"

"Yeah?"

"Me wantem bush tucker. Me look round where pokupain been diggin' at."

"Yu-ai," Calum said. And then murmured to himself, "I wish you wouldn't eat those ant eaters, mate. I reckon they're nice, little fellers."

He rose to his feet, walked across and took over from Jalyerri. Brian joined him. Brian was clearly hungover; the sickly look on his now pale face indicated the extent of his suffering.

He hung his head, and held both hands against his temples. "I don't suppose you'd be a real mate," he said, "an' make a pot of tea?"

"You're trying to get round me," Calum accused. "And I can't forget you agreed that I shouldn't have any beer."

"Are you sure I said that?" Brian asked with a frown. "I must've been terribly thirsty to have been thinking like that."

"And now you're not even sorry."

"Well, my head's hurting," Brian complained. "An' my tongue feels like the floor of a parrot's cage."

"Have a swim."

"No way! There's gators in that damn river."

Calum's eyes widened in alarm. "Now you tell me. Did you see one?"

"No. But that doesn't mean there are none in it. I reckon a big, fifteen-foot bugger is probably lying in wait for me."

"Jesus, what happens when a person gets grabbed?"

"You mostly get taken in quiet water. You don't have a lot of worries when the river's running a *banker*."

"Well, this river's *not* running a banker."

"They swim slow," Brian said dramatically, laying it on thick, "and the only things that're showing are their eyes and nostrils. An' when they're near enough, they'll move *fast*, grab you an' then go into their death roll till you're drowned. Then you get eaten."

Calum was getting more and more spooked. It showed on his face. "For Crissake," he exclaimed. "You couldn't pay me to go *near* that water."

Brian shook his head sadly, and his dark eyes showed amusement. "I can see you're not at all brave. Not even to get a bucket of water. Hell, it's not as if I'm asking you to sit an' dangle your feet in the river, am I?"

"But what the hell do I do if I see a gator swimming toward me?"

"Throw the bucket at it," Brian said in an offhand voice, grinning evilly. "Then bloody well run."

"Oh, shit."

Brian smiled, walked over to the bucket and grabbed it. "Hell," he said scornfully, "I've seen some nervous Nellies in my time, mate, but you take the biscuit."

"Do you want me to sit there with my rifle while you put the bucket in the water?"

"Now you're trying to make me nervous."

Brian returned with a bucket of water, made himself a pot of tea and then settled back, with the heel of one boot atop the toe of the other. "I've never seen Mum so happy, you know," he offered. "She's rapt."

"Bit sudden, wasn't it?" Calum grumbled. "Heck, no sooner is Hank near a priest than he and Jan get married."

Brian grinned at his mate. "I reckon you've always fancied my sister. Just a tad like, know what I mean?"

"Brian, shut up."

Brian took another sip from his mug. "Anyway, it makes sense to get married quickly," he said. "Otherwise, it could be a long wait till they see each other again. Yeah, it's best not to muck around." His face brightened. "Come to think of it, they're probably mucking around right now."

"You're disgusting, thinking like that. And about your own sister too."

"Yeah? Well, it's on account of her that I've got this sore head."

"Well, you shouldn't have spent most of the night and, I quote, 'wetting the baby's head.' Jeez, they've only been married for one day. No wonder your mum kept telling you to shut up."

Brian took another long sip of tea. "You know," he said. 'Hank's an okay bloke to have married my sister. Mum told me Jan wasn't expecting it."

"And why not? He's real lucky, 'cause she's a beaut person. And she's real good-looking, too."

"Yeah? And you know, I was really happy we got one or two smiles out of Aunty Lil. It's been a long time since she got out of her cottage an' sat drinking an' joking around a campfire."

"She's sad, isn't she?"

"She has her reasons."

They saw Jack Kelly's familiar figure, on his buckskin, riding toward them.

"Hey, look who's turned up," Calum said.

"No way Jack'd miss the races and a chance to catch up with old mates. How're you going, Jack?" Brian called out.

"Not bad. An' how're yer drinkin', fellers? Left any beer in O'Hara's?"

"A heap. An' it's all there waiting for you, Jack," Brian said.

"I'm thankful. I was worried O'Hara's would be dry by now," he joked.

Calum stood up and went and got Stupid. He asked Jack to stand by his head while he cleaned out the grey's hooves. Brian then headed off to see if he could find a suitable rope for Curaidh. Then, while Calum held a front hoof steady against his lower thigh, he scraped out its compacted muck. The big grey promptly swung his head round and nuzzled Calum's shirt collar and then his hair.

"Now, you leave me alone, Stupid. Do you hear?"

Stupid continued to nuzzle Calum's hair.

"That horse likes yer, son," Jack Kelly remarked.

"Just so long as he runs well, this arvo, Jack."

Calum finished Stupid's hooves, stood erect and reached for the lead rope. He saw Jack Kelly shake his head in irritation. Calum looked round and recognized the approaching, uniformed rider.

"Well, lookee here," Jack said softly. "If it's not Mounted Constable Sean Fitzpatrick! I wonder what the hell *he* wants."

Sean Fitzpatrick didn't dismount. He looked down from the back of his big, black mare. "G'day, fellers," he said. "I'm lookin' for Murranji. You seen 'im?"

"He's give it a miss this year," Jack answered. "Says, now he's married, he's got ter act responsible, like."

"Yeah, I heard he got silly an' married some creamy piece."

"I reckon she's a real nice woman. An' I was honoured ter be at their wedding."

"That right, Jack?" Sean Fitzpatrick asked sarcastically. "Now, Ed Smith was doin' a bit of drinkin' last night. Says he owes Murranji for a broke nose an' ribs."

Jack's eyes narrowed. "You tell Smith ter start with me if he wants someone ter shoot at," he said quietly. "Course, I'm liable ter shoot back."

"Now, now, Jack." Sean Fitzpatrick smiled a thin smile. "That's not the way, an' you know it. I already told Ed we don't want any trouble 'tween us white fellers. Hell, us whites need ter stick together."

"Well, I don' go along with the way you expect us ter stick together, Sean. And nex' time I see Murranji, I'll tell 'im I'm backin' him."

Sean Fitzpatrick gave Jack a cold stare. "Looks like I better have another word with Smith. Yer a real stubborn bastard awright, Jack."

"An' how come yer don' pick up that mongrel fer what he does ter Murri women, eh?"

"Well, I haven't heard anything, have I?"

"No?"

"No." Sean Fitzpatrick looked coldly at Calum. "An' we never got that young creamy. You sure you can tell south from north, boy?"

"Course he can," Jack Kelly emphasized. "Hell, I was the one who bloody well taught him, wasn't I?"

Sean Fitzpatrick wheeled his mare. "See yer," he said tersely and rode off.

Jack said nothing. He turned his back on Sean Fitzpatrick and mounted his buckskin.

"I'm off fer a wander, young feller," he said.

"See you, Jack. And did you hear Hank and Jan got married?"

"No, I didn't, Calum. I'm real pleased. That's happy news."

Jack raised his hand in farewell and touched his heels to his gelding.

Brian returned with a rope and gave Jack Kelly a wave. "You know what I just heard?" he said.

"What?"

"That bastard Ed Smith is sniffing around, looking for a woman."

"But how does he get hold of a woman," Calum asked, "if they won't let him into their camps?"

"He finds a feller that's a grog eater an' gets him drunk. An' then buys the use of his woman with more grog. By Crise, he's a bad bastard."

Once again, Calum found that he was anxious and filled with foreboding. His thoughts turned to Doreen. Yes, he reminded himself, she was his girl, and it was up to him to take care of her. He remembered the disgusting way that Ed Smith had spied on her, and his foreboding turned to anger.

****

Hank was lying naked on top of the sheets. He had his hands behind his head and was watching his wife who'd just emerged from the shower. And the more that he thought about it, the more he was convinced that marrying Jan had been about the most sensible thing that he'd ever done. Not only did his wife have a lovely, serene personality, but she also had a lovely body. And as far as he was concerned, the only other thing that a man could ask was to be able to trust his wife. Well, she'd find that she could also trust him all right. Too damn right she would.

"What are you thinking?" Jan asked.

"That you look like a painting by that Norman Lindsay guy. You know, of a proper, full-bodied woman. Only you're alive. And your breasts keep moving while you're drying your hair."

She smiled at him and half-raised an eyebrow. "So you've decided I'm full-bodied, have you?"

"I think you're beautifully full-bodied."

"How come you're looking at my body?" she asked. "And probably getting sexy thoughts? And all I'm thinking about is combing tangles out of my hair."

Hank grinned like an adolescent boy who's been caught looking too intently at a Goya nude during a class excursion to an art gallery.

She stopped drying her hair and considered him with soft eyes. "I think you're lovely," she murmured.

They continued to look at each other. After a moment, he reached for her, and she came into his arms, and their lips met. Soon, their kiss became increasingly passionate.

Quite some time later, when he opened his eyes, he saw that she was smiling down at him.

"These walls aren't very thick, my love," she murmured. "People in the street will wonder what I'm doing to you."

"Lady, you're driving me totally insane. It was never this intense before. Never!"

They lay still. She held him, and his arm lay across her and down, and he was conscious of the fine hair beneath his hand. He savoured the intimacy of the moment and felt very much in love.

"I don't want to move from this bed," he said with a grin.

"You will, soon. I'm sure you'll want your wife to get you something to eat."

"I'm just pleased you can cook, because my cooking is only campfire stuff."

"My aunt Lil's the one. She's the real cook."

"I found her very quiet. And she seemed sad."

Jan looked away and frowned. "She's never got over losing my cousins, Jonno and Evonne," she said. "That was bad. You know, I can still remember playing with them."

He gently brushed a wayward lock from her eyes. "How old were they?" he asked.

"Jonno was six, and Evonne was five."

"Jesus. That's young to die. How tragic."

She gave a start. "No," she said, "you don't understand. They're alive, but Aunty Lil doesn't know where they are. That's why she hardly ever leaves her cottage. She keeps waiting and hoping they'll come knocking on her door one day."

Hank looked at her intently. "I don't get it. What do the police say, for heaven's sake?"

"It was the police who took them away, my love."

"Oh no," he groaned. "Not them too."

"The Old People stained their faces and bodies, but the trackers weren't fooled."

Hank stared toward the window, noticed specks of dust that were suspended in the sunlight, and tried to concentrate on them. He became aware that Jan was speaking again. She spoke very matter-of-factly.

"It's unbelievable for my aunty Lil, you know. Sometimes, I think it would've been better for her if Jonno and Evonne had been killed. Then she would've been able to mourn them and move on. This way she just suffers and suffers, and waits and waits."

When Hank spoke, his voice was bitter. "I never knew. I just never knew. And tell me," he asked, "what sort of jobs does the Church of England, my Church, find these kids when they eventually leave their institutions?"

Jan answered unemotionally, "A lot of the young men go to towns and get work as labourers. And the girls get jobs as domestics. And as you've seen, many have problems with alcohol."

"But you and Brian were never taken?"

"It's the one thing we can really thank my father for. He kept tellin' Native Affairs, he was goin' to marry my mother. Of course, he never did. And later, the sisters taught us at the little, church school. Of course, the old Father knew Mum wasn't married. She cooked for him, but that's not all she had to do for him. And I don't mean normal sex either. He was a strange one. But as she says, she would've done a lot more if she'd had to."

Hank shook his head in disgust, put his arms around his wife, and gave her a long hug. And then he got out of bed and padded over to the window. He stared thoughtfully out onto the street, through a narrow opening in the cream-coloured curtains.

Jan continued matter-of-factly, "But there was a young Father. His name was Father John. He soon worked out what was going on. And he put a stop to it. He was the one who made sure that we went to the parish school. And you know, Brian and I were the only half-caste kids there. All the other kids were full-bloods."

Hank shook his head, nonplussed. Then he brightened. "I haven't had the chance to tell you," he said, "but my share of the ranch, in Texas, will go quite some way toward buying the lease of a good run. So I've told my Adelaide accountants to put in a standing offer for Long Creek. Not in my name of course."

"Oh." She drew in her breath sharply. "I do hope First Northern'll sell to you. And I'll keep what you've just told me to myself."

"I know you will, sweetheart."

He returned to the bed. She considered him carefully. "But I do want you to know," she said, "that it doesn't matter to me, whether you have money or not. It's you that's important, not money. And besides,

I've a good job with the Commonwealth Bank." She smiled. "I could even support both of us if that was ever needed, you know."

He grinned. "Now, being a kept man could appeal to me. As long as it was you who was doing the keeping. And I was getting the fringe benefits I'm getting now."

She stroked his hair. "Anyway, I'm pleased you're not one of those men who think that they're the only one who can earn a living and that their wife's place is only in the kitchen or bedroom."

"Now, that is an interesting thought," he said. "But tell me, how come you're accepted, and doing so well at the bank?"

"I think the bosses see me as some sort of prize. I'm an example of how our Government-owned Bank is helping to make this assimilation business work."

"And how do you get on with the bank's customers?"

"Most prefer not to deal with me directly, but that's all right. There's always plenty to do behind the scenes."

He kissed her cheek. "They don't know what they're missing. And tell me, what do you want to do when we have our own station?"

"I'll leave the bank and work alongside you."

He smiled at her, and his eyes softened. "I'd like that," he told her. "My mum worked alongside my dad when they were building up their ranch."

She looked at him with a frown and changed the subject. "You know," she said, "not all priests are bad. It was Father John who persuaded the Catholic bank manager, at Tennant Creek, to start me off. He even arranged for me to board with a couple of elderly, Catholic ladies." She smiled serenely. "You'll always find good, as well as bad, if you look for it. And I'm sure a lot of good is done by your Church too."

He kissed her again on the cheek. She looked at him questioningly.

"I think you're marvellous," he said, "the way you always manage to look on the bright side of things."

"That's the way Mum brought us up."

"She surely is a fine lady. And I do like her."

"I'm glad. Because she thinks the world of you."

****

Races Week was normally held early in October. Nobody was sure why it was late this year. Whatever the reason, it didn't matter to the large number of Territorians who journeyed from Katherine, Darwin, Tennant Creek, Alice Springs and other towns or to the big influx of South Australians. Or to those Western Australians from Wyndham and the Ord River. Or even to Broome's, punting pearlers who, when their cash ran out, had been known to bet in pearls.

Leaping Lena, the steam train that huffed, hissed and hooted her way from Darwin to Birdum and back again did her best to ensure that all who wanted to could get to Catriona: though many drovers, ringers, head stockmen, miners and station managers came on horseback.

Races Week also was a mecca for Murries and part Aborigines, as well as those who possessed Asian backgrounds. Chinese Australians were recognized as fearless punters. And among them were those who always came equipped to set up their "Take Away" stalls. They knew from experience that inebriated whites would dine heavily on their chopsuey and rice.

One consequence of having such a large, hard-drinking and free-spending crowd was that it attracted a number of Adelaide and Darwin-based bookmakers. And though most visitors were hell-bent on ensuring that the end of the Territory's cattle-working year would be given a rousing and inebriated send-off, some would inevitably manage to enter into the spirit of the occasion too enthusiastically. And when that happened, Mounted Constable Sean Fitzpatrick was notorious for his lack of forbearance.

"I have tell you, mate," Brian informed Calum, "that bastard Fitzo locked up one poor ringer last year that'd annoyed him, for the whole week."

"That was a bit rough, wasn't it?"

"I reckon. It was little Alfie Speight from Wickham. Fitzo arrested him and charged him with being drunk in charge of a horse."

"You're having me on?"

"No, I'm not. The Court Solicitor tried to plead that the horse wasn't complaining, but the Beak wouldn't have a bar of it. He fined Alfie three pounds and banned him from riding for two months. Just as well the Wet was coming on, eh?"

Cup Day was traditionally a Bank Holiday, and only O'Hara's remained open. Its takings, during the week, were rumoured to rival that which it took during the rest of the year. Rum and beer were the big sellers with many a rum, followed by many a beer chaser, regarded as the norm.

The Cup dance, held on Cup night, was the culmination of the week. It was *the* premier event for those wishing to be seen. The Catriona Cup, of course, was the feature race and was run at 2:40 PM.

Calum had decided to take Stupid to the racecourse early to get him used to all the colour, noise and commotion. So promptly at noon, riding Socks and with Stupid on a lead rope, he and the small, Long Creek contingent headed along the narrow track to the racecourse.

Brian constantly checked his pocket to reassure himself that the five-hundred pounds, suddenly produced by Calum, was still there. It was a huge some of money, and Calum's instructions had been succinct.

"It's all I've got, mate. Put it on Stupid for a win, with the Adelaide and Darwin bookies that're here. We win, and the money goes into our joint account in Jan's bank. It'll go toward our station."

"Mate, I've got nothing like this to put toward a run."

"So what? We're partners, aren't we?"

Les Jackson was staying at O'Hara's and, so far, hadn't visited the Long Creek campsite. Brian, who had taken it upon himself to act as their news hound, informed the group of what he had seen.

"Mr. Jackson's staying at O'Hara's, an' he's as thick as thieves with some townie spiv. Anyway, I reckon they're up to something."

"Yeah?" Calum said. "That wouldn't surprise me. Anyway, I'm glad he hasn't been hanging around giving us orders all the time."

The accommodation, for racehorses, consisted of a collection of tin and sapling lean-tos. Calum settled Stupid and Socks in adjoining lean-tos, and Jalyerri volunteered to stay with them, while the rest of them placed their bets and had another look around.

Already, a temporary O'Hara's "Racecourse Pub" was doing excellent business, and the crowd was in high spirits. It was a noisy, constantly moving, and lively crowd, brightened by a strong sprinkling of colourful dresses that dotted the racecourse.

The Long Creek group headed for the bookmakers to execute their "plunge." Because so little was known about Stupid other than that he was a Long Creek stock horse, he was being offered at fifty to one. And even after the Long Creek plunge, executed to spread the bets evenly, his price still stayed as high as ten to one.

"It's his damn name," Brian whispered. "They probably reckon he's been entered for a joke." He moved closer to Calum. "With what I had, it means we stand to collect eighteen-thousand-five-hundred pounds. We'll be well on the way to leasing our own run."

"I feel sick in the guts."

"Come off it, mate. You're startin' to act like a nervous Nellie again."

"You're not riding the bloody horse."

"What's up with you?"

"I told you, I feel sick in the guts."

"Come off it. I know you're an amazing rider."

Then it was time to head for the mounting yard. Once there, Calum had a good look about him. A noisy, motley crowd had gathered to get a close-up look at their selections. And the loudest and most unflattering comments, aimed at the horses, were clearly alcohol induced. Those that he heard amused Calum and helped to take his mind off the race.

"That grey there, looks like he's bin stolen from a glue factory, mate."

"Yeah? Well, the bay what you backed'll *still* be runnin' termorrer mornin'."

Most of the jockeys wore a jockey's shirt though some had been kitted out with a full set of silks. Calum noted that the four, white professionals were controlled and expressionless. The only horses that seemed to interest them were those of their fellow professionals. They didn't give Stupid a second glance.

Ten minutes before race time, Brian, who was acting as Stupid's strapper, gave Calum a leg up. They joined the other mounted horses in a parade around the mounting yard. Calum's stirrups were short, and he tried to look unbalanced and uncomfortable. That wasn't lost on the professionals. One gave him a wink and shook his head mockingly.

"What's your plan, mate?" Brian asked.

"Stay out of bloody trouble and hope that Stupid has the legs for the run home."

"Are you still nervous?"

"For Crissake, shut up. And watch where you're leading this horse. You nearly went into the one in front."

The course was bone-dry, just red earth with the odd patch of dry, brown grass. And the rails were unpainted, bush timber.

When Calum cantered Stupid up the straight toward the starting line, the grey felt good. He was strong and free in his action, and the animated crowd didn't worry him. That pleased Calum because the noise had now swelled to what sounded like a sustained, baying roar. And it seemed to pursue the horses, right up to the start.

The Long Creek group, having arranged to meet at O'Hara's "Racecourse Pub", was watching the race together. Theirs was a mixture of anxiety and anticipation. Jan was hanging on to Hank's arm with both hands, and Brian had an arm round his mum's shoulders.

"What can yer see, son?" Alice asked. "Your eyes is better 'n mine."

"They're at the start, waiting to be called into line, Mum."

"Oh, I hope that boy don't fall off. I'll never ferget what happened to yer father."

"Don't worry, Alice," Hank assured her. "Calum sits a horse like he's been glued to the saddle."

"Well, my money says he's goin' ter win," declared Jack Kelly. "I seen how that grey likes 'im."

At the starting line, Calum held his grey back. Stupid was on the bit, was alert and was showing a keen interest in what was going on around him. His coat was glowing, and its dapples stood out. *Well, feller, I did the best I could*, Calum thought, *and you look a picture. And you're just as fit as any horse here.* He kept stroking the big grey on the neck and talking to him in order to relax him.

"Now it's what's called a walk-up start," Calum told him. "And when all the horses are roughly in line, the starter'll let us go. You and I are going to settle in behind 'em and let 'em cart us along. Then, when we approach the home turn, we'll watch for horses that swing wide on the bend and give us an opening. We'll take any opening, and then, mate, you have to stretch your neck out and pin your ears back. I think you can do it. But if I see you can't win, I won't use this whip on you. You won't be hurt. All right? Now, it looks like we're being called up to the line. Mate, it's one and a half miles. That's six quarter miles, and I'll be checking how we go every furlong."

Calum shut out the noise. He watched the other horses and jockeys. Now the starter seemed happy with the line. They were off! It was a mad dash from the starting post: jockeys yelling, drumming hooves, billowing red dust and flying bits of red earth. Riders were jockeying for position and cursing and swearing at one another. Now the field had flashed past the first, two furlongs. The pace slowed, and the field bunched. Calum looked through gaps between those ahead and saw that the four, professional jockeys were leading. They'd slowed the field to a dawdle. They were watching one another and playing cat and mouse among themselves. Calum saw his chance and didn't hesitate. He gave Stupid more rein, and the big grey loped round the bunched field to take the lead. Soon he'd opened up a five lengths' lead. Wind and the grey's swirling mane were in Calum's face. He felt the bounding power of that long, rocking stride beneath him. And he was concentrating so hard that the crowd's roar could have been a million miles away.

Nugget turned to Brian. "What the hell's Calum doin', Brian?" he asked. "Why's he so far in front?"

"Calum knows what he's doing, mate," Brian admonished. "There's a long way to go yet."

"Come on, son," Alice shouted.

Hank felt Jan's nails dig into his arm. He glanced down at her. Her face was a picture of apprehension and excitement. He saw her open her mouth and heard her scream.

"Faster, Stupid. Faster!"

Now, it was just Stupid and his rider in harmony. Calum was so low over his mount's neck that his nose and forehead were wet from Stupid's sweat. Calum had a new strategy. He'd gambled that the four professionals would stay preoccupied with one another and would dismiss him as a young ringer seeking a brief moment of glory by recklessly going to the front. There, he would be the focal point of every eye till his mount, spent and exhausted, dropped back quickly through the field.

Now Stupid had reached the mile marker, and Calum judged that his lead was fifteen lengths. The grey was happy to slacken pace when Calum slowed him for a breather. Calum glanced back over his arm.

He saw that they'd passed the ten furlong mark and saw that, at last, the four professionals had realized the danger. They'd begun to chase. Now the race was truly on. Calum still had Stupid on a firm rein even though the others were closing. He could hear their pounding hooves getting louder. His heart started hammering. He was conscious of the sweat running down his forehead and cheeks, and he had to keep blinking his eyes to clear them.

"They're catching him," Jan cried. "And he's not riding. He's just sitting still."

"Calum knows what he doing, sweetheart. He's saving his horse."

"Too right," Brian agreed loyally. "Course he's saving Stupid. Anyone can see that."

"He's ridin' real light," Jack said. "I reckon that grey'd hardly know that Calum was on him. By hell, that boy's got the lightest hands I've ever seen. I bet that grey feels like he's runnin' free in a paddock."

"But they're catchin' him bloody fast now," exclaimed Nugget in shocked voice.

Calum forced himself to keep on concentrating. *Hold him*, he told himself. *Hold him till you're two hundred yards out and then hope to hell their hard run to catch you means that Stupid's got more left in the tank than they have.* He concentrated on riding the big grey.

Between his legs he could feel that great heart pounding and pumping great arteries of blood to huge lungs and massive muscles. He looked along the familiar, strong neck with its lacework pattern of little, pulsing veins. The grey's silky, furry-inside, wet-at-the-base ears were flat against his wet neck. Calum could feel and hear the evenly spaced, great gulpings for air and knew that Stupid's nostrils would be dilated and showing pink. And all the while, those great, low-to-the-ground, loping strides never faltered. *Just hope he can hold them off*, he told himself. *Hope to hell your training was spot on. That you peaked him right.*

Jan clutched at Hank even more tightly. "I can't bear to look," she wailed. "They're right behind him now."

"Them other jocks are whippin' their horses, an' Calum hasn't moved," Nugget said. "I tell yer, I'm getting' nervous."

"I'm not givin' up on him yet," Jack said. "I like what I see. An' by hell, that boy does ride light."

Calum could hear that the pursuing hoofbeats were now right behind him. Adrenaline was coursing through his body. His hands were wet, and their sweat had made the reins slippery. *Don't grip the reins*, he reminded himself, *ride with cotton fingers*.

He risked a quick glance behind. His lead was just over a length. Now they had reached the final furlong marker. He quickly gave Stupid rein and simultaneously gave him a solid rake with his spurs.

"Go, boy!" he shouted. "Go!"

Incredibly, he felt the big grey lengthen stride. He shut out everything else and concentrated on riding hands and heels. *Not far now. Stay balanced. Help your mount. He's holding them*, he told himself. *Jesus, he's holding them. Christ, he's pulling away!*

"Go, boy! Come on. Go. We're nearly there!"

When they passed the winning post, Stupid was two and a half lengths clear. Tears of relief were running down Calum's cheeks. He was laughing and crying at the same time. His arms and legs felt like lead, and he was exhausted. The big grey was blowing hard, and he was trembling, but he had his ears pricked, and he was toey. Calum felt totally drained. He didn't hear the screaming, yelling crowd.

"It's over, boy. It's over. You gave 'em weight, and you still beat 'em."

Unbelievable relief! Unimaginable happiness! Calum sat up straight in the saddle. He felt just a little bit taller, and excitement had now replaced that drained feeling.

In the winner's enclosure, Brian took off Stupid's bridle and put a headstall on him. Calum couldn't understand why the crowd had started to boo.

"It's not you, mate," Brian happily explained. "They're giving those professionals a payout for letting you steal the race. Jeez, mate, but you did well. You should've seen the others. Mum an' Jan were bawling their eyes out. Hank was struck dumb. An' Nugg just kept saying over an' over, 'Strewth! Yer little ripper! Yer little ripper!' Fair dinkum, mate, you've done us all proud."

Tears of happiness and relief again started to run down Calum's cheeks. That didn't worry Brian. He was just proud to be leading his mate's horse.

Later, they stood and watched Mr. Jackson receive the cup on behalf of First Northern and Long Creek. After he'd thanked the Committee for organizing such a successful Races Week, there was some fitful hand clapping from the crowd. This was quickly replaced by loud booing, directed at those professionals who'd ridden the place getters.

****

Calum was washing Stupid down when Les Jackson, accompanied by Hank, stopped at the lean-to. Even though he'd removed his jacket, he was still sweating profusely. He was excited. And it soon became clear why.

"Good ride, Calum. You certainly stuck it up those pros," he said with an expansive smile.

"Thanks."

"When you've finished with that grey, I want you to put him in the new float I've bought. Hank'll show you where it is."

Having said what he wanted, Les Jackson turned on his heel. He was about to leave when he swung round and addressed Calum, "By the way, has this grey got any vices?"

"Only one. He'll try to put the boot in every so often," Brian said quickly.

Les Jackson nodded and walked off. He didn't bother to say good-bye.

"Why did you say that?" Calum asked. "You know Stupid doesn't kick."

"Well, he just might kick that bastard for all I know. Nothing wrong with hoping, is there?"

"What's all this about, Hank?" Calum asked, puzzled.

The tall Head Stockman grinned. He was looking very happy. "Take a deep breath, both of you, and I'll fill you in. Seems that Mr. Jackson has resigned. Coincidentally, he bought Stupid a fortnight ago. He showed me the receipt, and I have to say that he paid First Northern an excellent price for a stock horse."

"The cunning bastard," Brian said.

"Bloody hell," Calum groaned. "Stupid deserves better."

"You could say that."

"Where's he off to?" Calum asked.

"Adelaide. It's his brother whom he's got here with him. His brother's a racehorse trainer. They want to leave right away so that they can make Katherine tonight."

"Yeah? And who's going to be carrying the whip on Long Creek, now?" Calum asked.

"Me. I've been on the phone to Brisbane. They're even happy for me to have a ten-day honeymoon in New Zealand. But they want Nugget and Brian to keep an eye on things."

"What about the other Head Stockmen and ringers?" Calum asked.

"Jackson paid 'em all off a fortnight ago, till after the Wet."

"Oh, I see. Well, I reckon you and Jan should have a great time in NZ," Calum said.

"We're looking forward to it." Hank grinned. "There's been a fair bit of intermarriage between Maoris and whites, so we think we should be okay." He paused. "And the first thing you can do when you get to Long Creek, Calum, is take a couple of weeks off to visit Big River."

"Thanks, Hank. Thanks a lot."

"Forget it. Just check out the condition of any cattle you might happen to see along the way. That'll be work, and that means you'll be paid for being on holiday. And don't forget to give Doreen our best regards."

When they put Stupid in Les Jackson's horse float, Calum gave the grey a pat and a hug around his neck. "I hope they treat you well, mate. And don't race you into the ground. You're a fine horse. Yeah, and about the only vice you've got is not trusting horse floats."

The grey moved his ears at the sound of Calum's voice and then nudged him aside, with his head, so that he could get at his hay net. Calum gently stroked his neck while Stupid was eating his hay.

****

Brian and Calum were finally able to make the rounds of the bookmakers in order to collect their winnings. And Mr. Donald, the mousy, little bank manager, was happy to open up the bank for them.

They entered via the manager's residence. Mr. Donald was excited. He gave the impression that he couldn't wait to have such a large sum deposited in his branch. Calum noticed that Mrs. Donald appeared to

look the other way when Brian passed her and that Mr. Donald made
no effort to introduce his wife to them. But he did look enviously at
their money before he locked it in the safe.

"What are you fellers goin' to do with all this money?" he asked.

"Just leave it in the bank," Brian said. "We're in no rush to spend
it."

They farewelled Mr. Donald, collected Socks and headed back to
camp.

"Where are Curaidh and Jalyerri, Brian?"

"They were with Nugg the last time I saw 'em."

"Yeah? Well, I think I'll lie down. I've had it."

****

Nugget arrived back in camp, minus Jalyerri and Curaidh. He was
loaded up with beer. He'd already been celebrating heartily at O'Hara's
and had been sneaking out beers to Jalyerri and a couple of his new,
Murri mates. Nugget couldn't stop burping.

"Good on yer, Calum," Nugget managed after yet another burp.
"But I need ter rest. I'm pissed, an' I promised ter see a sheila later, what
I got talkin' ter."

Jalyerri returned at dusk with Curaidh. He was very drunk and soon
collapsed, snoring, by the fire. He was certainly in no condition to keep
an eye on things as he'd promised.

"What do you reckon, Calum?" asked Brian.

"You go to the dance. I'll stay here."

"Are you sure? I'm only going to take a quick look through the
windows to see Hank wearing the suit he bought. That'll be a laugh.
Not to mention all the other buggers an' their sheilas, carrying on like
two bob watches."

"I can't be bothered," Calum said. "I'll prop here and keep an eye
on Jalyerri, Curaidh, and Socks. But give me a hand now to pull Jalyerri
away from the fire. I'm worried he might roll into it."

"All right. An' I'll wake you when I get back an' tell you who got
into fights with whom. An' over what sheilas."

Later, after the others had headed off to the dance, Calum lay in
his swag with Curaidh beside him. Before he drifted off, he wondered
idly if he now felt more comfortable with Murries instead of with any

whites that he didn't know well, now that he'd a girlfriend whom most whites would disparage. He knew somewhat fearfully that the future wasn't going to be easy. And he couldn't help wondering just how well he'd be able to cope. And he also couldn't help wondering if Doreen would be able to cope better than he himself could. He went to sleep thinking about his Dor and how beautiful she was. And how he couldn't wait to be with her again.

Calum woke with a start. He was bathed in sweat. Curaidh had also woken with a jump. He pushed against Calum and licked his hand. Calum lay still and, unable to sleep, thought about the comments Brian had made before heading off to the dance.

"Mate," Brian had said. "The money's now in the bank. Let's forget about it for now. Anyway, we both need to learn this business properly. Like all the book-work stuff, know what I mean?"

"Who've you been talking to?"

"Hank. An' he said he'll teach both of us the whole bijnitch about running a station."

"I suppose it makes sense not to rush in and spend our money," Calum said.

"Too damn right."

Before he managed to drift off again, his thoughts turned to Doreen. Now, he'd be able to tell her that he and Brian had a real future. And he also wanted to share with her what it'd been like to win the cup. And he found that if he concentrated hard, he could remember everything about her, especially the sound of her voice and the way that her skin smelled faintly of the bush, with just a touch of eucalyptus. And how lovely her bosom had felt and looked.

PART TWO

Let us roll all our Strength, and all
Our sweetness, up into one Ball:
And tear our Pleasures with rough strife,
Thorough the Iron gates of Life.
Thus, though we cannot make our Sun
Stand still, yet we will make him run.

—Andrew Marvell

CHAPTER 16

WALKABOUT

LONG CREEK, 1950

Calum had turned twenty. And Jan had watched approvingly during the intervening years, as the prickly, inward teenager that Perce had delivered to Long Creek had rapidly matured into a lean, personable and broad-minded young man. She'd grown very fond of him and now regarded him pretty much as a younger brother.

He was now over six feet tall, self-confident and outgoing, and walked with that distinctive slightly bowlegged gait of a man who spends long hours in the saddle. His striking, blue eyes now looked out of a deeply tanned face from behind a permanent, sun-induced squint.

His relationship with Doreen had deepened. They hadn't yet become lovers and that, he confided to Brian, was no thanks to Alasdair Macdonald who continued to watch over Doreen as though "I've got no bloody business at all, going over there to visit."

"Old Alasdair must think your intentions are not honourable."

"Thanks a heap, mate."

Although Calum liked to blame Alasdair, he acknowledged to himself that there was a much more significant reason. Very simply, Doreen was petrified of having a child that could be taken from her forcibly. And both of them knew only too well that Calum had about as much hope of gaining his father's approval to marry as a snowball has of prospering in hell. Indeed, Calum had explained to Doreen why he'd stolen his father's money and had told her that he never wanted to see his father again, having long ago convinced himself that his mother had purposely tempted fate with that stallion, because she'd been so desperately unhappy in her marriage.

Jan thought that Doreen had developed into a beautiful and vivacious young woman. And clearly, she was so in love with Calum that her world revolved around him. Sometimes this caused disquiet within Peg.

"Listen, love," Peg said, "yer look inter that boy's face an' all yer see is the sun, moon an' stars."

"I love him, Mum."

"Yer still young, yer know," Peg said, testing. "An' there's better fish in the sea than ever come out."

"Did *you* have somebody else while you and Dad were apart?"

"No. I tried, but wasn't able."

"So? Don't fuss, Mum. I'm the same as you, for heaven's sake."

Within all of Doreen's close relationships, the one dark area that sometimes caused disquiet was her complete refusal to talk about Cord River. And if questioned, she would sullenly retreat into silence or, on occasions, erupt into tears and tantrums. The one, bright spot though, within that poisonous episode of her life, was that the mission had called off the search for her, once she'd reached sixteen.

Doreen and Jan had grown so close that they could easily have been sisters. And in Jan, Doreen had found someone younger than her mother in whom she could confide.

"I feel bad, Jan," Doreen confessed, "when I have to stop him, because I know how much he wants to. And it's getting harder and harder because I love him so much."

"Don't you dare feel bad, Dor! And don't you dare do it till *you're* good and ready."

"And did you and Hank do it before you were married?"

"No." Jan pecked Doreen's cheek. "But the big difference between you and me, love, is that I wanted to, and you don't." She gave Doreen a reassuring hug. "You'll know when it's right for you, Dor, truly."

Jan remained worried about Doreen's refusal even to acknowledge that she'd been held in Cord River. She'd discussed it with Hank on a number of occasions.

"I suspect she's suffering from what psychologists call post-traumatic stress, sweetheart," Hank always replied. "And she's the only one who can start the healing."

"How?"

"Talking about it could help to flush it out her mind."

"What do you think happened to her there, darl?"

"I'd only be guessing, and that'd be unfair to Dor."

What nobody knew was that Doreen's panic attacks were usually brought on by uncontrollable and horrific flashbacks of the callous, sexual assault perpetrated against her, plus Sister Rose's attempted seduction: the latter being all the more damaging because it'd happened, at a moment, when what Doreen'd really needed was the comfort of healing and understanding arms. Additionally, to make matters worse, Doreen had become convinced that she'd brought it all upon herself. That somehow she'd encouraged both perpetrators.

Curaidh, at three, was in his prime. He'd matured into a magnificent-looking dog and was taller than the norm. He sported a handsome, reddish-yellow coat, and his dark, intelligent eyes were steady and gave the impression that they could see right through a person. He was devoted to Calum and, even when resting, with his head on his paws, he'd position himself so that Calum was in view.

"That damn dog of yours won't even let you, his owner, have a piss in peace," Brian mischievously remarked. "He has to tag along. An' God help you if you ever get Dor into the cot. I tell you he'll drive her out before you've even got your fly undone."

"Oh, shut up, Brian."

"And I hear you're still spending plenty of time with Maudy? Seems to me she must reckon she broke you in pretty good."

"For Crissake!"

Brian was still the same easygoing person. He and Calum rarely had a disagreement, and the years had only served to strengthen the bond between them.

Hank often gently teased Jan about how easygoing Brian was. "I just wish he wasn't so slow to stand up for himself. Yet he's always the first to stick up for Calum or Nugg," Hank'd say.

"He's always been like that, darl. Mum used to say that even his dreams must be slow moving."

Hank had purchased Long Creek nine months ago, when First Northern had decided to divest itself of some of its noncore assets. But the mortgage that he'd required was extremely hefty. He, Calum and Brian knew that the Macs wanted to retire and that they'd made a commitment to sell to Calum and Brian the day that Calum turned twenty-one, which was when he and Doreen could legally marry. The Macs had offered their hands on the deal. Similarly, the three, Long Creek friends had shaken hands and had agreed that when Big River had been bought, it'd be amalgamated with Long Creek, and the three of them would become partners. And that both bank loans would be combined and secured by both titles. They'd worked out that it'd be a fair-enough deal given the size of the loan taken out by Hank.

"More than thirteen-and-a-half-thousand square miles should be enough to keep the three of us out of trouble. What do you guys think?" Hank had observed dryly.

Hank was widely respected by most of the other pastoralists in the region but, behind his back, townies often made unflattering comments about his wife. Typical were those that Calum overheard one evening in O'Hara's back bar. John and Bill Anderson, the brothers who owned and operated Catriona's highly regarded emporium, were the culprits.

"The poor bugger's a Yank, yer know; an' he don't know the score up here. I reckon that bank creamy trapped him, fer sure," Bill observed.

"I wouldn't mind bein' trapped by a creamy piece like her," replied John. "But only fer a couple o' nights, like."

Instantly, Calum lost his temper, threw beer in their faces and invited them to join him outside. They declined. And Sean Fitzpatrick, who was also in the bar, gave Calum a clear choice.

"Head fer Long Creek *now*, McNicol, or cool off in a cell," he suggested with a thin smile. "Take yer bloody pick."

On the drive back to Long Creek, Calum found himself wondering why most ringers were a lot less racist than townies. He decided that it was probably respect born out of working alongside skilful Murri ringers: also, living in cattle camps, with Murries, for months on end allowed a man to get to know them as people.

Hank and Jan now had a delightful daughter whom they'd named Janice. She was two years old, and there wasn't anyone on Long Creek who hadn't been captivated by her. Charlie was by far the most besotted. He acted like a doting grandfather and was always cooking her little treats, like chocolate-chip biscuits, as well as finding the time to play with her. The little monkey knew it and had managed to get herself thoroughly spoiled. This fact prompted Jan to vow that it was about time that she became pregnant again in order to stop her daughter from becoming permanently ruined. Alice, though, wasn't concerned in the slightest.

"She'll have ter get used ter sharin' soon enough, love," she said. "So let her have her time as the centre of everybody's attention."

"An' Hank's no help. He's the worst when it comes to spoiling her."

"Jus' count yerself lucky, love, yer've a husband what cares so much."

"Yeah," Jan replied, and her expression softened. "He is very thoughtful. You know, sometimes he's content just to hold me."

"By Crise, love, yer don' want ter knock back yer man *too* often. It don' pay, I'm tellin' yer."

"Mum, husbands and wives talk to each other these days."

"Jeez, love, yours is more 'n more sounding like a real strange marriage. I tell yer, yer ol' man knew awright when he wanted it. That was it. Onter the bed immediate, an' no beg pardons. An' sometimes all he took off was his boots and pants."

"Oh, Mum. I didn't know."

"It's long ago now, and I never knew anythin' differen'."

Jan placed her arm across her mother's shoulders. "Mum, would it make you feel any better if I told you we do it most times, because we both want to?"

"Course. But jus' remember, my girl, it don' do ter knock back yer man. It's not natural, love. An' it'll cause yer a heap o' trouble."

Jan had resigned from the bank following her marriage. Mr. Donald was sorry to see her go and mentioned her departure to his wife.

"That Jan was a good worker," he said. "And nothing was ever too much trouble for her."

"If you ask me," his wife said, grimacing, "that damn half-caste didn't know her place. Why the Bank ever hired her is beyond me."

One of the first things that Jan did, following Long Creek's purchase, was to provide Hank with the bullets that enabled him to negotiate a more favourable mortgage for Long Creek. Mr. Donald was furious, but Hank was delighted. And he was even more delighted when Jan volunteered to free him from all of Long Creek's paperwork. She quickly proved, courtesy of her bank training, to be a first-class secretary cum bookkeeper.

Somewhat unexpectedly, Nugget became infatuated with Mary, a fifteen-year-old kwee-ai. Mary had fled back to Big River after the miner, with whom she'd been cohabiting, had gambled her away during a drunken, poker game. Unfortunately, the miner, who'd won her, had infected her with a nasty dose of gonorrhea, which she'd then unknowingly passed onto Nugget. Calum and Brian listened, in morbid fascination, to Nugget's tiny tale of woe.

"I swear, fellers," he complained, "it felt like I was pissin' fishhooks. Then there was all this puss what came out!"

"Are you being dinkum, Nugg?" Brian asked, visibly whitening.

"Too right. An' that new quack stuck huge needles inter our bums, every day like. An' I reckon each would've held 'bout a quarter pint o' penicillin!"

"Ugh," Calum winced. "I'm not brave with needles."

"But we're both cured now," Nugget cheerfully told them. "An' we'll be sticking tergether, 'cause neither of us want ter put up with that lousy, damn bijnitch ever again"

Murranji took over as Big River's Head Stockman and kept complaining that he was always being pestered by Nugget for work, because Nugget was so anxious to be near young Mary. Actually, it suited Murranji because he was spending more and more time with Peg and Doreen and less and less in cattle camps. In fact, Murranji's position at Big River was pretty much as Station Manager.

Additionally, Jan had taught Doreen how to do the Big River books. Soon, both Calum and Murranji were in awe of her ability with figures; not so the Macs.

"Didn't I tell yer she was a bright spark?" Alasdair chortled to Iain.

"Yes," Iain agreed. "Calum's lucky. He'll be gettin' a dinkum partner awright."

Murranji didn't quite see it that way. "Now, Calum," he warned. "Don't you teach my daughter how to mark bull calves, all right?"

"Why?"

"I need to keep a few things up my sleeve. You know, things I'm better at than Dor."

"Too late. Alasdair's already shown her."

"Bugger."

"But don't worry, Murranji. I know she won't go near any truck's engine. She says they're smelly and dirty and greasy."

"Thank Gawd," Murranji said, brightening. "I'll be able to boast I'm an expert. Course, I am a passable, bush mechanic, you know."

Calum didn't begrudge Doreen her cleverness. He just liked to be there for her, especially when she had her panic attacks. Lately, large spiders were able to bring on mild ones. These started after one, the size of her father's hand, had stood up on its back legs and had confronted her and Jan threateningly. It had a burrow in the bank of a dry, creek bed, and Jalyerri had told her that this kind often caught and ate small birds.

When suffering such panic attacks, a shaking Doreen would seek Calum's arms.

"Just hold me, darl," she'd whisper. "I always feel okay when you've got your arms round me."

When Murranji returned to Big River, from the floodplains, for this year's bullock muster, he left Peg and Doreen up there with Peg's people. Both had told him that it'd be a pleasant holiday for them. But what Doreen didn't tell her father was that Calum planned to join her.

"That Murranji's always pestering Calum an' me to give him more and more of a hand at the River, you know," Brian informed Hank.

"Is that right?"

"Yeah, it is. But now that he's back, I told him to forget this coming bullock muster 'cause Calum an' me an' Jalyerri are having a holiday. And we're going on a long walkabout. Course, I didn't tell him we were headed for the floodplains. Peg and Dor are still up there, you know."

"Why not tell him, for heaven's sake?" Hank demanded.

"Well, sometimes dads get funny when it comes to their daughters, know what I mean?"

"I see. And when're you leaving?"

"Soon. We want to get there by the end of February." Brian grinned wickedly. "I reckon Calum can't wait to be with Dor when she's well away from old Alasdair an' her dad."

"I don't doubt it," Hank agreed dryly.

Hank, realizing that Calum, Brian, Murranji, and Nugget would be more help to Big River than to Long Creek, had hired three, new Head Stockmen. The only one of Les Jackson's men that he'd retained was Potato Bob, so called because of his love of potatoes. Potato Bob was tall and skinny, was liked by his Murri ringers and always refused to have any whites in his crew. By contrast, Sophie, his light-skinned, mixed-descent de facto, was extremely stout—so much so that her mode of transport, by necessity, was a cart drawn by a pair of mules. She drove her mules skilfully and did all the cooking in camp. She made sure that Potato Bob always dined extremely well. It puzzled her that he never put on any weight.

Jack Kelly still stopped at Long Creek looking for work. He always got it and at Big River too. Murranji and Peg had kept working on him and had found that they were managing to get him to stay for longer spells.

****

Murranji became quite irritable when Brian finally got around to telling him that Calum, Jalyerri and he were bound for the floodplains.

"Hell," he complained, "I reckon *I* should be heading back, while you lot should be doing the bullock muster."

"Are you sure you're not dirty 'cause my mate's off to see your daughter, an' you won't be there?" Brian asked with a sly smile.

Murranji glowered but said nothing.

The three of them left early the next day, and it wasn't a minute too soon for Calum. For days, he'd been impatient to start; his thoughts constantly on Doreen.

Peg's people had made the long trek up to the floodplains from time immemorial because, at that time of the year, food was more than plentiful there. Now, though, fewer and fewer were making the journey. Mission experiences, mining camps, different groups mingling on cattle runs, jobs with buffalo shooters and the lure of white townships were just some of the reasons. Murranji frequently bemoaned the changes that he could see taking place before him.

"You know," he'd complained to Calum more than once, "soon Peg's lingo'll have gone. An' so will lots of the thirty-odd lingos that're spoken from the Gulf to the West Australian border."

"How come?"

"Creole, mate. Creole. Already some of the pics speak it as their first lingo. I reckon it's real sad. And nothing's being done to save these languages. You see, when a people's language is gone so, too, is their culture."

"But will they all disappear?"

"Yeah, except for the main ones like Warlpiri. Hell, that's spoken from the Katherine region down to Alice Springs almost."

Their spelled horses stepped out, and the three made good time. But by late afternoon, most days, dark clouds would appear, and shortly thereafter the heavens would open, and they'd cop a deluge. Then the air would grow sweet and dank with the smell of saturated vegetation.

"It's good to see you with a smile," Brian told Calum. "Never mind, I'm sure we'll get to see more than a few once Dor happys you up."

They lived off the land, and Curaidh proved himself to be an excellent, tucker dog. His tenacity, strength and cleverness impressed Brian. He even knew instinctively the folly of chasing a big 'roo into the water, in which it'd taken refuge. Regrettably, excitable, station dogs often weren't so savvy and any that stupidly swam out to the standing 'roo would be grabbed, by the neck, and held beneath the water till they drowned.

They arrived before the end of February. Calum was amazed. He halted Socks and stared. The Wet had flooded the plains to create a vast, inland lagoon that stretched as far as the eye could see. Tall, bright-green Cane Grass grew to the water's edge and imposing, ninety-foot-high Paperbark trees, with their wide-spreading branches, fringed the margins, and many now stood in water. Farther out, smaller, half-submerged trees, rising from the water, resembled little islands of bushy, green foliage. Brian pointed to the nearest one.

"Can you see what're clinging to the branches?" he asked.

"Hell yes. I can see a snake, a feral cat, and a couple of goannas."

"They ran up that tree to escape the rising water. And that's where they'll stay till the water drops."

Wide, green, water lily pads covered significant portions of the lagoon. And long-legged, long-toed Lotus Birds, with their fleshy, red, forehead combs, were stepping from pad to pad. While grey-headed, rusty-brown-backed, and crimson-breasted Crimson Finches contrasted prettily with the green, Cane Grass stems to which they clung.

Scattered Swamp Buffalo fed on the floating grass beyond the green, reed beds, and their black-grey, slow-moving bulks contrasted with the brown-green water in which they grazed or swam. Others rested among Paperbarks, immobile and camouflaged by dappled shade. And only the movement of a flicking ear or swishing tail betrayed their presence.

The impact, scale, movement and majesty of the scene were incredible. There were hundreds of thousands of Magpie Geese alone, and their resounding dissonance, even on its own, would've been deafening. But added to that was the combined cacophony created by all the other species—including cinnamon-brown Wandering Whistling-Duck; Pacific Black Duck; white-faced, Pink-eared Duck; grey-brown Grey Teal; black-faced, white Royal Spoonbills; as well as pink-legged Black-necked Storks; and very large White-necked Herons that stalked the shallows. And as if the din made by this huge gathering of waterfowl wasn't enough, drinking flocks of little, chattering, multihued Zebra Finches; Galahs; grey and white, yellowish-crested Cockatiel parrots and flocks of largely-white Little Corellas added their voices to the racket. And nearby, Calum noticed a dozen black-and-white Pelicans, which had all upended themselves in the water as they fished in unison.

Brian indicated six, feral, black pigs that were swimming, in a tight-knit group, toward the nearest shore. All that could be seen, above the water, were their black heads, ears and snouts.

"They were trapped on a small island," he said. "Now, they're swimming to shore."

Suddenly, the knobby, dark head of an Estuarine Crocodile broke the surface beside one pig. The big reptile opened its long, jagged-toothed jaws and clamped them over the pig's head. Then, with a huge splash, its entire body momentarily broke the surface as it turned on its back, before quickly submerging with the pig in its jaws, leaving behind only a short-lived swirl of sunshine-dappled brown water.

"Bloody hell!" Calum exclaimed, wide-eyed.

"Now, you've learned why you only swim where the Old People swim," Brian dryly remarked.

This was the tribal land of Jalyerri's wife, Janey. He was welcome, but she wasn't. Brian told Calum the story. "It's all to do with tjarada," he said. "An' the terrible punishment given to both when a man takes another's wife. You see, both of 'em have got to front their people next day. That's when the spears, throwing sticks an' stones start flying. Course, they both fight back, an' if they survive, they head for what's called ''Nother Place.' That's where you'll find the living dead, those who've been banished. They're the living dead 'cause they can never go back to their own country."

"But why is Jalyerri welcome if he's married to Janey?" Calum asked.

"She never left her husband for him, an' he's from a different mob. He came across Janey in Tennant Creek, where the feller she left her husband for was selling her an' was also making her beg. You know the sort of shit. 'Gibbit flour. Gibbit bacca.' Anyway, Jalyerri fancied her. He said he'd take her to live at Long Creek if she wanted, and he wouldn't sell her to anyone. Course, she's happy for him to come up here 'cause he can tell her about her own mob when he gets back."

"And she can never return?"

"No. All she can hope is, when she dies, her Shade'll be taken back to her own country."

****

Rather than have a couple of strangers barging into their encampment, Jalyerri went on ahead to make contact with Peg and Janey's people, while Brian and Calum set up camp. When he returned, he was grinning and asked them whether they wanted to collect goose eggs. Calum was indifferent about going because he was impatient to see Doreen, but Jalyerri insisted. To refuse would be rude, he said.

They followed Jalyerri. The sky was clear, the sun hot and the air muggy. Quite a large group of Murries was waiting for them, beside three, dugout canoes. They were chattering animatedly among

241

themselves. Many were naked though the women either wore calico *lap-laps* or the odd skirt made from Cane Grass that'd been split into fibres. Perhaps the reason why Calum initially didn't notice Doreen was because he was so used to seeing her dressed in a shirt and baggy, cut-down moleskins.

"There's Dor waving to you," admonished Brian. "An' you're ignoring her."

Then he saw her. She was standing at the far edge of the group, dressed only in a lap-lap. She was smiling at him and waving shyly. He thought that she looked lovely and found it hard to stop looking at her breasts. He was embarrassed when he stumbled while getting into his dugout because he hadn't been concentrating on what he was doing. Doreen laughed gently at his discomfort. She kept watching till his dugout disappeared from sight.

Jalyerri held his arm to get his attention. "Soon, you be getting' good missus, awright!" he announced with a happy grin.

Countless thousands of Magpie Geese nests had been built in close proximity to each other. They were bulky platforms of vegetation, structured atop trampled-down, reed tussocks, in among the upright, green reeds. The yellowish-white eggs were bigger than duck eggs. Most nests contained between five and eight, but some had as many as fourteen. Calum asked Jalyerri if there was an easy way to distinguish between the sexes because, to his eye, every Magpie Goose looked identical. All were big, lanky, boldly patterned, black-and-white birds with that notable knob on their crown. And all had red bills and orange legs. Jalyerri just smiled. You could tell by the way that they looked, he said. And he also told Calum that, unlike other waterfowl, the gander often had two mates. *No wonder*, Calum thought, *there are so many of them.*

It didn't take long to fill the canoes with eggs. And Calum soon found himself, alongside his full dugout, splashing his way through the squelching reeds and brown-coloured shallows back to dry land. Initially, the thought of gators worried him but the Murries, with him, weren't concerned, so he relaxed.

Doreen and Peg, together with an excited mob of adults, teenagers and pics, were waiting to carry the eggs back to their encampment. When Calum reached dry land, Doreen joined him. She looked down at his soaking, muddy boots and moleskins, and her dark eyes sparkled mischievously.

"You're not a pic anymore," she chided. "And you're still playing with mud."

"Why don't you tell me you're pleased I'm here? And that you missed me?" He grinned. "Hell, it's been over two months."

"Take off your pants now, darl, and I'll wash 'em," she teased.

"No way! I'm not going to run around in my underpants in front of everyone."

"You're chicken, my love. Is that the right word?" She pushed her hair back, from dark eyes that crinkled, at the corners and reached out and held his arm. "Of course, I missed you." She smiled. "Lots and lots. And every day I don't see you means another ache inside. And I hope you missed me just as much."

"I did miss you, my love. And you *are* beautiful."

"Because I'm not wearing a shirt?"

"That helps."

"Calum McNicol! I don't know what I'm going to do with you. You've been looking at my breasts ever since I was fifteen. How come you're not used to them by now?"

"That's what being in love does."

"Oh, darl."

Brian and Peg walked over to join them. "G'day, Peg," Calum said and gave her a peck on the cheek.

Peg hugged him warmly. "G'day. How yer goin'? Awright, mate?"

"Couldn't be better."

"As you can see, Dor," Brian said. "I brought you up a feller."

"Thanks heaps, Brian. I reckon fellers are great, and *every* girl should have one."

"Come on, love," Peg said, smiling. "We better help with the eggs."

Later, Brian told Calum that he and Jalyerri would be spending most nights at the Murri encampment. "The elders see us as guests, mate," he explained. "An' they'd be showing real rudeness if they made us hold back our manly feelings."

"Oh."

"Look, I'm sorry to leave you looking after the camp by yourself, but just say the word an' I'll be back."

Calum smiled at the lack of enthusiasm in Brian's voice. "It doesn't worry me, mate. I know you can't refuse their hospitality. Anyway, it'll give me a break from your terrible snoring. It's getting bad, mate. Specially after you've had a couple of rums."

"I don't snore," Brian protested.

"Pigs bum, you don't!"

"Well, if you're going to be like *that*, telling lies about me, right to my face. Heck, I'm sorry I offered to come back."

Calum laughed happily. His mind was on Doreen and how pleased she'd been to see him. And the way that she'd been dressed and how lovely she'd looked with her sunshiny, dark hair being blown about by the breeze.

The last of the day swiftly passed. The sun quickly dipped below the horizon. Nightfall then descended just as quickly, bringing with it its own still and balmy, night air.

Calum was lying on his back, gazing up at a shimmering, white-yellow Igulgul and the teeming, sparkling stars that dotted a velvety, blue-black sky. He looked at Kunapipi and Wanjin, listened to the chorus of nearby frogs, and wondered what was keeping Doreen.

When she did come, she arrived so noiselessly that he didn't know that she was there till he dropped his glance. She was standing, looking down at him, her only garment a calico lap-lap. He looked at her in wonder. Igulgul's creamy light had cast a soft sheen over her flawless, olive skin and was reflecting tiny glimmers from her dark eyes. He was speechless. She knelt beside him and unbuttoned his shirt and moleskins. His eyes looked at her questioningly. She kissed him to reassure him, unwound her lap-lap and moved into his arms. And for the first time, he knew all of her smooth, cool length. Neither spoke. She kissed him, and her familiar, brown nipples puckered and grew erect under his hands. He lowered his mouth to her breasts, and she cradled his head in her arms. Then out of habit, he pulled back. She placed her fingers over his mouth.

"It's all right," she murmured. "Both of us have waited a long time for this."

"Are you sure, Dor?"

"Yes. And I want to, darl."

He lifted his head, looked down into her eyes and smiled at her. "I think even the stars are happy for us," he murmured.

"Why?"

"They're still shining down on us. They haven't found a cloud to hide behind."

"Oh."

"I was just thinking that neither of us can ever have this night again."

"Yes." She held his face in her hands and kissed him. "You're talking a lot, darl. I hope that means you're a little bit nervous." She gave a tiny giggle. "'Cause I know I am."

"I love you, Dor. And somehow, I don't want this moment to end."

"Tell me again, you love me."

"I do love you, Dor. I love you so much it hurts."

She kissed his chest and then gently held his face in her hands. He saw that her eyes were filled with wonder and tenderness and love. She started to tremble ever so slightly. Their kissing became more passionate. Her hips pushed harder against him, and he could feel the heat where her thighs joined. Then, when he entered her, he felt her go tense and give a tiny cry. But suddenly, she thrust against him and grasped his back hard, with rigid fingers that dug into him.

Afterward she lay still in his arms. He held her tenderly, and all the love that he had for her seemed to rise up through him till he felt as if it was choking him.

"I love you lots and lots and lots," he murmured. "Do you know how much that is?"

"No."

He pointed at the Dog Star, shining brightly, far above them. "I love you all the way to Wanjin and back again, Dor."

"And that's how much I love you too, my darling." She wrapped her arms around him and held him tight and whispered, "What do you want me to do now?"

"Tell me you'll marry me the day I turn twenty-one," he said.

"You know I will."

"Gee, I wish I was as patient as you."

"We both have to be patient. But I'll be at the River often, and we'll go into the bush and do what we did just now. Would you like that?"

"Oh my word, yes." He kissed her tenderly. "And you know," he said, "when we're married I'll go crazy being apart from you when I'm in camp."

"I've thought about that. I'm going to be in camp with you." She giggled. "I'll be your drover's 'boy,' and I'll warm you on cold nights. And you can put your hands down my shirt whenever you want."

He hugged her and kissed her on her cheek. "Dor, having you in camp will be terrific. God, I wish the Macs'd sell now."

"They told Mum they were looking forward to retiring in Adelaide."

"Really?"

"Yes."

He turned on his side and looked down at her. "You asked me if there was anything you could do for me," he said huskily.

"I think I know what you're going to say. Yes, my love, I also want to. But first, I want to feel your darra, not moving, inside me."

"Yes."

****

In the morning, they decided to move camp because Doreen was sure that she'd heard the splash of a big gator nearby.

"And when we've finished setting up camp, I'll show you how to cut into a Paperbark tree to get a couple of pints of water," she told him.

"Yeah?"

"And you better pay attention," she warned. "It could save your life one day. And you're very precious."

After that first night, they were rarely apart. She often teased him. She claimed that he was too serious and loved it when she made him laugh.

One time, he discovered that he was enjoying just holding and kissing her. Her body seemed to melt into his. He felt her arms go around his neck, and her hands stayed against the back of his head. There was no passion to his kissing, and he became more and more aware that he was delighting in the feel of her arms, around his neck, and her lips against his. Abruptly, she pulled back and looked at him. He saw that her eyes were puzzled.

"What's happening?" she asked.

"What do you mean?"

"Well, we've only been kissing. And usually, by now, you've got your hands on my breasts."

"I don't believe you," he teased.

"It's true. I think you're losing interest now that you've had what you wanted," she pouted.

"No way, Dor."

"Well, what is it, then?" she asked.

He took both of her hands in his and began to look sheepish. "I know this sounds silly, Dor," he said. "But I've only just discovered how nice it is just to kiss and cuddle my girl."

She came into his arms and hugged him. "That's the nicest thing you've said all morning," she murmured.

Later, he lay stretched out in the sun, eyes closed, as he dried off after a refreshing swim.

"I can see you're not busy, darl," she said.

He half-opened an eye at the sound of her voice and looked at her. She was standing, looking down at him. She was naked and was smiling.

"I've heard there's a certain type of woman who's quick to get her clothes off," he remarked conversationally.

"Well, aren't you the lucky one! But I was asking if you were busy."

"Flat-out. Flat-out, love, like a lizard drinking."

"Well, how about coming in the water and helping me to look for File Snakes? They're those fish-eating, light-brown snakes with lots of browny-black, coloured bands on top. They've got a really rough skin, which they use to trap fish so they can't get away. And they're terrific eating."

"Are you sure you haven't come to flirt with me, dressed like that?" he asked. "'Cause I'm sort of hoping you have."

"Come on," she said laughing, and held out her hand to him.

****

Jalyerri and Brian made a point of calling in most mornings. The first time that they came, both were all smiles after realizing that Doreen and Calum had spent the night together.

"It's about time you put him out of his misery, Dor," Brian laughed. "You know, sometimes he used to sulk when he came back from seeing you."

"Oh, the poor dear," Doreen teased.

Often the four of them would sit and yarn over a cup of tea. Jalyerri always wanted to be reassured that they had enough to eat. This particular morning, Doreen remarked that she'd enjoy a duck for their late-afternoon meal. Without a word, Jalyerri got to his feet and signalled for them to follow. Doreen took Calum's hand.

They watched Jalyerri arm himself with a hollow, lily stalk. Then, totally naked, he eased his lanky, ebony frame into a safe billabong, from which the women always collected their edible, water lily tubers. He disappeared from sight and stayed below the surface.

"What's he up to?" Calum asked.

"He's breathing through that lily stalk," Doreen answered.

"Oh."

Calum watched the nearest Grey Teal unconcernedly swimming on the surface. Unexpectedly, it flapped its wings and splashed and struggled frantically. But the strong hand that had gripped its legs relentlessly dragged it under. Then another duck flapped and squawked before it, too, disappeared below the surface.

"That's two," Brian remarked. "Walk to the edge an' take them from him so he can go back for more."

After Jalyerri had caught four ducks, he stood up in the rib-high, brown-green water and then came ashore. Clear, water beads on his black hair and black skin dripped and glistened in the bright, morning sunlight. He was grinning from ear to ear. Then he indicated Brian.

"That Brian feller, he want me to spear Barra'," he said. "Me spear Barra' by 'n' by."

Later, Doreen and Calum roasted two of the ducks that Jalyerri had caught. They were delicious.

"This beats the corned beef we eat in camp, Dor, I tell you." He rubbed his stomach and sighed contentedly. "Oh, mate," he sighed,

"I'm as full as a *goog*, and you're a pretty good cook. I have to give you that."

She smiled at him very sweetly, and when she spoke, her voice was just as sweet. "Have you decided I'm not a bait layer, after all?"

"I never said that," he exclaimed, shocked.

"No? Well, Brian told me you did."

"What a rotten, fibbing rat. Jeez, he'll keep."

True to his word, Jalyerri sometimes spent the early mornings spearing Barramundi. He chose dawn's stillness, before the breeze sprang up and ruined his visibility by riffling the surface of the water. They'd watch as he sat motionless; his lanky legs dangling on each side of a sturdy, tree limb that stretched out over the glassy surface. And there he remained, looking for all the world, like a wonderfully sculpted, life-size, ebony carving. His slim, right hand, above his head, gripped his woomera and long, three-pronged, fish spear. Then suddenly he'd drive downward, and they'd see the shaft of his spear weave crazily through the disturbed water. And when he jumped down to retrieve his spear, there'd be a good-sized, silver Barramundi wriggling on the end of it. He'd present it to Doreen with a wide grin that displayed very white teeth.

"Goot tucker. True!"

The two of them ate their first Barra' meal at dusk. Calum had no idea how to cook it. Doreen smiled at him and pecked him on the cheek.

"Didn't I tell you you'd be lost without me, darl? And put away that frying pan, my love. We won't need it."

He watched her lay the whole fish flat on red coals that'd had some sand placed over them.

"When that side's black, it'll be cooked," she told him. "Then we turn it over."

When the Barra' was cooked, she took it from the coals, cut it into portions and filled his plate.

"Amazing," he said. "Look, the skin and scales are just falling off the flesh."

"That's how you can tell it's properly cooked. Best-tasting fish your woman'll ever cook for you," she asserted.

"Mm. Specially when it's eaten with beaut, just-made damper."

Later, Curaidh, who'd been investigating something beyond the firelight's radius, appeared from out of the shadows. His eyes glowed like embers in the firelight. He crouched as he approached, with apparent humility.

"Don't move, Dor," Calum said quietly. "I want to see what he's up to."

Curaidh kept his eyes on Doreen. When he got to within two yards of her, he lay down with his head on his paws. His gaze stayed fixed on her. He rose after a minute and resumed his slow, crouching approach. When he reached her, he dropped his ears and gently rested his head on her outstretched thigh. He remained there, quite motionless. Doreen reached out and placed her hand on his head, and every now and again, his intelligent eyes glanced up before looking away once they'd met hers.

"I'll be blowed," exclaimed Calum. "And I thought he was a one-man dog. You have to believe it, but he's never done that before. Not even to Brian."

"He's decided I also belong to you."

"Yes?"

"He's learned to trust me. And he has a lot of love to give."

****

When Jalyerri and Brian arrived next morning, Calum had newly returned from walking Doreen to the encampment. Jalyerri told him that he'd never seen him so happy. And he wondered, with a twinkle in his eye, whether Doreen had taught him new ways of making love. Calum laughed and wandered off with Curaidh, quite lost in the world of Doreen's tjarada. He wondered whether Igulgul, Willie Wagtail, and her tjarada had all conspired to make him want her more every time that he saw her. For he'd never before realized just how marvellous a physical relationship could be when two people truly loved each other. And the depth of their relationship astonished him, as did its intensity. However, there was one problem. Doreen had become increasingly worried. She told him that the happiness that she felt frightened her. She hadn't known that becoming his lover would so increase her love for him. And she'd begun to believe that she was too happy, and that so much happiness could only come from a wrong-side love.

Calum told Brian of her fears, and Brian listened attentively.

"You've got to remember, mate," he said, "the Murri part of her is saying you're related to Tchinek-tchinek, so what's between you two has got to be wrong-side." Brian thought before continuing. "An' of course, her white half is saying that's all nonsense. An' remember, she's been fucked up because of her years at Cord River. Crise, it must've been bad if she still won't talk about it. An' can you imagine what it's doing to her inside?" He nodded to himself. "But after what she's been through, I reckon she's doing all right. An' don't ever forget, mate, you're her rock."

"Yeah?"

Brian suddenly brightened. "Hey, I've just had this beaut idea I'll put to Peg," he enthused.

"What is it?"

Brian grinned. "If her uncle Henry told Dor she's been promise-married to you, then everything'll be all right. Because there'd be no wrong-side love, right?"

"Of course."

"I think I'll go and talk to Peg."

Later, Calum walked to the encampment.

Peg's near-black eyes regarded him with amusement. "What've I got ter do ter keep yer away from me daughter?" she teased.

"Too late, Peg. Like I always say, you should've done something about it when we first met."

"I blutty well tried, mate, but you is a dreadful, persistent feller."

"Well, that's love, isn't it? And the day I'm twenty-one, I'm going to ask you and Murranji to give me your permission to marry Dor."

Peg threw back her head and gave a throaty laugh. She rested her hand on his arm. "Mate, as far as I can see, you two is married already. An' of course, you'll get our permission." Her face grew serious, and she looked intently at Calum. "Marriage is fer always, mate. Yer do know that, don't yer?"

"I know I'll always want to be married to Dor."

"An' are yer real sure yer want a creamy fer yer wife? An' how're yer goin' ter introduce yer little creamy ter yer white mates in town an' on other runs?"

A ripple of anger crossed Calum's face. "That's enough, Peg. You know me better than that."

"Awright." Peg sighed. "An' another thing, her uncle Henry has already told her she's been promise-married ter you. So there's no blutty worries on that one."

Calum smiled hugely. He put an arm round Peg's shoulders and gave her a hug. "So we really are married, eh, Peg?"

"As far as me an' my people are concerned, yer are."

He gave Peg another hug. "Thanks, Peg," he said sincerely. "You'll do me for a mum-in-law."

"Yeah? An' another thing, I'm tired of Murranji hangin' around Dor an' me when he should be doin' what he likes. An' that's bein' in camp with you fellers."

"So?"

"So now you an' Dor is married, me an' her will also be in camp."

"Yeah?"

"Yeah, we'll do the cookin' an' look after you lot, proper like." Peg's eyes grew dreamy. "It'll be like when I first met an' looked after my man, all those years ago."

Calum walked slowly back to camp. He decided that he liked the feeling of being married, and he resolved that he'd take his Murri marriage just as seriously as he would a white feller one. He was disappointed that Doreen wasn't waiting in camp when he got back. She still hadn't arrived by the time he'd decided to put out the fire and turn in.

He awoke at piccaninny dawn. When he opened his eyes, the first thing that he saw was Doreen's face looking down at him. She'd obviously come back to camp after he'd fallen asleep and hadn't wanted to wake him.

"I love looking at you when you're asleep, darl," she said. "Your face looks innocent, like a baby's."

"And are you really sure you don't mind being a wife?" He grinned.

"I've decided I like my husband's face. But I'm still working out whether or not I'm rapt in being a wife," she teased.

"Dor."

"What?" she asked innocently.

"Bloody hell," he exclaimed. "I love having you for my wife."

She smiled at him. Her eyes were still teasing. "Maybe I could get to like it. It all depends on if you're going to be nice and not hire me out to other white fellers."

"Dor!"

"And you'll have to remember to scratch my back when it's itchy. And get the tucker I like. You know, those sorts of things."

He started to smile. "I can see you're going to be a demanding wife," he said. "Just my rotten luck."

High in a Paperbark, a Blue-winged Kookaburra cackled in the day. Curaidh approached them and nudged Calum's elbow. They both gave him a reassuring pat. Calum sat up, rubbed the sleep from his eyes and looked around. Socks had been lying on his side. Now he rolled over, thrust out his front legs, and used his back legs to push himself to his feet. Like Lady, next to him, bits of grass and dirt clung to his muddy coat. He stood looking at them with his ears pricked. They heard him noisily make wind.

"You're a rude bugger, Socks. It's far too early for me to cop that nonsense."

"Poor Socks. You can't help it, can you?" Doreen told him.

****

They were the first to arrive at the smallish waterhole, which was known to harbour gators. Not a breath of air stirred its still-dark surface. Nearby was the raft made yesterday from thick sheets of Paperbark lashed together with strong, green vines.

It was the day before he, Jalyerri and Brian were due to leave. And he sensed the change that had suddenly gripped Doreen. Her unease was now palpable, and he could feel the tension that hung between them. It was always the same on their last day. On the outside, they affected a cheerfulness that neither felt but, underneath, the tension simmered and grew. But this time it was worse. Now that they were lovers, it seemed that an added strain was stretching and pulling at them. Then all of a sudden, Doreen's emotions got the better of her, and she became as churned up as just-made butter.

"I hate it," she unexpectedly cried out. "What's the point of having a husband when he leaves you?"

"You know I promised to help your dad, and I won't let him down."

"And why're you always so damn white feller calm? Why don't you let me see what's inside you?"

She started pummelling a small fist against his chest. He could feel her frustration, and he knew that she was as tightly strung as an overwound watch spring. He held her fist. He was beginning to feel edgy himself.

"There's no point in both of us being jumpy, is there? And I just don't understand why you're also like this if I ever bring up Cord River," he said.

It was the wrong thing to say. He instantly realized that he'd been stupidly insensitive, and he could've bitten his tongue. She looked stunned. Her face grew tight, and then she suddenly exploded.

"Calum, you're a bastard for even mentioning Cord River. You're nasty and cruel!" she cried, deeply wounded. "And I suppose," she scornfully continued, "like any man, you'll be fucking those women at Long Creek who're told to go to you? Or would you prefer a nice, white girl? Yes, a white girl who can give you nice, white babies?"

"I've never heard you use that word before," he said weakly, suddenly worrying that somebody had told her about Maudy.

She was pummelling his chest again, and her lovely face was distorted with anger and frustration. "Well, isn't that what you've been doing?" she cried. "Haven't you been fucking your creamy while you've been up here? And now you're pissing off."

He grasped her shoulders hard and shook her.

"Stop," she cried out. "You're hurting me."

"I'm sorry."

"You hurt me," she cried accusingly.

"I said I was sorry. And I meant it. And why in hell are you so edgy? And why can't you talk to me?" he angrily demanded.

She stayed sullen and silent.

"Come on," he demanded, still angry, "tell me, for God's sake!"

Tears came to her eyes. "I can't talk about Cord, and you know that," she cried. "And it was very different when we weren't sharing the same swag." She sniffled. "Now, sleeping with you is all I seem to think of. I hate it because I've always got this ache in my stomach. And I hate you for making me feel this way. And now you're leaving. It's just not fair!"

"And are you going to sleep with visiting Murries while I'm away?" He grimaced, coldly.

"Only my husband can tell me to do that."

"And will you want to fuck anybody else while I'm away? Perhaps a blow-in white feller?" He was struggling to hold onto his anger.

"No," she said in a tiny voice.

"Now you hear me good, Dor," he stated viciously, his face set and hard. "There's no damn way I'll be fucking anyone else, while we're apart. And if I ever find out you've been fucking another man"—his face tightened—"Jesus, I'll gut that bastard like a fish, and you'll find yourself in 'Nother Place. And so damn, quick smart you'll have skid marks on the bottom of your bloody feet."

She looked up at him with big, round eyes. She'd never before seen him this angry. "But just tell me you won't want white babies, because that's something I can't give you ever."

His voice softened. "You're the only woman I'll ever want, Dor. And when I'm seventy, I'll still want to have my darra in you. And by then, if we're lucky, we'll have brown-skinned, freckle-faced granddaughters, who'll love staying with us at the River."

Her face cleared, and an impish look appeared in her dark eyes. "But your darra might be worn away by then," she said.

He'd settled down. "No, it won't." He grinned. "And that's just wishful thinking on your part."

"No, it's not." Her smile was gentle and caring. "So long as you still love me, I won't mind at all when your darra's inside me."

"Good. Because for better or for worse, we'll always be together."

"I try to tell myself that, darl. Often."

"Believe it, my love. Please."

They heard the approaching Murries before they saw them. Brian and Jalyerri then appeared. They were surrounded by a chattering mob of men, women and children. Brian held the sturdy, mug-shaped, harpoon head that carried three, strong prongs; each, of which, had a razor-sharp barb at its point. Instructed by Jalyerri, Brian had made the harpoon head and had toiled over Long Creek's furnace and anvil till Jalyerri was satisfied. On the harpoon head was a socket, through which a green hide rope had been tied. Jalyerri carried the long, wooden shaft onto which the harpoon head fitted. Brian had explained that when the barbs were embedded in a gator, the power of its escape surge would pull the head free of its shaft. Then the men, onshore, holding the end of the green hide rope would haul the gator from the water. And when they'd hauled it out of the water, Calum would be expected to shoot it in the head.

As soon as Jalyerri calculated that there was enough light to see the thin line of bubbles made by a gator, he stepped onto the floating raft. His sinewy, black arms effortlessly poled it to the deepest part of the billabong. Once there, he stopped poling and used his pole to beat upon the surface. Almost immediately a thin, moving line of bubbles rose to the surface to indicate that a gator was gliding slowly over the billabong's muddy bottom. Jalyerri carefully followed the bubbles till they stopped moving. Abruptly, he thrust down powerfully, with the harpoon, and then quickly poled to the grassy bank. He leaped from the raft and joined the men holding the end of the straining rope. The men commenced to haul on the rope. They were urged on by the excited mob of shrieking, gesticulating women and children.

"Be ready with your gun," Brian warned.

"This looks like a dinkum fight, mate. Will it be a big one?"

"Not real big. But they're all strong bastards."

It didn't take long. The harpoon barbs were deeply embedded in the back of a tail-thrashing, twisting, open-jawed, ten-foot gator. It was slowly dragged from the billabong. It was the first time that Calum had seen a gator close up. He was repulsed by it. He saw it solely as a stalker and killer of man and beast, and he found the sight of its wide-open jaws and rows of big, uneven teeth quite chilling. He glanced at Doreen's face and saw a mixture of fear and excitement. He waited, still appalled by the immense power of this knobby-skinned, prehistoric monster. It stilled its head for a moment, and he shot it. That was the signal for several pics to leap onto it and jump up and down in excitement.

When the harpoon head had been cut out of the monster's back, Jalyerri got back onto the raft. Before the breeze sprang up and spoiled his visibility, he'd harpooned another one. It measured eleven feet in length.

That night, there was a feast in the Murri encampment. And, in accordance with tradition, when it came to gator, Jalyerri, as a hunter, was offered his "vow" choice.

Calum was aware that if somebody else ate Jalyerri's "vow" choice, the Murries believed that it'd turn to poison in that person's gut.

Following the feast, Calum and Doreen returned to their camp. Doreen was still unable to shake off the anxiety that gripped her, and Calum held her all through the balmy night. He listened to the night sounds around them: the distinctive plop of a Barramundi, the breeze rustling through the grass and the never-ending croaking of frogs. And then, from a long way away, the far carrying, plaintive and primordial howling of a dingo family.

Before daybreak, Doreen turned and clutched him, and Calum sensed her inner turmoil. She indicated that she wanted him inside her, with minimal preliminaries. Then she thrust and thrust against him.

"I'm sorry. I'm sorry. I'm sorry."

"There's nothing to be sorry about," he murmured.

"I just need to get used to our new love," she whispered. "I'm happy and aching and frightened all at the same time."

"I can't wait to finish off Big River's bullock muster, Dor, and get back to the homestead. You will be coming, won't you?"

"I promise. And promise me, my husband, you'll be waiting, for me, when Mum and me arrive."

"I promise, Dor. You have my word."

"Promise me again that you'll be waiting when Mum and me reach the River."

"I promise, Dor."

CHAPTER 17

BUFFALO

Within minutes of Calum and Brian arriving, back at Big River, Murranji thrust Hank's note under their noses. It didn't thrill them.

> To Murranji, Brian, and Calum. Could you guys please meet me at the stockyard on Little Georgina Creek? It's important. And bring a week's rations with you. We'll be waiting. Thanks guys, Hank.

"Jeez," Brian complained, "another bloody, long ride. I reckon my bum'll soon be growing onto my saddle."

"Yeah, well get some rest tonight," Murranji told him. "Because we'll be heading off at first light."

At dawn, they ate the breakfast that Mr. Ah Lee silently put in front of them. And though the freshness of a sou'east trade breathed on them, they knew that the day was stubbornly headed toward the high eighties.

Later, as Brian, Murranji and Calum, helped by Alasdair and Iain, loaded provisions onto a packhorse, the banter was nonstop and not always gentle. Hank's message, carried by Tarpot, had them all puzzled.

"I'm pleased the bullock muster is about finished," Alasdair said.

"Yeah?"

"What I mean," Alasdair explained, deliberately inviting comment, "is we're not up to it now 'cause we're old. Come ter think of it, I reckon I'm tempting fate if I even pick green bananas off my tree."

Murranji looked exasperated. "That so?" he asked. "Well, you'd better stick to tomatoes. They ripen quicker than bananas, don't they?"

Alasdair appeared shocked by Murranji's terse comment. "I reckon yer do want ter see the end of me, Murranji," he dolefully complained.

"Well, I will," Murranji shot back, "unless you stop being a morbid, old man, you hear?"

"An' why isn't Peg here?" Alasdair continued plaintively. "She an' Dor are the only two people in the whole Territory who like me. They never tell me ter pick green tomatoes, and I'm *always* happy when they're about."

"Yes," Murranji agreed. "They like you a heap. And I also like you, but only when you're cheerful."

"Well, yer don't show it, you know. An' I am cheerful sometimes."

Iain gave his brother a sour look. "Yer do say some terrible, depressin' things, Alasdair," he complained. "An' it beats the hell out of me where yer get them thoughts."

"It's 'cause I want ter retire ter the place we've bought in Adelaide. An' I'm happy to sell even before Dor gets round ter making an honest man out of Calum."

"You heard him, Calum," Iain said. "We'll set a price as soon as you two get back."

"I'm glad he's decided I'm not a rogue." Calum grinned. "Now I won't have to worry about dodging his bullets."

"Maybe," Iain suggested, "Alasdair's depressed because your Kaditje man's been hanging around. An' how was he this time, mate?"

"Fine," Calum said. "We shared a feed last night, and I gave him a little axe. He was rapt. He's all right, you know. I don't know why people are so scared of him."

"You're the one who's awright. But the rest of us is still waitin' ter see who he picks on next," Iain complained. "An' it won't be ter adopt us."

"Relax, Iain. You don't have a worry."

"Beats me how he always knows where you are, Calum," Iain complained. "But I'll be glad when he moves on. All our Murries are shit scared of him. Me also, come ter think of it."

"He'll turn up again when I get back," Calum said. "I reckon he's told the Murries to keep track of me and tell him where I'm headed."

"Mm."

"I did tell you Henry was bringing Peg an' Doreen down, didn't I, Alasdair?" Murranji asked.

"I'm not losin' my memory, yer know," Alasdair flashed. "I'm only old."

"Yeah?"

"Yer said they was due in about two weeks, didn't yer?" Alasdair pugnaciously asked.

"Yeah. An' I reckon they'll be real shitty because Calum an' me promised we'd be waiting for 'em when they got here," Murranji said. "An' if they're early," he continued, "you tell 'em they're not to go wandering around. Your Murries tell me Ed Smith's been hanging about here and there."

"Fer Crissake. But he won't come anywhere near the homestead, I promise yer," Alasdair said.

"No?"

"Guaranteed! He knows he'd cop the rough end of a pineapple if he did," Alasdair threatened. Then he added excitedly, "Jesus, I better oil me rifle."

Hank's message had irritated Calum. All he wanted was to help wrap up the bullock muster quickly and then be back at the homestead when Doreen and Peg arrived. He consoled himself by imagining what it'd be like when she was living in camp during the calf branding. Then he grimaced to himself as he pictured her disappointment when she discovered that he and her father weren't waiting at the homestead as promised.

He briefly stroked Socks's neck, shortened his reins and swung himself into his saddle. He looked down at the brothers. "See you when we get back," he said. "And Alasdair?"

"Yeah?"

"I'm trusting you to look after my girl and her mum."

"I hear you," Alasdair grumbled.

"Hooroo, fellers. See you when we get back."

They wheeled their horses and headed off at a brisk walk. Trotting beside Socks was Curaidh who, as always, kept glancing up at his master's face.

They hadn't ridden far when Calum halted Socks and turned him. He enjoyed the view from beyond the homestead, down to the river. It was a panoramic vista that encompassed the slow-moving, coffee-coloured river and the undulating, grassy slope, which reached down to the heavily wooded flats. Just before the flats were two, seventy-foot-high Woolly Butts, with their ever-present, squealing Black Flying-foxes. These large, furry bats dined on fruit as well as eucalypt and melaleuca nectar. And the way that they dangled from the upper branches always made Calum think that they themselves resembled some sort of strange overripe, black fruit. While beyond the Woolly Butts, an ever-present flock of pristine-white Cattle Egrets, sporting their long yellow, head, neck and back plumes, were scattered among the grazing Shorthorns.

"If anyone reckoned this place was only easy on the eye," Calum remarked, "they wouldn't be within a bull's roar of telling it right."

"You're not wrong there, son," agreed Murranji Bill. "An' my Peg also reckons it's extra special."

"Dor does too."

"An' don't worry about Dor being upset if you're not at the River, son," Murranji said. "I'll square things for us, no worries."

"It's just that I promised her."

"A man needs to know when he has no choice but to break his promise. An' his woman needs to understand."

"Yeah?"

Calum was grateful that Murranji had volunteered to square things with the women. It was typical of the man. He'd always been considerate as far as Calum was concerned, and from the start, Calum had liked him. Nowadays, Calum regarded him with a deal of affection.

They turned their horses and recommenced their journey. Sunshine, their packhorse, was happy to bring up the rear. He was everyone's favourite because he never needed a lead rope.

The black mare that Brian was riding danced skittishly sideways upon spotting a motionless Short-beaked Echidna. The thoroughly alarmed, toothless, little eater of ants and termites, clad in its straw-coloured, black-tipped spines, was already burrowing downward, and soon, only its spiny back would be exposed. Brian's mare stood snorting and looking at it with pricked ears. He gave her a reassuring pat.

"This mare doesn't miss a thing," he remarked. "She saw that *pokupain* long before I did."

Calum smiled and didn't bother to mention that Socks had spotted the Echidna way before Brian's mare. The horses continued to step out, and Murranji calculated that in the three hours that they'd been riding, they'd covered close to fifteen miles.

Suddenly, the shrill squealing of fighting stallions erupted ahead of them.

Brian put his mare into a canter. "Come on, fellers," he urged.

They cantered up the small rise in front of them. When they breasted it, they had a clear view. Eighty yards on was a little creek, and beside it were four, feral, Brumby mares and two foals. These stood with staring eyes as two stallions fought over them. Calum slid off Socks, passed his reins to Brian and grabbed his rifle. He looked down at Curaidh.

"You stay with Socks, pup," he ordered.

He walked away from their horses, sat down and rested his elbows on his knees. He noted that the mares and foals were poor specimens. They were inbred and wouldn't have been worth the trouble of catching and breaking in, even if a man did happen to fancy the excitement offered by a bit of Brumby running.

"This scrap is a fair dinkum one, fellers," Murranji murmured.

A chunky, black stallion with feathers on its feet was going hammer and tongs with a clean-looking bay. They were standing rear end to rear end and were kicking out viciously with both hind legs. Then simultaneously they swivelled, reared up on their hind legs and chopped nastily, with their front hooves. Both squealed continuously. The bay was struggling. It had blood pouring from wounds on its neck and was giving ground more often than the black. The black continued to press hard.

The end came suddenly. Exhaustion caused the bay to stumble. In a flash, the black, with its neck low and long, grabbed a vulnerable front shin in its mouth. It snapped the bone as easily as a man snaps a thin branch. The bay stood unable to move. It was anchored piteously on its three, sound legs. Instantly the black wheeled and kicked out viciously.

One of its back hooves caught the bay a sickening blow high up on its cheek. The bay's skull was crushed as easily as the tap of a spoon crushes the top of a boiled egg.

The black squealed a challenge at the world and then trotted, head high and tail up, around its dead foe. It continued to squeal shrilly, in triumph. When it dropped its head and snaked its neck to round up the mares, Calum shot it. He managed to shoot three of the mares and a foal as well. But a mare and a foal escaped into a thick clump of scrub before he could get off another shot. He rose to his feet and returned to the others.

"Poor bastard," he remarked. "He wins his fight and gets shot for his trouble."

"We don't need thieving, Brumby stallions breaking into the breeding paddock, stealing Big River mares an' scattering the rest hell, west an' crooked," Brian dryly observed.

****

They reached Little Georgina Creek on the fourth day, at sunset. Hank, Jack Kelly and Jalyerri were squatting on their haunches around a fire, waiting for a slab of near-ready, corned beef to finish cooking.

Jack Kelly gave them a cheery wave and called out, "Bush yer horses, fellers. The damper's about done. An' did anyone think to bring a bottle or two?"

"Have I ever let you down, Jack?" Murranji called back.

Jack Kelly was the only one to whom Curaidh went. He briefly sniffed at Jack's leg and accepted a couple of pats before returning to Calum.

After washing their hands, they cut themselves meat and helped themselves to the just-baked damper.

"How're you fellers going?" Murranji asked.

"Okay," Jack replied. "What about you lot?"

"Good, mate. Now tell us what's so important, Hank?" Murranji asked. "But don't start till I pour myself a rum," he said. "Hell, I'd best enjoy a grog now, seeing as I'll have my missus watching me, like a kite, when she reaches the River."

"Jan asked me to remind you, Murranji that too much rum'll poison the body," Hank smilingly observed. He shook his head "Isn't it amazing how these women stick together?"

"So, how come she reckons it's bloody poisonous?" Murranji truculently asked.

"Because," Hank smilingly explained. "If you put a worm in a glass of water it'll live. But if you drop a worm into a glass of rum it'll die. It's as simple as that."

"The only thing that proves," Murranji indignantly told him, "is that a feller who drinks plenty of rum will *never* get worms!"

Hank couldn't help laughing. "Let's forget worms and rum and get back to why we're here," he said. "Look, I went up with a pilot who came looking for work, just for the ride, but also to look at our boundaries from the air. And we went a good bit farther north and flew over that large bit of Crown land with all the water. And we saw buffalo there."

"So what?" Murranji said. "Don't tell me you brought us here to tell us you've seen buffalo?"

"I'm worried they'll drift south, so I got permission from the Department to shoot them."

"Why in God's name would a man want to go chasing after buffalo?"

"Because they're riddled with Brucellosis, Murranji. And it's contagious."

"What the hell is *that*?" Murranji asked.

"We've got it in Texas. There, it's called it Texas Fever."

"And?"

"There isn't a station here with boundary fences, is there? I'm worried they'll drift south and infect somebody's herd. Next thing you know, Big River'll be infected, and then so will we."

Hank looked around at their faces. They stared back at him blankly. He drew on his cigarette and blew out twin streams of smoke. "Brucellosis is carried by goats and cattle," he explained. "And anyone who comes in contact with infected beasts can catch it. People like ringers and abattoir workers. Even kids who drink infected milk."

"For Crissake," Murranji exclaimed. "Is it bad?"

"I had friends in Texas who caught it. They had chills, bad fever and painful joints. But they were lucky because it can also affect the brain and spinal cord."

"Jesus! Can cattle be cured?" Murranji asked.

"No. But I heard they're working on a vaccine for calves, in the States."

There was silence. The potential risk to the vast, Long Creek herd was now sinking in.

Murranji gave voice to their fear. "That's no help, for Crissake. Hell, the Long Creek herd's got to be fifty-thousand-plus."

"I know," Hank said quietly. "And in Texas, you can't sell your cattle unless a vet's tested your herd and it's Brucellosis free. And that'll happen here, sooner rather than later."

"How come they've got so far south?" Calum wondered.

"Beats me." Hank shrugged. "Maybe it's population growth. They've never been culled by the Government." He saw their concern and tried to sound reassuring. "Jack was a buffalo shooter before the war. He's come along to help."

Calum looked at Jack Kelly. "I've seen 'em, of course, but I've never shot them," he said.

"Wounded ones need ter be followed up an' killed," Jack said ominously. "They're dangerous. And they've killed hunters and their horses."

Calum didn't like the thought of that, so he changed the subject. "The Macs are going to have a sale price worked out for us by the time we get back," he told Hank.

"Wow."

"An' we shook on it, Hank."

"That *is* great news."

"Yes," Calum agreed. "And I just want to clean out these buffalo quickly, because Dor and Peg are due to arrive in about two weeks."

****

The following afternoon, after they'd set up camp, Jalyerri invited Calum to go hunting with him. Calum was touched. He was well aware of the honour, which such a renowned hunter as Jalyerri had accorded him. He walked behind Jalyerri and tried to tread in his footsteps.

265

Jalyerri had told him that he was after Corellas and had, with him, a yard-long boomerang, fashioned from a piece of Coolibah root. For some reason, Calum assumed that Jalyeri would throw it at Corellas, rising into the air, and if he missed, it'd come whirling back to him. Calum couldn't have been more wrong. When they came upon a flock of ground-feeding Corellas, Jalyerri threw his boomerang powerfully, parallel to the ground. It skidded along, like a stone skimming over the surface of a billabong, and collected four of the birds before the flock could take off.

Later, they roasted them on the campfire. Calum thought that they made a delicious entrée.

****

On their third morning, they were squatted around the fire, breakfasting. Hank looked determined.

"I want to run through our plan once more," he said. "Now, Jalyerri is horse tailer, and you three are the foot shooters." He paused. "Jack and I won't move on our horses till you guys are in position and have got off your shots. Your rifles'll spook the rest of them. They'll start running, and that's when Jack and I will take off after 'em." He glanced at Calum. "You stick with Brian, my friend. And both of you need to keep Murranji in sight, so you can help him out with your crossfire."

Jack nudged Hank's arm. "There's one thing I forgot ter mention, mate. Buffalo get cranky when they're bein' chased. They'll often stop, swing round an' charge yer horse. An' if they hit yer horse, they'll knock it over. Next thing yer on the ground, an' the bastard's onter you, quicker 'n a cat on a mouse. They're real fast."

Hank breathed in deeply and raised his eyebrows. "Now you tell me, Jack. And you did this for a living?"

"Hank, yer can always tell if the one yer chasing is goin' ter turn back on yer. Like, it'll slow up, keep lookin' back at yer an' start swingin' those big horns from side ter side. So don't get took by surprise. Course, when it turns and comes at you, yer horse'll turn around quick an' start fightin' fer his head, 'cause all he wants is ter put distance between himself an' the bull. That's when yer got ter hold him back. Yer not lookin' ahead because yer watching that bull over your shoulder. An' when it's 'bout one and a half tail lengths from yer horse's bum, yer lean back an' put a bullet in its head."

"Jesus!"

Jack Kelly contemplated Hank. "But most times it's like I said. You can gallop up alongside the beast an' lean over an' put a bullet in its spine. That anchors it till yer've finished yer run. Then yer walk yer horse back an' lean over an' put one in its head."

"Yes."

They mounted and headed for the spot where, late yesterday, they'd come upon the fresh, buffalo tracks. Brian went ahead to scout. When he returned, he filled them in.

"It's a small mob," he told them. "I'd reckon maybe thirty."

"Are they all grown?" Hank asked.

"No, mate. It's a mixed mob of cows, calves and bulls."

Brian pointed to a low, heavily timbered ridge that was ahead and to their left. "They're behind that ridge an' around a billabong that's drying out. We'll approach 'em from the right. That way they'll be upwind."

Jack Kelly and Hank rode off to the right.

Calum watched Brian hop off his mare, Poss, and tighten her girth.

"Why're you doing that?" he asked.

"I want to know my saddle won't slip if I have to get on in a hurry."

They remounted and, accompanied by Murranji and Jalyerri, rode to the low ridge, rounded it and halted their horses. They found themselves looking at a wide, flat plain broken up by a shrinking though still expansive, sun-sparkling billabong. The grey-black mud that bordered it had dried and had cracked into innumerable, different shapes. To their right was a forest of Paperbarks. The high-water marks on their trunks indicated that during the Wet, this billabong had been joined to others to form a huge, freshwater lagoon. Farther to their right and beyond were heavily timbered, low ridges.

"As Hank'd say," Murranji remarked. "Ain't this something else again?"

Areas on the billabong's surface were covered by a dazzling array of exquisitely coloured, purple, white, and yellow water lily blossoms. These stunning blooms, atop their long stalks, nodded in the breeze above broad, green pads and the floating, green grass with which they shared the water.

The billabong teemed with an array of noisy waterfowl. And Calum noticed a number of clever Galahs. They were hovering just above the water, like giant pink-and-grey hummingbirds, while dipping their pale-coloured beaks beneath the surface to drink.

Interestingly, Calum thought, *the buffalo, while in small groups, had by and large stayed as a herd.* Three, not far from the water's edge, were wallowing in a wet-mud wallow that they had dug and enlarged, and nearby, a number were grazing above the dried mud. Their bodies were caked with the dry, blackish-grey mud.

Jalyerri touched Calum's arm and indicated by extending his lips, to ensure that no part of his body would be projected in the direction that he indicated. Calum picked up the three, resting bulls just inside the timber's edge. One was lying down, and the other two were standing motionless in the shade. Jalyerri was not impressed.

"No goot bugger, dat t'ree feller."

Calum thought again about the brief conversation that he and Brian had had.

"I want you to stick close, mate," Brian had said.

"Why?"

"Something about this doesn't feel right to me." Brian's brow had been furrowed. He'd looked at Calum, hard. "I can feel things, mate. I can feel the earth like you can feel the wind. An' water is like my own blood."

"Yeah?"

"I'm telling you something is not right about this. You stick close, okay? I reckon we need to look out for each other."

"I understand."

Calum looked at Jalyerri. Jalyerri held two, Ironwood-shafted, hunting spears in his slim left hand. He was alert and relaxed.

"All right," Murranji said. "Brian, you and Calum need to get into position and shoot those three bulls at the edge of that timber. You two fire first, an' then I'll start shooting at those in the billabong."

"Right."

Calum stroked Curaidh. "Now you stay here with Socks, pup," he ordered.

Brian and Calum moved closer, sat down and rested their elbows on their knees. The bulls hadn't moved. They stood resting and chewing the cud. Their only movement was when their ears flicked or when they shook their heads to rid themselves of the flies that'd clustered around their eyes. Now that he was at such close quarters, Calum found himself surprised by their size. It wasn't only their height, but it was also their bulk. He estimated that each would have to weigh over a ton. And the horns! He'd thought that some Shorthorns grew big horns. Hell, compared to these, those were tiddly.

"I'll take the two on the right. You fire first," he suggested to Brian.

As soon as Brian fired, Calum fired twice, and he levered the Winchester so quickly that his second shot was not more than three seconds behind his first. He fired a third time when he saw that Brian's bull was still standing. Then he heard Murranji start to shoot and jumped to his feet.

"Come on," he yelled to Brian. "Let's check these bulls and then go and help Murranji."

The three bulls were dead from brain shots, so they ran for their horses. And as Calum mounted, he noticed Curaidh sitting on his haunches, ears pricked, wide-eyed and swivelling his head to ensure that he missed none of this new excitement. He'd stayed with Socks as ordered.

"Come on, pup," Calum said. "We're off to help Murranji."

For an instant, at the sound of Calum's voice, Curaidh's ears dropped, and his oval eyes looked up at his master. And when Socks moved, he tucked in beside him.

They reached Murranji and saw that sensibly, he'd been shooting the calves to prevent their mothers from galloping off with them. Confused cows were calling and sniffing at their downed offspring. Then, like Murranji, both began to shoot the cows and calves still standing. Behind them they heard the *crack* of Hank's and Jack's rifles. When Calum reloaded, he did it by feel, with his eyes on those buffalo at the billabong's margins. He was aware that the teeming waterfowl had risen from the billabong and now were circling, like some porous, dark cloud, high above it.

Not a single buffalo had attempted to escape by heading for the billabong's opposite shore. All had rushed inshore toward the shooters and then had thundered off over the plain on a course that for about forty yards kept them parallel to the rifles. *It was almost like shooting those moving cut-out ducks in shooting galleries,* Calum thought. *There was no challenge; it was simply a cull.* Lever the Winchester and aim, lead, fire, and see the small puff of dust between the animal's eye and ear, where the bullet had struck. And watch the momentum of the huge beast abruptly halted as its legs lost power. See it twist sideways and collapse to the ground.

Calum reloaded and heard more shots coming from behind and to his left. He glanced over his shoulder and saw Jack Kelly's buckskin. It was galloping and was being firmly held. A big, mud-covered bull was so close behind that the buckskin's flowing tail was literally brushing its nose. *Hell,* he thought, *that's damn scary.* Then he recalled what Brian had said to him, and his heart started to hammer a bit faster.

Calum watched Jack Kelly lean back. He held his rifle at arm's length, in his right hand, and then poked it in the bull's face before squeezing the trigger. Calum saw the bull start to collapse, even before the rifle's *crack* reached him. He breathed out, relieved, and noticed lying upright, in Jack's wake, four more buffalo. They couldn't move because their spines had been shattered.

No more buffalo were standing. Calum rose to his feet and checked to see if any of the downed buffalo were wounded. There was only one, a young heifer, and he shot her in the head.

When he turned around, he saw that Brian and Jalyerri were coming to join him.

"That's the lot," he called. "I'm heading for that rise there so I can see what Hank and Jack are up to."

From the low rise, they had an uninterrupted view. Jack Kelly was riding at a walk, some two-hundred yards from the nearest crippled buffalo. Hank was ninety yards from Jack Kelly. He warily approached a prostrate buffalo that he'd shot before leaning over and dispatching it.

"Just mopping up," Brian said.

"I don't reckon this was anything to write home about," Calum observed.

"Just another job, mate."

Murranji gathered his reins, mounted and rode over to the nearest of Jack Kelly's crippled buffalo. He shot it and then dismounted, loosened the girth on his horse, tied its reins round its neck and set it free to graze. Then he walked to the buffalo that he'd shot, leaned his rifle against its shoulder and sat down on its rump. He took out his makings and rolled himself a cigarette.

"Wouldn't it be funny if that bugger that Murranji's sitting on suddenly got up," Brian grinned.

"Don't laugh, mate," Calum warned. "That's exactly what happened to Jack. He told me he and one of his Murries were sitting on a cow they thought was dead, when suddenly she got up from under 'em. It was bloody coola, and Jack had to shoot it in a hurry. And he said his Murri nearly shit himself he was laughing so much, at the look on Jack's face, when that cow got up."

They relaxed, uncocked their rifles and put on the safety catches. Murranji, his back toward them, inhaled deeply. He raised his face skyward and exhaled cigarette smoke. At that moment, a large, black, feral boar casually walked out of a clump of scrub, some thirty yards in front of Murranji. It continued on in an unflustered, minding-its-own-business way toward another bit of scrub. It seemed to be largely indifferent to its surroundings and, what's more, didn't appear to be in any hurry.

"By Crise," Brian exclaimed. "Will you have a look at that big bugger? It's got to be going on five-hundred pounds. An' look at those tusks. Mate, I've never seen bigger ones, I tell you."

Murranji noticed the boar for the first time. He casually reached for his rifle, transferred his cigarette to his left hand, aimed and fired. They heard the *whump* as the bullet struck. Instantly, the huge boar started to squeal in rage and pain. It set its little eyes upon Murranji and went straight at him, with its tail up. Calum was amazed to see how fast it charged over the ground. Murranji stood up quickly. He levered his Winchester, took aim and squeezed the trigger. The resulting dull click was quite audible. It was either a misfire or else the magazine was empty. Murranji obviously thought that it was a misfire. He frantically levered the rifle to clear the chamber, but no shell was ejected. Alarm registered on his face. He turned for his horse, but the gelding had taken fright. It was trotting away nervously, with its head up and its eyes wide.

It was all happening very fast. Neither Brian nor Calum could shoot. Murranji was in the line of fire. He was still frantically trying to feed a cartridge into the rifle's breech when the squealing boar hit him.

The huge pig's impact knocked him backward and onto the ground. And the enraged boar continued to squeal all the while that it was biting him and gutting him with its long tusks.

Jalyerri was the first to move. Yelling continuously, he ran forward with great, bounding strides and held aloft a hunting spear. As he bounded forward, Calum moved to his left to create the angle that he needed. On hearing Jalyerri's yells, the boar looked up, focused on him and immediately charged. Calum fired twice, and by the time Jalyerri reached the boar, it lay dying in the blood that was pumping from bullet holes in its neck, chest and shoulder.

Hank galloped to Murranji. He pulled his black to a sliding halt and leaped off to kneel beside him. He placed two fingers against the side of Murranji's neck but, after a moment, shook his head, reached down and closed his friend's eyes. After Murranji's body had been covered with a square of canvas, Hank stood up and reached for his makings. He rolled a cigarette, put it between his lips and lit it with his Zippo.

He stood, filled with anguish, and gazed out over the wide expanse of water. Then, abruptly, he became angry with Murranji. *Murranji had no right to be so absent-minded,* he told himself. But of course, that was part of Murranji's charm. During a task, he could be relied upon to be conscientious and dedicated, but when the job was done, he had a tendency to drift off into his own little world.

When Hank returned to the others, his face was composed and his voice was matter-of-fact. "We'll bury Murranji here, where the ground's soft. And when we get back to the home station, I'll put a stone in the graveyard."

Once the grave had been filled in, Hank asked everyone to take off their hats. He spoke quietly. "Lord, I don't know why you put a pig in that place. And Murranji was being absent-minded when he shot at it, with only one shell in his rifle. Maybe he just forgot to reload. But whichever way we look at it, we've lost a good friend and you've lost a good servant. Murranji Bill Taylor was a decent, honest man. He couldn't abide hypocrisy, and he was without prejudice. He and I had a shaky start, but when I got to know him, I was proud to call him a mate. May he rest in peace. And, Lord, please extend your comfort and support to his loved ones, Peg and Doreen. Amen."

Jack Kelly also spoke. "Mate," he said, "yer won't be havin' any more nightmares now 'bout goin' on them dispersal shoots when you was a youngster. An' any black feller blood that shoulda been there was well an' truly bred out of yer. But yer heart stayed the right colour as soon as you got older. You was always a good mate, an' you was true blue. We'll miss yer. An' I can tell yer now, yer can rest easy 'bout yer family 'cause I'll be lookin' out fer 'em."

"Too right. We all will," Brian added.

Hank replaced his hat and once again surveyed the scene around him. Dozens of white-eyed, shiny-black Torresian Crows, as well as light-coloured Whistling Kites, had already joined the feast. They were tearing greedily at the buffalo flesh beneath their feet. And a large Wedge-tailed Eagle sat on the dead boar's shoulder and ripped at the flesh around a bullet hole.

Hank turned away and headed for Murranji's horse. When he returned, he was carrying Murranji's rifle. He handed it to Brian. "Give me the one you got from the store," he said. "This is a fine rifle. Treat it well because it belonged to a decent man."

They watched Hank mount his black and lead the way back to camp. Jalyerri rode beside him. Hank felt shattered. He couldn't wait to get back to Jan and his little girl. He thought about his wife, and he knew that whatever she chose to say about Murranji's death would make a lot of sense. *God, he was lucky,* he told himself, *because Jan wasn't just his wife; she was also his best friend.*

Brian noticed that Poss was with Hank and Jalyerri. And that Murranji Bill's bay, now hobbled, was cropping grass nearby.

Curaidh sat and watched the riders depart. He seemed puzzled that his master wasn't going with them.

"Brian," Jack Kelly said, "I reckon that's Hank's way of tellin' yer Murranji's horse is yours now." He looked at Calum. "I'll ride with you ter the River, mate. I want ter tell yer girl I was her dad's mate an' that I'll be watchin' over her an' her mum from now on."

"I'm going with Hank," Brian informed Calum. "I need to check on Mum."

"Yes."

Murranji's death was now hitting Calum hard. He was very conscious that from the start Murranji had treated him like a son.

Chapter 18

The Macs of Big River

On reaching Big River, Calum felt sombre as he and Jack slowly rode up the curving driveway. The Murries that they'd earlier passed had told them that Peg and Doreen were back. He looked up at the homestead, but couldn't see either. From below, the old, timber-walled and iron-roofed homestead stood out starkly against the afternoon's brilliant-blue skyline. When they got nearer, they saw that the brothers were on the verandah and were watching their approach. Each was leaning long legged against a verandah post.

"I don't see the women, Jack."

"Me neither."

"G'day, fellers," Iain called. "Take yer saddles off an' put yer horses in that yard, there."

Jack and Calum dismounted and shook the brothers' outstretched hands. Iain peered at them and shook his head sadly. Then he and Alasdair helped them to wash down their horses.

"We heard 'bout Murranji soon after it happened," Iain said. "That Murri grapevine travels a lot faster 'n a horse can walk. Bloody shame; he was as straight as they come."

"Yeah," Jack said. "He was a one-off all right."

"Did yer come ter break a few colts, Jack?" Iain asked.

"Yeah. An' I also come ter tell Murranji's family I'm backin' 'em."

"That's carin' of yer. An' where's Brian?" Iain asked.

"He'll be over," Jack said. "After he's checked on his mum and Jan." He paused. "How did the women take it?"

"As yer'd expect," Iain replied. "Lucky they come down with a mob o' their people. They wailed an' hugged, of course, before takin' off ter do their sorry bijnitch."

Calum looked sharply at Alasdair. "We came across Ed Smith's tracks on the way here, mate."

"Don' yer worry, Calum," Alasdair said. "Henry was with 'em. An' Iain went an' set up his own camp where he could watch out fer Smith. *He* went 'cause he boasts he's a better shot 'n me these days. An' the ladies come home last night," he continued. "I reckon Peg was let off light 'cause Murranji's a white feller. She says she's dirty on Murranji now, 'cause he probably decided he'd be happier in the Dreamin' Place than bein' married ter her."

"She's always been a strong woman," Calum said. "Where are they now?"

"We had a big lunch. Mr. Ah Lee went mad," Alasdair said. "He knows Peg wasn't allowed ter eat red meat when she was doin' her sorry bijnitch, so he was determined ter feed both of 'em up. The ladies decided ter sleep it off."

"I don't blame them."

"Anyways, come on up an' join us in a rum," Alasdair said with a twinkle in his faded eyes. "I don' know 'bout you, fellers, but it's not too early fer us."

They'd no sooner reached the verandah than Peg and Doreen walked out onto it. Peg ran into Calum's arms. He looked past her to Doreen and held out an arm for her. She kept her distance, looking hurt and angry.

"I'm sorry. So sorry," he said to Peg. "He really loved both of you. You meant everything to him."

"Yes."

"On that day at breakfast, you know," Calum told them, "he was saying he couldn't wait to get back to you both. He said having you'd changed his life, and he was determined to make up for all the years he'd missed out on."

Peg looked up into Calum's face. She was clear-eyed. She'd already endured whatever grief she'd allow others to see. "Was it quick? Did he suffer?" She paused. "An' give it ter me straight, like."

"He didn't suffer," Calum lied. "And before he passed away, he told me to tell you, Peg, he was rapt that you'd married him. And he said being a husband and a father was the best thing that'd ever happened to him. And he wished he'd had the sense to marry you years ago so he could've had a couple more children." Calum smiled. "And then he said, 'Course, that would've been up to Peg, and I'd have gone along with whatever she'd of wanted.'"

Peg gave Calum a long hug and then a peck on his cheek. "Thanks fer tellin' me that, mate," she said. "Yer've given me somethin' ter hold on ter." She paused and then added quietly, "An' I'd have given 'im all the children he'd have wanted. An' now I won't even get ter look after 'im when he's old."

"He could've been a cranky, ol' bugger, Peg," Alasdair said.

"Not with me, he wouldn't." Peg turned and moved to a verandah chair. She sat down heavily. "I'm awright, Calum," she said. "Why don' yer take Dor fer a walk? Yer both must've lots ter talk about. An' I'm goin' ter make me old fellers here a cuppa before I let 'em open that bottle."

"Now, Peg," Alasdair said. "I'm wishing you'd come out ten minutes later; then I'd 've had that bottle open already."

"Looks like today *isn't* yer lucky day, mate."

Calum and Doreen said good-bye, left the verandah and walked toward the river. Curaidh led the way and, every now and then, trotted back to check on them. Once they were out of sight of the others, Calum stopped and leaned his rifle against a tree trunk. He put his arms around Doreen and held her close.

"Aren't you going to give me a kiss?" He grinned.

She looked up at him and gave him a quick kiss. He studied her face. He'd known that she would be badly knocked about by her father's death, and during their walk, her voice and her manner had revealed a brittle edge. The way she now held her shoulders told him that inside, she was stretched as tight as a violin string.

"Will that do you?" she asked and met his eyes defiantly.

"Not really," he said easily.

"Well, it'll have to, won't it?"

"What is it, Dor?"

She turned on him angrily, and her face was tense and hard. "You promised you'd be waiting here when we arrived!" She cried. "And you weren't. Instead, you and Dad go chasing after buffalo. I'm surprised *you* weren't killed too. How am I supposed to trust you?" She laughed sarcastically. "And now you expect me to be all over you like a rash."

She started to walk on ahead, but he didn't move. She looked back and didn't speak. *The air within the riverbank bush was still and heavy,* he thought, *like the gulf that now lay between them.* And there were often butterflies here. And today they seemed to be everywhere, especially the big, greyish ones with a large, black spot on each wing. He shook his head, bemused. *Yes,* he thought, *sometimes, Dor was no damn different to a butterfly. Like now, when she looked just as fragile and with her mood dipping and fluttering and rising, like a damn butterfly's stuttering flight.*

"Well?" she asked and started to cry.

He studied her. "You tell me," he said.

The angry, sullen look left her tear-blotched face, and suddenly, she appeared lost and vulnerable. Her voice was tremulous. "And I suppose you'll be next," she cried. "They say bad things always come in threes."

"I don't follow you."

"Well, all the people I love get taken from me. First, Cord River took Mum away. And now a stupid, damn pig kills Dad." She glared at him. "And I never had him for long. And when'll you be taken from me? Or are you just going to disappear when your darra's tired of my mouth and kumara?"

"Cord River didn't damn well take your mum from you. You were taken from *her*, Dor."

"And don't you dare ask me about Cord. You couldn't take it if I told you what really happened there," she shouted hysterically.

He steadied himself against his starting anger. "Stop it, Dor. And don't you bloody well fly of the handle. I wasn't the one who mentioned Cord."

Big teardrops started to roll down her cheeks and great, convulsive sobs wrenched at her body. He desperately wished that somehow, he could take away all her pain and endure it himself. He walked to her and put his arms around her and held her. She pulled away.

"Don't you dare touch me!" she cried. "You broke your promise. And you've never done that before."

Tears were still rolling down her cheeks. She was standing, slightly bent over. She'd crossed her arms and was hugging her shaking body. He was left to stand and watch her pain.

"I love you," he told her urgently. "And nothing'll ever change that. But I can't give you any guarantees. Life's not like that. And I think this business of bad things happening in threes is all bullshit. And as far as those buffalo go, we had no choice. We couldn't let Hank down." He paused and studied her. "I take you the way you are, Dor. So please take me how I am."

"You still broke your promise to me," she cried. "How can I trust you? Or maybe being manly in front of Hank is more important to you than I am!"

"Dor, I'm really sorry I broke my word, but please try to understand. Truly, we did have to go."

Without warning, she turned, ran to him and threw her arms around his neck. "I'm sorry too," she wailed. "And sometimes I hate me for telling myself I hate you, because that's when I'm mean to you. But you've made me love you so much. And sometimes, I hate the pain of loving you. And then at the same time, I get frightened and worried that something's going to happen to you. And then I panic and don't ever want to be apart from you. And I can't eat or sleep. And I wouldn't blame you if you thought I was crazy. Because even I start to think I must be a little crazy to be like this."

"You're not crazy. I also worry that something could happen to you. Then I make myself stop thinking like that. And I force myself to think of all the happy times we've got ahead of us. And I make myself believe we're going to grow old together."

All her anger suddenly left, like a fleeing, dark cloud after a brief, rain-filled, wind gust.

"I've been horrible to you. I'm sorry, my darling. I don't mean to be nasty. It just happens, and I can't help it."

"Dor, it must be real hard for you to lose your dad. I'm also hurting because he was like a father to me."

She frowned and looked away. "I can't talk about that now," she said tremulously. "I just need to feel close to you." She looked up at him and gripped his arms hard. "Will you do it to me, now?"

He kissed her, but she didn't respond. "Just do it," she commanded. "Now."

When it was over, they walked back to the homestead. They took their time. She held his hand all the way and didn't speak. At the old, driveway gate they turned and waited for Curaidh to catch up. He'd killed a small, dark-grey Ground Goanna. He dropped it at their feet.

"No, we don't want it, pup," Calum told him. "You go ahead and eat it if you want to."

Curaidh picked it up and moved under a nearby bush.

Doreen stood on tiptoe, looked up into Calum's eyes, and then kissed him. "I've never seen so many butterflies before," she said. "Today was a real butterfly day, wasn't it?"

"Yes." He grimaced. "It really was."

The others were still on the verandah. Peg and Jack Kelly were still absorbing the just-announced decision by the Macs that they proposed to retire to Adelaide forthwith. Calum did his best to quell his rising excitement, sat down on a verandah step and made himself listen to what was being said.

"An' yer really are goin'?" Peg asked, stunned.

"Too right," Alasdair said. "Course, Mr. Ah Lee's also comin'. He says he's worried an Adelaide cook'll poison us. But the truth is, he's like us: he's got nobody else."

"But you've got me and Dor," Peg said. "Course, yer might not want us visitin' yer in Adelaide. Yer neighbours'll probably complain that havin' Abos stayin' with yer will drop the house values in the street."

"Bugger 'em!" Alasdair swore. "I'll get my rifle out."

"That wouldn't be wise, Alasdair," Peg said. "Look, mate, Adelaide's not the Territory. You'd end up in jail. Anyway, it'll be good practice ter turn the other cheek. 'Cause that's what I've been doin' all my life." She looked at Doreen. "And that's what you need ter learn too, my girl."

"I'll think on that, Mum," Doreen answered, "while I go and make a cuppa for my feller. And I won't take your cups 'cause I'll make a big pot."

Alasdair still had Adelaide on his mind. "But I will want ter see you when we're there, Peg," he insisted.

"Well, suss out yer neighbours first, mate. An' tell 'em we won't be stayin' long at all."

"Oh, all right."

"You know," Calum said, turning to Iain and changing the subject. "I never realized your parents were Gaels till I saw how you spelled your names. Has anyone ever called you Alexander and John?"

"No, and don't you start either," Iain said.

"I might if Alasdair starts talking again about still being alive when his green bananas ripen."

"Cheeky young bugger."

When Doreen returned, she was carrying a tray with a couple of mugs and a large pot of tea. There was an abrupt silence as everyone looked at her. She'd changed and was now wearing a dark-cream dress with matching shoes. And she'd brushed her hair and had put on a touch of lipstick. Iain was the first to speak.

"My!" he exclaimed. "Dor, you look prettier 'n a newborn foal, love."

"Too right. But one thing's got me tossed," Alasdair said, "I don' see how a woman can run in these modern dresses. They look tighter 'n the wire round a snared rabbit."

"Yer mus' be blind, Alasdair," Iain remarked. "Anyone can see Dor don' intend ter run from Calum."

Calum was speechless. Like the other men, he'd never before seen Doreen dressed in anything but too-big moleskins and a shirt or a lap-lap. Doreen said nothing. She just continued to pour their tea.

Peg was watching Calum, and her eyes showed amusement. "I have ter say, mate," she said kindly, "yer eyes put me in mind of a coupla dinner plates."

"And I'm noticing, Calum," Iain said, "yer can't take yer eyes off what that dress is wrapped aroun'. And Dor's being polite," he continued. "She's not lettin' on she's seen that silly look on her man's face."

Doreen still said nothing. Her demeanour suggested that she was quite used to being attired in the latest fashion, ordered from Adelaide's John Martins Department Store. Calum's was the last cup that she poured. When she'd finished pouring his tea, she looked at him impishly from under her long lashes. And she made a point of pulling down the tight dress and smoothing it over her hips. His eyes stayed glued to her hands and then her hips.

"I didn't wear my high heels," she told him demurely, "so as I wouldn't be looking down on you, darl. I know a wife's place, all right."

There was a moment's silence before the Macs and Jack threw back their heads and roared with laughter. Peg smiled at Calum as Doreen exited wordlessly, with a fluid swing of her hips, to refill the teapot.

Iain wiped his eyes. "The little devil!" He exclaimed. "Look down on him? Why, she'd be lucky if she's two bricks and a penny high."

Doreen soon rejoined them. As she walked past Calum, she rested a passing hand on his shoulder. Then Mr. Ah Lee arrived and interrupted their conversation.

"Ellybody, come now. Gitchim tucker!" he told them loudly.

"Thank you, Mr. Ah Lee," Iain said.

After their meal, they adjourned to the living room, and Alasdair filled their glasses with rum. Calum saw that his heavy hand hadn't lightened, not one bit.

Big River's living room was friendly and welcoming. It was comfortably furnished.

"You said your grandfather first took out this lease, Iain?" Calum said, seating himself and stretching out his legs.

"Yes. He migrated from an Outer Hebridean island called North Uist, an' he copped a spear, in 1888, fer his trouble."

"Good grief."

"Too right. But he'd a different attitude to what we have today," Iain said. "You see, he reckoned he'd caught one of the Murries stealing an' laid into him with a stock whip. That same evening, he was killed. The spear took him clean through the throat. Grandma and Ma buried him up there behind the house. Pa was off musterin' at the time."

"Oh."

"Tell me about your father, please," Doreen asked.

"Doreen!" Peg admonished. "Yer bein' nosey. That's family bijnitch."

"That's awright, love," Iain said. "Pa was killed, in 1899, by myall blacks. They'd speared a bullock. He came up on 'em and fired his rifle in the air to frighten 'em off. Only they didn't frighten. They threw their spears instead." Iain shook his head. "He's also buried up there."

"And even after all that, the Macdonalds still didn't allow coppers on Big River," Doreen murmured and shook her head in surprise.

"That was Ma an' Jawoyn's doin'," Iain informed them. He looked at Jack. "Yeah, I know that's the name of the tribe from around Katherine, Jack. But Ma called him that 'cause she couldn't pronounce his real name. And she made a deal with him. The deal was, there wouldn't be any dispersal shootin' on this run, and in return, there'd be no more spearin's. She was a God-fearin' woman, and she was determined ter keep the rest of her family alive."

"I'll be damned," Jack Kelly said. "I've known you two fer thirty years, an' I never knew it was yer ma what stopped them shootings."

Iain smiled at him. "We're no different ter you, Jack," he said. "We also keep our own counsel."

There was a pause in the conversation. Then Calum said, "If you don't mind me asking, why did your grandparents come here?"

Iain studied Calum, and his faded, blue eyes crinkled at the corners. "Not only do we have ter feed yer, but here you are, young feller, demanding a history lesson as well."

"I didn't mean to sound nosey."

"I'm teasin', son." Iain gathered his thoughts while he opened another bottle of rum. "Our grandfather proved to be a born overlander," he said. "And no sooner had he taken up his two-hundred acre selection at Emu Creek on the Darling Downs, in Queensland, than he packed up and brought his family here. He was the first person ter take out a Government lease on the Big River."

Calum had been listening intently. "That would've been one helluva journey in those days, Iain," he said.

"I reckon. And I was born here in 1878, and Alasdair was born in 1876."

Calum stood up and topped up Iain's glass. "Were there many spearings in the old days?" he asked.

"More than a few," Iain said. "And it's understandable. We, white fellers, rode roughshod over the Murries." He paused. "But Alasdair an' me was all right, 'cause after our mother died, both of us had our women livin' with us. Funny thing though, neither of us ever had children. An' when our women passed on, we never found others who suited us as well. But why we never had children has got me tossed." He looked at Peg. "I would o' liked a daughter or two like you, Peg."

Peg reached across and rested her hand on his. "Looks like yer'll have ter make do with what yer got now, mate," she said.

Calum's curiosity about spearings hadn't been satisfied. "When did the spearings slow down?" he asked Iain.

"Not till just before the war." Iain thought for a moment. "The last big one would've been in 1936, I reckon. It was at Caledon Bay in Arnhem Land."

"Yeah?"

"Two Jap pearling luggers anchored there. They were collecting Trepang."

"Trepang?"

"Yeah. That's the black, sea slug they eat in the east. An' five out of the six Japs were killed in a shower of spears. But their crew, who came from South Goulburn Island, got away with the sixth Jap. Some weeks later, they turned up at a mission called Milingimbi. Now, Milingimbi was two-hundred miles away through the scrub."

"Jeez."

Doreen stood up and stretched. "I reckon I must be good hearted because I'm going to make a pot of tea to save my Calum from drinking more grog."

"Well," Peg told her, "if yer good hearted, yer better learn ter wear that dress on'y round the homestead. 'Cause if yer wear that dress in Catriona, yer bound ter cause trouble fer yer man."

Peg smiled at Calum's sudden look of astonishment. Calum hadn't given a thought to the effect that her dress could have on other whites. And that included some white women who wouldn't hesitate to egg on their fellers, if they felt threatened by a good-looking, half-caste girl. Calum put it from his mind. Hell, if any suggestive comments were made by whites, well, he was big enough and old enough to handle them. Peg's voice got his attention.

"Yer best remember, Doreen love, that one o' the things a woman like you has always got ter think about is makin' sure her man don' get inter fights over her."

Doreen looked at her mother thoughtfully. It was obvious that she'd been told something to bear in mind.

Iain quickly broke the silence. "I'll be happy ter tell you lot 'bout Fred Brooks," he said in a bright voice, "providin' yer able ter take yer minds off Doreen's dress."

"I'm listening, Iain," Calum said.

"Now, this was only twenty-odd year ago," Iain recounted. "Fred was a battler, yer know. An' he'd made the usual bacca and flour arrangement with a Murri for the loan of his wife ter wash his clothes and sleep in his swag. The only problem was, at the end of the agreed time, Fred reneged on the agreement he'd made. He didn't cough up the bacca and flour. And the Murri just couldn't understand how a man wouldn't keep his word. He felt he'd been cheated."

"Oh no," Calum said. "What happened?"

"Well, I can state with total honesty Fred never reneged on another deal."

"How come?" Calum asked.

"That Murri cut Fred's throat and stuffed his body down a large hole Fred'd been digging lookin' for rabbits."

Peg gave Calum a wicked grin. "Us blacks is bad, Calum. So don' even think 'bout reneging on the deal you an' me made when I promise-married my Doreen to yer."

"You never told me about any deal you and Calum made, Mum?"

Peg grinned at her daughter. "Now, wouldn't yer like ter know, love?"

"Yes, I would."

"Are yer sure?"

"Mum!"

"Awright, I'll tell yer, love," Peg said, her eyes twinkling. "I tol' yer man yer'd be promise-married ter him if he gave me a few, coloured beads an' a blanket. Course, I didn' think you was worth much more ter tell the truth!"

"Mum!"

The Macs and Jack burst out laughing.

Iain wiped his eyes. He regarded Peg, Doreen, and Calum affectionately. "Well, if that don' beat all," he said. "I reckon I've heard the lot now." He turned to Calum. "And will that do yer, young feller, about spearings and the like?"

"I just like to listen when you talk about the old days," Calum said.

"Nothin' wrong with that, son. Nowadays folks don' care about what it was like back then. Soon it'll all be forgot because the world will've moved on."

"I reckon he's a bloodthirsty young devil," Jack said. "I can't understand what Doreen sees in him."

"Me neither," Calum agreed. "But she doesn't have a choice. Peg told me not to return Dor. Because, even if I did, I wouldn't get the beads and blanket back."

Jack grinned then his face took on a serious look. He nodded at Calum. "Would yer like ter know the outcome o' that Fred Brooks' killin'?" he said. "It's not a pretty story."

"Yes, I would, Jack."

Jack shook his head sadly. "A police party, led by a Constable George Murray, set out ter bring in Brooks's killer. Now Murray was a Gallipoli veteran. I don't know if he did anythin' heroic there, but a lot of folks here an' even one Adelaide newspaper thought he was a hero for what him an' his party did at Coniston."

"Coniston?" Calum asked.

"Yeah," Jack said. "Coniston's sou'west o' Tennant Creek, on the Lander River."

"What happened, for Crissake?"

"Murray's party caught up with a mob of Murries there. He thought it contained Brooks's killer. Anyway, his party massacred most of 'em. The number killed was officially thirty-one. But Murray claimed privately, I'm told, that it was a lot more. The survivin' Murries said it was nearer *seventy*. And a white, mission lady backed up what the Murries said."

"Good God!"

"Yeah," Jack continued. "That was the last, big massacre that I know of. An' it happened in 1928. And that Murray damn well got off total scot-free."

Peg turned to Jack. "Yer know, my man admitted ter me he took part in them murders," she murmured. "An' also how regretful he was.

I tol' him we couldn't change the past, an' it's how people act *now* what matters. He found it hard ter believe I never held it against him." Peg paused. "I know I changed him in lots o' ways, but then, he also changed me."

There was a long silence before Alasdair broke it. He had a serious look on his face. "Let's get back ter the present," he said. "I've seen a few gators recent, yer know. So I might ask you fellers to see if yer can shoot 'em. That river's the main water fer the cattle."

"Those gators'll be a worry to my feller," Doreen said with a grin.

"I'm with you, Calum," Alasdair said. "I don't like 'em either. Not one bit. It's awright, yer know, fer those folks livin' safe in their fine houses Down Below ter say gators shouldn't be hunted. But they don' have ter cross our rivers or see their cattle and horses bein' taken."

"I agree."

"Hell," Alasdair said. "I've had two horses took when crossin' that River."

"Frightening," Calum said, with feeling.

"That's fer sure," agreed Alasdair. "One moment yer swimming nice an' yer holding on to yer horse's tail. An' yer getting a good pull along. Yer horse's got its neck stretched out o' the water, an' it's snortin' an' swimmin' good. Next thing, this bloody, great gator rises up, with its head an' shoulders out o' the water. An' it grabs yer horse's head in those bloody, great jaws. An' yer left there, swimmin' an' wonderin' if another one's comin' ter get yer." He paused and stared at the glass in his hand. "An' the worst thing is yer don't even see the bastards coming." Alasdair looked at Calum with his faded eyes, smiled and changed the subject. "Yer know, this place could do with the sound of kids," he said. "It needs ter come alive. Fer too long all it's had is old men livin' here."

Both brothers stood up and stretched sleepily. They'd decided to turn in. Peg thought that they really looked their age. And the affection that she felt for both suddenly welled up inside her.

"Good night, all," Iain said. "Just put out the lamp after you fellers've managed ter empty that bottle of rum."

"Good night."

Calum rose to his feet and stretched. "I'm going to check on Curaidh, Dor," he said. "Do you feel like some fresh air?" He turned to Peg and Jack. "We won't be long," he said.

"Don't worry about me, love," Peg said. "I'm goin' ter turn in too."

"An' I'm off as well," Jack said.

Doreen joined Calum, and they went out on to the verandah. Curaidh was lying on Socks's saddle blanket, next to Calum's saddle. He raised his head and looked at them, and his eyes shone in the light coming through the window.

"How're you, pup?" Calum said.

Curaidh's tail made a couple of small thuds against the wooden, verandah floor when he wagged it. Calum leaned over and stroked his head before straightening up.

Doreen put her arm around Calum's waist. "Curaidh's happy," she said.

"Yes. So long as he's next to my saddle he won't move."

He looked down at her. In the moonlight, he saw a tiny frown on her face. "What is it, my love?" he asked.

She smoothed her dress over her hips. "Do you think this dress is too tight?" she asked. "An' shows too much of my shape?"

He was careful to keep his voice neutral. "It's the latest fashion, and you got it from Johnnies, so it'll be what everybody's wearing."

"I'm not everybody. And I don't want white fellers staring at my shape when we're in Catriona."

"I'll look after you."

"That's one of the things I'm worried about. And you're the same when it comes to Jan. Mum's right. Jan and me need to watch we don't cause trouble for our men."

"I can look after myself."

"It's not only that. No, I need to learn us half-castes mustn't draw attention to ourselves. It seems I'm learning all the time."

He was quiet. Her mood had changed.

"Anyway," she said in a tight voice. "I hate white fellers staring at my shape. It makes me think of Cord River."

"I see."

"You couldn't. You're a damn man, and you're white."

He stayed silent. She looked up at the night sky, her face suddenly brightening. "Isn't it good now the Macs have given us our own room?" she said.

"Yes."

She grinned at him, her face no longer tight. "Let's go to bed now," she suggested, winking naughtily. "Because I don't mind it, at all, if you stare at me when I undress."

"That's about the best offer I've had all night."

****

Brian arrived four days later. The Macs then insisted that Brian and Calum take a good ride around their run and informed them that they would put a price on it when they returned.

"We want yer to have a good look at what yer buyin'," Iain said. He grinned. "We don' want yer ter say later that you were dudded."

"Okay. We'll head off tomorrow," Brian said.

Brian and Calum set off at first light, and they didn't get back till late, next day. They'd seen all that they needed to see.

"The ladies're out ridin' with Jack," Alasdair informed them on their return. "Come an' sit on the verandah, an' we'll talk business over a rum."

They headed for the verandah and joined the two brothers in a drink. Brian raised his glass. "Cheers," he said with a wide grin. "An' all the best when you get to Adelaide. But they tell me the Big River's the same as the Georgina. Once you drink from it, you'll be back, no worries."

"That's why two of the chairs on this verandah will always carry your names," Calum said.

"Thanks, fellers. An' cheers."

"You've got a nice run here," Brian said. "All it needs are bores and the Shorthorns to breed up and recover their numbers, because that last, dry spell thinned 'em out."

"Yes," answered Iain. "Put in the bores and she'd carry five times as many head."

"I'd agree with that," Brian said. "And you've got nice horses too. They look to be about three quarters Thoroughbred?"

"You're not wrong there, son," Iain said.

Calum, lazily looking around him, noticed a Black-Headed Monitor that was lying along a limb of a nearby Mangan. He couldn't help thinking that this thirty-inches-long lizard would give a monkey a run for its money, because it was such a speedy and agile, tree climber. *It also had a serious set of teeth*, he thought, grimacing. And he felt relieved that it wasn't on the ground anywhere near Curaidh because, doubtless, Curaidh would immediately take it on.

Then he looked down over the slope toward the river flats. He felt happy. Life was good. A dream was about to come true. And it wasn't only the fact that he and Brian would finally have their own run. It was because he and Doreen would now have the home that they'd both grown to love. Relief and contentment flowed all through him. A wonderful future beckoned. And it stretched even further than he was able see up and beyond the wide, coffee-coloured river below.

Alasdair leaned forward in his chair. He looked keenly at both Calum and Brian. "Well, boys, we've written down our selling price for yer to look at," he said.

He passed the sheet of paper to Brian, who glanced at it, before handing it to Calum. Calum read the neat writing carefully.

Big River Sale Price to Doreen Taylor, Brian Wilson, and Calum McNicol

Rental = 8 shillings per square mile and set till 1968

Station plant and stores	£10,000
Buildings and improvements	£12,000
150 horses @ 6 pounds	£900
5,000 shorthorns @ 2 pounds	£10,000

Total	£32,900

Calum looked up from the sheet of paper and spoke to Brian. "I reckon these old-timers've understated by at least two-thousand beasts. And the going price is three pounds a head, not two pounds!"

"We won't argue the toss," said Alasdair. "Let's round it off at thirty-three-thousand pounds and call it quits. Here's my hand on it."

"Why?" asked Calum, puzzled.

"That's our weddin' present to Doreen." Iain grinned. "An' you fellers better remember she owns a fifth of all the cattle on this run. An' there's one more important condition."

"Yeah?"

"Peg is ter have a home fer life in this homestead."

"That goes without say," Brian said.

Calum held out his hand. The four of them shook hands, and the deal was done.

"You've bought yourselves a station, fellers," said Iain.

"Yes." Calum grinned. "And it looks as if we've inherited most of the dingoes in the Territory too."

"We don't allow that dog stiffener on the place." Iain shook his head. "That mongrel's bloody dangerous."

"I agree," Calum said. "And we'll also warn him off when we see him."

"And I suppose the dogs have bred up a bit," Iain mused. "But yer know, I've watched the breeders drinking. These Big River Shorthorns is good at lookin' after themselves. 'Cause, always, there's a nursemaid cow what stays back with the calves and keeps the dogs off." He glanced at Calum. And his smile was affectionate. "Tell me, son," he said. "What does it feel like to be part owner of a Gulf Country, cattle run?"

"It feels good, mate. Real good."

"If yer look after it like we did, it'll never let yer down. It's never let us down, yer know."

Alasdair and Iain contentedly nodded to each other. Then Iain nodded at Calum. "An' I've got one last piece of advice fer you, Calum."

"Yeah?"

"If you and Dor do happen ter have a baby before yer can get married, make certain you register its birth proper."

"Yeah?"

"That was the mistake Jack made. He never registered the birth of his son. Yer see, after his wife died, his boy was stayin' with the grandparents while Jack was off buffalo shootin'. Yeah, he told me he was making good money, selling the hides to leather merchants. Anyway, that was when the boy got grabbed."

"Jesus!" Calum exclaimed.

"Yes," Iain said. "An' the bastards wouldn' give his son back. Yer see, Jack couldn't prove the boy was his."

"Good God," Calum said. "I'd no idea."

CHAPTER 19

A WHITE FELLER WEDDING

The Macs, accompanied by Mr. Ah Lee, left for Glenelg, an Adelaide beach suburb, just prior to Big River's calf branding. They promised that they'd be back for any planned festivities, following Calum and Doreen's wedding.

"Yer didn't think we wouldn't check up to see if Dor's made a proper, honest man out of yer, did yer?" Alasdair truculently demanded.

"No, Alasdair," Calum replied, grinning. "And you can be sure none of your green bananas'll be picked. Because now you've got *me* spooked."

"Are yer trying ter make sure I'll have a shocker of a day?" Alasdair demanded.

As they waved off the brothers' truck, Doreen grew teary. Calum gave her a hug.

"I'm all right, darl," she told him. "But it's like saying good-bye to both of my granddads at once."

Brian clapped Calum on the shoulder. "Let's get with it, mate," he said. "We now have a station to run."

"I know. And when Hank suggested we ran Big River while he ran Long Creek, it really hit home. It's a big responsibility."

"Well, aren't you lucky you've got me," Doreen said, smiling cheekily. "Gee, you get me for free to do the books, pay the bills and keep a check on the money. That means you'll both have stacks of time to grow the best beef in the Territory."

"Do you think we can trust her with the money, Brian?" Calum asked, winking.

"You're being horrible, darl!" Doreen pouted. "And I refuse to marry you now."

When Calum got a lift into Catriona to pick up the truck, parked there by the Macs, he went to see Andrew Blades, their resident Flying Doctor. Andrew was easy to talk to, and Calum described Doreen's panic attacks in detail.

"Somehow, they have to be fixed, Andrew. It's crazy; they've been going on much too long."

"What she's been going through reminds me of the problems some flyers experienced after being traumatized. You know after being shot down, wounded, or getting burned while escaping from their flaming kites. Men can get traumatized too, Calum. So what Dor's suffering can happen to anyone. She needs to open up."

"Oh."

"And you're the best person to get her to talk about it, Calum."

"Right."

"But whatever did happen to Dor, it's important that you convince her that it wasn't her fault. And once she tells you, make sure you tell her it's made you love her even more. All right?"

****

Calum and Doreen were duly married, in Catriona, the day after Calum turned twenty-one. It'd been agreed that only Peg and Jack would attend. They'd be the witnesses, and the real celebration would take place back at Long Creek. Doreen wore a simple, peasant skirt and blouse. Calum thought that she looked lovely. And it hadn't been hard to get permission from Native Affairs to marry because Calum's skin was lighter than hers.

Kev Luscombe, their area's new Protector of Aborigines, was an enthusiastic advocate of the Government's assimilation policy. Importantly, though, he'd helped short-circuit much of the usual, red tape and had assisted Calum and Doreen to obtain the necessary, written approval for their marriage. When they dropped into his office to pick up this approval, he looked at Doreen's olive skin and freckles and then looked askance at Peg's obvious darkness.

"I reckon yer gran'children'll look white, Mrs. Taylor." He sniffed. "Well, not properly, like. Maybe more like these Greeks 'n' Eyeties who're startin' ter flood inter the place these days."

Jack Kelly waited till the notification of approval was safely in Calum's hands before he grinned at the bespectacled, young bureaucrat. "It won't matter what yer kids look like, Calum," he said. "Peg's mob'll be happy ter accept 'em. An' if yer take my advice, yer'll have yer kids live with 'em when they is young ter learn their ways an' be taught about the bush."

Kev Luscombe looked aghast. He was horrified and put a hand to his ear as if to block out what he was hearing. "I'm sure the Department wouldn't be happy about that," he stressed. "In fact, I know it wouldn't approve. It'd want any children yer might have ter be properly assimilated."

Peg gave Jack Kelly a solid nudge and smiled sweetly at the horrified Kev Luscombe. "I'm sure my daughter'll mind yer words, Mr. Luscombe. It's good advice."

"Thank yer, Mrs. Taylor."

"Right, we're off, Kev," Calum said. "Noel Mulholland'll be waiting for us at the Registry Office. Thanks for your help. It's appreciated."

"That's all right. An' tell Hank I'll be out next week ter renew his permit ter employ Abos."

"I won't forget."

When they were outside, Peg looked puzzled. "Calum, love, I thought yer woulda been bubblin' over like on yer weddin' day?"

"Peg, I reckon we're already married. We got married up north, but I'll be happy when we're back at Long Creek and can celebrate with our mates." He smiled. "And I'll bet Charlie's gone and prepared a beaut feast, now he's got to like Dor."

Doreen pretended to frown and gave Calum a small punch on his arm. "Don't you dare act so casual, Calum darl," she cried. "This is our wedding day, and I want you to be excited like me."

"I was only saying that I'm really looking forward to celebrating with our Long Creek mates."

"Maybe Charlie's even made a wedding cake?" Doreen excitedly wondered.

"I wish I was as certain of the next Melbourne Cup winner as I am of that," Calum told her.

"Mm," Jack admitted, "I've got a terrible cravin' right now fer chocolate icin'."

They headed up the street, in bright sunshine, to Catriona's cramped and hot Registry Office where Noel Mulholland, the area's perpetually perspiring Registrar of Births and Deaths, was waiting to marry them.

Word of their impending marriage had rapidly spread among Catriona's white community, and disapproval and dismay were expressed in roughly equal proportions. And nowhere were these sentiments expressed more vehemently than in the back bar at O'Hara's, where the town's luminaries met, at lunchtimes, to drink and discuss business.

"I never would've believed what young McNicol's gone an' done," Kev Luscombe sadly stated. "It's awright for Chinks and wogs, mind you, but McNicol's a good bloke. I coulda puked when I first seen his new mother-in-law. Not a gin, mind yer, but still awful, bloody black-lookin'."

"Could yer imagine takin' somebody lookin' like a gin home ter meet yer parents, Kev?" young Ned O'Hara asked, horrified.

"The silly young bugger should've known better," Sean Fitzpatrick declared. "Why a man'd want ter marry a creamy is beyond me. Most of 'em will come across anyway, no worries."

"Is that the voice of experience speakin', Sean?" Kev Luscombe asked, grinning.

Sean Fitzpatrick stuck out his chest. "A man'd be stupid if he knocked back what was dished up ter him, Kev, wouldn't he?" he bragged. "But no dinkum white feller'd want ter wake *every* mornin' an' see a black head on the pillow beside him. Anyway," he predicted, "that's the beginnin' o' the end fer Long Creek an' Big River. There's nothing surer than their kids'll be like all them other half-castes. They'll get on the grog an' piss them cattle runs away against the nearest wall!"

"McNicol should've got himself an Adelaide sheila, like my Liz," Ned O'Hara opined. "Funny, but my Liz had never really seen Abos till she come up here. Now she looks down on niggers an' half-castes worse 'n me."

"And she's not the only sheila, mate," Noel Mulholland said. "You should hear my wife when she gets wound up. She reckons Abos are nothing but lazy, dirty buggers what stink."

****

Immediately after the simple wedding ceremony, the four of them headed back to Long Creek in the old, Bedford truck. Jack enjoyed the most comfortable ride because he lay on the new double bed strapped down in the back, which Jan and Hank had ordered as a wedding present.

"It'll be hard to hold on to an argument," Jan had told Calum, "when the two of you are lying close in a double bed."

"Jan, bed is the *last* place I'll start arguing!"

"Mm."

"You know, Jan, there is one thing you could do for me, and that's order a nice dress from John Martins."

"I'll be happy to, love. What's Doreen's dress size?"

"How would I know? You've seen her. Heck, she's not as tall as you and doesn't stick out so much in front. What else do you need to know?"

"Calum McNicol! How do you know I'm not pregnant?"

"Are you?" he'd asked with a cheeky grin. "I didn't think you looked any different."

"Calum! You're a young devil."

On the trip back to Long Creek, Calum and Doreen continued their ongoing discussion about where to honeymoon. Calum favoured Adelaide because neither had been there. Peg didn't speak; she just kept looking out of her window. Doreen, who was in the middle, left her hand resting on Calum's knee.

"You don't sound keen on this Adelaide idea, my love," he ventured.

"Of course I'll go if you're set on it, no worries. But I'm not excited."

"How come?"

She turned her head and looked at him. She saw that his face was impassive and that his eyes were fixed on the red dirt road that stretched before them. *He's so damn blind*, she thought *and wondered if he truly appreciated what a mixed-race couple would be up against.* Adelaide worried her. She imagined all the hostile stares, the nudges, the deliberate refusal to make room on pavements, and the muttered insults like, "Bloody boong!" No, she'd long ago decided that the best way to protect their relationship was to avoid, where possible, such hurtful bigotry.

"Don't you want to talk about Adelaide, my love?" Calum asked.

"I'm sorry, darl," she answered. "I was miles away."

"Well?"

She sighed. "I don't want us stared at by townies just because you've married a half-caste."

"People in Catriona stare at us now."

"It's other things too."

"Yeah?"

"Like if you felt like a beer, I couldn't go into a hotel with you. They'd refuse to serve me and would probably ask me to leave. And where'd that leave you? Feeling you have to walk out beside your wife with your tail between your legs?"

Calum stayed silent. Her words had burst through his daydreaming like a clarion call.

"And what about Curaidh?" she asked. "He'll only put up with being left with Brian for so long."

Calum didn't speak.

Peg looked across at them and finally broke her silence. "Do yer min' if I add my thoughts, mate?" she asked him.

"Go for it, Peg."

"Murranji an' me talked 'bout this sort o' shit often. We decided we had ter look after each other. He never wanted ter see me insulted, an' I never wanted ter see him get inter a fight over me."

"And?"

"We jus' decided ter avoid places where we wasn't wanted." She smiled at Calum, and her eyes crinkled. "The bush don' worry 'bout the colour of a person's skin, yer know, mate," she said.

There was silence in the truck's cabin, and the roar of the Bedford's, noisy engine suddenly seemed louder in the confined space. Calum glanced across at Peg, smiled, and gave her a wink. She'd hit the nail on the head.

Calum covered the small, slim hand on his knee with his own. "What would you say, my love," he asked, "about honeymooning at Rock Wallaby Waterhole?"

Relief covered Doreen's face, and he felt her hand squeeze his knee.

"Yes please, darl. You know it's my favourite place. We'll camp there and eat bush tucker and sleep under the stars. That's us, my darling. Adelaide's not us!"

"You're a real bush lady, aren't you?" He grinned.

Peg continued to look out of her window. A small smile stayed on her lips.

****

When Calum halted the truck outside the homestead, the Long Creek mob rushed out and surrounded it. And the newlyweds clambered out to shouts of "congratulations!" and many a "it's about bloody time!"

Everyone wanted to kiss the bride, especially the Macs who'd arrived that morning, courtesy of Perce.

Doreen hugged them both. Tears came to her eyes. "Thank you both for coming," she told them. "It means such a lot to me. Truly, it's sort of like having my granddads here."

"No way we'd miss it," Iain said. "An' it's great to catch up with Hank an' Jan again."

"Didn't I say Calum wasn't a rogue?" Alasdair announced triumphantly.

Calum shook their hands and grinned at them. "I was always going to turn up on the day," he said. "It was Dor whom I was worried about!"

Brian gave Calum a bear hug. "Good on you, mate," he said. "You've married a beaut sheila."

Curaidh was running around. His brown eyes were shining, and he kept trying to reach up and lick Calum's hand. Calum patted him.

"How're you, pup? Have you been behaving yourself?"

"He's been miserable, son," Alice said. "He's been lyin' aroun' mopin' on my verandah."

Jan came and hugged them both. She was delighted for them, and her eyes were a bit misty. "I'm thrilled, Dor," she cried. "It's wonderful. I've known him since he came here. He looked like a lost puppy then, and now I love him like a brother. And he's so lucky to have you."

"We're both lucky, Jan. And how's little Janice."

"Fine. The little monkey's asleep right now."

"Calum told me you and Hank are maybe trying for another."

"Yes. And did he also tell you that he said I wasn't good-looking like you, 'cause I stuck out too much in front?"

"Calum!"

Charlie appeared on the kitchen verandah and rang a small, hand bell loudly. He glared around him till there was silence. "Didn't I say," he asked, "ter come inside right away? The tucker's already on the table. An' it's getting' cold."

Once inside the big kitchen, Nugget grabbed a couple of beer bottles from a tin bath filled with ice and bottled beer. He quickly opened both and, with a bottle in either hand, started filling glasses fast.

"Fill yer glasses, everyone," he yelled. "We got ter have a quick toast so's we can start the serious drinkin'."

Brian grinned and nodded to Hank. "How about doing the honours, mate?"

"Of course," Hank said and rose from his chair. "Now, as we say, in the Territory, would everybody be upstanding, please! And please raise your glasses. To a fine partner," he toasted. "And to his lovely bride."

"Hear, hear," the Macs loudly agreed.

Jack had seated himself next to Peg. He eyed all the food that'd been heaped upon the table: chicken, small, beef sausages, roast potatoes, peas, carrots and gravy, plus fried steaks, thick rashers of bacon, and fresh bread. And in the centre of the table, looking dark brown and delicious, stood a huge, square, chocolate cake. Spidery looking, white icing traced the words "CONGRATS TO DOR AND CALUM."

"How soon before I can have cake?" he asked Peg.

"Don' yer touch it till I tell yer." She turned to Charlie. "All this tucker looks wonderful, mate. Yer've dinkum spoiled us."

"Course," Charlie said pompously, "I only done it 'cause Dor is Murranji's daughter. An' I knew young Calum'd have the manners ter say his appreciation."

"Charlie, we feel very spoiled," Calum told him.

"See," Charlie glowed. "Pity you other fellers don't have Calum's manners."

"Yer a bloody crawler, mate," Nugget quietly whispered to Calum.

Brian picked up Nugget's whisper. He grinned at him. "I didn't hear what you said, Nugg. Could you speak up, please?"

"I jus' remarked this feed is better 'n what yer'd get in an Adelaide hotel," Nugget quickly explained, with one eye on Charlie.

"Are you sure that's what you said?" Brian asked, grinning. "It didn't sound like that to me."

"I refuse ter speak ter you any more, Brian. I want to concentrate on this tucker."

"Come on, you lot," Charlie urged. "An' siddown those as is still standin' an' get it inter yer! Yer can eat as well as drink, yer know!"

Charlie's feast was consumed nearly as fast as a seemingly limitless number of cold bottles of beer were drunk. And the conversation flowing around the big table seemed to increase its decibel level in direct proportion to the number of beer bottles that were detopped. Hank, who was sitting next to Doreen, rested an arm around her shoulders briefly and had to shout to be heard.

"Did Calum remember to pass on Brian's message to our hospital's new nurse?" he asked.

"I had to kick him," she said. "He told her Brian'd be drunk for a week and wouldn't be able to make it to the dance."

"I heard that," Brian said. "The rotten rat! I reckon your husband's *not* trustworthy, Dor. An' I'm pleased you found that out so early in your marriage."

"Don't worry, Brian. I rescued your romance. And I think she's nice."

"He tells me it's not a romance, Dor," Hank said. "He says they're only good friends. Anyway, I'm wondering when you two'll be back from your honeymoon?"

"Give us about three weeks," Calum said. "Why?"

"Well, it wouldn't hurt to have Nugget help Brian keep an eye on things."

"Makes sense."

Calum nudged Doreen and indicated Perce. "I'm glad Perce could make it," he said.

"Yes, and wasn't he sweet the way he delivered all our letters and never charged a penny?"

Perce and Alasdair were having a long and amicable conversation. To look at them, one would never have thought that a cross word had ever passed between them, let alone the odd, rifle bullet. Perce, as always, overflowed his chair, and his expression was almost avuncular.

He noticed that Doreen and Calum were smiling at him. He gave them a happy wave and shouted up the table, "You tell yer man, Dor, that if he don't treat yer good, I'll take him back ter where I found 'im."

Doreen gave Perce a big smile and blew him a kiss.

Brian stood up and loudly tapped a spoon against an empty glass to get some quiet. Then Peg rose to her feet.

"I reckon someone has ter make a speech," she said. "An' as I'm the on'y parent here what these two has got, I'm going ter say some words fer both of 'em."

After some more clapping and a few whistles, Peg took a deep breath, looked at all the faces before her, and began speaking. "If Murranji was here," she said, "he'd say we was looking at the new Top End. I don't know 'bout that, so all I'll say is that these two love each other enough ter take whatever life throws at 'em." She paused and looked at Calum. "You'll do me fer a son-in-law, mate. Yer a strong man inside an' strong enough, like, ter go yer own way an' do yer own thing. An' yer've now got a wife who on'y sees the sun, moon and stars when she looks at yer. She's a real fine person, an' she'll be a won'erful wife ter yer. An' I'm certain yer'll both make a real success of yer marriage. God bless yer both."

"Well said, Peg," Hank called out.

"Hear! Hear!" the Macs chorused.

"An' now you can get back to your drinkin'," Brian told everyone. "Because there'll be no more speech-making. Anyway I wouldn't allow it."

Finally, replete with food and drink, Calum and Doreen excused themselves. They reminded everyone that that they planned to set off before first light and insisted that everyone keep their seats and continue celebrating. Charlie angrily scolded Nugget for his suggestive comment and smirk about brides with wedding-night nerves.

"Yer bein' a dirty bugger, Nugg," he clicked. "That's not the British way."

"No, mate, but it *is* the Aussie way."

****

It seemed to Doreen that they'd been riding for days, but now, thankfully, Calum had told her that they were only half an hour's ride from Rock Wallaby Waterhole. They were in country that abounded with gorges, boulders and slabby cliffs, as well as billabongs, *Boabs*, Woolly Butts and water lilies; and with clean, clear air and small, cotton wool clouds that lazily moved across an azure sky.

Doreen remembered that Alice had told her that after marriage, the bedroom side of things quickly settled down for a woman because of the constant demands made by her husband. But her mum had just laughed when Doreen had recounted what Alice had said.

"It was differen' fer me, love," her mum had told her. "After we was married, I wanted yer father in me bed more 'n before. Yer see, he was *now* my husband."

"I don't understand, Mum."

"Yer dad stood tall, love," her mother had said. "An' I thought, here's this white feller showin' the world he wants me fer his wife. It felt real good. An' I felt he belonged ter me, *properlee*. An', love, I wanted him in me bed awful bad."

Doreen glanced across at her own husband. She saw that he was looking at their packhorse, Sunshine. Then he looked at her.

"That Sunshine's got to be the most cheerful, little packhorse I've ever come across," he said.

She didn't say anything, but held his eyes while she undid the top three buttons of her shirt. Then she took off her hat and fanned herself with it.

"Are you that hot?" he asked.

"I can feel myself getting that way," she said enigmatically.

301

She watched him out of the corner of her eye. He kept glancing at her open shirt, and he looked a little puzzled. She moved her hand to her throat. She knew that her wrist would conceal the swell of her breast from him. She smiled to herself when she saw him shift uncomfortably in his saddle and then look ahead determinedly. *That's my Calum*, she thought, *he's got his mind set on reaching Rock Wallaby Waterhole.* She felt her desire increase.

When they arrived, they stayed on their horses and looked out over the broad stretch of water. *This billabong is just plain beautiful*, Calum thought, *with its small, sandy beach and its mauve, white and yellow, water lily blossoms nodding in the breeze.* He took in the sun-dappled water that was fringed on their side by stately Paperbarks, interspersed with the odd Boab. The far side was bounded by a cliff that looked as if it'd been constructed out of thick, red-brown, rock slabs, which some giant had carelessly piled one on top of the other.

"I'd almost forgotten just how beautiful this place really is," he exclaimed.

"Mm," she agreed.

"Let's make camp and put up the tent fly quick smart, my love. That water looks very inviting."

They unsaddled, watered and bushed the horses, and then made camp beside a nearby full-bellied Boab, which would remain leafless till the rains came. Its leafless branches resembled spreading roots, which was why the Murries had labelled it "upside-down tree."

Doreen watched her husband place their swags next to the saddles and his rifle and smiled at his neatness. Then she became aware again, of her desire. Her legs were starting to feel weak.

"For heaven's sake, darl," she scolded. "Can't you tell when your wife wants you? Are you going to unroll that swag now, or do I have to?"

Afterward, they swam and splashed in the cool water like a couple of kids. He watched her when she stood up after she'd swum closer to the little, sandy beach. And it suddenly hit him that this lovely woman was now his wife in the eyes of the whole world. The water, where she stood, was thigh-deep, and her body was silhouetted against the sun-splashed, red-brown cliff behind her.

Then it struck him, with incisive clarity that this image of his wife would stay with him forever: the dripping, black hair plastered to the shape of her head, the soft, dark eyes, olive-brown skin, and laughing, white teeth. And with sparkling droplets of water that clung to her shoulders, high firm breasts, and slightly curved belly: and with her legs lapped by a sun-dappled billabong whose water beads clung to the tuft of wet, black hair between her thighs. He continued to look in wonder at his wife, dressed only in sunshine and water beads. And realized, with a start, that she'd changed from a girl into a woman. And that she was now less pretty and much, much more beautiful.

"You're really beautiful, Dor," he called.

She looked at him from under her lashes and smiled shyly at the compliment. She pointed to Curaidh who was acting as if he was torn between them. First, he'd run up the little beach till he was opposite Calum, Once there, he'd lie on his stomach with his head on his paws. He'd watch for a short minute before jumping up and running along the shore till he was opposite Doreen.

She held out her hands. "Come on, pup. Come on," she called.

Curaidh rose and advanced till the water reached his stomach and then stopped. He looked at Doreen, lowered his ears and fastidiously held his gently wagging tail above the surface.

"You're a sook, pup. Go to Dor," Calum ordered.

At the sound of Calum's voice, Curaidh turned his head toward his master, hesitated for a moment and then rushed toward him with bounding, splashing leaps, till deeper water forced him to swim. When Curaidh reached him, Calum's strong arms held him above the water. He wriggled and tried to lick his master's face.

Calum grinned at Doreen. "Now's as good a time as any to wash him. But I bet, when I'm finished, he'll roll in that sand and grass till he reckons he's got back to being normal dirty."

"I'm going to sit and sun myself on that big, warm rock over there and watch you."

****

That evening, after they'd eaten, they relaxed and watched the orange-yellow, dancing flames of their campfire. While beyond the flames, stepped white clouds were being splashed a myriad different orange, yellow and red hues by the departing sun. Calum sat with his back against the Boab's trunk and had his arms around his wife. Her head rested on his chest.

"And now we're married," he gently said, "shouldn't we make a fresh start and put Cord River well and truly behind us? Besides, I'd like to understand what you had to go through."

He felt her go tense. But this time she didn't sullenly clam up or yell at him to leave her alone. Instead, anguish filled her voice.

"Please, don't make me talk about it."

"I only want to understand. And don't you see, it'll always be hanging there between us. And me worrying and never knowing when you'll have your next, fear attack. Dor, please," he begged.

When she spoke, her voice was flat and cold. "But could you really understand, my Calum?"

"Please, please trust me."

"Which means if I don't tell you, it's because I don't trust you, doesn't it?" she said sarcastically.

"Don't, Dor, please."

"And are you *sure* you need to hear this?"

"Yes, I am."

She sighed deeply. Right now, safe in Calum's arms, Cord River seemed a million miles away. And that's where she wanted it to stay. But Calum was her husband, and she knew that she couldn't have him thinking that she didn't trust him. That'd only drive a wedge between them, which would grow and fester. She understood *that*. She sighed again. It was a resigned sigh. Calum felt her tense some more and then start to shake. He held her protectively. Then, amid great gulping sobs, she started to speak and slowly told him everything that the Big Father and Sister Rose had done to her.

"And I still don't know what I did to invite them," she sobbed. "Maybe it was the way I walked? But I must have done something. I know it had to be my entire fault."

"You never invited them!"

"And I'm still so ashamed, because I found I liked what Sister Rose was doing."

"You've nothing to be ashamed about, Dor. You were young, and they had power over you. They took advantage of you."

"Do you think so?"

"Definitely. And Hank told me that those two are called by a special name. And they always worm their way into places, like Cord, so they can practice their shit on children or young teenagers."

"You're not having me on, are you?" she asked in a strained voice.

"No way!"

"Are you really sure there are others like them?"

"Dor, the mongrels are all over the place. Hank calls them paedophiles."

She let out a deep sigh. She continued to speak. He thought that she sounded a bit more settled. "I've always thought that it was my fault," she repeated.

"No, Dor. No."

She closed her eyes, took a deep breath and clutched his arms hard.

"God, Dor, I love you so much."

"Still?"

"Even more," he told her and held her very tenderly. "And that'll never change."

"You're not just saying that?"

"No, Dor. Definitely not."

****

Their honeymoon days seemed to merge into one, halcyon spell. The southeast trades hadn't yet been replaced by northerlies. And above them, blue skies beamed benignly on Blue-winged Kookaburra mornings, butterfly and water lily afternoons and starlit, camp fire nights.

Neither could remember a happier time. Her white feller wedding had given Doreen a sense of security that she'd never before known. And being able to talk freely more and more about Cord River had stripped away a choking burden and had lifted her spirits. Calum thought she suddenly seemed more carefree and laughed a lot more. And her sense of fun was infectious.

This particular morning, he was sitting on a rock, drying off in warm sunshine, while watching her. She was parading up and down in front of him. She was dressed in his shirt and rolled-up pants. Her eyes were radiant, and she was clearly enjoying the effect on him of her thrust-out chest and the exaggerated swing of her hips. He was finding it hard to contain his mirth.

"You're not supposed to be laughing," she scolded. "You're supposed to love me no matter how I look."

"But you look like a mixture of some tramp and Charlie Chaplin."

"And you're meant to feel sexy when I swing my hips."

"How can I? I can't stop laughing."

She halted abruptly and glared at him. "I know what it is. It's because I'm over eighteen now."

"What the hell's that got to do with it?"

"I think you prefer young girls because you tried to get my pants off that first time you visited the River. And I was only fifteen."

He burst out laughing. "And I didn't get anywhere for my trouble."

"Ha! I bet you thought I'd be easy!"

He sat up, beetled his brows and did his best to look threatening. "No, I didn't. And you've got two seconds to start thinking nicer thoughts about me."

She started to giggle. He got to his feet and began to advance. She stood and watched him. Her eyes were sparkling, and the smile on her lips widened. Suddenly, she turned and ran into the water, with a girlish shriek. He chased and caught her. They tumbled over in the shallow water, splashing and laughing and holding on to each other. He kissed her wet lips. She put her arms around his neck and kissed him for a long time before she drew back.

"I'll tell you one thing." He grinned. "I like you better now you're eighteen."

"How come?"

"You've filled out."

"Now, you're telling me I'm *fatter*, aren't you?"

He started laughing again. She pretended to struggle against his arms. He held her and kissed her.

"Hell, I can't win with you," he said. "I was trying to say you look much sexier now."

The way she narrowed her eyes was plainly theatrical. "Cross your heart and hope to die, darl?"

"I swear, Dor."

"Well, that's all right then."

"You look very womanly," he said. "And I love it."

She stood up, took off his wet shirt and pants, and looked down at herself. "But I'm not as womanly as Jan, am I?" she asked.

"You reckon?"

"I bet you wish I stuck out as much as she does."

"I don't know about that."

"You're just saying that. I'm sure men prefer women with big bosoms."

"I prefer women about your size."

She looked again at her breasts and studied them. "You know," she said. "I think I am bigger than normal for someone my build."

"Too right," he agreed, smiling.

"Honestly?"

"For sure," he said innocently. "And I reckon you'll even be as big as Jan one day."

"Calum!"

"What?"

"You're being naughty now," she told him as she sat down again.

Curaidh had been sitting on his haunches, watching them intently. He looked as if he was wondering what his two humans were doing, just sitting and chatting in waist-deep water. He got up and trotted to the water's edge and stood looking at them. Doreen noticed him.

"Come on, pup," she called.

Curaidh obeyed her and daintily stepped through the water to join them. Calum told him to sit. And when he did, he sat between them. And any onlooker could've been forgiven for thinking that they resembled the timeless nomads, who had used this billabong down through the ages: a naked hunter, his naked woman and their land's first dog.

Doreen was wondering about Brian's Nurse Alison Noiret. She'd seemed, to her, to be like a breath of fresh air that'd blown in from somewhere else. "Tell me more about Nurse Alison," she told him. "I like her."

"Brian didn't say much. She's French, but her mum's English. And she was in the Resistance in Paris. Her fiancée got captured and killed by the Gestapo."

"How awful."

"And since the war, she hasn't been able to settle. She was in Tahiti for a while and then worked as a cook on a big yacht that was headed for Darwin."

"She sounds like the right sort of girl for Brian."

"That's what I said. He just laughed."

Her brow furrowed slightly. "I was thinking," she said. "Brian could bring her to the River if she had a week off. I like her 'cause she never looked at my skin."

"I'll mention it to Brian."

Doreen leaned past Curaidh and gave Calum a peck on the cheek.

"What was that for?" he asked.

"'Cause I love you." She looked at him questioningly. "What do you think of the bras and knickers I wear?"

"I don't know. I don't think about them much. Why?"

"Well," she continued, "when we get back to the homestead, I think you should help me look through a Johnnie's underwear catalogue. Then you can tell me what sort of bras and briefs turn you on."

"Heavens."

"It'd mean," she said impishly, "I'd be a bit more naughty underneath for your eyes to undress."

"You'll end up turning me on like a tap, Dor." Then he grinned. "Do you know what one of Hank's army mates told him?"

"No."

"He said it was a pity women didn't realize it'd pull the wrinkles from their faces if they didn't wear bras."

"That's awful!"

He studied her face. He'd never seen her looking so relaxed. "Happy?" he asked.

For a moment, her face took on a faraway look. "Yes. And you know what I'd really like to do?" she asked.

"What?"

"I'd like to go to the ballet just once. I saw pictures in a magazine, you know. It looked just like a fairyland."

He grinned at her. "*Fairyland*'s the right word," he said. "I know, because my mother made me go with her one time in Melbourne."

Her face lit up. "Tell me," she asked, "was it like a fairy dance?"

He grinned mischievously. "You *could* say that. There were all these sheilas on stage with muscular legs. And they were wearing wings. Then, while the orchestra played, they started chasing this pansy-looking feller all over the place."

She frowned and smacked him lightly on his arm. "Calum, you stop that. You'll spoil it for me."

He saw the disappointment on her face. "Sorry, Dor," he said. "I was only kidding."

Her face turned dreamy. "Could we pretend I'm white just for a little while, please? And let's pretend we're in Adelaide now, staying with the Macs? And you've asked me if I'd like to go the ballet?"

"Of course, my love," he said, playing along.

"What'll the theatre be like, darl?" she eagerly asked.

"It'll have tiny balconies above the side of the stage that're called boxes. And I'll have hired one, just for us. The orchestra's playing, and all the men in the audience are wearing suits while the women are wearing beautiful dresses."

"You're not just saying that, are you?"

"My word, no. I'll be in a dark suit, and you'll be wearing a terrific-looking dress."

Her face started to glow. "Could we sit in our box," she asked, "and eat chocolates?"

"My word. And ice cream, too."

"And can we walk along the Macs' beach, next morning?" she asked excitedly.

"I don't see why not."

Her face brightened again. "I haven't seen the sea, you know. And like you said, it'll be just like a huge, blue billabong."

"And you'll need to wear a swimsuit on the beach, my love."

"I know. But I won't wear one of those tiny, two-piece ones. I'd be too worried about fellers perving on me."

"But I'll be with you." He grinned. "Anyway what's wrong with a bit of perving? I'm always looking at your body, aren't I?"

She glanced at him, and her face softened. "You don't count," she said. "You're harmless. Besides, you're my husband."

"Me harmless? Bloody hell!"

****

The following day dawned hot, and the air was still and heavy. They decided, for the first time, to explore the deep gorge below the billabong.

The ragged, red-brown cliffs, on either side of the gorge, were high and sloped away from it. They were full of caves, and as they descended into the gorge, they began to see little, rock wallabies, which fled in terror when they saw Curaidh. They stood and admired their sure-footed speed and agility. The cliff-face caves and depressions, in which they lived, ensured that they were pretty safe from dingoes. But the fact that they fled from Curaidh meant that dingoes preyed on them. *Probably,* Calum thought, *when they ventured away from their rocky fastness to feed.*

"They've got such sweet, little faces," Doreen exclaimed.

"Hank reckons these are called Black-flanked Rock Wallabies."

"They're just so pretty with their silver flecks and that white stripe down their sides."

She led the way to a vast, shallow cave that'd been formed by a large, rock overhang. Calum was fascinated by the ancient, rock art on the cave walls and studied the stick men, kangaroos and goannas.

"I bet these are thousands and thousands of years old," he said.

"Yes. Even the Old People, whose land this is, don't know who painted them."

"Look, there's no dingo. Maybe these people were here before the dingo arrived. Hank said the dingo has only been here for about five-thousand years. And that it probably came from Indonesia. You know, that new country that used to be called the Dutch East Indies."

"Isn't that a long time ago, though?"

She leaned back against a large boulder and watched him. When she spoke, she tried to keep her voice neutral. "Tell me," she asked, "would it worry you if we had a baby?"

He stopped looking at the rock art and regarded her questioningly. "Are you pregnant, Dor?"

"No."

"Then, there's nothing to get fussed about, is there?"

He continued to study an emu. *I'm not handling this very well*, she thought. *Then she wondered, with dismay, if he mightn't want children.* She went to him, put her arms around him, and leaned against him. He held her and kissed her cheek briefly. He was absorbed in the rock art.

"You see, my darling, I want to have a little Calum growing inside me," she told him quietly.

He stopped looking at the rock art, considered her and appeared to think carefully before answering. "One of the reasons my old man and me didn't get on was because I liked my mum more than him. And he was sure it was always us against him."

"I know you'll be a great dad. And to me, you'll always be just as important as our children."

"Anyway," he told her, with a hint of a smile, "I reckon I might prefer a daughter, maybe even two."

"You've got to be joking. *Every* man wants a son."

She looked up at his face. Yes, he was serious. *God, this husband of mine*, she thought. *He's full of surprises, but wanting daughters instead of sons? Well, that does throw me.*

"Tell me, why you'd prefer a daughter?" she gently asked.

He started grinning. "I'm only being selfish, mate," he said. "You see, if I do have to grow old, I want to be surrounded by beautiful women in my old age."

"And I suppose." She grinned. "You think we'd spoil you rotten by waiting on you hand and foot?"

"Of course."

"You're a devil, darl. You had me worried, you know. And would it worry you if I got pregnant real soon?"

"No." He grinned disarmingly. "So long as you order a daughter that looks like you." He tightened his arms around her and kissed her tenderly. "You are serious about wanting a baby now, aren't you?" he asked.

"Yes. Even before we got married, white feller way, I wanted my own, little Calum."

He kissed her again, this time more passionately. She looked at him questioningly.

"What's happening, now?" she asked.

"I suppose," he suggested, "we could always start our first son or daughter, right now."

"You often say things I don't expect."

"The way you're yapping," he complained. "We're *never* going to get our family started!"

"You mean you want to do it *now*? Standing up?"

"Well, you said you wanted to start a family straight away, didn't you?"

"Blutty hell," she exclaimed. "All right. But hang on, darl. I need to find somewhere higher to stand."

****

The following afternoon, they were sitting on a rock, with their feet dangling in the water.

"I've been meaning to ask, Dor. Do you think your mum likes Jack Kelly?"

"Only as a friend. It's too soon for anything else. She told me he reminds her of Dad, because he tries to make sure she's happy."

He looked at her quizzically. "Do you try to keep me happy?" he asked.

"Sometimes." She smiled.

"How?"

"I think of ways to make you laugh."

"Yeah?"

"I can read your moods, so I know if I need to be listener or lover or mate."

"You do all that for me?"

"Because I love you."

He looked at her for a long moment. When he spoke, he sounded a trifle mortified. "I must be as thick as a brick," he said, shaking his head. "I never thought about these sorts of things, Dor. Will you help, love, by telling me the sorts of things that make you real happy? You know, to keep our marriage good like it is now."

She kissed him and gave him a long hug. "I think that's nearly the nicest thing you've said to me since we got married," she told him. "And you've said lots of nice things." She suddenly pointed to Curaidh. "I think you should call our dog, darl. I'm getting nervous just watching him."

He looked in the direction that she'd indicated. Curaidh had found a six-foot-long Perentie Monitor and was attacking it. The giant lizard, creamy-white with brownish-yellow markings, constantly swung round to face him. Its movements were deliberate, and it kept flicking out its forked tongue. And its beady eyes never left Curaidh, who kept leaping at its neck and then jumping back quickly to avoid getting bitten. Curaidh was enjoying himself. He was also looking very determined, but he'd taken on an extremely dangerous adversary. Even Murries, who regarded it as delicious eating, acknowledged that it was more than capable of defending itself.

"Here, pup. Now!" Calum shouted.

Curaidh immediately left the large monitor and loped toward them.

"That's a good pup," Calum called. "You better leave that lizard alone. Its tail is a weapon too, mate. You cop a swipe from that, and you'll get a broken leg."

****

It was their last day before breaking camp. Calum could tell that the day was going to be hotter than yesterday. And till the rains came, in December, the country would continue to dry out. Soon it would be as dry as desert dust and then some. And he remembered again that Brian'd told him that they were due for a bad drought, and that he was sure that he could feel one coming on.

"Do you want to do anything special today, my love?" he asked.

"I want to wash my hair 'cause it's starting to feel oily."

"I think I'll wash the horses and take 'em for a swim. It'll be a good break in their routine."

"Mm. And would you wash my back? And I need to cut your hair. You're starting to look hairier than a draught horse's feet."

"Oh, it'll keep," he told her.

"No, it won't. I don't want Jan or Alice seeing you looking like this. They'll think I don't look after you."

"All right, but give it a real quick trim, eh? What if I go and get the comb and scissors to hurry things along?"

They sat waist-deep in the billabong. Curaidh joined them. He walked around slowly, looking at the small fish beneath his nose. And every so often he'd raise a paw and bring it down tentatively, as if he expected to trap one under it. He persisted despite continuing failures.

When Doreen had lathered her hair, Calum offered to massage her scalp for her. He knelt behind her.

"Mm," she murmured. "That's nice."

"I like doing this."

"Hey," she cried. "You're supposed to be doing my head and back. How come your hands have got round to my front, all of a sudden?"

"Sorry." He grinned. "I think they must have slipped."

She smiled mischievously under her head of lather. "You better concentrate on what you're supposed to be doing, darl," she threatened. "Remember it's your turn next, and I'll have the scissors in my hand. Heavens, I'd hate my hand to slip under the water, all of a sudden, while it was working those scissors something fierce. You could end up getting your manhood snipped."

"For Crissake! Where do you get such terrible thoughts?"

"Just think though. If it happened, I'd never have to worry about you ever being unfaithful, would I?"

"Come off it, Dor. Who said anything about being unfaithful?"

"Well, I'd only be taking wifely precautions, wouldn't I?"

"That's it. I'm not letting you anywhere near me with your scissors."

"Don't you trust your wife, my darling? Your dear wife who loves you so much?"

"No. She gets these evil thoughts all of a sudden."

She leaned back and kissed him on his cheek. "Just tell me you trust me, darl, and then I promise to be good."

"No way."

He lapsed into silence. When it was his turn, he wouldn't let her near his hair till she'd promised him that she wouldn't snip an ear or, indeed, any other part of him.

"But what if I have an accident, my Calum?" She asked sweetly.

"There you go. You're at it again."

She batted her eyelids at him. "Accidents will happen," she told him sweetly.

"That's it. Now, you have to promise you won't have an accident."

"All right," she promised brightly. "Cross my heart. But don't you dare fidget, or all bets are off."

He agreed, after more cajoling, to trust her. She wet his hair, combed it straight and proceeded to snip quickly and confidently.

"I've done this so often I can snip very quickly now, can't I?" She asked mischievously.

He ignored her.

"You're sitting very still, my darling. None of your usual little-boy fidgets. None at all."

He continued to stare straight ahead and continued to maintain what he thought was a dignified and long-suffering silence.

"This is the quietest you've been all morning. What a peaceful last day. There, I think I've finished. Now that didn't take long, did it?"

He continued to regard her with suspicion.

****

That night they lay wrapped in each other's arms. Igulgul's white-yellow light shone on them. The countless stars were bright, and night insects added their chorus to the bush, night sounds. She snuggled closer to him and cradled his head against her breasts.

"I never knew I could be so happy," she said.

She reached down with both hands and felt him and then giggled against his chest. "There's nothing much happening down there, darl," she said. "But if I can get you going, would you like to try again for your daughter?"

He kissed her on the cheek. "I'm not fussed, my love. Honestly, I think I'm about honeymooned out, right now."

She turned over on her other side and fitted her back and buttocks to the shape of his body.

315

"That's better," she said, "I'm going to sleep now, 'cause I'm tired, darl. And I don't want to be tired when we're travelling tomorrow. And tomorrow night, I want us to try for my son."

"I see. Good night, my love. Sleep tight."

"Goodnight, darl."

CHAPTER 20

DROUGHT

Brian was right. The Wet didn't come, and dust and drought had taken over the land. It was as if they had decided to terminate pastoral leases by malevolently ruining the heartland and rendering it uninhabitable for man and beast. And the colour of drought never changes.

Some leaseholders decided to pack up and leave before utter despair enslaved them. Others decided that it'd be more prudent to give up the soul-destroying struggle and quit their land before they found themselves owned, for the rest of their lives, by some faceless bank.

Calum was shocked. Not even in his craziest imaginings could he have visualized anything quite as devastating as this. "Talk about it being as dry as desert dust," he complained to Brian. "Hell, Long Creek's already been turned into a desert. We might as well have a run that's slap-bang in the middle of the Tanami Desert."

"And I reckon this is only the start, mate."

Week after week, the sun blazed out of a pitiless, acrylic-hard sky. And each day, it was a debilitating 105 degrees plus in the shade. That is, if you could find any. Waterholes were either dry or else rapidly drying quagmires of sludge. Any feed around them had already been eaten out for a radius of some twelve miles. This meant that only the strongest cattle, the bullocks and dry cows, were able to survive both the long hike out to sparse feed, like Mulga leaves, followed by the hike back in to the watery sludge.

317

Long Creek, because it carried more than six beasts per square mile, was faring far worse than Big River, with its single beast per square mile. It was currently losing an estimated two-hundred head a day. The partners were keenly aware that this figure would continue to increase till hard rain eventually arrived.

"It's hurting us bad, sweetheart," Hank confessed to Jan. "God knows how many horses and cattle'll still be alive when the rains do come."

Jan looked at her exhausted and drained husband and found herself hating the drought that'd etched such deep worry lines on his face. She went to him, wanting to comfort him and put her arms around him.

"All you can do is to hang in there, darl. Keep on fighting and don't give up. And I know my husband's a real fighter."

"Yes, sweetheart, we'll all keep fighting because this is our land, and it's our daughter's future. I just thank my lucky stars I'm married to such a strong, Territory girl, because I don't think an Adelaide girl would've been able to cope." He shook his head. "What a hard lesson though. We must restock with a more drought-resistant breed. Maybe a Brahman cross."

Dead and dying cattle were everywhere and, in particular, around virtually dry waterholes. Calum would frequently see an emaciated cow stagger into the sludge in search of water and then become bogged in the holding mud, because it was too weak to drag itself free. Then death's harbingers, the hordes of waiting, black crows, would descend and peck out its eyes, before swarming all over the terrified, bawling calf that'd been left helpless at the quagmire's edge. He shot every bogged cow that he came across and developed an almost-pathological hatred toward crows. Brian saw him one time, obviously enraged, empty both barrels of a shotgun into a flock before walking away, seemingly oblivious to the wounded ones that were left fluttering on the ground. Brian knew, deep down, that Calum had lost his temper but chose to put it down to a temporary, drought-induced aberration. He picked up a stick and dispatched the wounded crows.

"Those crows are only doing what comes naturally," he gently reminded Calum.

"Fuck 'em!"

Calum found it interesting that the long, broad, weight-distributing back feet of Red Kangaroos and Euros, so different from the sharp and cloven hooves of Shorthorns, prevented most of their kind from getting bogged. And they were often to be seen lapping as daintily as cats at what little surface water remained.

The nauseous stench of thousands of maggot-infested, cattle carcasses rotting in the tropical sun was appalling. It hovered over the burned-up countryside and permeated everything, even clothes and swags. The horses were also suffering. They were gaunt, listless and dull eyed. Many were badly girth-chafed and carried seeping, saddle sores. And always, there were swarms of flies plus unrelenting heat and choking dust. They forced a man, Calum thought, to hold on to himself hard in case he did anything silly.

Birds were dropping in the thousands, especially those cute, yellow and green, little Budgerigars. Prior to the drought, their dense, chattering flocks had swarmed erratically over the countryside. Now, they couldn't cope. But the carrion eaters, like crows, kites, falcons and eagles, prospered. It was as if all their Christmases had come at once.

"Didn't I tell you," Brian said to Calum, "the Budgies would cop a pounding?"

"Yeah, the poor little buggers. And I've never seen so many crows and eagles and kites."

The only animals still in good condition were also carrion eaters. Because there was so much putrefying flesh around, dingoes could be spotted boldly scavenging during daylight hours. Normally, they holed up during the day before emerging at dusk to hunt. Feral pigs also appeared to be much more numerous. They could be seen tearing at fly-blown, cattle carcasses as well as at those cattle still alive that'd just given up and had lain down to die. Because that's exactly what cattle did do when they gave up, and there wasn't a damn thing that you could do to get them back on their feet again. But that didn't mean, Calum told himself, that you had to put up with wild pigs eating at still-alive Shorthorns. He took pleasure in culling those that he could and, while doing so, he balefully recalled what had happened to Murranji. And he never hastened to put out of their misery those that he'd wounded. It was almost as if he was taking a malicious and prolonged revenge.

"Don't you ever give up practicing with that rifle?" Brian asked.

"Not when it comes to pig," Calum replied grimly.

Brian thoughts turned to Murranji Bill, and he said no more.

Calum had no quarrel, though, with those big Perentie Monitors, with their gore-encrusted heads and shoulders, which he saw pulling at and then eating the entrails of dead cattle. He recognized them for what they were: Kunapipi's garbage collectors.

This was a drought to end all droughts. It would soon develop into the most horrific one that old-timers, like Charlie, could remember. It would be one that the Territory's pastoralists would never forget. In years to come, this 1951 drought would be seen as the yardstick by which all future droughts should be measured.

****

When Calum returned from his honeymoon, Brian, strongly convinced that drought was on the way, quickly persuaded him that they should muster and then drove Big River cattle to the river. There were no bores, of course, on their run. Initially, Peg and Doreen had been in camp with them. Calum liked to recall that time. He thought that it was the happiest, cattle camp that he'd known. And thinking about it now was a pleasant way to alleviate the appalling, current, working conditions.

Peg and Doreen had shared the cooking. Peg had encouraged Doreen to be his mustering mate, and he'd discovered that Peg's tongue could border on the coarse when it suited her. And maybe she hadn't been as tolerant as she could have been about Doreen's desire to become pregnant. This desire had festered so much in Doreen's mind and had become so pervasive that her thinking had had no respite from it.

"You go an' help yer husban' muster, love, 'cause I can manage the cookin'," Peg had suggested. "But you make sure he's got no blanket; otherwise, the two of yer won't bring back a mob. An' this camp is about musterin'. It's not about baby makin'!"

"Peg, she's my wife."

"That's exactly what I'm sayin', mate. Marriage has changed her. Now she's like a hussy when she's with her husband."

"Mum!"

"Don't yer mum me, love." Peg'd grinned wickedly. "An' now I've said me piece off yer go."

He'd shaken his head in amusement. "Peg," he'd complained, "I reckon my mother-in-law has become a real nark."

"Well," Peg'd replied in a conspiratorial tone, "Now, yer well and truly married ter my girl, I can afford ter let yer see the real me, can't I?"

"Jesus!"

"An' yer can ferget about Him helpin' yer, mate, 'cause *I'm* the one as goes ter Mass." She'd laughed. "Now, come an' give us a peck, like a good boy, before yer go."

"Hm. I still reckon the Government's being slack not being like Murries, and having a law that says mothers-in-law can't speak to their daughters' husbands."

"Yer cheeky, young devil!"

****

It'd been late-morning, and Doreen and Calum had been droving back the little mob that they'd mustered.

"I bet your mum'll complain that this mob is too small," he'd said.

"Yes. And she's been telling me I get too carried away, sometimes."

"About what?"

"About wanting too much to have a baby."

"Well, you do think about it a lot, don't you?" he'd asked carefully.

"You still want to have a baby, don't you?" she'd replied quickly.

"Of course. I just don't want us to get all lathered up about it. I'm sure you will get pregnant when it's right for you."

She'd looked across at him. What he'd said hadn't really registered.

"You do know, for starters, that I'll need to stop in camp with the bub, don't you?" she'd said in a slightly anxious voice.

"Yes." He'd frowned. "But I reckon your mum's right. You are thinking about it all the time. And maybe if you stop thinking about it so much, it'll just happen."

"All right, I won't think about it," she'd said in a brittle voice. "And you know you'll only have to do without it for the first six weeks or so, don't you?"

"Dor! For Crissake, that's the last thing I'll be thinking of. Anyway, at least I'll get some proper sleep when I hit our swag."

"Calum!" she'd admonished. "You tell me now if you reckon you'll feel left out."

"No way, Dor, 'cause I'll be the dad. And I'll want to cuddle my bub just as much as you two women'll want to. You don't think I'd let you, two, get all the smiles and cuddles, do you!"

"And if we don't share?" she'd asked brightly.

"I'll sulk. Maybe for weeks."

"Oh good. I haven't seen you sulk before."

"In that case, I think I'll start practicing, right now!"

****

Now, month after month, as the rains continued to stay away, Calum, Brian, Jack and Nugget spent every daylight hour mustering Big River Shorthorns before droving them to the river.

Peg and Doreen started to get a bit niggly with each other. The heat and the dust were getting to them; besides, the men were never home. They were still battling against time to save as many of their herd as possible. Peg decided that a change of scenery would do them both good. So she asked Doreen to accompany her and Jack up north, to Adelaide River, for a break.

"Jack reckons it should still be a bit green up there. Besides, yer man is never home."

"He's working his guts out, Mum. For us all."

"I know, love. An' I didn't mean it the way you took it, fair dinkum."

"It's all right, Mum. And I'm sorry. It's just that I'm edgy." Doreen laughed. "And I shouldn't be. Heck, I haven't even started to bleed yet this month."

"Maybe yer pregnant?"

"No, more's the pity. I know I'm not pregnant, 'cause I can feel my period coming."

Doreen didn't want to leave home. But she agreed to go when Calum and Brian, briefly returning for fresh mounts, had told her that they now felt obliged to go on to Long Creek to help Hank. That night Calum and Doreen walked arm in arm down the driveway, to the old gate. It was stinking hot, and the night air felt light and dry. They could smell the parched, red earth beneath their feet.

"I don't want to leave our home, darl," Doreen cried.

"You and your mum need the break. Besides, all I'll be doing over there is droving and eating dust. And I don't know how long I'll be."

"And you promise to come for me when the drought breaks?"

"Nothing'll stop me. And I'm looking forward to it, because I've never been to Adelaide River."

"Tell me you love me."

"I love my wife," he said and suddenly felt very emotional. "And, God, I love her body."

She held on to him tightly. "You better, darl. It's the only one she's got."

They leaned against the gate. Those cattle that he heard lowing sounded weak. He cursed the drought and cursed the fact that he and his wife were destined to be apart for God knows how long.

"You're quiet," she murmured. "What are you thinking, darl?"

He exhaled and then grimaced ruefully. "I was thinking about you being in Adelaide River. And how far away that is."

"Darling, I won't go if you don't want me to," she said anxiously.

"No, it's not that. It's just that I'm beginning to think there must be something wrong with me, the way I miss you all the time. And then, when you're with me, I can't keep my hands off you. No wonder you need a break from me."

She hugged him fiercely. "Oh, darl," she murmured, "you can't really believe that, surely?"

"I do wonder about it sometimes," he admitted grudgingly.

She leaned back and looked up into his extraordinarily blue eyes. It pained her to see how tired and remote and lost they looked. "Do you know how much I love you?" she asked.

He gave a distracted smile. "Maybe to Wanjin and back?"

He felt her shake her head against his chest. Then she looked up at his face. "No. Now you listen to me, Calum darl," she told him softly. "I want you to remember always, I love you *so* much that sometimes I can get wet just looking at you."

He stared at her for a long moment and then rubbed his eyes with the back of his hand before smiling ruefully. "That's not fair," he complained. "It doesn't show on you, does it?"

She burst out laughing and stood on tiptoe and kissed him. "Oh, my darling," she cried. "Honestly, I never know what you're going to come out with next." She wiped her eyes. "And I needed that laugh, because I think I've just started to bleed."

But she hadn't, and her period didn't come.

She took his arm and hugged it to her as they turned and walked toward the homestead.

"When will you leave for Adelaide River?" he asked.

"As soon as you head for Long Creek."

"I'm exhausted, my love. And I also, want to see if I can get some condition on Socks. Brian and I must have a few days off before we head for the Creek."

"Good. That means we'll have those days together. That'll be lovely."

That night they agreed to meet in Adelaide River during the fourth week, after the start of any hard rain. Jack told Calum that they'd be staying with a mate of his who'd retired there, with his Murri woman.

"You'll like old Tom," he told Calum. "He enjoys company an' a rum, an' what he don't know 'bout catching fish, in that river is somethin' else again. Course, there's more 'n a few gators in that water, like."

"Big ones?"

"About as big as I've seen."

"Shit."

When Brian and Calum set off for Long Creek, Doreen, Peg, and Jack said their farewells. Nugget stayed to be with Mary and, of course, to keep an eye on things.

Peg hugged her tearful daughter. "Cheer up, love," she said. "And think how excitin' it'll be when yer meet again."

****

As usual, the Long Creek day had dawned hot and airless, and the dust was thick and choking. Today would be no different, Calum gauged. He and Brian, helped by Tarpot and Jacky Jacky, were droving seven-

324

hundred-head of drought-stricken beasts to the Number 8 bore. And that was some twelve miles from the dry billabong, at which they'd mustered them two days earlier. The billowing red dust, being raised by the moving cattle, was becoming increasingly thick. It was irritating his eyes and making them water. No wonder, he thought, so many old ringers were either dust blind or needed to wear very thick lenses. He wondered if his own eyes would one day be similarly affected. That prospect disturbed him, so he concentrated his thinking on the job at hand.

Droving cattle, from dry waterholes to already-overstocked bores, was the only task that Long Creek's ringers had been doing since the drought had dried up the billabongs. And a dry billabong was something that happened long after the creeks had stopped running.

The mob that they were now droving was strung out over some four miles. Bullocks and dry cows were in the lead while breeders with older calves straggled along behind. Droving this mob wasn't hard, Calum thought. Most looked half dead. He touched his heels to Meg, the mare he liked riding when Socks needed a spell, and caught up to Brian. The usual distance that you could drove cattle was about ten miles a day, but today they'd be lucky to manage half that. Brian flashed him a wry, dust-covered grin.

"Do you reckon we should slow the leaders and give the rest a chance to catch up?" Calum asked. "Otherwise, they'll be all over the bloody shop when we reach that bore."

"Yeah, I'll give you a hand."

They steadied the leaders till those lagging had caught up. Nevertheless, Calum estimated that the mob was still strung out across a mile and a half of country.

"Bloody shithouse, this drought, Brian." He grimaced. "And not a drop of rain to be smelled."

"Yeah."

"This drought is supposed to be the worst one yet." Calum grinned ruefully. "And I was just thinking that the people Inside wouldn't have a clue what we're going through. They'll just turn up at their corner butcher to buy their steak and mince, complain about the price, and then Bob's your uncle; they're off home to cook up a beaut feed."

Brian nodded his agreement. He didn't speak. His throat was too parched.

At that instant, they were hit by a huge blast of wind that'd come from nowhere. Calum quickly glanced around him. A powerful Willy Willy, one-hundred-feet high, dark and twisting fast, swept by on their left sucking up dust and debris in its path. Now the wildly gusting wind really went crazy. It swung about erratically, as if it was trying to cover all the points on the compass at once, and fast-flying pieces of grit and bark badly stung their faces.

"For Crissake," Calum grumbled to himself, "this shit is so bad it'd blow the damn stripes off a zebra."

Wildly-swirling, red dust blanketed the sun. Daylight faded. And through the dust and dark, the confused, bawling cattle became hazy outlines. Calum tied a kerchief over his nose and mouth. *This is one hell of a dust storm*, he thought, *and we need it right now like we need a hole in the head.*

He saw that Brian had moved his brown gelding, Bucko, next to Meg. He'd also tied a kerchief over his face. Conversation was impossible. Calum gave him a thumbs-up. Brian's eyes crinkled, and he nodded his head. Then the wind howled from the north and held steady, and the sky grew ever darker as a huge, black cloud rolled up and completely covered the sun. *This is eerie*, Calum thought, *here it's midmorning, for Crissake, and it's as dark as all hell.*

He allowed Meg to swing round till her rear end faced the wind. She stood, head down, with her mane blowing around her head and her tail flat against her rump and side.

Brian and Calum nodded to each other, dismounted in unison, and firmly holding their reins, they squatted at their mounts' heads, hoping that the horses would act as a windbreak. Curaidh lay on his stomach next to Calum. Calum rested a hand on his shoulder. A distant rumble of thunder reverberated loudly. Calum looked at Brian, passed his reins to him and stood up. In no time, he'd unsaddled both horses. Then they took off the bridles and replaced them with halters. Brian held their horses while Calum carried the saddles and bridles, with their Tom Thumb bits, steel buckles and stirrup irons thirty yards away. When he returned, they squatted beside their horses' heads and waited.

Calum left his hand on Curaidh to calm him, because thunder had always alarmed him. A lull in the wind preceded the initial flash of lightning. This was followed by deep, rumbling thunderclaps that reverberated all around them. Then the sky lit up. Continual, blinding, lightning flashes forked and arced and jaggedly rent the heavens as more and more thunder followed. It rolled and roared and rumbled. More than once, the horses panicked, neighed shrilly, backed away and fought for their heads. And the two men had to rise and hold tight on to their halters and then pat and stroke them to calm them. They looked at each other. Brian winked, and Calum smiled back, under his kerchief. Both continued to cower beneath what they thought could well turn out to be one of the worst *Cockeye Bobs* that either had ever encountered.

The air around them became heavy and very close, and it contained so much electricity that they could hear it crackling in their ears. Both felt insignificant. They were awestruck and rigid as they watched the heavens being illuminated by such dreadful and incandescent savagery. They knew fear and, at the same time, felt humble in the face of such terrifying power and violence.

Calum noticed that much of Brian's hair was standing quite upright. He touched Brian's arm and pointed. Some exhausted Shorthorns had collapsed onto the ground, and blue electricity was arcing over and between their horns. He glanced at their bridles. The same, blue electricity was stuttering over the steel Tom Thumbs. He pointed it out to Brian. They hastily took off their spurs and tossed them toward the saddles and bridles.

Calum crouched lower. He'd never heard of lightning being conducted along a green hide halters, but then, he'd never before seen blue electricity stuttering on horns and Tom Thumbs. He told himself that this had to be Nature at her most terrifying. Then he saw a tree being struck by lightning. It first flashed against a limb and then a loud crack, like a sharp explosion, immediately followed. Flames then burst from the struck limb before it crashed to the ground. *Thank God this mob is exhausted and weak*, he thought. *Otherwise, we'd have one hell of a rush on our hands.* He waited fearfully, convinced that it'd be only a matter of time before either he or Brian would be struck by lightning.

Then suddenly, the storm passed them by. It departed as quickly as it'd come. And it left behind a brief, tantalizing splatter of huge raindrops. The sky lightened as the huge, black cloud moved on, and then, thankfully, the wind dropped. They stood up and looked about them.

"Thank Crise!" Brian exclaimed. "And thank Crise we're both still standing."

"Yes, thank God."

About a sixth of the mob was on the ground, with their legs tucked under them. Calum knew that they'd have trouble getting them to their feet. They walked their horses over to the saddles and bridles. Calum pointed to a cow that'd been struck by lightning. She lay dead, on her side, with her legs stuck out at right angles from her body. Her head and shoulders had been scorched black. Her mouth was open and grotesquely twisted to reveal her teeth and blackened tongue. Brian, breathing heavily, looked at the clear heavens with raised eyebrows.

"Do you reckon we were being teased?" he asked.

"Tchinek-tchinek?"

"Well, I caught a glimpse of a rainbow."

They mounted. Tarpot and Jacky Jacky rode up smiling. The four of them then went in among the cattle, cracking their stock whips. It was largely a futile exercise. Barely a dozen Shorthorns struggled to their feet.

"We're wasting our time," Calum stated flatly. "And we don't have any to waste. We've got to save those that're on their feet."

"You're right, mate."

They were forced to leave behind around one sixth of their mob. It was heartbreaking. Those that they left didn't move. They lay in the red dust and waited to die.

Calum wheeled Meg. "I better get back to my place on the flank, Brian. We've got to keep the rest moving. Hell, we don't need any more lying down."

The Number 8 bore had been visible from five miles out. It consisted of a towering, sixty-foot-high windmill that pumped artesian water into a huge, earthen tank from where it was then released into a fifty-foot-long stock trough. They calculated that they'd reach it by early afternoon.

The leading mob, for some reason, had doggedly swung over to Brian's flank. Calum cut through to help straighten them. Both saw the solitary figure at the same time, and Calum's sharp eyes immediately recognized Ed Smith. The dog poisoner was sitting with his back against the trunk of a spreading, thin-branched, Gidgee acacia. His saddle and rifle were on the ground beside him. He appeared to be unconcerned and watched their approach with minimal reaction.

"You better do the speaking, Brian. I don't trust myself."

"We'd be bastards if we didn't help, mate."

"Yes."

Ed Smith continued to watch them as they rode up to him. Finally, he got to his feet and stretched his legs. "G'day, fellers," he called. "I've been watching your dust coming, for a long time. Those cattle of yours don't move real quick, do they?"

"G'day, Ed," Brian called back. "Struck a bit of trouble, eh?"

"My horses gave out yesterday. I've been resting up during the day and walking toward that bore at night. I've still got half a bottle o' water left. I woulda made it, you know."

Calum said nothing. He thought that the man's expression looked a bit wilder than usual. Now and again, his mouth opened, but no sound came from of it. And his stink hadn't changed.

"I see you still got yer dingo," Ed Smith said to Calum.

"And I aim to have him for a lot longer, no worries."

"That Murranji Bill got what he deserved, you know. If that pig hadn't got him, I would've."

Brian moved Bucko smartly in an effort to place himself between Calum and Ed Smith. He wasn't quick enough. Calum looked down at Ed Smith. His temper surged uncontrollably, and he spoke between gritted teeth.

"Murranji was good mate, Smith. And you got what you deserved. If I ever see you on Big River land, I'll finish what he started. So help me, I'll bloody well gut you like a fish, you filthy bastard."

Brian finally managed to push Bucko between Meg and Ed Smith.

"We wouldn't leave a feller in strife, Ed," he interjected quickly. "We'll sell you one of our spares."

Ed Smith turned his attention to Brian, his eyes glowering. "How much?"

"Have you got three quid?"

"I won't argue. Beggars can't be choosers."

"We don't see any beggars," Brian told him. "Only a human being afoot in rough country."

"Yeah? But that wouldn't be how that Murranji woulda seen it. An' me, a white man too, mind you."

Brian took a sheet of paper, from his saddlebag, and scribbled a receipt. Ed Smith stuffed it in his shirt pocket, handed over three pounds and picked up his rifle and saddle.

"Show me this horse," he said. "I want to get moving." He kept on staring malevolently at Calum. "I won't forget what you said, McNicol, so help me!"

"Yeah? Now, you've got me terrified, you mongrel."

"I won't forget, McNicol. Yeah, I won't forget. You'll see."

Ed Smith saddled up quickly and swung himself into his saddle. He barely looked at them and certainly didn't acknowledge the presence of Tarpot and Jacky Jacky.

"Hooroo," he said shortly. "Tell that Hank I'll do him a favour now I'm back from Western Australia, an' thin out the dogs for 'im. I tell you that Yank's a real man. Pity there aren't more like him," he observed and gave Calum another malevolent look.

They briefly watched him as he rode toward the bore. Again, Calum experienced that strong sense of foreboding that contact with Ed Smith always generated.

"These buggers are not like 'roos," Calum said, referring to their mob and shaking his head. "And now we're just about there, help me sprinkle a water trail to the trough. It'll take their minds off giving up, and it'll speed 'em up too."

"Yeah, anything to speed things up."

"But it'll still take us three hours to water them."

When the thirsty leaders smelled the water trail, they quickened their pace and followed it to the trough. Eighty or ninety, at a time, were cut out and watered, and the others held back till those at the trough had drunk their fill. It was tedious, dusty work, and it was dark by the time the whole mob had been watered.

It'd taken the ringers well over two hours to put the mob through. *What a bastard of a day,* Calum thought, *nasty too, when a man had to leave behind so many of his mob. Then stand by and watch some of those he'd saved discover that once they'd a full belly of water, they were too weak to continue standing and got the staggers before they dropped. Yes, Calum thought, it was bloody crook because there wasn't anything you could do for the poor bastards. You just had to hope that they'd find enough strength to get back on their feet again.*

That night Calum left the fire early. Sleep was tugging him toward his swag. He was beginning to hate the unrelenting stench of rotting, cattle carcasses. And, God, how he'd come to hate crows, while his admiration for kangaroos increased. Yeah, when there wasn't much feed about, 'roos automatically stopped breeding.

He wondered how much longer this drought would last. He shook his head and let his memory savour that idyllic time that he'd spent at Rock Wallaby Waterhole: a time that'd been spent against a benign backdrop of lush greenery and clean, fresh water and with his olive-skinned wife beside him: whose body fitted into his better than his hat fitted his head, who often laughed, and who loved him passionately—and who longed to be carrying their child.

When he awoke, the first thing that he wondered was how many more cattle had died during the night. And how many would die during the coming day because it'd be the same as yesterday. He rose, put on his shirt and boots and walked some distance away to relieve himself. Curaidh, resembling a ghostly outline in the half light, padded along next to him. He bent over and gave his dog a caring pat.

"I know you want a drink, pup. But let me get my whip first, just in case any of these half-dead beasts can summon up the strength to have a go at you."

They walked to the trough. Calum watched Curaidh stand on his hind legs, front paws resting on the rim and lap thirstily.

"You're a noisy drinker, pup. And that's not polite."

Curaidh listened to him. Calum saw that his dog's eyes were on his face, even while his long, pink tongue lapped thirstily.

When he returned, Brian was up and had the fire started. He welcomed Calum with a cheerful grin. "The damper'll soon be ready," he said.

"Great. I'm starving."

"I'm worried about having to go on to Victoria Waterhole and then Number 9 bore," Brian stated. "Look, I don't know whether the horses'll make it. Maybe we should head straight for the home station and get fresh ones? What do you reckon?"

"These have had it, mate."

"That'll do me," Brian agreed. "We'll go back. Okay?"

"We've no choice."

After they'd eaten, they broke camp and rode for Long Creek.

****

Three days later, they arrived at the home station when it was going on for dusk. Helped by Jan, Charlie, and Hank, they took the shoes off the horses by lamplight before turning them out. Jacky Jacky and Tarpot then headed for the Murri camp, carrying a bag of flour and a sack of beef.

"I'm looking forward to a meal," Hank said wearily. "And it shouldn't be too long, because Jan said she'd help Charlie." He smiled at her. "For a pregnant lady you've sure got a lot of energy, sweetheart."

"I don't mind Jan in me kitchen," Charlie said. "She's not like you fellers, 'cause she notices the trouble I go to."

Jan put her arm round Charlie's waist. "Come on, mate," she told him. "You're in charge. I'm only the kitchen *useful*. Let's get to work, while Hank pours these dry and tired drovers a cold beer."

She looked at them. All were exhausted, their faces drained and pinched. And the fact that they were losing so many head was dragging them farther down. *What they needed right now,* she decided, *was a good meal, a few cold beers and a bit of mothering.* She looked at them, smiled and took control.

"You fellers go and throw some water on your faces and hands," she told them, "and by the time you come back, Hank'll have poured *big,* icy-cold glasses of beer."

"We'll go and sit at the table, fellers, after we've washed up," Hank suggested. "Knowing my wife, a hearty meal that tastes terrific won't be long in coming."

Hank was right. They ate in the glow of soft, electric light made possible by the generator, bought just prior to Doreen and Calum's wedding that was Hank's pride and joy; and which, he claimed, had brought much needed civilization to Long Creek in the form of a huge freezer and a very large fridge.

"It's good ter sit back," Charlie said, "an' eat what someone else's cooked."

Jan had finally managed to get little Janice to go to sleep. She came back, brushing a loose strand of hair from her forehead. She rubbed her tummy. "I hope this next one won't be such a little monkey," she said and grinned companionably at Calum. "And you're right, mate. I'm already sticking out a bit."

"That's only to be expected," Brian said, glancing at her stomach. "After all, you'll soon be five months pregnant."

Jan kept smiling conspiratorially at Calum, who quickly looked down, at his steak.

"This steak's the best I've had since before the drought," he hastily said.

"We've had pics tail a few killers down at that little waterhole," Hank said. "There's always a bit of grass there."

"Yeah?"

"And I was just thinking," Jan remarked, "how fresh the air felt, when we were taking the shoes off those horses. And the wind had swung round and was coming from the north, like the start of the Wet."

"Promises, promises," Hank suggested

"I don't know about that," Brian said. "The clouds were certainly building up."

At that precise moment they all heard the sound for which they'd been praying. It was the unmistakable noise of heavy rain hammering down on the corrugated iron roof, almost like something that was alive. Calum left the table and headed for the verandah.

"Please excuse me, but I need to see this." Once outside, he exclaimed, "You little beauty!"

For a long minute, he stood on the verandah. In the light from the windows, he watched big raindrops strike the ground, in a puff of dust, and form small craters in the dust layer. Soon, the parched earth was transformed into a vast sheet of water. The deluge far exceeded Long Creek's immediate capacity to absorb it. Soon, Calum knew that the rivers'd be running bankers, and the creeks would flow again, and the billabongs would fill. And the stench of death would be swept from the heartland. Then he'd head for Adelaide River and the wife who'd taken his heart with her when they'd kissed each other good-bye.

Brian joined him. He looked at Calum and nodded at the downpour. "That's hard rain, mate. Looks like the drought's broken."

"Thank God for that!"

****

Mostly, in the afternoons, massive, rolling clouds rode the nor'westerlies like living juggernauts. They were dark and threatening and overloaded and were in a hurry to dump their heavy burden of illimitable gallons of hard rain onto the parched earth below. In the Gulf Country, particularly, these deluges were often preceded by violent, electrical storms. The drought was well and truly broken, and hard rain was now regenerating a burned land and the life that it was required to sustain.

Those pastoral lessees who'd not been driven from their land would never again be the same. They'd been tempered in that hellish furnace called drought, and they'd survived. They had also learned a valuable lesson. The day of the Shorthorn must come to an end.

The Shorthorn was a European breed, and sensible lessees realized that a more suitable breed was needed for such an unforgiving land. Soon, Brahman and Brahman crosses would rapidly increase in popularity, being more drought and tick resistant. And during the following year, the first Santa Gertrudis would be imported into Australia, from the King Ranch in Texas. It was a breed that'd been created following an infusion of Brahman blood into a Shorthorn herd.

****

There wasn't much for ringers to do during the wet, so they tried their best to amuse themselves. They often played poker, for imaginary millions, and an overconfident Brian was always the biggest loser. Then he'd seek an alternative diversion. Right now, he gave Hank, Charlie and Calum a withering look, promptly shed his clothes, armed himself with a bar of soap and strutted, stark naked, out into the latest downpour. He continued to bellow lustily and tunelessly, while he energetically soaped himself.

My Mabel waits for me

Underneath a clear, blue sky,
Where the dog sits on the tucker box
Five miles from Gundagai.

"Yer'd think he'd worry about his mum seein' him. The bastard's got no shame," Charlie sniffed.

In Alice's cottage, Alice and Jan were sitting, chatting, and having a cup of tea. Alice loved these occasions because Jan had glowed ever since her marriage and Alice had found that she was able to bask in her daughter's happiness. Jan watched her mum nurse her granddaughter and felt very relaxed. She enjoyed the Wet. It made her feel more married, because Hank was around most of the time. She especially liked the evenings. She enjoyed being able to cook the things that Hank liked, things that he'd never have in camp. And then after little Janice was asleep, they'd often sit and listen to the wireless. She'd discovered that he liked to draw the blinds and persuade her to spend the rest of the evening in her bra and briefs. He got enormous enjoyment from just watching her when she wore few or no clothes. She smiled to herself. *If that's what he wants,* she told herself, *I'm happy to give it to him.* Heavens above, it wasn't that much to give to one's husband, especially one who was now her best friend, who frequently sought her advice and who always treated her as an equal. And who absolutely adored his daughter. She'd decided, too, that what he liked wasn't sinful, which meant that she didn't have to bring it up when she went to Confession, in Catriona.

Jan's thoughts switched back to her shape. She would need to make sure she got it back quickly after the new bub was born. Heavens, if Hank made the effort to be such a caring father and husband, then she'd make sure that she didn't let herself go. She made a mental note to ride her mare more often. It'd be an opportunity for her mum to have little Janice all to herself, and besides, she loved her mare. She'd been chosen by Hank, because she was so docile, and Calum had put in a lot of time schooling her. Not surprisingly, Brian had named her Spitfire.

Brian's tuneless bellowing interrupted her thoughts. She could hear him above the sound of the rain. She looked at her mum and raised her eyebrows. Alice couldn't resist having a look. She got to her feet and

335

stuck her head out of the front window. Her son's nakedness didn't faze her. She yelled in the direction of the ringer's hut.

"What's up with Brian, you fellers?"

"His brain's waterlogged. Must be the seven inches we've had," Calum yelled back.

Alice lost much of Calum's answer in the beating rain. But this much she did hear.

"Must be … seven inches."

"You blutty men," she yelled back. "Yer always boastin'. From what I seen, it's not even *two* inches."

Alice returned to her chair and sat down again. She turned her attention to Jan. "My grizzlin' granddaughter is very cuddly this mornin', love."

"She had a tummy ache, and she didn't sleep well last night."

"Poor baby." She nodded toward Jan's stomach. "Any sickness or anythin', love?"

"No, it must be the black feller blood. I don't even feel pregnant. And it probably wouldn't worry me if I was like you an' gave birth on a sheet of Paperbark and then, afterward, wrapped the baby in a Paperbark shawl."

"Things is much differen' now, love." Alice reflected. "An', tell me, how does Hank feel 'bout yer bein' pregnant?"

"You've seen him with Janice, Mum. I can't have another quickly enough as far as he's concerned." Jan smiled. "An' now my breasts are getting bigger, and there's no tenderness; he's like a kid with a new toy."

"Blutty men. They never grow up."

"And I've got lots of love left over for him, so he'll never feel left out."

"That's good, love. Anyways, I reckon yer've got yourself a good man, my girl."

****

Calum was relaxing on the verandah. He looked out, through the rain, at what he could see of the surrounding countryside. Miraculously, it seemed that the entire country had been transformed. Wherever he now looked, he saw green, green, and more green. Already the grass was shin high, and the cattle were rapidly putting on condition. And he knew that after that first night's rain, they would've drifted away from the bores and would've scattered themselves over the countryside.

Calum wondered what Doreen was doing at this moment. Maybe she was wondering if he'd already left for Adelaide River. He felt rested and decided that he'd leave on the day after tomorrow. Then his thoughts turned to the Kaditje man. The old man had turned up the day after it'd rained. Jacky Jacky had helped him, and between them, they'd forged steel heads for the old man's spears. He grinned to himself when he recalled the terror on Jacky Jacky's face and how invaluable he'd been as an interpreter. It still puzzled him, though, why the old man had wanted to know the route that he'd be taking when he travelled north. All the old man would say was that they might meet up and that they might share a pig, because now that he had these new spearheads, spearing a pig would be easy. The talk of spearing had caused Jacky Jacky's eyes to roll in terror. He'd made a point of repeating a number of times that he wouldn't be travelling with Calum. Then it'd all become too much for him, and he'd asked to be excused.

Calum noticed that the rain had stopped and that Hank was walking toward the ringer's quarters.

"G'day, Hank," he called. "Come and talk to me, because I'm bored."

Hank joined him. "I was thinking, there's nothing to stop you heading north now," he said. "I had a look at Socks, and he'll get you there okay. Just remember to put plenty of cattle dung on your fire to keep the mosquitoes away. There's always a lot around after rain."

Hank settled himself in a verandah chair. Calum thought that he'd never seen him looking so at peace with himself.

"Marriage agrees with you, Hank. You're looking great."

"I'm lucky. Jan's a wonderful wife and mother. You know, she's always the same. And she always has a smile on her face. She makes living with her kinda easy."

"She and Brian are peas in a pod, like that."

"You're not wrong, there." He grinned. "And tell me, Calum, how are *you* finding married life now that you've been married for all of ten months?"

"Real good. Except I'm dirty at being wiped by most of Catriona's whites."

Hank smiled, and Calum saw his look of understanding. "But that's something you knew would happen, didn't you?" Hank said.

"Yes. But it still eats at me," Calum replied irritably.

"I understand. You know," Hank said wryly, "it'd be okay if we just wanted to sleep with our women. But to marry them! And want kids by them!"

"Yes."

They sat silently immersed in their own thoughts.

"I guess," Hank finally said, "when you get back, we should talk about getting Brahman herd bulls for both runs. Also Nugg needs to be one of your head stockmen, because he's so keen on young Mary."

"And we should train and employ as many local Murries as possible."

"Yeah, they make great ringers!" Hank took his watch from its pouch on his belt and looked at it. "I'm feeling hungry. I think I'll go and see what's happening about lunch," he said.

"Right, and is there any beer left?"

"Plenty!"

"Great. I feel like a beer." Calum smiled. "And you can all wish me a safe trip."

CHAPTER 21

UNDESERVED

Calum headed north for Adelaide River at first light. Daybreak promised a fine morning, with white clouds polka-dotting the golden sky. He'd put his pack saddle on Sunshine and smiled as he watched the little, black packhorse contentedly walking along just behind Socks. Curaidh, alongside Socks, kept checking on Calum's face. And now and again, Calum would look down and give his dog a smile.

Then, they headed nor'west, and soon, behind Calum's right shoulder, the emerging, red-gold sun swiftly swelled till the surrounding, green plain had been transformed into a glistening vista of green and gold.

He thought that this wasn't a bad time to be travelling across these sparsely-treed plains, because it offered a man the clean, fertile smell of damp earth to go with the sweet smell of new, green grass. And ahead, frequently taking flight, would be massive flocks of shaggy-crested Little Corellas, all white and shiny except for those few, pink feathers between bill and eye. He'd always thought that their departing flocks resembled a blizzard of giant snowflakes that was being blown willy-nilly before his horses.

And he found it very satisfying to watch healthy calves, part owned by himself, approach out of curiosity and then friskily flee from his horses, with their tails stiffly held straight up in the air.

By mid-afternoon, on the second day, he was not far from where the Big River meandered east through Crown land. It was broken country, part hilly and stony, but which offered Mitchell grass on its intervening flats. And which also contained dense patches of Ironwood and Lancewood.

After he'd made camp and bushed his horses, he headed out, with Curaidh, to see what they'd come across for their late-afternoon meal. Ahead on a large flat, feeding on Mitchell grass, was a small mob of Red Kangaroos. They were a hundred-and-thirty yards away and there was no cover for a stalk. Momentarily, he regretted being afoot because approaching 'roos on horseback wasn't hard. But then he had needed to stretch his legs after being in the saddle for nine hours. There was nothing for it, he decided, but to take the shot. He sat down, raised the rifle's back sight, rested his elbows on his knees and got off his shot. The bullet's impact knocked over a young male. Almost immediately, it rose to its feet and headed after the fleeing mob. He saw that it was steadily losing ground but, nevertheless, was moving well enough to be soon out of sight. He sent Curaidh after it and tried to follow at a jog, but the green grass underfoot was polishing the leather soles of his riding boots, and causing him to slip repeatedly.

As he ran, as best he could, he worried about the 'roo's big toe. Three of its four toes, on each foot, were small and insignificant, but the remaining one was big and had a long, strengthened nail. This was the nail that gave the 'roo leverage, to bound, by hooking into the ground. It was also its primary weapon and could inflict hideous wounds by ripping deeply through hide and flesh.

When he was close enough to get a clear view, he breathed a sigh of relief. The 'roo was on its side, and Curaidh had it more by the neck than throat. He'd hamstrung it and was in no danger from either back foot. Now that Curaidh wasn't in any danger, Calum relaxed and admired his dog's cleverness. He saw that Curaidh was tugging at such an acute angle that the 'roo was finding it impossible to reach back and grasp his head with its front paws. Obviously, it wanted to pull Curaidh's head forward so that it could bite. And under his glossy, reddish-yellow coat, Curaidh's shoulder muscles were bunched, and those on his thighs were corded with the strain. Every now and then his back pads slipped forward on the downtrodden grass. But he reset his feet immediately and continued with his tugging and his small grunts.

When Calum, breathing heavily, finally reached them, he saw that the battle was over. Curaidh stood over the dead 'roo, with his eyes on Calum and with his dribbling, pink tongue lolling out of his mouth. He was panting heavily and gulping in such deep lungfuls of air that his ribs showed with every gasping breath. Calum leaned over and patted him on his shoulder.

"I have to tell you, pup, there's no way that I could've got here sooner. And I'm proud of you, 'cause I reckon another dog that's not as smart would've been ripped open from its neck to its tail. But look at you, mate. There's not even a scratch on you." He stooped over and gave Curaidh another pat and then stroked his head gently. "And, gee, if it wasn't for you, we wouldn't be eating this well. And no bush tucker tastes better than roasted 'roo tail that's washed down with a mug of tea."

After Calum had caught his breath, he took out his clasp knife, knelt down and butchered off the parts of the 'roo that he wanted.

"Come with me, pup," he ordered when he'd finished. "We're heading for camp. That's quite enough excitement for one day, don't you think?"

Later, beside his companionable, flickering campfire, with a full stomach and with Curaidh stretched out asleep beside him, Calum listened to the night sounds and stared into the dancing flames. Now, the orange-red coals seemed to conjure up images of his wife within their shimmering heat. And once again, he saw the concern that'd been etched on her face when he and Brian had ridden in that last time after having headed out, during those days, when they'd planned to rest prior to leaving for Long Creek. But a Murri couple, on returning from their walkabout, had told Brian where they'd seen a fair mob of cattle beside a dry waterhole.

On their return to the homestead, he and Brian had sat, parched and aching and exhausted, on the verandah. Doreen had placed a cold bottle of beer and a glass before each of them. He'd barely drunk one glass before he'd begun to slur his words.

Peg'd laughed at him good-naturedly. "I reckon yer man's a one glass screamer, love." She'd grinned. "Look at him, he's unsteady already."

"Mum, be kind. Can't you see they're both out on their feet?"

Then she'd gone to him, made him stand up and had taken his arm. "You come with me, darl," she'd told him. "It's a bath for you and then something to eat." She'd looked over her shoulder at Brian. "What about you, mate?"

"Calum's welcome to the bath first, Dor. I'll take my time enjoying this beer. It's cold, an' it's wet, an' it's what I need right now."

They'd gone into the spacious, white-painted bathroom and she'd closed the door, filled the big, footed bath and had helped him to undress. He'd lain back while she'd soaped a sponge. Then she'd washed him as if he'd been a baby. He'd felt very spoiled.

She'd smiled at him. "I'm only spoiling you 'cause you've saved so many of my beasts, you know."

"Mm."

The water had soothed and relaxed him. He'd felt his strength returning, and his head had cleared. He'd watched her take one of his feet in both hands.

"What are you doing, Dor?" he'd asked.

"I need to wash between your toes. I can see it's been a while."

"There wasn't a lot of water out there."

"I know."

"I reckon I could go a good feed now," he'd told her. "I'm starting to feel hungry as well as halfway human."

She'd smiled at him. "That's not going to make me hurry up, darl. I'm going to get you clean before I feed you."

"Yeah?" He'd looked at her. "Tell me, Dor," he'd asked in all seriousness, "do you think I'm a boring husband?"

"What made you say that for heaven's sake?"

"Well, Brian was teasing me this morning. He said life must get boring for you, 'cause you have a dull husband who never looks at other women. And who doesn't drink too much and always remembers to shave and brush his teeth."

"And tell me, what brought all that on?" she'd asked, amused.

"Well, you remember the week Brian's Alison spent here? How you both stripped down to your knickers and had a dip in that small billabong?"

"Yes."

"Yeah, well, Brian said I hardly perved at all on Alison while he had the sense to look at both of you."

She'd grinned at him. "Are you wishing now you'd had a good look at Alison? And do you think she's got a nice figure?"

He'd given her an exasperated look. "How come we're talking so much about Alison? I reckon I was asking if *you* thought I was a boring husband like Brian says."

She hadn't replied till she'd finished washing his foot. "No," she'd said quietly, "you don't bore me. And it would've really hurt me if you'd kept on staring at Alison's body. Does that answer your question?"

"Sort of."

"My love," she'd said and had kissed his wet lips. "I don't find you boring at all." She'd grinned and passed him a towel. "Come on, darl. Out you get now," she'd emphasized with a shake of her finger. "Because everyone is hungry. And they'll be waiting for us."

He'd stood up and had started to dry himself. She'd considered him, and a look of amusement had crossed her face. "Now, what's on your mind, Calum darl? You've got your little boy look, so I *know* you're going to ask me something."

He'd held her close. "Will you marry me again, Dor?" he'd murmured.

"What! We've been married less than a year!"

"No, we haven't. We've been married longer than that. We were married up north, remember? But I was talking to Hank," he'd said, his voice growing animated, "and he said that married couples often renew their vows. It's like getting married all over again, and I've decided I'd like to marry you three times." He'd smiled. "You see, *good* things always come in threes."

She'd leaned back in his arms, looked up at him, and had shaken her head in feigned astonishment. "I think you're sunstruck, darl. Anyway," she'd continued loftily, "I reckon husbands should be no different from driving licences. And when he's expired, the wife should be able to decide whether or not she wants to renew him. Course, she shouldn't have to *pay* to renew him, you know."

"Dor!"

The impish smile had stayed on her lips as she'd moved toward the bathroom door. "Yes, my love," she'd murmured, "I do think it's a lovely idea, but can we talk about it later, please? Now off you go and get dressed, because I'm going to put on a new dress. And it's one you haven't seen before. And I'm also going to tell Brian that I think you're the most unboring husband in the whole Territory."

After they'd eaten, they'd gone out on the verandah. He'd looked up at the calm, steady stars, watching over them, and then at Dor in her new, dark-blue, silk cheongsam that was slit halfway up her olive thighs. Her matching shoes were high heeled, and she'd tied her hair back. It'd struck him then just how compellingly beautiful she was, and he hadn't been able to speak. He'd just stared and stared.

"Do you know that Chinese couple who've opened the café and shop in Catriona?" she'd murmured.

"Yes."

"Well, her name's Mrs. Wang. She took my measurements and ordered it for me."

"Dor, it's real beautiful, and you really do look a million."

She'd come into his arms and had raised her face. "You're allowed to kiss your wife, you know, if you want to."

They'd kissed, and when she'd pulled back, he'd watched her eyes slowly flutter open.

"I told Mum, you know, that you wanted to marry me again," she'd murmured.

"Yes."

"She got tears in her eyes, and she said that it was just the same sort of silly thing Dad would've asked *her*. And she told me Jack had said there was a retired, Methodist minister living at Adelaide River."

"Truly?"

"Yes." She'd stood on tiptoe and had given him a peck. "Now, if you do make it to Adelaide River, when the drought breaks, I will marry you again." She'd kissed him once more. "And, my love, thank you for asking me. And I'm sorry, but I just had to tease you when you first asked; otherwise, I would've cried. And I didn't want to cry, because you'd made me so proud and happy."

At that moment, a song, on the wireless, had drifted out onto the verandah. Peg must've turned it up because she'd known that it was one of his favourites. It was Frank Sinatra singing "Polka Dots and Moonbeams."

He'd held out his arms. "I'd love to dance with you, Dor."

She'd smiled, had come into his arms and they'd danced, lightly and easily, in amongst the moonbeams that shone along the whole length of the verandah.

"Oh, darling," she'd said. "I do wish we could dance away this drought."

Then the song had ended, and Peg had turned off the wireless. And only bush, night sounds and night, cattle noises could be heard.

At that instant, the large coal at the base of his fire, at which Calum'd been staring, cracked open in a shower of sparks and burst into flames.

He stretched his shoulders, looked away from his campfire and came back to the present. He sniffed the air. It smelled and felt like rain, but so far there was no sign of it. He looked at Curaidh. His dog was stretched out on his side with his stomach toward the fire.

"I'd better get some sleep, pup. But do you know why we have to get to Adelaide River in a hurry? No? You see, Dor and I are getting married, and it's going to be a special sort of wedding; because she's the most special wife in the whole Top End. And getting married again is my way of telling her just what a terrific wife and mate she is."

Sleep headed toward him with laggard steps. He was still thinking about his wife when it finally reached him.

****

The day that Calum headed for Adelaide River, Ed Smith made camp beside a small creek that was situated some two miles from the Long Creek homestead. He sat and talked to himself while he roasted a young dingo and kept one eye on an approaching rider. He'd first started to talk to himself a couple of years back. Now he did it continually.

"Fuckin' dogs is hard to trap. Yeah, them dogs is hard to trap." He laughed his high-pitched laugh. "'Cause they know they'll get ate if I trap 'em. Bloody whites don't know what they're missing." He laughed again. "No way them dogs'll eat me, 'cause they know I eat them."

The rider that he'd been watching was Jan. When she reached his campsite, she reined in Spitfire. Ed Smith kept staring at her, and though his lips continually moved, no sound came from his mouth.

Astonished to see him, she nevertheless greeted him politely. "G'day, I thought it was Nugget. Be just like Nugg to make camp when he's only a couple of miles from the homestead."

She was relaxed. After all, she *was* Mrs. Hank Nelson.

Ed Smith remained seated. Jan found his manner disconcerting and his smell nauseating. Revulsion swept over her. *This man is awful,* she thought. *Yes, he really is disgusting, and I don't understand why Hank allows him on the place.* She forced herself to be pleasant.

"You've picked a nice spot to camp," she told him.

She glanced around her and took in the Coolibahs and was conscious of the trickling sound coming from the little creek. She decided to appear nice, one more time, before she departed. After all, Hank would want her to be polite. She looked again at Ed Smith.

"What's that you're cooking?" she asked, feigning interest.

"Young dog."

A picture of Curaidh flashed, unbidden, into her mind. "If anyone ever wants a feed of steak," she quickly said, "they're welcome to stop by our stock camp kitchen. My husband says anybody passing through is always welcome."

She saw Ed Smith's face abruptly contort with rage. She was stunned. Then he started to laugh in a crazy-sounding, high-pitched way. *God,* she thought, *I have to get out of here.*

Suddenly, Ed Smith began to scream at her. "You *fuckin'* creamy whore! You're not married. You fuckin' *whores* can't get enough of us whites! I know your mob 'cause I'm white. Yeah, I'm bloody white. An' I bet you wish *you* were, you yeller slut!"

Jan saw that spittle was running down the sides of Ed Smith's mouth, and suddenly, her skin felt very cold. She stood her ground and forced herself to sound self-assured.

"I'm Mrs. Jan Nelson," she told him. "And my husband is one of the owners of this run."

"*Fuckin'* liar!" he shrieked. "Well, I'm Edward Hugh Smith, slut, an' *I'll* give you what you're lookin' for!"

Jan gathered her reins and started to pull Spitfire around. But Ed Smith leaped to his feet, grabbed them with one hand and simultaneously dragged her off Spitfire. Confused, she tried to push him away and, at the same time, tried to stop herself from gagging. At such close quarters, his stench was overwhelming. Oddly, she became aware of the serene, blue sky above, and she couldn't help wondering why this was happening to her. And on such a lovely day too.

"Stop it! Stop it!" she screamed. "I'm going to have a baby!"

"Whore liar. An' you're *lovin'* what I'm doing!"

Then he was cutting her moleskins off her, and she began to struggle determinedly. Without warning, he cocked his fist and punched her brutally in the face. She felt him ripping the buttons off her shirt before biting her breast. Searing pain knifed through her. She screamed and screamed. Ed Smith punched her again, hard. This time it was below her eye. When he entered her, she lay still and started to whimper. He didn't take long. He rolled off, and she thought it was over. Then she felt the excruciating pain. It shot right up her body and then exploded, within her brain, in a shower of white and red stars. She screamed and, deeply shocked, realized what he was doing. Then, mercifully, she blacked out.

When she regained consciousness, she was lying on the ground in a foetal position. Her breast hurt, and she saw that it was bleeding. She remained curled up because the terrible pain, down below, made her frightened to straighten her legs. She saw that that her bra was gone, there were no buttons on her shirt and that she was naked from the waist down.

She started to cry. "Oh, Hank, help me, please!" she sobbed.

After a while, she raised her head and looked around. There was no sign of Ed Smith, just the guttering fire and the sickening smell of roast dingo. But Spitfire was standing there quietly, with her reins dangling on the ground. She forced herself to sit up and focus on her plight.

"You're hurting bad, girl," she numbly told herself. "And that blood an' stuff running down the insides of your legs is probably the baby you and Hank aren't going to have. But you must get to Mum."

She bit her lip hard, shut her mind to the agony and dragged herself onto Spitfire. More blood ran down her thighs to congeal on the saddle flaps. Soon, countless flies were settling on her blood.

Just sitting in her saddle sent severe pain shooting from her vagina up through her body. Often she became so light-headed that she thought she'd faint or fall off. *Hang on*, she kept ordering herself, *you have to hang on.*

When they reached Alice's cottage, she slid off Spitfire and fell against the front door, fainting almost immediately. Alice heard the noise, opened her door, and, in shock, screamed to Brian.

Stunned, Brian cradled his sister in his arms, carried her inside and laid her on his mother's bed.

"Get the Flyin' Doctor on the radio, son," Alice cried. "An' tell 'em it's urgent!"

Alice rushed for warm water and towels. *Crise*, she thought, *what sort of mongrel'd do somethin' like this? Oh, Mother of God, it looks like she's lost the bub.*

She washed her daughter tenderly and then placed towels between her legs to try and stem the flow of blood. And her heart lurched when she saw how pale Jan looked.

Brian returned, and his face was set and hard. Alice stood up and straightened her shoulders. She looked skyward and then silently cursed. *Oh God*, she cried inwardly, *why do we women always cop this blutty shit? An' we never ask for it!* She forced herself to concentrate.

"Listen ter me, son," she told him. "I want yer ter go ter Charlie an' tell 'im ter hold on ter Janice till I come. Last time I seen 'em they was makin' chocolate biscuits. An' find Hank an' warn 'im what's happened ter yer sister." She gave him a hard look. "An' get Hank ter go with yer when yer track down this bastard. Yer'll need ter have a white feller with yer, 'cause no way was this done by a Murri!" She paused. "An' when yer fin' the mongrel, I don' want 'im brought back ter a court, 'cause his lawyer'll put yer sister through terrible hell. An' he'll likely trot out some whites what'll swear yer sister was a creamy slut an' everyone knowed it 'cept her husband."

"I'll get Jalyerri to pick out fast horses," Brian said. "I'll ask him to come too."

"Yes. An' come back in a half hour, son. Maybe yer sister will've come to an' tol' me the mongrel's name."

"Right, Mum."

Alice was about to place a cold, damp cloth over Jan's discoloured and swollen eye when her daughter's eyes flickered open. She smiled reassuringly and waited for Jan to say something. When Jan did speak, her voice sounded very weak.

"Oh, Mum, I'm hurting bad inside."

348

"I want yer to take these aspirins, love. They'll help a bit till the Flyin' Doc gets here."

Jan started to cry. "Mum," she cried weakly, "Ed Smith raped me. Then he used the handle of his knife on me."

Alice was stunned. She could not have been more shocked had she suddenly burned herself with a red-hot, branding iron. She willed herself to stay calm and struggled to control her breathing. *Ed Smith.* It was as if the name had been burnt into her brain. She spoke reassuringly.

"Yer have ter believe yer'll be awright, love. 'Cause I *know* yer will! And I want yer ter say two men done this. And one was red haired. Now, *don't* mention Ed Smith ter *anyone* except Hank. Awright?"

"Yes."

She watched the tears rolling down her silently sobbing daughter's cheeks.

"I hurt so much," Jan whimpered. "And I don't want Hank to see me like this."

"Oh, love, Hank has ter know. An' I promise yer he won't think it's yer fault. No blutty way!"

By the time Hank arrived, Alice had dressed Jan in a pajama top. He sat on a chair next to his wife and took her hand in his. Little Janice held on to his other hand tightly.

"Why my mummy in jamies?" she asked.

Alice picked her up and held her on her hip. Janice continued to look at her mother with big, round eyes. She kept her thumb in her mouth.

"Mummy's sick, darling, and she needs to see the doctor," Jan answered her weakly. "Please go with Gran, darling."

"Yes," Alice said. "We need ter get clean clothes fer you, my little possum, 'cause we're maybe goin' ter Catriona. Now, you come an' help Gran find yer prettiest dress."

"Yes, please go with Gran, darling," Hank said.

"Dolly come too?" Janice asked.

"Too right," Alice told her. "We *couldn'* leave yer dolly behind, could we?"

When they'd left, Hank held Jan's hands in his. "I've spoken to Dr. Blades, sweetheart, and you're going to be all right," he told her. "And

I love you so much. And please, please don't let this change anything between us. Oh, God, I do love you, sweetheart."

"I need you to tell me you love me, darl. An' I think you're going to have to tell me often."

"Yes."

While she was packing, Alice heard the engine of a light plane as it circled and then came in to land.

"That's the Flyin' Doctor's plane, possum. He's here, already."

When Andrew Blades walked into the bedroom, he greeted Jan and Hank cheerfully. "G'day, Jan. And how are you, Hank?"

"We're getting there, Doctor," Jan replied weakly.

Andrew Blades was in his early thirties. He'd learned to fly while a member of his university's flying club. And by joining the Royal Flying Doctor Service, after the war, he'd been able to combine his two great loves: medicine and flying.

He casually addressed Hank while he opened his bag. "Hank, my nurse is getting some hot water. Would you mind seeing what's keeping her? And please close the door behind you, because I'm going to examine Jan."

Andrew Blades was shocked, although he didn't show it. He'd delivered little Janice and genuinely liked Jan, whom he regarded as a sensible, loving mother. He'd been warned that Jan had been violated, but he hadn't anticipated this degree of brutality.

When Andrew Blades finally opened the door, he asked Hank to come in. Hank saw that Jan had a drip attached to the back of her hand and that her eyes were closed.

"Hank, I've given Jan a painkiller and a sedative. She's suffered a lot, and I'm sorry to tell you, she's lost the baby."

"But will she be all right? That's all that matters."

"I'm going to fly her to Catriona right away. Luckily we have a visiting O and G Specialist, and I want him to do the surgery that Jan needs. What I've done is to stop the bleeding. Also she described to me the two men who did this, so I'll be able to pass on those details to Fitzpatrick." Andrew Blades rested his hand lightly on Hank's shoulder. "Hank," he said gently, "I do believe that Jan's going to be all right. But she'll be some time in hospital."

"Yes."

Alice, Hank and little Janice watched the small, twin-engine plane taxi down the runway, gather speed and then become airborne. Hank glanced at Alice. She was watching the plane, and he saw that little Janice was still waving it good-bye.

"I'm to blame, you know," Hank said in a bitter voice. "Jan asked me to go for a ride with her, but I was too busy fixing that goddamn truck."

"*You* weren't ter blame, mate. It's the feller what done this who's ter blame," Alice replied.

Now, Hank felt rage and remorse seep through his body like drops of acid. They stayed with him, and they seeped and seeped. "Yes," he said. "And, Alice, you'll need to drive little Janice to Catriona because I'll be going with Brian."

"We'll leave right away, and we'll stay with Lil."

Hank put their bags in the boot and then opened the new, Ford's doors for Alice and Janice. Brian and Jalyerri stood nearby holding six horses. Three were saddled, and their saddlebags bulged with provisions. They hadn't bothered with a packhorse because they planned to travel light and fast. Alice started the motor, and Hank gave little Janice a hug and a kiss good-bye. The waiting three watched the Ford head toward the rutted red road that led to Catriona. They waited till it'd turned the corner and was out of sight.

"Right," Brian urged, "let's move it an' go an' catch the pig that did this!"

They mounted their horses. Each had a spare on a lead rope.

Brian glanced at Hank. "I'm asking you again, Hank. Are you sure you want to be in on this?" he asked.

"I feel responsible."

"You weren't told before, mate, but we're after Ed Smith. He was the one that did it," Brian said calmly.

"Sweet Jesus," Hank cried. "I've made a terrible mistake. I should've done what Calum wanted and ordered him off the place."

"You know Smith's going to die out there, don't you?" Brian said.

Anger at how his kindness had been repaid merged with the rage at what'd been done to Jan. It didn't leave, and an overriding need for revenge flooded right through him.

"If you don't kill him, I will," he said tersely. "And all things considered, it's probably better if I did it."

"Why, for Crissake?" Brian asked.

"Well, in case it ever gets out." Hank glanced at him. "I'm white, and you're not. I could always plead self-defence, and I'd be believed."

"It's not going to get out. An' you know Jan, mate. Crise, she'll stick to her story till bloody hell freezes over!"

Brian and Jalyerri picked up Ed Smith's trail at the little creek. He had headed nor'west. His horses' shod hoofprints were very obvious in the rain-softened ground. They were easy to follow, at a fast canter.

Brian nodded at Hank. "The bastard's pushing it," he observed. "I reckon he's got the shits up. But we'll catch him all right, 'cause he's only got one, riding horse. An' it'll be carrying his weight *all* the time."

After every twenty minutes, they stopped and changed horses. And after every hour and a half, they halted and rested. They kept up the pace till it was too dark to see. Then they stopped and made camp at a bore.

They sat around their small fire and ate some of the cooked, corned beef and bread that Charlie had packed for them. It was a pleasant night.

"Did you know we lost the baby?" Hank asked Brian.

"No, I didn't. An' I'm sorry, mate."

Brian met Hank's eyes and held them. "Hank," he said quietly, "did you know that the bastard used the handle of a skinning knife on Jan?"

Hank looked stunned. He closed his eyes as if trying to shut out what he'd heard. "Oh, Christ!"

Even from where Brian was sitting, he could feel Hank's rage. *Isn't it funny,* he told himself, *'cause when Hank's really cranky, his voice goes real soft and has no feeling.*

"Goddamn," Hank observed quietly, "I wish it was possible to track in the dark!"

"No goot bugger, him feller," Jalyerri said.

"You're damn right, Jalyerri," Hank said tersely, momentarily forgetting to speak in Creole. "He is filth, and soon, he's going to wish that he'd never set eyes on my wife." He paused. "And he's goin' to take a Goddamn, long time to die!"

Jalyerri looked blankly at Hank. Brian rattled off a translation, and Jalyerri turned and looked at Hank with wide eyes. At that moment, the appalling screech of a Barking Owl suddenly rent the quiet darkness.

"Muddrin' bird," Jalyerri nervously observed.

"Yes, and it's an appropriate omen," Hank murmured to himself.

That night, Hank lay on his swag and listened to the nearby, steadily-creaking windmill. He was mentally tired, but his thoughts kept returning to what Jan had suffered. He found himself in the same icy rage that used to fill him whenever one of his soldiers had been killed. It was a rage that initially alarmed him, because its intensity compelled him to look forward eagerly to taking the fight, even more savagely, to Jerry. Now he was resigned to the fact that it surely wouldn't leave him till Ed Smith had been caught and killed.

****

Calum was in no hurry because he'd decided to give his horses half a day's rest. The sky was dull and overcast, and he hoped that the sun would burn away the cloud cover because he preferred travelling under a blue sky. *A man on his own always felt more alone,* he decided, *when it was raining or dull.* He watched Curaidh going through his getting-warm routine beside the fire.

First, he sat front on to it, with his muzzle pointing to the sky. And when he'd decided that his throat and chest were warm enough, he turned, with a contented sigh, and lay on his side with his stomach toward the fire.

"And after we've eaten," he told Curaidh, "we're going to have to find Sunshine. What tracks that brief shower didn't wash away tell me he's wandered into that bit of scrub, over there. I tell you, pup, I've never come across a horse that covers so much ground with hobbles on."

Calum was feeling very relaxed. He wondered what Adelaide River would be like, and he tried to imagine the delighted look on Doreen's face as soon as she saw him riding toward her. Suddenly, out of the blue, the shocking screech of a Barking Owl disturbed his thoughts.

"Did you hear that, pup? That's that owl with the brown streaks underneath. It makes a murderous racket, eh? No wonder the Murries call it 'muddrin' bird.'"

Calum finished his tea. He noticed that the first exploratory rays of the sun were touching Curaidh's shoulders and that his ruff was glinting red-gold in the yellow light.

"You're a handsome dog," Calum told him as he rose to his feet. "Yeah, I reckon we were lucky we found you when you were little: because you give me such a lot, and you don't expect much in return. Seems to me that all you expect is a decent feed, some company and to be treated like a dog should. And you've really taken to Dor too, haven't you?"

Calum picked up his rifle, checked that the magazine was full —out of habit— and then rested it on his shoulder.

"Come on, pup," he said. "We'd better go and find Sunshine."

He had to track Sunshine for a good fifteen minutes before he came upon him. The little packhorse was in a small clearing, dozing with his eyes closed and with his weight on three legs. Above, in a tree, a couple of crowlike, black-and-white Magpies were musically sounding their melodic, fluting yodel. Then suddenly, he was startled by the sound of something large crashing its way noisily, through the scrub. Immediately the Magpies gave harsh shrieks of alarm and noisily flapped their way through the high twigs and leaves above. Calum levered a cartridge into the breach of the Winchester. It was a reflex action and coincided with the bursting entry of a large, brown, scrub bull. He noted its flaring nostrils, wild eyes, foam-flecked mouth and tossing head. He couldn't help thinking that its enraged look contrasted oddly with its soft-looking, furry ears. He stood very still and studied it. He noted the wide horns that were growing almost at right angles to its head.

The incensed bull's entrance coincided with the speedy exit of a quickly awake and thoroughly alarmed Sunshine. *Hell,* Calum cursed under his breath, *this is one big, coola bugger all right! And, little wonder, with that bloody, flint-head spear sticking out of its off-side flank. Damn the spear, and damn the young, myall Murri that'd thrown it! Hell, it was probably some kid who was showing off in front of his mates. And who'd soon found that he'd had to run laughing, for the nearest tree after it'd struck home.*

Calum glanced round the clearing without moving his head. He felt trapped. It was a very small clearing, and that made things awkward, because this furious bull would obviously charge the moment that it saw him. *Yes*, he thought, *once it's out in the open, that'd be the time to go after it and shoot it. So it's best to stand still and make sure I don't meet its eyes. Christ! Even meeting a strange dog's eyes means you're challenging it.* Unfortunately, at that moment, a threatened Curaidh chose to move in front of his master. He'd raised his hackles and exposed his teeth. The bull saw him immediately and began to paw the ground. Then it picked out Calum and didn't hesitate. It lowered its head and charged. Calum raised his rifle while out of the corner of his eye he saw Curaidh gather himself, leap forward and fasten his teeth onto the bull's nose. Calum quickly moved sideways to give himself the angle for a shot. But before he could shoot, he watched in horror as the bull dropped to its knees and began to crush Curaidh against the ground. Calum fired, and the mortally wounded bull lost coordination and slumped over onto its side.

Curaidh lay still on the ground. Panicking, Calum ran to him. His breathing was shallow and punctuated by gasps and wheezes. To his horror, Calum saw blood start to trickle from his nose, and he was shocked to see broken ribs protruding through Curaidh's skin. The urge to take Curaidh into his arms was just about overpowering, but he knew that Curaidh shouldn't be moved. Instead, he rested his hand, very lightly, against Curaidh's cheek. He watched as his dog struggled to move his head and then try weakly to lick his hand. A hard lump came into his throat, and tears filled and stung his eyes. Then he was crying freely. And he watched helplessly as the light, within those splendid, oval eyes, slowly faded. He spoke in a voice that was hoarse with pain.

"Oh, mate, you were always too brave. It's the *only* fault you ever had. And, pup, you were such a fine, fine dog."

Calum rose and slowly returned to his camp to get the small shovel that he always strapped to his rolled-up swag. He walked back to the clearing in a daze. He'd just started to dig Curaidh's grave when he heard a voice behind him. He waited a moment for his eyes to clear before he turned around. Ed Smith was standing there, holding his rifle.

"I hear you're looking for me, McNicol?"

"No. And I didn't know you were around," Calum replied wearily.

Calum could smell the man's pungent odour. And he saw that his mouth was opening and closing, fishlike, and that dribble was running down his chin. He moved forward a couple of steps and looked down at Curaidh. Then he laughed his peculiar, high-pitched laugh.

"I knew I'd get his scalp. Knew it'd be just a matter of waiting. I may as well take it now, eh?"

"No, you bloody won't!" Calum yelled, livid with rage. "And piss-off now, you mad, stinking bastard! And don't you ever let me see you again. You're already finished on the River, and now I'll make certain you'll also be finished on Long Creek!"

Ed Smith's eyes opened wide. His mouth gaped, and his lips started to quiver. Without warning, he raised the muzzle of his rifle and squeezed the trigger. Calum felt a huge force slam into the side of his chest, and then his legs went from under him. *For Crissake*, he thought, *this is like being kicked by two mules at once.*

"Dor …" he managed to gasp. Then the huge force slammed into him again.

****

The three pursuers were closing fast. And it was just as well Hank thought, because their horses were feeling the effects of the long, hard ride. All six were now covered in lather and were starting to stumble through weariness.

"How much longer, Brian?" he asked.

"We'll get him inside ten minutes, mate." Brian grinned. "Jalyerri an' me haven't been *blind stabbing,* you know."

Abruptly Brian pulled up Poss and leaped from her back. He and Jalyerri studied the ground intently before they conversed briefly.

"What is it?" Hank asked anxiously.

"That mongrel's cut across Calum's trail. He's turned, an' now he's tracking Calum."

"Jesus," Hank said, alarmed.

"I'm not worried." Brian replied as he remounted. "It'd take a better man than that bastard to spring Calum. Besides, Curaidh'll warn Calum, no worries."

Jalyerri was also alarmed. "Eh, look out him feller!" he warned.

They continued to push their labouring horses till thicker scrub slowed them. Then it opened up, and they found themselves at Calum's campsite. Socks and Sunshine were dozing in the sun. They stopped to unsaddle and hobble their spent mounts. If Calum was afoot, they wouldn't need horses. They relaxed. Soon they'd be able to fill him in on what Smith had done.

Two shots abruptly shattered the silence of the bush. Cockatoos screeched in fright and took to the air.

"Come on," Brain yelled in alarm. "That's not Calum's rifle!"

"Oh Jesus."

They started to run through the scrub. Not long later, they came upon a little clearing. At the edge of it, they saw a large, recently killed, scrub bull.

"That's Calum's work," Brian said, panting.

Hank watched as Jalyerri and Brian carefully checked all the signs on the ground. A small movement, on his left, caused him look in that direction, and he was astonished to see a slight, dark figure materialize out of the scrub. The figure leaned on his woomera and stood and watched them. Hank studied the skeletally thin, old man. Long, matted, grey hair fell around his face, and the split septum of his nose held a bone, nose peg.

"Christ," Hank said, "what's *this* all about?"

Jalyerri looked alarmed. "Eh, look out!" he warned.

The old man signalled with his lips toward some newly cut branches. Brian and Hank walked to them briskly. Brian reached them first and pulled them aside.

"Oh Christ!" he cried out and recoiled in horror.

Hank saw him gag and then start to vomit. Hank took a couple of steps forward and looked down. His face blanched, and for a moment, he stood with his eyes closed. When he opened them, he spoke in a quiet, matter-of-fact voice.

"I'd like to bury Curaidh quickly before we go on," he said and reached for Calum's shovel.

Brian looked, unseeing, at Hank, and when he spoke, his voice was filled with incomprehension. "That bastard even scalped Calum's dog."

The old man stood silently and watched them quickly bury Curaidh. His face remained impassive. When they'd finished, he indicated with pursed lips. Only then did they see the cleverly concealed *gunyah*. They walked over to it and were shocked to see an unconscious Calum, prostrate on a Paperbark mattress, with two, naked, young lubras sitting beside him. They were taking it in turn to keep the flies off him with goose feathers. Hank steeled himself, quickly knelt beside Calum and felt his pulse. Thankfully, it was steady. Then he saw that his shirtless friend had been shot twice, once in his left shoulder and also through his right side. The bullet holes had been plugged with healing pipe clay, and Calum's breathing, though shallow, remained even.

Brian touched Hank's shoulder. Hank looked up and saw that the old man was motioning to them to follow him. They walked after him for some five minutes before they saw the two, naked, warriors. Then they saw Ed Smith. He was sitting with his back against the trunk of a big River Red, and his hands and feet were bound with vines. When they looked from Ed Smith and back to his captors, they saw that they'd vanished. The old man walked across to Ed Smith, looked down at him, and uttered a few words. Then he leaned two of his spears against the River Red. Hank noticed that Jalyerri's face had gone grey and that his eyes were wide with fear.

"Do you know what the old feller said, Brian?" he asked.

"He told Smith a gator was going to eat him. An' that the heads on those spears there, were made by Calum."

Hank looked back to where the old man had been standing, but he had vanished. One moment he'd been there, and then he'd just disappeared. Hank decided that everything about the old man was eerie, and he felt the hairs, on the back of his neck, start to prickle. He sensed that an unseen presence was now standing right beside him.

Ed Smith cleared his throat, looked at them and gave a high-pitched laugh. "I'm bloody pleased to see you fellers," he called. "I reckon those niggers were going to kill me! Course, you've done what all white fellers would've done. An' we, white fellers, have got to stick together against these niggers, don't we?"

Brian gave him a quick glance. "I'm not white," he said quietly. "I'm half-caste."

Ed Smith was puzzled. He was sure that they hadn't heard about that creamy from Long Creek. Hell, with the start that he'd had no horse could've caught up to him. Especially not after the way he'd pushed his own horse. *Yes,* he reassured himself, *anyone chasing after him would still have to be half a day's ride behind.* And as for that yellow slut, who'd take her word against that of a white man? And about what had happened to McNicol? Well, that'd be easy to explain. Hell, the man's dog had gone for him, and he'd had to shoot it. Then McNicol had gone crazy, and he'd had to shoot him too, in self-defence. He looked again at Hank, and when he spoke, his voice was a pleading whine.

"All right, fellers, fair go. You can cut me free now. I'm bloody thirsty I tell you."

Rage and hate coursed through Hank's entire body. "You just have no Goddamn idea how much I loathe you, do you?" he said quietly.

"What're you talkin' about?" Ed Smith regarded Hank with shrewd eyes. "I demand you take me to Fitzpatrick *now*. He's the law, an' I want to tell 'im what really happened. An' that's my *right*."

Hank turned on him angrily. "You have no Goddamn rights, and you're going to die."

"You have to be lying, don't you?"

Hank's eyes narrowed, and he moved to Ed Smith and, very deliberately, smashed him across the face with the back of his fisted hand. Then he repeated the blow with his other hand.

"You filthy, depraved bastard!" he ground out.

"Why won't you take me to Fitzpatrick?" Ed Smith pleaded. "An' let a court decide?"

Hank smashed Ed Smith across the face again. "Get fucked," he said.

Hank turned away and returned to Brian and Jalyerri. He watched Brian strip off his shirt and sit on the ground, in front of Jalyerri. Jalyerri commenced to decorate him with a mixture of white clay and water. The design started at Brian's forehead and ended at his navel. Jalyerri didn't speak.

"You don't have to do this, Brian, you know. Just tell me what you want done, and I'll do it. It'd mean about as much to me as swatting a fly."

Hank saw the anguished look return to Brian's face. "It has to be my call, Hank, after what that mongrel did to my mate an' to my sister." He glanced at Hank, puzzled. "But why? Why? Of course, we both know none of this shit would've happened if Fitzo had gone an' done his job properly in the first place."

"Yes."

"You know," Brian said, half smiling, "Calum's the only ringer that Bitch never tried to bite."

"Yes. And he's very fit, so I think he's got every chance of pulling through."

"Too right. 'Specially if that Kaditje man's got anything to do with it!"

"Yes. And I've been thinking," Hank said. "After this, you better head for Adelaide River. I'll stay with Calum, and Jalyerri can head back and tell Alice about Calum and why I'm here."

"Yes. An' tell me again, we do have to do this, don't we?" Brian asked in a quiet voice.

"Yes," Hank answered bitterly. "But make sure it's Goddamn slow. I'll feel a helluva lot better if I can watch the bastard suffer for a while."

"It'll be slow, mate, no worries."

Hank looked about him. He couldn't help thinking that it was a pity that this tranquil, little glade was being asked to witness what was coming. Yes, he thought, the bloody War had goddamn changed him all right, and so would this. Then the rage that'd briefly left him returned and grabbed at him so hard that, for an instant, he thought he was about to choke.

CHAPTER 22

TOGETHER AGAIN

Hank farewelled Jalyerri and Brian and then returned to set up camp not far from Calum's gunyah, which was close to a clump of Mulgas. He noticed that the two lubras had left and that the old man was sitting next to Calum. Instinctively, he knew to keep his distance. When he turned in for the night, he saw by the glow of the man's, little fire that the old man still hadn't moved.

That night, Hank kept tossing and turning. Images of his devastated wife, a dying Ed Smith and his badly wounded friend kaleidoscoped around in his mind. And guilt, coupled with an undiminished hatred for Ed Smith, continued to fester inside him.

When he awoke, the melodious warbling of those pretty, whitish-brown to chestnut Rufous Songlarks were offering a musical accompaniment as the sun painted in a magnificently coloured, bright-gold dawn that totally filled the sky. Hank, feeling exhausted and mentally drained, rose to check on the horses. He saw that the old man was wide-awake and didn't appear to have moved. He also noted that the old man never glanced in his direction.

And that was the pattern of the days and nights that followed. Hank kept his distance, constantly worried about his wife and daughter and watched as the old man diligently nursed his patient who appeared, by turn, to be delirious, feverish, thirsty, or testy.

But Hank wasn't surprised by what he was witnessing. After all, Murries had been dispensing their own, bush medicines for thousands of years.

Soon, Hank lost all track of time. He filled his days by keeping an eye on the horses, grooming them and shooting for the larder, while wishing that Brian and Doreen would turn up so that he'd be free to rush back to Jan and Janice.

This particular day had dawned muggier than usual, and Hank sensed that something was afoot. Then suddenly, he saw the old man collect his belongings before putting some cooked, leftover pork into a dilly bag. Finished, he returned to Calum, grasped his hand and silently peered into his eyes, for a long moment, before rising to his feet. Then, effortlessly, he just disappeared into the bush, without as much as a backward glance. One moment he'd been clearly visible; the next, he'd vanished.

Hank immediately went to Calum, saw that his friend was clear eyed, and that his face no longer had its deathly white pallor.

"How do you feel, Calum?" he asked, finally able to speak to him.

"Sort of weak and still bloody sore. But I reckon I'll be up and about in no time," Calum replied unsteadily.

"There's no rush, my friend. It'd be shame to undo all the good that old man has done."

"It was that bastard Ed Smith who shot me," Calum said, his voice hardening. "And I'm going after him as soon as I'm able."

"You won't need to, pardner. He's already dead."

"How come?" Calum asked, looking intently at Hank.

"Brian and I saw a gator grab him. He was trying to escape us."

"If any bastard deserved that, he did."

Hank didn't feel sufficiently comfortable to tell Calum about Jan's horrific rape. Besides, he remained acutely aware that Calum had implored him to bar Ed Smith from Long Creek.

Just then, a nearby Socks flung up his head, pricked his ears and neighed loudly. Hank quickly looked up and saw that Brian and Doreen were riding toward them.

"Now, don't get too excited, pardner," he told Calum, smiling. "It's only Brian and Doreen. And just as I was about to tell you that Brian had gone to get her."

He saw Calum's face light up. Doreen put Lady into a fast canter before pulling her to a halt, some twenty yards from them. She leaped, from Lady, and joyfully ran to Calum; tears of happiness were streaming down her face. Hank rose to his feet, put an arm around her shoulders and gave her a brief hug before quickly walking toward Brian, in order to give them their privacy.

Doreen immediately knelt beside Calum, took his hand, and clasped it to her bosom.

"Now just look what happens, darl," she sniffled, "when I let you out of my sight."

"Is that right?" He grinned. "Anyway, I'll soon be on my feet."

"No, you won't. Not till I tell you."

He moved his hand and tried to reach beneath her shirt. "I just need to hold you, Dor."

"Yes."

She couldn't help thinking, momentarily, that his action resembled that of a three-year- old, who was seeking the reassurance that his mother's breast had always offered. She dismissed the thought. Heavens, her Calum would never feel *that* vulnerable. She looked down at his face. And again, she was shocked by his drawn and wan appearance.

"I love you, Dor," he said in an unsteady voice.

"Darl," she joyfully told him as more tears came to her eyes, "soon, you'll also have our baby to love. Because now, I *am* well and truly pregnant."

Calum suddenly felt all choked up. He could only stare at his wife, in wonder, as her news slowly sank in. He continued to look at her lovely, tear-stained face.

"I bet you're wondering, my darling," she said, "whether I'm going to give you your daughter? But just remember, if it's a boy, you can't send him back."

"I see," he said, smiling weakly.

"But our bub's been no trouble so far, so it's probably a girl. I've been told little boys can be quite naughty, you know."

"Dor, I have to tell you I'll love a naughty, little boy just as much as a beautiful, little girl."

"Oh, darl."

"What is it, my love?" he asked.

"I love you. And I know you'll be a terrific father."

"Yeah? Well, I hope you love me nearly as much as I love you."

"I do. I love you all the way to Wanjin and back, darl."

"I'm lucky."

"We both are, my Calum, because soon we'll be a family, and we have our whole lives to be happy." Her eyes suddenly clouded. "Brian told me about Curaidh, darl. It's so sad."

"I'll tell you about it later, Dor. Right now, I'm too happy to talk about it."

"Yes. And now, I'd better make some lunch. That'll give Brian a chance to talk to you." She buttoned up her shirt. "And then it's more rest."

"Bloody hell. You've started your nursing already!"

Smiling, Doreen started to walk away. *That's my Calum*, she thought. *Sometimes he can be just like a rebellious, little boy.* She thought about the baby growing inside her and wondered whether she could find herself mothering two, rebellious, little boys. She smiled again. Calum would be horrified if he realized that sometimes she did mother him. Anyway, she was quite certain that there were times when all wives mothered their husbands. She started giggling to herself. She couldn't help it. She was so happy that her happiness seemed to be bubbling right up and out of her.

GLOSSARY OF ABORIGINAL, KRIOL, AND OTHER WORDS AND PHRASES

ant beds: Termite mounds
bacca: Tobacco
banker: In flood (river)
boab: Baobab tree
bijnitch: Activity
billabong: Waterhole
black velvet: Sexualized description of a lubra
blind stabbing: Tracking by guessing
Beak: Magistrate (Australian slang)
Big Run (The): Victoria River Downs Run
bludger: Person who evades work
boong: Aborigine (derogatory)
brass razoo: Worthless coin
breaker: Horse breaker
bush (The): The Australian wilderness
bush the horses: (To) turn them loose
cattle duffing: Cattle stealing
cheeky: Dangerous
cleanskins: Unbranded cattle or horses
cockrag: Male genital linen covering
cockeye bob: Violent, tropical storm
combo: Caucasian who lives with a lubra
coola: Angry
crook: Bad (Australian slang)

Crown land: Land owned by Government
darra: Penis
Debuldebul: Devil, bad magic.
dilly bag: Small bag made by Aborigines
Down Below: All of the Australia that lies
south of the Northern Territory
drover's boy: Drover's *lubra*
dry gully: Anywhere whites dumped murdered
Aborigines
fair dinkum: Real, genuine.
fats: Prime bullocks
gator: Estuarine crocodile
gin: Aboriginal woman (derogatory)
goog: Egg (Australian slang)
go up a gully: (To) make oneself scarce
gunyah: Aboriginal shelter (traditional)
green hide: Untanned leather
horse tailer: Person responsible for horses
humpy: Aboriginal shelter (non traditional.)
Igulgul: The Moon God
Inside: Civilization in the form of cities and towns
in the white: Assimilated
Kaditje man: Wandering sorcerer
kirrikijirrit: Willie Wagtail (bird)
kumara: Vagina
kumbitji: Ironwood tree
Kunapipi: The Earth Mother
kwee-ai: Girl
lap-lap: Wraparound skirt
mangan: Native plum tree
mark: (To) Castrate
mix blankets: (To) Cohabit
moleskins: Thick burnished-cotton trousers
Murri: Full-blood Aborigine
myall: Wild, uncivilized.
narga: Male genital apron
on the wallaby (track): To wander

Outback: Sparsely inhabited back country.
pic: Piccaninny
promise-married: Arranged marriage
ringer: Stockman (cattle)
roany: Roan-coloured cattle or horse
rush: Cattle stampede
scrub bull: Feral bull
shade: Spirit
sheila: Woman, girl (Australian slang).
shimmy: Chemise
sorry bijnitch: Bereavement ritual
swag: Canvas roll with one's belongings
Tchinek-tchinek: Rainbow Serpent
The Old People: Aborigines who live traditional lives
on their traditional land
tjarada: Love magic
tjooloo: Baby spirit
tucker: Food
tucker dog: Hunting dog
spares: Spare horses
Wanjin: The Dog Star
warrigal: Dingo
woomera: Spear thrower
Yeller feller: half-caste male
yu-ai: Yes

ACKNOWLEDGMENTS

ABC TV, *100 Years. The Australian Story. Unfinished Business.* 2001.

ABC TV, *Australia's Frontier War.* 2001.

Arthur, J. M., *Aboriginal English.* Oxford Uni. Press, 1996.

Australian Newspaper, August 2, 2004.

Bennett, L., *Debuldebul Gadim Redwan Ai.* Barunga Press 1993

Berndt, R. M., *Kunapipi.* F. W. Cheshire, 1951.

——— and C. H., *End of an Era.* Aust. Inst. of Aboriginal Studies. Canberra, 1987.

Brown, D., *Bury My Heart at Wounded Knee.* Barrie & Jenkins, 1971.

Cartwright, M., *Missionaries, Abo'ls & Welfare Settlement Days in the N. Territory.* 1995.

Chambers, B., *Black and White'* Methuen Aust. 1988

Cole, T., *Crocodiles and Other Characters'* Pan Macmillan 1992

———, *Hell, West and Crooked.* Angus and Robertson, 1994.

Commonwealth Bank Aust., *The Northern Territory.* Issued 1949.

Davis, J., *Black Life.* University of Queensland Press, 1992.

Duncan, R., *The N. Territory Pastoral Industry 1863–1910.* Melb. University Press, 1967.

Elder, B., *Blood on the Wattle.* New Holland, 1998.

Flegg, J., *Birds of Australia.* Reed New Holland, 1995.

Fong Lim, A., *Memories of Pre-War Northern Terr. Towns.* Darwin State Ref. Lib., 1990.

Garadji, D., *Minjilung Groka Ailen Stori.* Bamyili Press, 1982.

Gilman, S. L., *Black Bodies, White Bodies: Towards an Iconography of Female Sexuality in Late Nineteenth-Century Art, Medicine and Literature.* Critical Enquiry Autumn, 1985.

Harney, W. E., *Life Among the Aboriginals.* Hale London, 1957.

Herbert, X., *Poor Fellow My Country.* Collins, 1975.

Johnstone, F. H. and O'Loughlen, *Cattle Country.* F. H. Johnstone, 1968.

Kelsey, D. E., *The Shackle.* Lynton Publications, 1975.

Kickett, E., *The Trails of the Rainbow Serpent.* Chatham Road Publications, 1995.

Laffin, J. A., *The J. A. Laffin Story: A Kidman Drover.* Laffin & Dargusch, 1996.

Lunney, B., *Gone Bush.* Harper Collins, 2000.

Makin, J., *The Big Run.* Rigby, 1972.

May, D., *From Bush to Station.* History Dept. James Cook University, 1983.

McGrath, A., *Born in the Cattle.* Allen & Unwin, 1987.

Menkhorst, P. and Knight, F., *Mammals of Australia.* Oxford University Press, 2001.

Merian, F., *Big River Country.* IAD Press, 1996.

Mitchell Gregory, *The Bush Horseman.* A. H. & A.W. Reed Pty. Ltd., 1981.

Nannup, A., Marsh, L., and Kinnane S., *When the Pelican Laughed.* Fremantle Arts Cen. Press, 1992.

Powell, A., *Far Country: A Short History of the N. Terr.* Melbourne University Press, 2000.

Prentis, M. D., *The Scots in Australia.* Sydney University Press, 1983.

Priest, C. A.V., *Glimpses of Bygone Days.* CAV Print, 1989.

Read, P., *A Rape of the Soul so Profound.* Allen & Unwin, 1999.

————, *Stolen Generations.* Sydney Gov't Printer, 1982.

Reed-Gilbert, K., *Black Woman Black Life*. Wakefield Press, 1996.

Reynolds, H., *Frontiers, Aboriginals, Settlers and Land*. Allen & Unwin, 1987.

———, *Dispossession*. Allen & Unwin, 1996.

———, '*Why Weren't We Told*. Penguin, 2000.

Rosser, B., *Dreamtime Nightmares*. Penguin, 1987.

Rudder, J., *Australian Aboriginal Religion and the Dreaming*. Restoration House, 1999.

Satterthwait, L., *Hunting and Gathering*. Government Publ. Service Canberra, 1990.

Simpson, B., *Packhorse Drover*. ABC Books, 1996.

Stringer, C., *A Gaucho Downunder*. Adventure Publ., 1994.

Torgovnik, M., *Gone Primitive*. University of Chicago Press, 1990.

Wharton, H., *Cattle Camp*. University of Queensland Press, 1994.